The
CHOCOLATE APOTHECARY

JOSEPHINE MOON

ALLEN&UNWIN

First published in Great Britain in 2015 by Allen & Unwin

First published in Australia in 2015 by Allen & Unwin
(under the title *The Chocolate Promise*)

Allen & Unwin
c/o Atlantic Books
Ormond House
26–27 Boswell Street
London WC1N 3JZ

Phone: 020 7269 1610
Fax: 020 7430 0916
Email: UK@allenandunwin.com
Web: www.allenandunwin.co.uk

A CIP catalogue record for this book is available from the British Library.

Paperback ISBN 978 1 76011 359 9
E-Book ISBN 978 1 92526 670 2

Set in 12.5/17 p
Printed and bo

10 9 8 7 6 5 4 3

For my dad, Brian, and stepmother, Pamela, for sharing so much of Tasmania with me, creating many treasured family memories of our time there.

1

Christmas Livingstone's Top 10 Rules for Happiness

1. Do what you love and love what you do.
2. Never let yourself get hungry.
3. There is almost nothing that cannot be improved by chocolate.
4. Nurture all five senses each and every day.
5. Share joy with others and you'll feel joyful too.
6. Massage is not a luxury but a necessity.
7. Ask yourself, 'What would Oprah do?'
8. Your destiny doesn't happen to you; you make your destiny.
9. Be on a quest at all times.

And, most importantly,

10. Absolutely no romantic relationships.

●

It was Thursday, Holy Thursday, to be exact—the day before the four-day Easter weekend, which also included the Evandale garden expo on Saturday—and The Chocolate Apothecary was a bubbling pot of activity. Easter, Valentine's Day and Mother's Day were the biggest chocolate events of the year, and this time around, Easter was late enough to be just a week before Mother's Day.

Cheyenne and Abigail were working the floor, selling and waitressing like their lives depended on it, carrying silver trays weighed down with mugs of hot chocolate, mochas, and pots of tea, apple pie and cream, chocolate fondants, chocolate-coated raspberries, chocolate brownies and pralines. Biscotti. Macarons. Meringues. The aromas of them all swirled together around the shop in a magical, intoxicating perfume and rolled out onto the street, stopping people in their tracks so they followed the scent inside, as if hypnotised.

Lots of visitors were in town for the Easter break, and it felt as though they'd all ended up inside Christmas Livingstone's stately Georgian building, hiding from the indecisive weather outside. She peeked out from the kitchen behind the swing doors, wiping her hands on her apron. The long communal table down the centre of the shop was full, with customers' chatter adding to the cacophony.

She'd be up all night replacing the chocolates and baked goods the crowd was consuming today. Maybe she should call someone in to help. But who? She couldn't very well expect Cheyenne or Abigail to stay into the night after working all day. Maybe her sister? Val couldn't cook a single thing, let alone temper chocolate or decorate it once it was set. But she was tremendously pragmatic. She would wash, clean, sweep, carry, lift and load. And she would keep Christmas's spirits up when the fatigue hit. But Val had a man and three boys to look after.

That really only left Emily. She was working today but she'd be up for an all-nighter. Christmas would only have to sell it to her as a girly sleepover like they'd had when they were kids, and give her a glass of bubbly, and she'd be in. It was one of the many things she loved about Emily. She was always so keen to help.

Christmas pulled her phone out of her pocket, then hesitated. She hated asking for favours, even when she knew the other person would be happy to oblige. But the crowd out there wasn't letting up and it was only going to get busier.

'Just do it,' she told herself, and tapped out a message.

Emily responded instantly. *Absolutely. Great timing! I've got a super surprise for you. I can't wait!!!*

A surprise? Christmas couldn't even begin to guess what that might be. And she had no more time to consider it, because the postman's squealing van had just pulled up outside the picket fence at the front of the shop.

'Excellent,' she said aloud, pushing open the swing doors into the shop, stepping around a little boy rolling a toy train on the floor and a number of steel walking frames propped beside chairs at the small round tables where senior citizens rested with their hot drinks. She'd put in an order for several kilograms of raw cacao butter to be sent express, just in case of a rush, and now she was exceptionally glad she had. She skipped the last two steps across the doorway to greet the postman, who was heaving out of his van a box with a *Caution: Heavy Load* sticker on it. He placed it on the ground while he fetched his paperwork and mobile scanner for her to leave an electronic signature.

Gordon Harding swooshed by on his penny farthing, his head bent low against the wind, his waistcoat buttoned tightly against the cold. She waved heartily. It was one of the things she loved so much about living in Evandale—the penny farthings, from another time entirely, still whooshing about poetically, refusing to give in to the pressures of time and technology.

'Sign here,' the postman said, handing her the clunky device and the electronic pen. She scribbled her initials and said thanks, waiting to see if he might offer to carry the box inside. He didn't. So she waited until his van had moved on, then knelt beside the box and tested its weight. It was fifteen kilos, according to the sticker. She knew she was strong enough to lift that much, but she was wearing a skirt and it wasn't easy to brace her legs as she needed to, and the box was large and the cardboard packaging slippery. She levered it a few inches off the footpath before it dropped down again with a thud. She glanced in through the door of the shop, half embarrassed and half hoping someone might help her, but both Abigail and Cheyenne were busy and most of the men inside were older than her ex-stepfather, Joseph.

She was considering her options when an orange taxi pulled up in the space where the van had just been. Through the window, she saw a man thrust a couple of notes at the driver; then he opened the door and stepped out, dragging a battered traveller's backpack that had certainly seen better days and looked as though its zips and buckles might pop open at any moment. The man straightened, adjusted a laptop bag slung across his body, closed the door, and the taxi left.

An easy smile broke through his dark beard, which was largely unkempt and messy but just within the bounds of still being rustic and attractive. But it was the way his smile reached all the way to his staggeringly blue eyes that hit Christmas hard. The air around her suddenly drained away and she was speechless for a couple of moments, unable to take her eyes off his.

'Hi,' he said. 'Is this the chocolate place?' He was walking towards her, his backpack abandoned on the footpath, peering through the window. 'I picked up a brochure at the airport. I can't believe I've never been here before.'

Christmas found some words. 'You live here?' Okay, not impressive words, but they were better than stunned silence.

He turned back to her, that smile still shining from his eyes. One side of his shirt was tucked into his pants but not the other, and for some reason this made Christmas feel wobbly. 'I come from Tasmania but I've been overseas for work a lot in the past few years, coming back to live in my grandmother's house in between gigs.'

'I've been open for three years.'

'This is *your* shop? Perfect. Maybe you can help me choose some chocolates for my grandmother. She's in a nursing home and has a terrible sweet tooth. All good up here—' he tapped his temple—'but the body's letting her down. On my way to see her now. And I'm starving so I thought I'd grab some lunch too.'

Christmas didn't know where to look. She couldn't keep looking at him because her body was reacting strongly to his presence. There was an aura about him—something magnetic. It was something she hadn't felt in a long time. Perhaps ever.

And it wasn't allowed. It was rule number ten—*absolutely no romantic relationships.*

This wouldn't do at all.

'Well, come inside and we'll sort something out,' she muttered, head down, marching towards the door.

'Hang on, is this your box?'

She turned around and he'd already heaved the box onto his shoulder as though it was a wildebeest he'd just slain and was carrying home for dinner.

'Yes. Thanks.'

'I'm Lincoln, by the way,' he said, following her through the door, weaving his way through the tables and displays and behind the counter and through the swing doors into the kitchen.

'Sorry it's such a mess,' Christmas said, taking in the spilled chocolate that covered the stainless-steel benchtops, splattered up the fridge doors, ran across the floor and was generally sprayed from one end of the room to the other. It was like a graffiti attack, but a lovely one, made with chocolate.

'I've just come out of the jungle in South America. Trust me, this isn't a mess. Where do you want this?'

'Huh? Oh! On the bench, somewhere, anywhere. Thanks.'

Lincoln dropped the box with a thud. Then he stood, calmly, looking at her, still smiling, as though he was waiting for something.

She began to shuffle and find flecks of chocolate to pick off the bench with her fingernail. 'Are you a musician?' she asked, remembering that he'd used the word 'gig'.

'Botanist. But that sounds like a great alternative job if I need one.'

She was silent for a moment, mesmerised by his eyes. 'Well, thanks for carrying that in. We should get your chocolates. And shouldn't you get your backpack?' she said, suddenly realising they'd left it outside.

Lincoln shrugged. 'It'll be right.'

Christmas wished her heart wasn't thumping so hard. 'So . . .' she prompted.

'You haven't told me your name,' he said, touching her arm and sending a twang through her as though he'd plucked a nerve, *blatantly flirting with her*! It was incredible. No one flirted with her.

6

Not here in sleepy old Evandale. She felt safe from romantic entanglements in this small town. With a population of only one and a half thousand, there simply weren't enough people for romance.

'Christmas Livingstone,' she said, as ordinarily as she could.

He whistled through his teeth. 'I like that.'

Oh boy, she needed to get out of this. 'Come on. We'd better get you some food and your grandma some chocolate before it all disappears. It's terribly busy out there today. You don't want to miss out.' And she turned on the spot and marched into the shop, not looking back but trying to sense the whole time how far behind her he was, whether he might be about to bump into her, if she stopped suddenly, for example.

Not that she would.

Not on purpose, anyway.

The rules, she reminded herself. The rules were there for her protection. The rules had served her well and kept her steady for the past three years. Now was not the time to abandon the rules. She had to get a grip.

Emily arrived that evening after The Apothecary had closed, pulling autumn leaves from her long unruly hair, and sniffing as though she was getting a cold. But still smiling.

'Are you sick?' Christmas said, tossing some bowls and spatulas into the kitchen sink and turning on the tap.

Emily sniffed some more, hung up her handbag on the coat hook by the door, dropped her overnight bag on the floor and took off her leather jacket. 'I think it's hay fever. Can you get it in autumn?'

'I think you can get it any time. Thanks so much for coming. I owe you.' Christmas headed to the fridge and pulled out a bottle of bubbly.

'Rubbish. Think of it as thanks for helping me move into the townhouse over New Year.'

'Oh yeah.' Christmas eased the cork out of the bottle with a satisfying pop and it hit the ceiling. 'That *was* hard work,' she laughed. In fact, it had taken her nearly a week to recover. Emily was such a collector and hoarder, and where most people would see moving house as an opportunity to reduce the number of items they had to transport, Em actually seemed to have collected more. She still had dozens of boxes that weren't opened or unpacked.

They clinked glasses. 'Cheers!'

'So what's this surprise?' Christmas asked, leaning against the bench. 'I'm intrigued.'

Emily's face lit up and she let out a little squeal. 'I *should* make you wait until the end of the night, after we've finished all the work, but I don't think I can.'

She placed her glass on the bench, went to her handbag and fished out an envelope. Returning to stand in front of Christmas, she held it in two hands by the top corners. 'Okay, so you know how in the past you've talked about Master Le Coutre?'

Christmas frowned in confusion. This was unexpected. Master Le Coutre was a world-renowned French chocolatier, known for his brilliance, eccentricity, and the annual scholarship course he opened to anyone, anywhere in the world, where they got to spend a week with him *absorbing his greatness*. The arrogance was breathtaking; the competition for the scholarship, hysterical. The itinerary for his course changed each year, and no one knew what it would be when they applied. Previous recipients reported poetry readings, surprise flights to African cacao farms, sleep deprivation and all-night chocolate making, opera lessons, and camping out in tents under the stars while

Master Le Coutre lectured by fireside and stirred melted chocolate over an open flame; some even claimed they hadn't seen
him once during their stay. He was mad, they said. He was
cruel, said some. He was a genius, said many. But nothing he
did ever turned people away from applying. It was as though
the stranger his behaviour the more people wanted to be in
his course. And as no promises were made as to what would
happen during the week, and no one actually paid for their trip,
no one could really complain too much. He was an enigma; and
his devoted followers, including Christmas, hung off every one
of his enigmatic words.

'Yeeess,' she said, instantly on her guard. Blood rushed
through her ears. She had spoken to Emily about him many
times, even showing her the magazines where the ads for the
scholarship were placed each year. And they had laughed about
how bizarre Master Le Coutre was.

'But would you go?' Emily had asked her in the past. 'If you
had the chance?'

Christmas had shrugged. 'Sure, why not?' But she'd never
considered the question seriously because she never thought she
would go as far as to apply. No matter how brilliant Master Le
Coutre was, going to France meant a whole lot more than professional development. Going to France was personal.

Emily's eyes brightened. 'You're in,' she whispered.

'What?'

'You're in! I got you a place in this year's scholarship course!'
Emily flung her arms around her and squeezed so tightly that
Christmas gasped for breath.

'Oh, sorry!' Emily said, stepping back, laughing. She thrust
the envelope into Christmas's hand. 'Read it!'

'But I didn't do this,' Christmas said, alarmed and confused.

'I know. I did it. I applied on your behalf and wrote an essay and everything. It took so long,' Emily finished, breathlessly, as though even the memory exhausted her.

'What did you say?'

Emily waved her hand. 'Oh, this and that. I've heard you talk often enough about your dream for chocolate to be used as medicine that I could recite what you've said.' She tilted her head to the side. 'It's a strange application form. They don't actually care too much if you have previous experience with chocolate making, though of course I sent photos of your greatest pieces,' she hurriedly assured Christmas. 'But mostly I just talked about your passion for chocolate and for the new frontiers!' She delivered the last sentence very dramatically. 'You're going to France! Finally!' And Emily launched herself on Christmas in another bear hug.

Christmas didn't know what to say. Every year, only a handful of applicants were chosen for Master Le Coutre's scholarship week. She'd be mad to knock it back. But it was in France, the great unknown, the place she'd dreamed about, romanticised, loved, and feared going to her whole life. At one stage a few years ago, she'd been quite motivated to go. But then everything in Sydney had happened and she'd shelved the idea, along with thoughts of romance and children. She'd changed her life— made it stable and predictable.

France was the home of the father she'd never known. For so long it had sat there on the other side of the world, taunting her with the possibility of discovery, and the terror of what that might lead to. And given her history, her family history, inviting the unknown into her perfectly neat life was not something to be taken lightly.

But with the trip literally in her hands right now, how could she not at least consider it?

2

A Little Piece of Chocolate Magic

By Peter O'Donnell

Is chocolate good for you?

At The Chocolate Apothecary, the answer is unequivocally yes. But its owner and creator, Christmas Livingstone, goes a step further than that. For her, chocolate is not just good for you; it's medicine.

It could be easy to assume from the outside that this is just one more chocolate shop among the delights of the gourmet food trails for which Tasmania has become famous. But as its name suggests, The Chocolate Apothecary is much more than a quaint, charming, French-inspired artisan's boutique.

Inside its stone walls is an abundance of magical enchantments, mystical wisdom, and potions disguised in smooth Belgian chocolate, home-made rose-petal meringues, and fine tea and coffee.

'I wanted it to feel as though when you eat something here you're eating a little healing potion,' says Livingstone.

Those potions are dispensed during a 'chocolate consultation', in which a person's character or life circumstance is matched to the particular properties of chocolate and the botanical extracts Livingstone combines with it.

The Chocolate Apothecary is the manifestation of the long-held dream of Ms Livingstone, a former Sydney-based public relations manager who was once in the media spotlight during her whirlwind relationship with tennis player Simon Barton.

A native Tasmanian, originally from Hobart, Livingstone seems to have transitioned into her new life here in the village of Evandale easily. And successfully. Her appointment list for private chocolate consultations is fully booked most weeks. She glows with the disposition of something akin to what her own name suggests—a little bit of magic.

Asked what drives her, she replies, 'It's one of my life rules to do what I love and love what I do. My goal for each day is to bring happiness to myself and to others. That's a huge motivation. I think we're a terribly stressed society and have lost the art of valuing simple pleasures and the wisdom of knowing just how important that is. What could be a better job than that?'

Well, possibly this: not only is Livingstone a chocolate apothecarist, but she has also carved out a niche for herself as a 'fairy godmother'.

'I started the website on a whim a few years ago, partly to give myself a feel-good project to work on while I was going through big life transitions,' she explains. 'I was soon overwhelmed by requests for wishes to be granted. I've had to restrict the number I take on, simply because of the time commitments involved in running The Apothecary, and that's the hardest part. Now some people pay me for services—such as helping them to throw a surprise party or do something nice for someone anonymously—and other wishes I do pro bono. I keep doing what I can in a small way but my ultimate goal would be for the paying clients to subsidise a part-time role for an assistant so we can get through more wishes. So many people out there are struggling.'

For now it's a small sideline operation, but one she finds immensely rewarding. 'It's great fun,' she says. 'And of course every wish is accompanied by gifts of chocolate. And any day that ends in chocolate is a good day.'

This travel writer can't disagree with that logic. So make sure you put a visit to The Chocolate Apothecary high on your to-do list when you're next heading to this wonderful island state.

What: The Chocolate Apothecary

Where: Russell Street, Evandale, Tasmania

When: Tuesday–Sunday each week, 9 a.m. to 4 p.m.

How to get there: Evandale is a short ten-minute drive from Launceston airport.

Christmas dialled Peter's number.

'Christmas Livingstone, I presume,' he boomed, the warmth in his voice sending a wave of nostalgia through her.

'I just read the article in the copy of the in-flight magazine you sent. It came in yesterday's mail but I only just got the chance to read it. It's really lovely, thank you. It's always so nerve-racking when someone does a story; they never seem to get it quite right. But I think that might be the best one I've read on The Apothecary yet.'

'Never trust a journo,' he said. 'You of all people should know that.'

She could hear the smile in his voice and she missed him. Solid, dependable Peter—one of the few people who knew why she'd left Sydney three years ago. He was an old-school journalist who should rightly be retired but who found the life far too exciting. 'You're brilliant, and a great friend. I should send you a portion of the extra profits that will surely come in after this.'

'Nonsense. Give them to some poor kid who needs a teddy bear.'

'Where are you off to next?' she said.

'Cambodia. I hear the noodles are excellent.'

'Well, have fun, and have a bowl for me.'

'Will do,' he sang. 'Bye, kiddo.'

'Bye. Make sure you drop in again next time you're in Tassie.'

'Will do.'

She was grinning as she hung up and slid her mobile phone into the pocket of her blue apron. Talking to Peter had given her the lift she needed, having spent much of last night listening to Emily enthuse about the scholarship to France and trying so very hard to pretend she was incredibly grateful and excited too. And she supposed she was, somewhere deep inside. But it was such a shock and she'd found it difficult to concentrate on the work; eventually she had apologised to Emily and explained that she couldn't stay up half the night talking because she had a huge weekend ahead. Emily had understood, of course, but Christmas had lain awake for several hours in her bed up in the loft, listening to Emily's deep breathing on the fold-out couch across the room, feeling anxious whenever she thought about France.

But now she surveyed her beautiful shop, buoyed by Peter's words, energised on this Good Friday public holiday, alone in the store and free to use her imagination. Her eyes fell on the store's logo.

At one point in primary school, it was all the rage among the girls in her class to take cold black coffee, dip a sponge in it and wipe it across white paper. After letting it dry, you took a lighted match and ran it around the edges to make them blackened and fragile. The paper absorbed the aroma of both the coffee and smoke, a heady combination that made Christmas feel rather mature. Then you wrote in ink across the paper, creating an ancient-looking letter.

These memories had inspired her when she was designing the logo for The Chocolate Apothecary; the result was a rectangular sepia-coloured label, with the corners blunted and the edges lined in black. *The Chocolate Apothecary* arched across the top in scrolled writing. Below the words was a sketch of a woman in Victorian dress atop a penny farthing—a nod to the town, famous for its annual penny farthing races through the village. The woman's basket overflowed with herbs and flowers—her medicinal tools—and her hair streamed out behind her in complete contrast with her prim Victorian clothing. Although the design was Victorian in feel, it coexisted harmoniously with the Georgian building she'd acquired to run her business.

When Christmas first saw the shop, it had a hand-painted sign tacked to a post and hammered into the overgrown front lawn saying, *For Sale or Rent by Owner*. At the time, she had enough money saved from her former career in public relations to place a deposit, but with no regular income now coming in, she knew that a bank wouldn't give her a loan to purchase the place. Instead she'd struck a rent-to-buy deal with the owner with the hope to one day own it outright. That was why articles like Peter's were so important. She was in this for the long haul, and failure was not an option.

'Most businesses fail in the first year,' her mother, Darla, had helpfully told her when Christmas announced she was opening the store. 'Well, I'm just being practical,' she'd said defensively in response to Christmas's dismayed expression.

But she was still here, three years on.

Like most small businesses—particularly those in sleepy towns off the popular trails—Christmas had known she'd have to diversify if she was to survive. While chocolate remained at the heart of what she did, she could never make a living just selling it; after all, people could pop into their local supermarket for a huge block of chocolate for a fifth of the price of hers. She had to entice people with a total sensory experience. So she found beautiful knick-knacks to sell and involved community members with small businesses of their own who needed a gorgeous place to sell their wares. In gilt letters on the front door, The Chocolate Apothecary now offered *Chocolate * Flowers * Homewares * Massage.*

In renovating the old building's front room, she'd sought to retain the essence of the original dispensary but also bring in a breath of fresh air and French country charm. Through a curly trail of paperwork with the council over heritage requirements, she'd replaced the solid wooden door with a glass one to make it inviting to customers on the street. To bring in as much light as possible and give the whole space a warm glow she'd hung rows of lamps and a couple of chandeliers from the ceiling.

She'd kept the original twenty-four-drawer dark wooden apothecary chest along the back wall. It still had some of its brass shell-shaped handles, though others had been replaced by silver replicas over time. On top of it, she'd mounted three tall white-washed hutches with shelves for products. The counter, which separated the apothecary chest and hutches from the customers, was a marble-topped affair, the kind on which you could grind, chop and mix ingredients and then scoop them off and into a mortar for further pounding. This was also where clients sat for chocolate consultations.

It was there at the bench that she'd first met Tu Pham, only weeks after opening the store, full of lofty ideas of chocolate as medicine she still wasn't really sure she could pull off. Tu had come to The Chocolate Apothecary to request a fairy godmother wish for her niece's thirteenth birthday.

At the time, Christmas had been making mousse. There was something so inspiring about turning unappealing egg white and sugar into a rich, snow-white, fluffy mound of foam. As Christmas whisked egg whites, Tu explained that her niece, Lien, lived with her because her parents had been killed in a car accident five years earlier. If that wasn't bad enough, Lien had juvenile arthritis, leaving her with stiff, swollen and painful joints, debilitating fevers and generally feeling unwell and fatigued. She was a smart girl and a big fan of Irish dancing, and whenever the medications were working and her arthritis was clinically under control, she took lessons.

Christmas, listening sympathetically, took a moment to enjoy the idea of a Vietnamese–Australian girl loving Irish dancing.

'But she's recently had a setback—her body's become immune to the cocktail of drugs she's been on. I'd take all her pain if I could.' Tu's knuckle caught a drop from her eye.

Christmas slid Tu a crystal glass filled with freshly made strawberry mousse, to which she'd added a drop of geranium essential oil.

'Thanks,' Tu said, taking the silver spoon from the marble counter and poking it into the shiny surface of the mousse.

'She must be missing her friends from school,' Christmas said. 'Thirteen is such a tough age.'

'It is. Her two closest friends come to visit her after school but it's like the light has gone out of her. She's depressed. And why wouldn't she be? She should be hanging out with her friends, wondering what dress to wear to the school dance, thinking about boys. Instead, she's basically bedridden like an old person.'

Tu sucked the spoon clean and her eyes opened wide. 'Mmm! That's really good.'

'Thanks. It's an experiment.'

'Well, consider me a willing guinea pig.'

Normally Christmas would have taken more pleasure in the compliment, but she was distracted by Tu's description of Lien's situation. It wasn't fair. A thirteen-year-old shouldn't be in that much pain. And depressed as well? Christmas knew only too well that dragging, empty, endless despair of depression. The way you became detached from everything around you, the fire extinguished. It was too much.

Her thoughts were interrupted when a woman in a bright yellow anorak approached the counter. 'Excuse me for a moment,' Christmas said, patting Tu's hand.

She served the customer, placing a dozen of her handmade chocolates into a box and tying it with ribbon. By the time she returned, Tu was halfway through the mousse and visibly cheerier.

'I'm serious. This is really good,' she said, waving her spoon in the air.

'Wait there. I'll give you some to take home to Lien.' Christmas popped out into the kitchen and spooned some mousse into a takeaway coffee cup, then snapped down the plastic lid.

She went back through the swing doors and resumed her position at her consulting stool. 'Apologies for the lack of presentation,' she said, handing over the cup.

'No, that's great. She'll love it, I'm sure,' Tu said.

'So tell me what I can do to help.'

Tu jiggled her leg beneath her on the stool, as though embarrassed or nervous. 'There's a big Irish dance company touring Australia right now and they'll be in Hobart next week. It will be hard for her to go—she can't get comfortable sitting up, but if we could get tickets, we could hire a special wheelchair, we can take her heat packs and pillows, we could organise special disability access. I know it's a lot, and we'd have to stay overnight because the long car trip would be really hard on her . . .' Her face fell then, reconciling all these challenges.

'Leave it with me,' Christmas said. 'I have a good feeling we can make it work and Lien will have a wonderful time. I'll try for tickets for her two friends as well, and hotel accommodation with a super-soft bed, all of it.'

'Really?' Tu's eyes welled with grateful tears.

'Absolutely. Lien needs as much joy as we can muster. Don't tell her yet in case it doesn't pan out. But I'll call you as soon as I can. In the meantime, if she likes that mousse you can come in every day and pick some up.'

Tu put her hands together in prayer position, her fingertips at her nose, and stared at Christmas as though she couldn't believe it. 'I don't know what to say. Thank you.'

'It's my pleasure. Truly.'

Later that afternoon, Tu had texted Christmas to say that Lien had loved the mousse, it had really lifted her spirits and she had been smiling ever since and telling jokes. *It must be magic mousse!* she finished.

And Christmas had stopped in the middle of sweeping the shop floor and leaned on the broom, a powerful, tingling wave rolling down her spine.

Geranium oil was well known for its effect of balancing the nervous system, lifting spirits, instilling a sense of hope, and relieving depression. Or so she'd read. Could the geranium oil in the strawberry mousse really have lifted Lien's mood?

It was possible, she'd realised with a turbo charge to her heart. It was entirely possible. And there'd been so much research into the health benefits of dark chocolate. So if both of those things were true, did that mean that her chocolate creations really could be medicinal? She'd been worried it was a bit fanciful, and her mother's eye-rolls didn't help, but maybe, just maybe, there was something in it after all. Tu's feedback certainly seemed to give the idea serious validation. And from that moment, she'd never looked back.

Everything had worked out perfectly for the trip to the Irish dance performance. Tu, Lien and her friends had had a great weekend in Hobart. Christmas's PR skills had combined with her journalist friend Mary Hauser's contacts to get free tickets, offered by the performance company. They'd also managed to secure hotel accommodation for all of them, with Lien's bed upsized to a king so she'd have lots of room to prop herself up with pillows as necessary. Tu and Lien had come in to see Christmas the day after their return, the young girl bubbling over with happiness. Soon afterwards, Lien became Christmas's taste tester.

'Dreadful!' she had declared about Christmas's German chamomile and lime chocolate shells.

'Lien!' Tu said, mortified. 'Sorry, Christmas.'

'No, no,' Christmas said. 'I need to know. Better to hear it from Lien than from a paying customer.' She winked at the girl.

Unabashed, Lien reached for her walking stick to go to the fridge for a glass of milk. 'Maybe sheep would like it?' she'd teased.

'Great idea. I'll take the rest to the animal sanctuary in Longford.'

Tu had handed Christmas a bowl of noodles. 'Stay for dinner?'

'Love to.'

Quickly, finding ways to help Lien had become one of Christmas's key motivations for what she was doing.

Rule number one—do what you love and love what you do.

And Christmas loved this store. She adored the crumbling brickwork and original fireplace, which she could never actually light because the heat would destroy the chocolate. She loved Cheyenne's glorious pyramid of fresh flowers next to the chocolate display case, with its blooms that mingled and cascaded down like a colourful fragrant waterfall. She loved the massage room in the back corner, the serene little hideaway for healing and relaxation, where Abigail eased muscles and minds every day. (*Rule number six—massage is not a luxury but a necessity.*) And she loved the nooks and crannies harbouring wooden trugs, wine barrels and metal bread bins, and the handmade soaps, floral linen water, ceramic birds, teapots, dried lavender, kitchen canisters, covered chairs, clocks, preserves, linen and lace.

It was precisely because of this that she should go to France. This career she'd built for herself was exciting; it was her life. She'd be mad not to go. She would just have to close the vault on any thought or emotion regarding her father. Stick to what was simple, the basic facts. And the facts were that she loved working with chocolate and Master Le Coutre was a virtuoso chocolatier.

Go to France, she told herself. *Go to France and forget your father. Simple.*

3

Over in Green Hills Aged Care in Oatlands, Elsa van Luc was waiting impatiently for her grandson to return. He'd come yesterday, straight from the airport, and stayed briefly, keeping a taxi waiting for him in the car park. She'd so wanted him to stay longer, but she'd quickly sent him home, telling him to get some rest. There was nothing worse than a clinging grandmother.

She'd heard Lincoln coming before she saw him, and her heart answered a loud hello. He'd called out when he reached the door of her detached bungalow but didn't wait for her to reply before coming in, just like the hundreds of times he'd ridden his bicycle to the farm to see her and eat her apple pie with raw sugar on top. Yesterday he strode in with a white box squashed under his arm.

She had known it was him by his voice and his smile, but not much else. There was so much hair.

'Hi, Nan,' he'd said, bending down to where she sat in her

wheelchair and kissing her cheek, wrapping her in a bear hug, his whiskers tickling her nose.

'Goodness, who is this come to see me? A yeti?'

He pressed the box into her hands and she clasped it in her crooked fingers with their enlarged knuckles. She could smell the chocolates inside and she brought the pretty parcel up to her nose and inhaled, her eyelids closing in a moment of bliss. At the age of ninety-two it was vitally important to make the most of each moment. The smell took her back to her teenage days working in the fancy cake shop in Hobart, where she had to wear a white lace cap, and polish silver, and stand all day long without a minute's rest off her feet.

'I came straight here, via the chocolate shop,' Lincoln said. He dragged a sturdy chair up next to her at the bay window where she'd been reading *Twilight* for the past hour. It was the latest on the book-club list. Lulu Divine—who occupied the private bungalow next to hers—had been so outraged by Elsa's choice that Elsa had begun to feel nervous about holding onto her position as captain, fearing that Lulu might lead a coup at the next election. She could already imagine Lulu's scathing diatribe on this one. Oh, what a chore she was. She was a former rodeo-riding, self-reliant girl (for, at seventy-two, she *was* just a girl compared to most of the residents) who, at just eighteen years of age, had left Australia to brave the tough rodeo opportunities in America. She wouldn't brook any of this Bella character's whimpering, simpering victim folly. No, Lulu Divine would have sent that Edward vampire on his way quick smart.

Elsa, on the other hand, harboured a soft spot for the Cullen boy. Typical really. Nothing had changed then. Sometimes she wished she'd been more like Lulu when she was young. Not that Ebe had been a vampire of a husband. Just a big kid who'd never grown up and didn't like to take any sort of responsibility in the world. He thought everything should come easily. Hard work was overrated as far as Ebe was concerned.

'You didn't need to bring me anything,' she'd scolded her grandson, but she knew Lincoln could see right through her pretend crossness. She'd missed him terribly. 'And you could have got settled at home first.'

She felt a stab of homesickness at the word 'home', the house she'd bought in town after Ebe had died, when the farm had become too much for her on her own. Now Lincoln lived there on an ad hoc basis between jobs. It suited her, knowing he had a place to come home to. A place not far from her.

'Bit jetlagged,' he admitted. 'Didn't trust myself to drive yet. My head's still on the other side of the world.'

'I got your email,' Elsa said. 'What luck for me that your project finished a bit earlier than expected.' Her eyes narrowed.

He sat casually, leaning forward with his arms resting on his thighs and his hands dangling between them. His blue eyes, the iridescent colours of a blue jay's back—so much like Tom's, yet alive and engaging where his father's were dull—drilled into hers. 'Yes.'

They regarded each other for a moment. Jenny would be behind this, no doubt.

'I assume you've cut your trip short because your sister asked you to,' Elsa said.

He hesitated as though trying to decide how much to say. 'She had reason to be concerned. The nurse, what's her name, Susan . . . ?'

'Sarah.'

'Yes, Sarah. She'd emailed Jen to say she was worried about you.'

'Did she?' Elsa felt a flicker of annoyance, but it was extinguished quickly. Her favourite nurse, Sarah, could do no wrong as far as Elsa was concerned.

'She mentioned that Dad had been making things difficult.'

Lincoln was fishing for information, she could tell. He didn't know much. But he'd cut his research trip short to come home for her. It was beyond flattering. But then, if someone *had* to come— and she was too proud to think for a second that they did—it probably would have to be him. Jenny couldn't travel easily from north Queensland with young Nathan in his wheelchair. As for the rest of the family: Elsa's eldest son, Matthew, had died in Vietnam; the next son, Jake, had left Australia forty years back for London; and the youngest son, Tom, was the one acting up.

'So how are you, really?' Lincoln asked, and the seriousness in his voice saddened her. He shouldn't be worrying about her. He had a life to lead, not to be wasted fretting over an old woman.

She began to untie the string around the box. ' "The Chocolate Apothecary",' she said, reading the sepia-coloured sticker. 'I don't think I've tried these before. Thank you.'

'You're welcome. But don't change the topic.'

She swallowed her annoyance. What the young didn't seem to understand was that no amount of moping or complaining could actually *fix* anything, so, really, there was just no point dwelling. All you could do was keep busy and strive for new goals, no matter how small. It was okay to keep wanting more, even at her age. Essential, actually. That's what she told herself anyway whenever she felt that vain thrill run through her at the sight of her name up on the board in the common dining room—*Book Club Captain: Elsa van Luc, Wombat Bungalow.*

'The physio-terrorist is exceptionally pleased with my work in the pool this week,' she said cheerfully, giving him some sort of answer in return for his concern. 'He says my hip range has improved out of sight. I'll be pole dancing by New Year.'

'That's a party trick I'd like to see,' Lincoln said. He was so easy to please.

She threw the focus back to him. 'Have you seen your father?'

'I only just got off the plane,' he said, eyeing her. 'I'll go see him when I've dealt with the jetlag. You were my priority. I wanted to make sure you were alright.'

Elsa had the box open and was clucking excitedly over the chocolates. Several had the most delicate floral stencil patterns on top. Some were the shape of a coffee cup, with white chocolate 'milk' inside. Some were wrapped not just in coloured foil but with tiny perfect ribbons as well. There were even tiny hand-painted fairies, with sparkling wings. 'They almost look too good to eat,' she said. 'Each one's a work of art.'

'It's an amazing little shop,' he said. 'It's run by this woman who's also a fairy godmother.'

'A fairy godmother?'

'Apparently. I picked up a brochure at the airport.' He started to pat his pockets, looking for it to give to her, but gave up when he couldn't find it. 'Anyway, she's a professional wish-granter or something like that. People hire her to make dreams or wishes come true for their family and friends. Isn't that a great idea?'

Elsa popped a hazelnut praline into her mouth and moaned as the velvety chocolate melted and washed over her tastebuds, the aroma wafting up her nostrils.

Lincoln smiled. She offered the box to him but he waved it away. Then he yawned.

'Clearly we have much to catch up on,' she said, running her tongue over her false teeth and sucking from them every last morsel of chocolate. 'But you obviously need to get home to bed.'

She arched a thinning eyebrow and gestured in the area of his face. 'And a shower and shave.'

He ran a hand through his long rumpled hair and yawned again, his eyes watering with fatigue.

'I want to hear all about the jungle, but don't tell me now,' she said. 'That way you'll have to come back and see me again. You should get home. That taxi's meter's running and it's getting dark outside.'

Lincoln reached out his big, roughened hand and placed it on her veiny, knobbly one. 'I don't need any excuses to come see my favourite grandmother.'

'*Pft.* I'm your only grandparent left. But I'll milk it for all it's worth. Come back and see me when you've found your face under all that fur.'

He stood and kissed her on the cheek again and she patted his shoulder. 'You're a good boy.'

He grinned and she was speared with the memory of him grinning just like that when he was six, fistfuls of leaves in his hands while helping her in the garden.

'Thanks, Nan. See you soon.'

With that, he'd lumbered out of the room, leaving behind a gaping hole in her chest.

Now she was waiting for him again, the opened copy of *Twilight* once more on her lap, except she couldn't muster the concentration to read it. Instead she was sitting at the window, watching for his car—her car, actually—to putter up the driveway. Waiting like a faithful hound and wondering if there was something she could do to encourage him to stay this time.

She hated being this excited about his return. And she felt unbridled guilt that she loved her grandson more than her son.

As well as deep shame that, if she were totally honest with herself, she wished he would change his life for her. No more tripping around the world. She wanted him to put down roots. Find a woman and get married and have children. For as much as she adored her grandson, sometimes his laid-back attitude to life reminded her of her husband—though Lincoln was far more generous and reliable than Ebe ever was.

Not that she wanted him to live his life around her, of course. She wasn't that selfish. She was an old woman; he was a young man. It was the law of nature.

But still, if it could all fall into place that way . . .

Especially with things as they were with Tom right now. Thinking of her youngest son was like being drenched with cold water. Not for the first time she questioned how Lincoln and his father could be so different.

There must be an answer. Certainly, Lincoln's globe-trotting would be partly due to his unwillingness to stay in the same place as his father for too long. Those two were made to rub up against each other like pieces of flint. Tom had always been too hard on Lincoln. Anyone could see that. And that was why Lincoln had spent more time at her house than his own as a boy. Tom was a fool and too stubborn to admit he'd been a bad father.

But she still had a chance with Lincoln. She just had to find a motivation strong enough for him to stay. It was a challenge, like a game of chess, and she loved a good challenge. It would keep her mind buzzing like a busy wee bee in the nightly hours of insomnia, as she lay in her bed with just the red glow of the emergency call buttons around the walls of her bungalow to remind her she wasn't really alone, that help was only a few metres away in the high-care building.

She heard the Honda crunching over the driveway and closed her book.

Challenge accepted.

●

To: Christmas Livingstone; Joseph Kennedy; Darla Livingstone
From: Valerie Kennedy
Subject: Save the date!

Hi family,

It's finally happened. Archie has popped the question! Actually, that's a bit dramatic. Basically we decided over fish and chips that after ten years and three kids it was about time we got hitched. So we've set the date for 29 July. Simple church wedding and backyard reception, nothing too fancy. Not too much tradition. Although, Dad, if it's okay I'd like you to walk me down the aisle. Christmas, will you be my bridesmaid? Mum, do you think you can come?

Val xx

———————

To: Valerie Kennedy; Christmas Livingstone; Darla Livingstone
From: Joseph Kennedy
Subject: Re: Save the date!

My darling girl, congratulations to you both. And of course I will walk you down the aisle. It would be my honour. Call me this afternoon.

Dad xx

Christmas felt like she'd swallowed a sponge. A big, fat absorbent sponge that was now sucking her dry. Her tongue stuck to the roof of her mouth. Thank goodness Val had shared this news via email rather than in person.

She dropped the block of chocolate on the marble bench, took a breath and ran her hands down her apron. She tugged at the lace around the sweetheart neckline of her dress, which was suddenly scratchy.

She was happy for Val. Of course she was. She and Archie had been together for so long and they seemed solid. And happy. Why shouldn't they get married? And it was an honour to be bridesmaid. So why did she feel like this?

It wasn't that she was losing her sister. Nothing was changing, really. Val and Archie already lived together and had the three boys, so it wasn't like anything major would come along to disrupt the sisters' relationship with each other.

She began to shave the chocolate into a small bowl. An unpleasant sensation spread slowly but unstoppably out from her middle, filling her chest and flowing down her legs.

Jealousy, she was horrified to realise. She was fiercely, achingly jealous.

But it wasn't the wedding.

It was Joseph.

To: Joseph Kennedy; Valerie Kennedy; Darla Livingstone
From: Christmas Livingstone
Subject: Re: Save the date!

My Tiny Val is getting married!!! How exciting! Congratulations!! Yes of course I'll be your bridesmaid. We'll chat soon!! ☺ love xxxx

———

To: Valerie Kennedy; Christmas Livingstone; Joseph Kennedy
From: Darla Livingstone
Subject: Re: Save the date!

Why would you change something that's not broken? Valerie,
I know you think you're doing the right thing, but honestly,
marriage isn't all it's cracked up to be. (Tell her, Joseph—you've
got two failed marriages under your belt.) You and Archie have
had a good run. Don't ruin it now.

I'm very busy with my work. I was due to be out in western
Queensland about that time. But if you insist on going ahead I'll
do my best to be there.

Mum

———————

To: Christmas Livingstone
From: Valerie Kennedy
Subject: What the hell is wrong with our mother?!?!?!?

•

When Christmas was nine years old, she'd pictured her
biological father as the Looney Tunes French skunk, Pepe Le
Pew. All her mother had ever told Christmas about her father
was that he had been a twenty-year-old travelling juggler
from France whom she'd known only 'briefly' (whatever that
meant). He wasn't listed on the birth certificate. No father was.
And as an adult Christmas was at times highly sceptical that
he existed at all, suspecting that Darla had fabricated him to
cover the fact that she couldn't actually remember who the real
one was.

But back then, before those doubts had crept in, Christmas had imagined that her father had black hair with a dramatic white stripe through it, styled with volume. His cheeks were large and expressive, mooshing and squooshing as he pressed them up against the object of his rampant affection—her mother. He clasped Darla's body to his, cartoon love hearts popping from his chest and stars shooting from his eyes at her outstanding beauty. He was dashing. Overwhelmingly romantic. He serenaded Darla with love songs, a rose between his teeth, and French poetry muttered breathlessly into her ear. Aside from the fact that Pepe Le Pew was actually blatantly sexually harassing the black and white female cat with whom he was smitten, and the fact that he smelled, well, like a skunk, he was every girl's dream.

Later, when Christmas was a teenager and Darla had made the shocking revelation that her father's name was Gregoire Lachapelle, Christmas's image of him had swiftly changed. He now looked like a French film star of the eighties she would watch on movies from her local video store and rewind to watch again. He had desperately soft, jet-black hair that framed his face with delicious curls that just begged to be coiled around your finger. Olive skin. A clean, square jaw. A husky, smoky voice. And eyes that smouldered with passion. She seethed with anger that her mother had carelessly let this man slip through her grasp.

Even as a mature woman, Christmas's vision of her father still changed regularly. In her most recent imaginings, his face was aged, lined. He would be retired now, with greying hair and silver whiskers that he kept artfully long, not long enough to constitute a beard but more than a couple of days' growth. Sometimes she pictured him as a farmer, out in the fields tending his sheep, or perhaps his vines. Sometimes he was an artist in Paris, living in a one-bedroom loft like hers, except he would be in the heart of the city, perhaps amid the cafes of the Latin Quarter. Sometimes she imagined him married, with not only other children but grandchildren too who he chased around in the park on weekends. Sometimes in her imaginings, Gregoire was gay—a lost juggler who'd headed out across the oceans as a young man to explore the world and himself, and her mother had been an experiment.

Darla was painfully sparse on details. Once, as a teenager, Christmas had asked her if Gregoire really was a juggler, and Darla said, 'Yes.' Then she looked off into the distance, her scissors poised above the magazine voucher she was clipping, and said, 'Or maybe a fruit picker who just happened to juggle his apples?'

Christmas was furious, raging with teenage angst. 'Was there more than one?' she demanded. 'Could it have been someone else?' After all, it *had* been the psychedelic seventies (and surely even Tasmania had been a little touched by the movement), and her mother's memories were clearly shaky.

Christmas had hoped Darla would be offended. Angry. Snap, 'Of course not, don't be silly.' But instead she considered it thoughtfully while Christmas waited, her heart threatening to spring out of her chest.

'No,' Darla said finally, slowly and deliberately. 'No.'

Christmas had stormed to her room and slammed the door anyway.

She'd never had a father, not even a photo of one. Not even one listed on her birth certificate to make it official in any way. It was as if she had just appeared from nowhere. She couldn't quite grieve for her father, because she'd never had him. Yet still she felt his absence. It was the cruel irony of losing something she'd never even had.

Joseph had married her mother when Christmas was six. He had been a stabilising influence on Darla, filling their empty fridge with pre-cooked dinners and fresh vegetables, and turning Darla's midnight neighbourhood rambles into reading time and warm milk before bed. Then, when Christmas was seven, along came Val, and it looked for a while as though they'd be a happily-ever-after family.

But a few years later, Joseph left. Twelve-year-old Christmas stood in the driveway watching the car, packed with him and her Tiny Val and their things, till long after it was out of sight, clutching the piece of paper with the phone number he'd written on it, telling her she could call any time. She'd refused to cry and her body burned with the pain instead.

Now he'd be walking Val down the aisle, proud as punch with his little girl on his arm.

He'd been the only father Christmas had known, and she'd lost him too.

4

The tail of summer, for what it was worth, had been shooed away with clouds and showers every day for the past week. It was a great relief for the farmers, whose land was parched from the prolonged drought through last winter, spring and late into summer.

Easter Saturday started early for Christmas, at seven am, with a special consultation for Rosemary McCaw With a Rather Wide Jaw. (After reading four *Hairy Maclary* books to her nephews last week, she'd started to think of her fellow villagers as larger-than-life rhyming storybook characters. And Rosemary McCaw, a flamboyant woman in her seventies, was by far her favourite.)

'My spirit is vexed,' Rosemary said now, sitting on the tall-legged stool at the counter. Her bejewelled fingers were pressed to either side of her unnaturally ruddy cheeks, the source of which Christmas was unsure, though she'd always suspected that Rosemary was fond of the sherry. Rosemary did her best, though, to hide it. She never left the house without caked-on white makeup, pencilled eyebrows, and blush swept so high on the cheekbones it almost reached her eyes. Her blue-grey hair peeked out from beneath an emerald-green scarf wrapped around her head like a turban.

Rosemary's grown children and their collective brood of offspring were staying with her for the weekend and she was feeling overrun already, particularly as it was also the Evandale garden expo today. Rosemary was on the organising committee and, as she kept telling Christmas, she'd been run off her feet picking up the slack for the other committee members, who didn't seem to care whether Evandale looked like a backyard garden patch, the Queen's own leisure grounds, or a pile of hay and manure mucked out of a stable. And today she needed to be out making sure everyone was showing Evandale at its best, not worrying about entertaining the family circus, who seemed to feel the need to come and see her all at once for safety in numbers.

Christmas listened closely to Rosemary's many complaints. 'I recommend plain dark chocolate,' she said at last, selecting a small block from the shelf. 'This is eighty-five per cent cocoa chocolate from Ecuador, made entirely from Criollo beans.'

'*Criollo*?' Rosemary rolled the word around her mouth as she reached for the chocolate life raft before her.

'Criollo beans are flavour beans, usually used for specific taste sensations rather than mass volume.'

'Like wine.'

'Similar. But it means it's not going to taste like a block of commercial chocolate you find in a supermarket, which are usually mostly made of Forastero beans.'

'All the better.'

'And the high cocoa content will make it drier and more intense,' Christmas went on. 'But what you'll get from it are high levels of antioxidants to help combat the negative effects of stress, and the release of endorphins in the brain will help you feel better. There's also research to suggest that chemicals in the chocolate can offer cardiovascular protection, also great during times of high stress. It's not cheap, but it's going to give you the biggest bang for your buck, with great nutritional benefits and without all the saturated fat and sugar of mass-produced chocolate.'

'I'll take it,' Rosemary said. 'How much should one consume?'

'That block should last you all day. And you can eat it on the run, wherever you are, no matter what you're doing. The caffeine in the chocolate might help keep your mind focused on your tasks too. But if you run out, you know where to find me.'

Rosemary raised the block to her face as if she were going to press her red matte lipstick to its smooth paper-wrapped surface, her features relaxing as she inhaled the scent of roasted cocoa. 'Christmas Livingstone, you're an angel,' she said, as she always did, in that husky resonant voice left over from her days in the theatre.

'Well, a fairy godmother, anyway,' Christmas said and smiled, as she always did.

'If only I'd had such nourishment on hand when I was playing Ophelia under that horrid director in Hobart who shouted and cursed with every breath he took.'

Rosemary then spent the next fifteen minutes explaining how important the annual garden show was for a small town like Evandale, and for Tasmanian tourism generally, lamenting the apathy of so many these days towards their town. Christmas nodded and assured her that she was doing great work. She'd always thought Rosemary was essentially a bit lonely and that she threw herself into community projects to pass the time.

'Also, I would recommend a massage as soon as possible next week,' Christmas said. 'You can't get much better than fine dark chocolate and massage for stress treatment.'

'My shoulder has been rebellious lately. I'm sure it's the weather. So changeable. I fell off the stage once and it's never been the same since.' Rosemary clasped her left shoulder and furrowed her brow.

Christmas looked in the appointment book and chewed the end of her pen. 'Abigail's free Tuesday morning if you'd like to come in then?'

'That sounds like a fine idea.' Rosemary slipped the chocolate bar into her metallic purple handbag and retrieved her change purse. She pulled out some notes and handed them to Christmas. 'You may as well take the money for the massage now too, to save bother later.'

Christmas wrote the time onto an appointment card and Rosemary chose a piece of West African salted milk chocolate from the tasting plate on the counter.

'Mmm . . .' She closed her eyes and sucked in her cheeks.

'Nice, isn't it?' Christmas said. 'The sugar hits you first and then the salt just lingers at the end and seems to enhance the whole thing.'

'There isn't a word that could adequately describe that,' Rosemary all but whispered.

Christmas laughed and accompanied her to the door.

'I can still count on you for the flower-inspired chocolates for the gourmet food tent?' Rosemary asked, her anxiety returning.

'Absolutely. Cheyenne is putting together flower arrangements and she'll be bringing them down soon, I should think. I'll be along shortly with the chocolates.'

'Marvellous. See you in a few hours.' Rosemary took a steadying breath before venturing forth.

Christmas gave her a wave as she strode across the coir doormat and down the single rendered step to the footpath, heading towards the park and the white expo tents that had been set up since yesterday, her long skirt brushing the pots of dancing fuchsia petunias as she went. She stepped off the path briefly to allow a more senior woman to pass unhindered, and was nearly knocked off her feet by Gordon Harding Who Rode His Penny Farthing. Rosemary shook her fist and bellowed at him for his reckless scooting around town on his silly old bicycle. At least, that's what it sounded like to Christmas. She suppressed a giggle and turned back inside the shop.

She was just opening the blue wooden window shutters to let in the mild day when Bert and Ernie bustled in the door. Those were their real names. She didn't have to give them rhyming names; she couldn't top what they already had. They'd been friends since they were boys and now played Canasta together every week with another couple of retired friends. They were fond of windcheaters and baseball caps. Bert still had his wife of more than forty years but Ernie's wife had passed on last year, and since then he'd struggled to smile as often as he used to.

'Morning, love, we heard you were opening early today,' Bert said.

'Yes, big day ahead.' Christmas patted him lightly on the shoulder as he passed. 'Busiest day of the year, I'd say.'

Bert and Ernie headed for the coffee plunger on the marble counter.

Christmas offered free coffee all day, every day. Real coffee from freshly roasted beans that were organic and ethically sourced, ground on site just prior to brewing. The smell wafted out onto the footpath, and the blackboard out front offering *Free Coffee From Real Beans* ensured that she capitalised on whatever pedestrian or motor traffic passed by her small garden of petu-nias, bluebells and daffodils within the white picket fence. And as Evandale was off the main thoroughfares, businesses had to capitalise on whatever they could. Too many small businesses had come and gone here over the years, so Christmas was deter-mined to do whatever it took.

She'd once read that during the Great Depression in America, cinemas offered free hot popcorn to patrons, the irresistible smell of butter and salt drawing people inside. That was a stroke of genius and exactly how you kept making money in difficult times, and she'd tucked that piece of information away in the back of her mind.

Coffee was currency. Coffee was her social media. Yes, you could make tidy profits on coffee by selling it, but only if you got customers in the door in the first place. Coffee drinkers were like wine drinkers and chocolate connoisseurs. If she wanted customers to invest in high-quality chocolate that cost ten dollars for a hundred grams instead of mass-produced high-fat, high-sugar chocolate at three dollars a block, she had to meet their refined needs and give them something to make it worth it.

And it worked. The constant stream of visitors made The Chocolate Apothecary one of the busiest shops in the street, right behind Jane Shaw's Ingleside Bakery, which filled Christmas with tremendous pride. She'd built something really special here, and life was good.

●

Lincoln had only been back in the country two days, finding his feet again with the norms of grocery shopping, miserable weather and the constant dread of visiting his father. He was still adjusting to this land—the complete opposite of the Amazon—and it wasn't helping his sense of place. It was disconcerting, and added to his restlessness to hit the road again.

As if to rub it in, his publisher, Jeremy Gilshannon, was flying off to Tokyo tomorrow and had asked to Skype this morning to discuss the new book. Lincoln assumed it wasn't good news, since Jez's email was sketchy and filled with promises of catching up for teppanyaki and cold beer when he returned. But it also gave him an excuse to put off dealing with his father for a bit longer, by convincing himself he had 'meetings' to attend to. And since Nan was looking well, there seemed to be no urgency to confront Tom about whatever he'd been doing to upset her.

Jez smiled smoothly at Lincoln from the computer screen. 'The sample chapters were good,' he said through a mouthful of cereal, his spoon chasing an errant raisin around the bowl. 'But we think you might benefit from a co-author.'

'What do you mean?' Lincoln asked, taken aback. 'As in a ghost writer?'

'No, not at all. A co-author. An equal partner. Someone who can bring an extra dimension to your writing. You've got all this amazing scientific knowledge of cacao and heaps of great history and wonderful street cred, having travelled Africa and the Amazon and all, it's just that, sometimes—and only *occasionally*—the facts get in the way of a good story.'

'You want me to lie?' In the background, Lincoln could see Jez's partner carrying a load of washing through the lounge room.

'No, no!' Jez gulped down tea from a mug, the teabag string and label stuck to the side. 'We want all your fabulous knowledge of cacao tree courtship rituals; we just want someone who knows how to spin it, weave it, into something that's so irresistible, so marketable, it will be the hottest non-fiction book of the year.'

Lincoln squirmed at the implicit criticism but managed to keep his cool. Jez was a graphic designer who'd crossed over to publishing five years ago. He thought visually. He thought in colour and with *pop*! When he read books he saw them as movies. Apparently, Lincoln's chapters had been a little black and white and grainy and Jez was looking for rich, surround-sound, multidimensional words. Words that could be eaten off the page.

'Your last book was different. It was a textbook, really. Which is why universities and TAFEs across the country have snapped it up as course reading material. But this is different. With the huge renaissance chocolate is enjoying right now, the general public is our target audience. They're the people who watch *MasterChef.*'

'But it's not a cookbook.'

'No. But it could be both. We could straddle two worlds, you with your botanical knowledge and emphasis on the economic, social and environmental aspects of sustainable cacao farming, and this other author focusing on the stuff we all love. The flavour. The smell. The colour. We want pictures. We want to vicariously taste all this wonderful chocolate that comes from the jungles of which you're so fond.'

'This is a different brief than we originally discussed,' Lincoln said, a needle of irritation in his tone.

'Yes, it is,' Jeremy said, pausing to offer the remains of the milk at the bottom of his cereal bowl to a Siamese cat who had just landed neatly on his lap, winding its tail up under his nose. 'And it's not your fault. Please don't think that. It's just that we're in the business of selling books and we react to what the market wants. And the market is voraciously consuming books about food.' He held up a finger and nodded sagely. 'Food is the new vampire.'

Lincoln snorted.

'But rest assured, we too want to go deeper than a how-to-temper-chocolate book. People have a thirst for knowledge now. They've moved on from that dashing devil in a purple coat.'

'Huh?'

'Cadbury.'

'Oh.'

'They want to feel *connected* to where their food comes from. And that's what you do so well.'

Lincoln's hackles lowered. He could see the sense in what Jez was saying. 'Do you have someone in mind?'

Jez shrugged. 'We've always got good writers floating around that could help out. If you like we can approach some, see how they feel. Unless you know someone already?'

'Leave it with me for a week or so to digest and I'll see if anything comes to mind.'

'Excellent. Well then, I'm off to Tokes.' Jeremy kissed the top of his cat's head. 'Let's chat when I get back. *Sayonara!*' He waved enthusiastically at Lincoln and disconnected from the call.

Lincoln sat in the chair for a while, staring at the blank screen. He felt deflated and tetchy. His grandmother's house, with its pastel furnishings and outdated laminate, felt empty and uninspiring.

Rousing himself, he texted his mate Rubble, arranging to meet him at the pub on Thursday, so that was something to look forward to. But right now he needed to get out of the house.

He grabbed a woollen jumper and the car keys and drove out of the driveway with no plan except to get some fresh air and clear his head. But it wasn't long before he found himself heading towards Evandale.

●

If Christmas hadn't been working so hard, running between the shop, where Abigail was managing the floor for the day, and The Chocolate Apothecary's tent at the garden expo, where Cheyenne was in charge, she'd have loved to wander around and look at the displays. There were trickling and bubbling water features; tiers of potted colour; bursts of fragrant herbs; shiny bronze garden ornaments; shovels and mowers, irrigation systems and chainsaws; neem oil for pest control; bird baths and feeders; beehives; and worm gardens. The Apothecary's tent was up next to the food vans, and the aromas of sizzling onion and wood-fired pizza drifted effortlessly on the wind and made her stomach rumble every time she scooted past.

Cheyenne's flower displays were elegant and simple, in white and pale pink, and she'd draped fine white gauze around the tent so it looked romantic and rather wedding-like. Christmas's handmade chocolates, all of them in the shape of flowers or boxes with flowers on top, sat in tiers on silver plates and attracted a lot of interest. She'd already received several orders for special occasions, and many people had taken photos and uploaded them to social media sites. She was also pleased to see that Cheyenne's flowers were generating plenty of interest too and she was fielding queries for special orders from the same people.

'What?' Cheyenne said, grinning, as she waved goodbye to a young couple who'd taken her business card with them.

'I was just thinking how much you deserve this,' Christmas said. 'You work so hard and you're such a great mum, your displays for The Apothecary are always sensational and add so much to my business. *And* you work in the convenience store as well. I don't know how you do it. It's great that people are finally seeing your true talent.'

Cheyenne fiddled with the silver bracelet on her wrist. 'Well, you just have to get on and do what you need to do. I'm lucky to have free space in your shop to sell my flowers.'

'It's not exactly free.' Christmas gestured around at the tent and the expo grounds. 'I couldn't get by without you stepping in to help out.'

'We need each other.'

'Definitely.'

'And I enjoy it. I like people,' Cheyenne said, reaching for a sandwich from under the table and chomping into it. 'I like networking and making new friends.'

Christmas checked her watch. It was nearing mid-morning and The Apothecary would be starting to fill. 'I'd better go back and see how Abigail's getting on,' she said. Abigail was capable and efficient, and worked under the same arrangement as Cheyenne, trading hours on the floor in the shop for massage space. But she wasn't as cheerful as Cheyenne. Abigail Ahern Who Seemed Rather Stern had less tolerance for busy work. She was a good massage therapist and was at her best in a one-on-one situation. Crowds of people rattled her, unlike Cheyenne, who seemed to shine brighter with every new person she spoke to. Abigail was younger and was studying to be an exercise physiologist—whatever that meant, Christmas was never quite sure. So everything she did day-to-day was broken down into small chunks of time, waiting for the next phase of life to begin.

'Yes, she'll be starting to fret,' Cheyenne said, not unkindly.

They paused to observe Rosemary McCaw sashay like a long-necked runner duck from one side of the lawn to the other, an emerald-green waistcoat hugging her thin torso, enunciating heroically into a megaphone as she urged people to buy up plants and ornaments. Then she stopped, lowered the megaphone, fiddled in the pocket of her waistcoat, retrieved a piece of dark chocolate and popped it in her mouth. Christmas cheered, and Rosemary turned and raised a graceful hand in salute.

Christmas was just slinging her cotton handbag across her body, preparing to return to the shop, when a tall bearded man approached the tent, two bags of plants in one hand and a sausage wrapped in bread in the other.

'Hi.' Lincoln smiled.

'Oh, hello.'

Lincoln smiled at Cheyenne too.

'Lincoln, this is Cheyenne, my friend and colleague. She's a florist.'

'Hi.' Cheyenne smiled and noticeably blushed, and Christmas felt inexplicably proprietorial towards him.

'And this is Lincoln, he helped me carry in a box yesterday. He's a botanist,' Christmas finished.

'Oh, wow,' Cheyenne said, her usual bubbliness squashed, Christmas assumed, under the total impressiveness of the man standing in front of her, tomato sauce on his fingers aside.

'Nice to meet you,' he said.

'I'm just leaving, actually,' Christmas said. 'I've got to get back to the shop.'

'I'll come with you,' Lincoln said. 'Can I carry something? I'm good at lifting.'

Cheyenne giggled and began to rearrange a display of lilies that didn't need rearranging.

Christmas smiled. 'That's okay, thanks. I unloaded every-thing this morning. But I've got to head back because it will be getting busy in there about now.'

They walked together through the throng of people and Lincoln finished off his sausage. 'Why are sausages so appealing when you're out in the open?' he said, licking sauce off his thumb.

'I know, right? I'd never buy sausages and take them home and cook them, but it's nearly impossible to walk past a sausage sizzle and not get one.'

They had a few blocks to walk to get back to the shop. The street was lined with cars on both sides, and the footpath was jammed with pedestrians weighed down with boxes of plants, garden tools, or prams and dogs. They had to keep breaking their conversation to sidestep someone coming the other way, or overtake someone going too slowly.

'You said you'd been in the jungle in South America,' Christmas recalled. 'What were you doing?'

'Working for a company called Neptune Enterprises.'

'As in the biggest producers of chocolate in the world?' she said, her interest piqued.

'Exactly. I've been doing research on their cacao plantations on and off for a number of years. The projects change but generally their attention always comes back to fruit production because that's where the bottom line is. So I spend a lot of time looking at the micro level of the mechanics of pollination: stamen, pistils, pollen, genetics, traits, nutrient transfer and mycorrhizal fungi.'

Christmas widened her eyes to suggest that she was impressed, but she didn't actually know what fungi had to do with cacao reproduction. 'That sounds interesting,' she said, 'and like a lot of hard work. What's it like being in the jungle?'

Lincoln took a couple of quick steps to catch up after stepping aside for an elderly woman and her dog. 'The jungle's intense. But my time there wasn't as hard as some others had it. The research station sits in the Amazon Basin jungle, on the banks of the Napo River. It shares infrastructure with the adjoining ecotourism lodge—diesel generators, solar panels, septic, water filtration and stuff like that. A lot of scientists out there use it as a drop-in centre to go to when they've struck bad weather, their research has hit a dead end or they're sick. I had a cabin in the station itself, basic but comfortable and even with wi-fi. But the ecology teams out there, who are often self-funded or working for universities, they trek for weeks at a time, sleeping in hammocks between trees and waking with boas on the canopy sheets, dealing with leeches and botfly larvae that burrow into the skin and have to be smoked out.'

Christmas shuddered. 'That's horrible. I need far too many of life's comforts to be doing that.'

'I only had to leave the station for day trips, mostly, or occasionally an overnight stay in one of the village huts. Sometimes I'd walk for half a day or canoe to one of the nearby fincas.'

'What's a finca?' she asked, shielding her eyes from the bright sun that had suddenly appeared again.

'They're family-owned cacao plantations, often only an acre or two,' he explained. 'Almost all cacao is grown this way, in small allotments. The family's out there every day, working to trade for cash. It's a tough life. What I do is relatively easy. I just blunder about under the trees and collect samples of pods, leaves, flowers, bark, soil. I count pods and chart weather patterns and growth rates. And sketch, you know, like in the old days! And I take photos. I catch pollinating insects and set humane traps to see what sort of arboreal animals are visiting the trees.'

'Like monkeys?'

'Yep. Cheeky buggers they are.'

They were at The Apothecary now and Christmas paused at the door. It was definitely busy in there. She could see Abigail, dressed in black beneath a red and white apron, moving swiftly through the crowd, picking up plates. Christmas knew she should get in there and help but she wanted to keep talking to Lincoln.

'You sound like you love it,' she said to him.

'I do,' he said. 'I never know when I'm going to get another contract, but that's okay. I've seen the uncertainty that the Ecuadorians live with from day to day. We're spoilt in a country like ours.'

There was so much she wanted to say to him then, about how she admired his bravery to just let go and follow his heart with no guaranteed reward at the end. But she needed to go. Abigail was trying to catch her eye.

'I'd love to keep talking but I need to get in there,' she said, indicating over her shoulder. 'I don't think I could live in the jungle, but I can make really good chocolate, thanks to people like you, I guess. And the farmers, of course. Though I almost feel guilty now, hearing about how hard they work.'

'No, don't. The trees give their fruit so it can be enjoyed. You're helping a tree fulfil its destiny, if you like.'

She hovered. 'That's a beautiful way of looking at it.'

'Actually, do you have any chocolate in there from Ecuador?' His eyes lit up.

'Yes.'

'Brilliant. I'll come in and enjoy the end result of my friends' efforts in the jungle,' he said. 'And I should get Nan some more chocolate for Easter. I'm seeing her this afternoon. She thought it was the best chocolate she'd ever tasted.'

'That's a lovely compliment. Tell her I said thanks.'

Lincoln followed her inside and her heart put in a quickstep.

And if she'd let herself, she would have heard a tiny, soft voice starting to wonder what it might be like to live without rules.

But she wasn't listening.

5

On Thursday, Rubble Jones, an industrial artist with a passion for creating pieces that fused art sculpture with functional furniture, ushered Lincoln into his dilapidated BMW—a car that had to be worth a total of four dollars, in Lincoln's estimation. Lincoln settled himself on the ripped seat and shoved the McDonald's detritus out of the way with his foot.

A pleasant drive through the countryside later, they found themselves in the sunny courtyard of Rosevears Tavern, looking out over the black mud sliding into the choppy, steely blue water of the West Tamar River. Across the expanse of water, green hills rose upwards, spotted with trees, houses and an elderly church down at the water's edge.

'Welcome home!' Rubble held up a schooner of amber liquid. 'It's good to have you back.'

'Thanks.'

'So what's next on the horizon for you, my friend?' Rubble said, leaning his bulk back in the seat.

'Not sure. I'm here to spend some time with Nan, mostly.'

'How is the old girl?' Rubble asked fondly.

'She's okay, I think. My dad's being a bit of a tool.'

'Nothing new there.'

'Nope. Nothing new.' It was a relief not to have to explain himself. Rubble had been there throughout his childhood and had seen enough of Tom's temper tantrums, sullenness and snide remarks to understand. And he'd been on the receiving end of more than a few cutting remarks from Tom too, particularly when his weight had started fluctuating in his teenage years. 'But I downloaded some job applications today, more research, similar fields.'

'The jungle's been good to you, then?'

Lincoln looked out across the water, still adjusting to the cool air and open spaces of home. 'It's fascinating. It never sleeps.'

'Like New York,' Rubble said, taking a handful of the hot chips that had just been delivered to their table.

Every part of Rubble's body wobbled as he moved—he must have put on fifteen kilos since Lincoln last saw him. A sure sign he was in 'famine' mode. Not literally, obviously. His popping shirt buttons and the flesh gathering under his chin were testament to that. It was the famine of artistic flow. Petulant silence from The Muse, which led to eating. And more eating. Until finally, usually at the point when Rubble had begun to despair of hearing from her again, The Muse (known to Rubble as Lydia) ended her punishing sulking and began to court him once again. Then it was nonstop, rampant creative union. Rubble would work feverishly day and night, channelling her siren song, forgetting to eat, sleep and (regrettably) shower, ultimately shrinking in size until his fretting agent began leaving frozen lasagnes on his doorstep. So it was necessary, this eating phase. It gave him reserves for the frantic pace to come. He was a grizzly bear, preparing for hibernation in his creative cave. And by the size of him, that was sure to happen any minute.

Rubble moved on to the calamari, shoving several greasy rings into his mouth. He licked his shiny fingers.

'What are you working on right now?' Lincoln asked.

Rubble screwed up his face. 'Nothing. I'm creatively constipated. Can't you tell?' He patted his girth.

'Maybe you should come to the jungle with me when I next go,' Lincoln said, suddenly realising, with a shock, that while he loved the jungle and his work, he did actually miss his family and friends quite a lot.

At the research station he was never alone. The Neptune team was big and always changing. On his last trip he'd made friends with Ernest, a German economics analyst, and Jasmine, a young New Zealand agribusiness researcher who'd also partnered with Lincoln on a project the year before. She was analysing a plantation in Costa Rica that had been planted with a new variety of cacao developed in West Africa that grew faster than the traditional varieties in South America. Jasmine was a fast, efficient researcher, an approach that transferred easily to her pursuit of love interests, among whom Lincoln had numbered for some months before she met a cacao trader from Switzerland and swiftly and good-naturedly moved on. The researchers were fun, easygoing, and they all passed their downtime pleasantly in each other's company. But no one knew him like Rubble, or Jen, or his mum, or his nan—especially his nan.

Rubble considered the suggestion. 'Huh. A trip to the jungle. How exotic. Maybe you're onto something there.'

They raised their glasses in collusion and Lincoln felt some of the tension of being between worlds ease just a bit.

●

To: Evandale Fairy Godmother
From: Dennis Chamberlain
Subject: Proposal

Godmother, I want to ask my girlfriend to marry me but I'm no good at romance.

———————

To: Evandale Fairy Godmother
From: Veronika Lambert
Subject: Washing machine

Help! I'm pregnant with our sixth child (I know . . . don't ask!!) and my washing machine's broken and we don't have a dryer and I've got morning sickness all day long and I'm DROWNING in washing and I can't cope anymore. We're broke, obviously. Please, please help!

●

Lulu Divine shouldn't have been in a nursing home. Not at her age. But here she was as usual, with pink lipstick and her long fair hair brushed till it shone. Must have been a benefit of never having children, Elsa thought. Her own hair had never recovered after the third baby.

Tom. Elsa felt her lips purse at the mere thought of his name.

Lulu tapped impatiently on the metal rims of the wheelchair, her single gold ring—worn on the middle finger of her left hand—clattering against the aluminium. Her copy of *Twilight* sat on her bony knees. As always, she'd been first into the room. Lulu was competitive about everything, from bingo to grabbing the salt shaker at dinner. Every book club meeting, she raced against imaginary competitors, spinning her chair from Potoroo Bungalow across the lawn and into the main building, zooming down the hallway with alarming haste to get the best position in the blue common room—the spot that commanded the view over the creek at the edge of the grounds.

Elsa tapped her false teeth together. She found herself equally annoyed with the bossy and combative Ms Divine and envious of her brazen candour and total commitment to her ideas, be they right or wrong. To admit uncertainty or error showed weakness, and Lulu was not one for weakness. Which was exactly why Elsa knew that Lulu would hate *Twilight* and the fainting Bella Swan.

Most of the residents of Green Hills had by now let go of at least some of the social niceties, and Elsa often found herself wincing at sharp words, dogmatic arguments and out-and-out insults. But with Lulu it was clear she'd always been that way.

Maybe Lulu should write a book. It seemed to be the thing to do in the *twilight* years. Ha ha. She chuckled at her own joke and parked her wheelchair next to Yvonne Murphy, former state parliamentarian and now forgotten great-grandmother with Alzheimer's.

'Do share the joke, Elsa,' Lulu snipped, her false teeth shiny in the fluorescent lights. 'We're all *dying* for a good story, some of us a bit more rapidly than others.' She glanced down towards the intensive care rooms where two old souls had begun their journeys homeward. 'God knows we didn't find it in this rot.' She triumphantly held up her copy of *Twilight*, commanding attention from the slowly forming circle.

Doris Laherty arrived to Elsa's right, having been wheeled in by Sarah, the youngest nurse in the home.

'Hello, Sarah.' Elsa smiled. 'How is your brother going?'

'Much better, thanks. The doctor says he'll probably have some relapse effects but the worst of it should have passed.'

Elsa *tsk*ed. The poor boy had picked up malaria on a trip to Papua New Guinea. His condition had been pretty serious there for a while. It made her queasy to think of Lincoln at similar risk.

Sarah stepped on the brakes and patted Doris lightly on the shoulder, leaving her with her head dropping to the side, her mouth open and snoring gently.

Lulu sucked in her cheeks in disgust. 'Old queer,' she muttered.

'What was that, dear?' Elsa asked, leaning forward with her hand behind her ear. She wasn't deaf. Not in the slightest.

'I said I'd love a cold beer,' Lulu said. Her eyes darted towards the window. 'Might get them to call me a taxi later.'

'You can't go out unattended,' Robert Graham (seventy-four, former civil servant, stroke victim, daily visit from wife) said with practised authority, though its gravity was undermined by his slurred speech. He had also lost much of his sight in the stroke, and he listened to the club's books on audio CDs, which his wife patiently tracked down for him at great expense so he could participate in the group.

Lulu studied Robert's lopsided face and smiled serenely. 'How can they stop me?' she said. 'This isn't jail, or had you forgotten? I'm not a ward of the state. I'm a paying customer.'

Yes, she was. The question of how each resident paid for their accommodation and care was always of interest to Elsa, and Lulu's situation fascinated her the most. Lulu's lips were tight as a drum when it came to sharing anything about herself other than her rodeo and trick-riding career. She never let slip personal information about family or the like. But she didn't seem to have any family, at least none that came to visit. As she was in the detached bungalow next to Elsa's, Elsa knew exactly how many dollars a day Lulu paid to stay here while she waited for her double knee replacement. Granted, it wouldn't be forever, unlike Elsa, who wasn't allowed a double knee and hip replacement due to her age and the potential anaesthetic complications—something that ignited a spark of jealousy towards the Lulu girl that sometimes kept Elsa tossing and turning at night. One day Lulu would walk out of here to get on with the rest of her life. But Elsa would not.

'Perhaps we should get started,' said Rita Blumberg (eighty-eight, widow, four children of varying levels of commitment, unknown number of grandchildren). Rita had been quite a successful painter, with a number of works hanging in galleries around the country. Though, as seemed so often the way with the arts, that public recognition didn't necessarily translate to dollars earned. She was now the unfortunate recipient of Parkinson's disease, and she shook and ticced and tremored in her seat at Lulu's left. Rita occupied one of the two slots in the home allocated for full grant assistance to the financially disadvantaged.

'So the book was ridiculous, obviously,' Lulu began, sitting up as straight as her arthritic back would allow. 'What a pathetic excuse for a woman Bella Swan is. Who would write such appallingly weak female characters these days? Haven't we come further than that? The popularity of this book is truly disturbing. The leading man is a murderer, and she can't do anything other than faint and mope and beg him to kill her so she can be like him.'

Lulu was one of those feminists who had emerged during the eighties and nineties, Elsa realised, the kind that gained power by dominating and outsmarting men. She'd obviously missed the *goddess revolution* of the new millennium, which seemed to be all about embracing and celebrating one's femininity. As for Elsa, her version of feminism was quite simple: let every person's true character show for what it was.

The way she was standing up to Tom, for example, might actually be applauded by the likes of Lulu. Her youngest son was being a brat and a bully, and the shame of her poor mothering lay heavily on her shoulders, as she was at great pains to admit. But she wouldn't let him manipulate her. She might be of advanced years and less mobile than him, but she still had all her faculties, and while there was breath in her body she wasn't going to let him push her around.

He wanted money. Well, in her day, if you wanted money you went and found a job and made it. He wasn't infirm. He wasn't useless. He might not be able to find work as a lumberjack anymore but it was up to him to direct his life. She'd worked hard, giving the better part of her productive years to the dairy farm she and Ebe ran, working in the rain, snow and wind all year round, from dawn till dusk and beyond, and the nest egg she now held, in the form of her house at Western Junction, was there as her insurance for a rainy day. If there was one thing she knew for sure it was that you could never know what was coming in the future.

At his core, Ebe had been lazy and dishonest. If there was a shortcut, he'd take it. If he could sell a twelve-year-old cow as a three-year-old breeder and get away with it, he would. If he could 'accidentally' send the cows to graze on someone else's lush pasture, he'd do that too. Tom, to her disappointment, seemed to also believe the world owed him. It was her duty as a parent, possibly her final duty, to teach him otherwise.

She had been sad at first when he'd told her he wouldn't come and visit her anymore. But that sadness quickly skedaddled, replaced by a tide of anger. How dare he? She didn't even like his company that much, to be honest.

'I admit I t-too thought it was *bupkis* at first. But I did get into it once I acc-accep-pted it for what it is. It's f-f-fantasy,' Rita stuttered, ticcing.

'Does that matter?' Lulu demanded. 'Bella is still a role model of sorts for girls everywhere.'

Rita smiled. 'I wouldn't be a t-true artist if I said someone else's work wasn't valid.'

Lulu snorted.

'So you don't believe in escapism?' Elsa asked Lulu.

'Not if it promotes women staying in abusive relationships, no.' Lulu's cheeks were red and the sun-damage lines on her face were deeper than usual. 'I thought—'

Elsa nodded and turned to Robert. 'And what did you think?'

Lulu huffed as her diatribe was cut short.

Robert took a deep breath. 'Can't say vampires are my thing,' he said arduously. 'I did read Bram Stoker when I was young, but nothing since.'

Robert's care at Green Hills was thanks to trauma insurance cover that paid out after his stroke. He also was too young to be here, Elsa thought sadly.

The debate raged on between Lulu, Elsa, Rita, Robert and Yvonne (whose Alzheimer's meant she couldn't actually remember reading the book or watching the film in the movie room last Friday night), while Doris continued to snooze, her steel-grey curls bobbing with each inhalation. Doris's doting family and her own personal pension paid for her high level of care. Her grandchildren seemed to love sitting in 'Nay-Nay's' lap and stroking her cheek and hair while she snored on.

Elsa was pleased with the robust discussion going on around her. Wasn't that what book club was all about? It would be so boring if everyone agreed. They were here to keep their minds active while their bodies took a back seat. Stave off Alzheimer's, for those who didn't already have it. She looked at Yvonne, struggling to keep up, and wondered if these mental games would help slow the spread of it in her.

She glanced at the clock. It was nearly afternoon tea time. Robert would want to get a move on soon, as his wife would be waiting to join him.

Beside her chair was a bag containing the next read. She always chose books with a movie tie-in, so that even if one of them couldn't read the book, or remember it, there was always the movie to give them another chance to be involved. And she knew exactly what they'd be reading for the June meeting, thanks to the idea from Lincoln. She'd ordered the books from the library straight away.

Next month, they'd be discussing *Chocolat*, and as well as the movie, she'd organised a guest speaker. She'd emailed that lovely Christmas Livingstone from The Chocolate Apothecary, who'd replied immediately, warmly accepting Elsa's invitation to visit the home. And not only would she speak about chocolate, but she'd offered to hold a chocolate-tasting workshop too. Which would be marvellous for anyone not on a diabetes diet. Elsa was dying for Lulu to end her tirade so she could make her announcement.

She was excited about the news for several reasons, one of which was that she wanted to be the best book-club captain the home had ever known. She was determined that her name would stay in gold lettering on the board in the dining room. It gave her a little lift to see it at each meal; if she were honest, she also took some satisfaction from the knowledge that it irked Lulu, who would have loved to take her place. But booey to her. She'd be out of here one day.

It was also a welcome opportunity to break up the monotony of the days, and a chocolate tasting sounded right up her alley, especially if the gift box Lincoln had brought her from Ms Livingstone's store was anything to go by. My, my! Wonderful work! Elsa would have loved to have had a job crafting chocolate, instead of milking cows and delivering calves. But those had been the golden years of dairying and eventually, unlike dairy farmers today, she and her husband had made enough money to take care of her now. (Thanks largely to her careful scrimping and planning, it had to be said.)

Of course, marriages were different back then, based on different values. The young people of today had so many more opportunities to pick and choose, and change their minds. But it did mean they could take their jolly time in settling down. Too long, if you asked her. Like Lincoln.

Just days after setting herself the challenge of finding a way to make Lincoln settle down, he'd arrived at her bungalow with potted plants for her room and full of chirpy conversation about Christmas Livingstone's chocolate shop, effusively praising its range and Christmas's careful consideration of chocolate brands and their origins. And not ten minutes later, he was telling her about his call with his publisher, and how Jeremy wanted him to find a co-author. Lincoln had looked a bit downcast at the prospect, while she'd sat there thinking, really, could it be this easy and obvious?

'What about Christmas Livingstone?' she'd gently queried, not daring to seem too eager. 'She sounds like she's got a lot of commercial sense and creativity. Might she not be a possible co-author for your book?'

And Lincoln's expression had changed in a second from morose to inspired. 'Yes,' he agreed, stroking the right side of his bearded cheek. 'She could well be.'

Elsa smiled inwardly while feigning nonchalance and already planning a visit to Rita; a good Jewish grandmother, known for her matchmaking, Rita could be a useful ally. But she knew Lincoln well enough to know it was better if he thought it was all his doing, so she said nothing more and casually changed the subject.

Now, she cleared her throat to call the book-club group to attention. 'I have an announcement to make about next month's novel and a special event.' She paused, enjoying their rapt attention. 'I'm sure you're going to love it. It's going to be delicious.'

6

Mother's Day was tomorrow—the first Sunday in May—so today would be another busy day in the shop. But Christmas had decided to squeeze in a quick early-morning jog before she met Emily for breakfast at Ingleside Bakery. It was exactly what she needed to work off some of the calories she'd inevitably consumed over the Easter weekend, through the necessity of sampling her wares before they went on sale.

On Easter Sunday, Val, Archie and the boys had come to The Apothecary, along with Joseph, for a big brunch set out on the long wooden table in the empty store, and as much chocolate as they could consume. There was much wedding discussion while her nephews hoovered up bars of chocolate and fine handmade pieces. No one had given her chocolate, of course, but the boys offered her a package of rough, unfired and largely unidentifiable clay pieces.

'Don't think your nephews don't love you,' Val said, sipping coffee and leaning back against Archie's chest while he wrapped his thick, hairy arm around her. 'It took them a whole half an hour to do that. Do you know how hard it is to get boys to sit still for that long?'

'Well, I think they're just wonderful,' Christmas said, although of course the clumps of clay were completely awful. She thought about giving specific compliments but was unsure how to identify each piece so decided not to risk offending. 'Thank you, I'm very touched,' she said sincerely; apparently satisfied, the boys ran through the swing doors, out through the kitchen and into the small backyard to chase each other around the birdbath.

She told Val, Archie and Joseph about Emily's surprise, and everyone was duly impressed and talked about how wonderful the trip would be. But then Joseph, arms crossed comfortably at his chest, quietly and perceptively asked, 'And how do you feel about the French connection to your past?'

Val's gushing had ceased instantly. 'Oh, crap, sorry, I hadn't even made that link yet,' she said, screwing up her face. 'I was just thinking about Paris and wine and baguettes.'

Archie was silent but scratched thoughtfully at his hairy face. The boys screeched out in the garden. And all eyes were on Christmas.

'It's confusing,' she admitted. 'I haven't had much peace and quiet to process it yet with everything going on this weekend.'

'But surely you'd like to try and look him up?' Val said. Archie cleared his throat and sipped his coffee and Val shot him a look, clearly wondering if he disapproved of the question.

'You don't have to do anything you're not comfortable with,' Joseph said. 'It would be perfectly okay just to enjoy the experience in France and the chocolate course and not put yourself under any pressure.'

Christmas smiled at him gratefully, warmed by his understanding.

Just then the middle boy, Nate, came in cradling an unconscious sparrow. Braxton followed, trying to take it off him, and Willis strutted importantly to the table as the oldest child to declare, 'It's dead.'

'No, it's not!' Nate countered. 'It's just sleeping. It's breathing. See!'

'What happened?' Val asked, jumping up.

'It flew into the window,' Braxton said breathlessly.

'And fell to the ground,' Willis finished. 'It couldn't have survived the impact.'

Goodness, Christmas thought, he sounded like a news reporter.

And so the conversation about France had ended there while the poor stunned sparrow was put into a cardboard box and placed in a quiet(ish) section of the room to recover its wits, which it did, thankfully, and a while later they'd all released it with great ceremony.

Now she pushed herself up to a slow jog, something she hadn't attempted since she lived in Sydney, and was soon puffing hard. Exercise was something she'd learned to do because it was good for her, like occasionally eating Brussels sprouts or mung beans. If she was going to devote her time to working with chocolate, she would be a fool to think she didn't need to actively burn off some calories. As it was, she was one and a half dress sizes larger than she'd been when she was in PR. She normally walked, sometimes took a class with Emily, but didn't jog. So she barely managed a wave to Gordon Harding on his penny farthing when she passed him in Pioneer Park and he smiled at her through his thick white moustache and tipped his Ivy tweed cap. Instead she concentrated on putting one foot in front of the other and defeating the stitch in her side. She also decided to take the opportunity to think about France, as her overriding physical need to breathe would prevent her from expending too much energy on unnecessary angst.

Of course she had always been fascinated by France. How could she not be? It was her only link to her history on that side of the family.

She'd had a pen pal while she was in high school, a girl her age called Miriam Deschamps, and Christmas wrote to her every week for seven months, going to the local post office for stamps and airmail stickers and fine, almost weightless, blue paper. Writing to Mim—even though it was always in English—had felt like some sort of validation of Christmas's ethnicity.

Mim lived in Paris, was studying for the *baccalauréat*, drank black coffee without any sugar, and read *Rolling Stone* magazine. They exchanged photos. Mim had mouse-brown hair down to her waist, thick eyebrows and a gappy smile. She was lanky and seemed to wear jeans all the time, in pink, orange, black, white and purple. One day, like so many things in childhood, they just stopped writing to each other.

Actually, now that she was thinking about it, Christmas remembered that Emily had always been dismissive of their contact, snatching letters from Christmas's school bag and reading them, snorting with derision at Mim's intensity and her passion for her city, and rolling her eyes at Mim's poetry. Christmas had enjoyed Mim's letters, but she remained silent while Emily sneered at them. If she could help it, she kept the letters away from Em's eyes in the first place. Perhaps it had been jealousy of Mim. Or maybe of her connection to France, which was exotic compared to Hobart.

She gritted her teeth now as she ran, and didn't glance at the antiques store on High Street or pause for breath when she hit her usual turn-around spot at the old brick water tower at the corner of Cambock Lane. To avoid the car exhaust fumes in High Street she cut through the back of St Andrew's church. In the quieter residential streets, families shuffled kids into cars, balancing mobile phones and cereal bowls.

Over the years, Christmas had watched lots of movies featuring France, both French films with subtitles and anything from Hollywood set in France. She particularly loved *Amélie*, *Midnight in Paris*, *French Kiss*, *A Good Year* and, of course, *Chocolat*. But she'd never gone so far as trying to learn French. She'd thought about it, naturally, but never done it. It was as though going ahead and learning the language would commit her to actually tracking down Gregoire Lachapelle. And while that idea was never too far from her mind, it was also quite scary. He might not exist, after all. And then the few tangents of a life she'd built in her imaginings would be gone and she'd be left with nothing.

Darla assured Christmas that his name was Gregoire Lachapelle, but she could—or would—give her daughter no more details about his life other than that he came from some-where in the south of France and that he'd spoken once or twice (in his heavy, sometimes indecipherable accent) about a younger sister, whose name Darla couldn't remember.

Christmas felt that familiar irritation with her mother now, jogging in Falls Park, where she spied Mary Hauser Who Carries Her Schnauzer and gratefully took a break, bending over with her hands on her knees and gasping for breath. Mary put Ferdy down and he jumped and licked at Christmas's hands while his mistress chatted on about the Easter weekend, the stories she was writing for the newspaper on the expo events and today's great weather before continuing on her way.

Setting off again at a pace more reasonable for someone who hadn't jogged in years, Christmas turned up Russell Street once more, heading to the bakery, where she'd organised to meet Emily. Her mind quickly returned to France and all it meant.

Sometime back in the nineties, when the internet had become the primary research tool, Christmas had gone through a phase of obsessive searching for Gregoire Lachapelle. But with nothing else to go on it was impossible to find him. There were more than a thousand Lachapelles listed in *Les Pages Blanches*. And even if he'd lived in the south of France at one time it didn't mean he was still there years later. It didn't mean he was even alive. She didn't know a single thing about him. And that was the problem. Not knowing gave her imagination far too much freedom to torture her endlessly. That was why she needed to keep busy; her mind left to its own devices found destructive ways to behave. It was something she'd inherited from her mother, sadly, and was why Darla had always taken physical jobs—cleaning, gardening, forestry work, fieldwork. Darla needed to be busy too.

Christmas staggered through the double iron gates into the courtyard of Ingleside Bakery, just a few doors up from The Apothecary. Emily was already there. She was always early, something that seemed incongruous with so many of her other disorganised traits. She wore a hand-knitted scarf (due to the gaping holes in it, Christmas concluded that it was probably made by one of her nieces going through a craft phase) that draped around her in a layered nest, entwined with her long, tangled hair.

Seeing Christmas, Emily jumped to her feet, scraping the metal chair along the brickwork. 'Hi!' Emily hugged her, and her hair tickled Christmas's nose. 'What have you been doing? You're all sweaty and red!'

'Oh, sorry. I've been jogging,' Christmas said, still struggling for breath and wiping at sweat beads under her eyes.

'God, why?'

'I probably consumed about five kilos of chocolate over the past couple of weeks. Thought I should do something about it.'

Emily grimaced. 'Fair enough, I suppose.'

Despite the runner's high—okay, maybe a runner's *lift*—she was on, Christmas felt awkward, suddenly feeling a bit needled by the memory of Emily mocking Mim's letters, and not really sure of Em's true intentions when she'd put in the scholarship application. How much of it had been to do with Gregoire Lachapelle? She didn't like feeling out of sorts with Em. She was like a second sister to her, indeed more of a sister in many ways than Val, since they were the same age.

'They have custard tarts,' Emily said.

'For breakfast?'

'Live a little,' Emily ordered.

They queued up at the long counter inside the bakery, which had been converted from the 1860s council chambers building and retained the original grand high ceilings and stately tall arched windows. It was warm inside, like most buildings in Tasmania, built to withstand the freezing cold rather than accommodate the few weeks of hot weather they got each year. Emily ordered them both custard tarts and lattes and they returned outside to sit beneath the pretty pale pink roses cascading down the brickwork.

'So you're back on the coffee?' Christmas said, gulping a glass of water.

'I tried drinking chai, as per your suggestion. Totally awful.

Imposter coffee. Bah!' Emily poked out her tongue and made a face.

'But how did you feel in that time?' Christmas prompted.

'Like complete shite. Migraines. Sugar cravings.'

'No different then.'

'Exactly. I'm writing that one off as a terrible experiment that should never be repeated. But I am making one concession: I've decided to try to give up sugar in my coffee at least. Commando coffee, I'm calling it.'

'That's clever.'

'I started with "bareback coffee", but then decided it was a bit rude.'

'Commando coffee is cute.'

'I thought so. And it makes me feel all brave and warrior-like. Speaking of warrior types, how's your mum? Where is she now?'

'Same as usual. Terse. Impossible. Frustrating. She's some-where in central Victoria right now. Her latest job is fieldwork for a PhD student who's examining the wear and tear on marsupials' teeth to study their dietary habits, or something like that.'

'Doesn't sound too bad.'

'No. Except that to study dental patterns, the PhD student needs teeth.'

Emily put a hand to her mouth. 'Oh no.'

'Uh-huh. Mum drives around by herself on lonely roads in the middle of nowhere, decapitating marsupial road kill and storing the heads in the boot of her car until she can deliver them to her employer.'

Emily paled.

'Apparently the trick is to make sure the marsupials have been dead for some time so they don't smell.'

'Can we talk about something else?'

'Definitely.' Christmas took a deep breath, releasing the tension that always gripped her body whenever she talked about her mother. Their coffees and tarts arrived and they both leapt on them. 'Hey, I met an interesting guy last week.'

'In Evandale?' Emily said through a mouthful of tart.

'I know, shocking, isn't it? He just got off a plane from Ecuador, where he's been working. He's a botanist but comes from Tasmania. He's staying around here for a while.'

'What's he like?'

'Tall. A bit scruffy. Interesting.'

Emily raised her eyebrows, which were in need of a trim. 'That sounds promising. But also a bit suspicious. Why isn't he married?'

'I don't know,' Christmas said.

'You better find out. If he's not gay or horribly dysfunctional— a little dysfunctional is okay, we're all a bit dysfunctional—then it could be good.'

Christmas bit into her own tart, thinking she'd have to go and run another block now to work it off, and talked through a mouthful. 'You know I'm not interested.'

'Oh, please. Look at you. You're totally interested!' Emily laughed. 'You're jogging, for God's sake!'

'That's just . . . good sense!' Christmas protested. *I'm not interested, am I?* 'And you know it's not allowed.'

'Yes. The rules. I know,' Emily said, with a bit of an effort to be nice, Christmas thought. She watched Emily for a moment as she scraped up crumbs with her spoon. Was there something going on between them that wasn't explicit? And if so, should it be brought out into the open? She was loath to ignite any latent friction. But it was bothering her.

She took a deep breath. 'Is there something . . . ?'

'Mmm?'

'Well, do you think I should be trying to look for my father while I'm in France? Is that the real reason you put in the application?'

Emily took her time to lick her spoon and sip on her latte, and it was so uncharacteristic of her to think before she spoke that Christmas knew there was something going on.

'Yes,' Emily said at last.

'Wow. I didn't actually expect you to just come out and say it.'

'Well, why not? You've only moaned for the past thirty years—'

Moaned?

'—about how you don't know him and how irresponsible your mother was for not helping you to know him and how there's this missing piece of your life. I've never understood why you don't just go to France and try to meet him instead of obsessing about the country and making up stories about him and building a little mini France all around you at home and in your shop!'

That stung.

'Shit, sorry,' Emily said, sighing and rubbing her forehead. 'You know I didn't mean it like that.' She looked stricken. 'I was trying to be a good friend. I knew you'd love the chance to do the scholarship course and it just seemed like the perfect opportunity to, I don't know, exorcise some ghosts of the past or something.'

Had Emily been a good friend in getting Christmas over to France? Or had she been motivated by something else? Was she—and this was a horrible thought—fed up with Christmas's *moaning*, as she'd put it, and felt Christmas had become self-indulgent, obsessed, whiny and addicted to this little family drama she kept playing out in her head?

And, mortifyingly, might Emily actually be right if she *had* thought all those things?

Christmas swallowed more water, uncomfortable. Guilty. Like she'd done something really mean and was now ashamed but unable to say sorry even though she knew she should.

Her chest was tightening in on itself. She knew this feeling and what was to follow—the heavy tethering weight of unidentifiable gloom. Depression. A lesson learned in the laps of her mother and grandmother. It was this very feeling she worked so hard to keep at bay. She was determined not to follow in their footsteps. The genetics might be there but that just gave her knowledge and the power to control the variables.

The rules for happiness were there precisely because of this. And it was exactly for this reason that she couldn't be interested in Lincoln and she couldn't look for Gregoire. The unknown was just too dangerous.

'You know why not, Em,' she said.

But Emily shook her head slowly. 'Once upon a time I might have accepted that.' She reached out and took Christmas's hand. 'But I don't anymore. You've come a long way since those days hiding in your room in Sydney. You're stronger now.'

Christmas couldn't answer.

'Look, I don't want to fight about this,' Emily said, releasing Christmas's hand and pushing her plate away and leaning back from the table. 'You've got yourself a free holiday and a week-long course with a master chocolatier. That's good, right?'

'Yes, and I'm grateful, I really am. I can't thank you enough. It's the most incredible—'

Emily held up a hand. 'Just think about the rest, okay? Will you do that? Just give it some thought?'

'Alright. I will think about it.'

Christmas checked the time. 'I've got to go,' she said, partly pleased they'd cleared the air and partly annoyed she had to leave now when there was still some lingering unease. She hugged Emily goodbye and just hoped time would smooth out the ruffles in their relationship that had been stirred up in the past week.

7

To: Evandale Fairy Godmother
From: Veronika Lambert
Subject: Re: Questions

I know you didn't ask, but I feel I need to explain about the many children.

The first one was a teenage pregnancy when I was 17. The second was an error in calculation, if you get what I mean, when I was 19. Then I went on the pill and I SWEAR I took everything just as I should, but I guess fate had other ideas because at 22 I found myself pregnant again, this time with TWINS!!! The next one was a bottle of scotch and a night out with my husband for the first time in six years (same father to all of them, by the way, and by this time we were married). And this latest one . . . sigh . . . well, let's just say a steamy romance novel in the middle of the day, too much visualising of Ryan Gosling, and your husband popping home unexpectedly early . . . and that afternoon delight quickly turns into afternoon de'fright!

Needless to say, we've taken care of this little problem for good now. ✂

Sam is a park ranger in Cradle Mountain and I'm a full-time mum. We've been through a rough patch lately. Anything you could do to help would be GREATLY appreciated. Thanks for taking the time to consider my request. I know you must be inundated with pleas for help.

Veronika

————

To: Evandale Fairy Godmother
From: Dennis Chamberlain
Subject: Re: Questions

Godmother Livingstone—Juliette and I are in our forties. She's a widow, so yes, she has been married before. I haven't. I'm no good at love. Juliette likes jazz music, wine, foreign films, spicy food, good chocolate, and cats. We both like staying in by the fire and touring wineries and gourmet food festivals. She doesn't like heights, water, having her feet touched or crowds. Yes, I think she'll say yes.

•

The old bell over the shop's door had been going all day, so constantly that Christmas was almost tempted to take it down. She was bunkered down in the kitchen madly crafting chocolates.

Cheyenne was serving at the counter again, cheery as ever, and looking every bit the jolly sales assistant with her orange ringlets and her neat but curvy frame, which filled a frilly apron perfectly.

'I think you've missed your calling,' Christmas said, bumping into her at the coffee machine as she went to get some ground coffee to add to a ganache.

'Oh no. I'm sure I was actually a princess swapped at birth.' Cheyenne giggled in a way that should have been far too girlish for someone in her forties but from her was delightful. 'I'm still waiting for Prince Charming.'

'Well, you're doing a fine job of getting on with things while you're waiting.'

'Once I'm a princess, and I sell the rights to my memoir, I'll need to have some ordinary times to write about so people can relate to me,' Cheyenne said, setting more coffee beans to grind.

Abigail was working extra hours too, serving on the floor, though not quite as cheerfully, checking her watch frequently.

Christmas's hands were busy but her mind was elsewhere, deep in the process of creating possible new potions for Lien, who'd gone back to school this week after an extended break at home. She was coping okay physically but was struggling to concentrate through the brain fog from the medications.

'It's like being hung-over,' Lien had explained one afternoon when Christmas was visiting. She was propped up to do her homework next to the fireplace in the family's cottage up on the hill behind Launceston, trying to focus on a science textbook while Tu peeled potatoes in the kitchen nearby.

'You don't know what being hung-over feels like,' Tu said, popping a potato into a sinkful of water. 'I hope.'

Lien let go of her pen and stretched her fingers. 'I read,' she countered, and Christmas smiled. Lien was a voracious reader and was never without a book, though Christmas sometimes suspected it was because it gave her a buffer against unwanted sympathy or, unthinkably, bullying. It was acceptable to be quiet and still while reading.

Since then, Christmas had been working on different chocolate recipes that included potent blends of the essential oils of basil, lime, lemon, peppermint and spearmint—all of which were uplifting and offered clarity and focus to the tired mind. She could do it easily enough. But she was hoping she'd stumble on something even more powerful.

Right now, though, she had work to do. She was setting bars of dark chocolate from Trinitario beans, harvested from an estate located in the Gran Couva area of Tobago, fermented and dried there before being sold to her newest supplier in America, who then roasted them and shipped the bags to her in Tasmania, where she ground them into powder. She was, as Lincoln had so grandly put it, an important part in the long journey of a tiny seed to fulfil its true potential in the world.

There were so many ways to wreck cacao beans—so many steps along the way in the beans' harvesting, drying, fermenting, packing and transporting where things could go wrong. But if a farmer worked hard and got the beans to her supplier in good condition, and her supplier did a perfect job of roasting them, then that just left her with the final responsibility to see it through to make marvellous chocolate. So many hands touched that one bean on its way to the consumer. Hers were just one pair.

She ladled out giant spoonfuls of gorgeously tempered chocolate from the tank and poured it into the moulds, removed the excess with the large steel scraper, and rattled the moulds seesaw-fashion, banging each end on the white marble slab on top of the workbench to remove the air bubbles, which rose to the surface and popped like tiny volcanoes.

The chocolate that came from this special region of 'the chocolate soils' in Tobago was highly prized, and rightly so; the next time she scooped up a ladle of thick brown liquid heaven, she let it cascade back into the tank just to see it fall. A shine on the surface. Ripples in the pool of chocolate below. The intense aroma.

The thermostat on the tempering tank clicked off and the sound reminded her she was working to the clock. She stirred the tank again, feeling the weight of the chocolate against the spoon, smoothing out the lumps that always formed the second the lid was removed and air met its simmering volume. Christmas had learned to keep her hands busy while her mind worked. It was like keeping a perturbed friend company while they talked. Her mind serpentined around the ghostly image of her father while her hands soothed—*everything will be okay; you just have to ignore it.*

It was challenging to separate the trip to France from the nagging notion of ancestral research. Now more than ever, she had to know what her priorities were. Studying with Master Le Coutre in France was the chance of a lifetime to blossom as a chocolate artisan. Well, possibly, depending on what his chosen itinerary held for that week. But even without Master Le Coutre, France was the hub of exciting and enriching food experiences. It wouldn't be possible to go there and not come away with a whole new vision for her future creations. And it would mean spending time in Provence in the French summer. Her mouth actually watered at the thought. If there was any tiny doubt left as to whether she would go, it vanished in that moment.

It was really very simple: Gregoire Lachapelle didn't matter.

She could absolutely separate her biological father from this trip. The two were not intertwined. They were different things. She wouldn't give one more minute to agonising over whether she should do something about finding him. She shouldn't. That was perfectly clear. She was going to France for this fantastic chocolate opportunity and nothing more.

The shop bell rang again as she turned her attention to the heart-shaped moulds, polished with cotton wool till they were shiny from the oils embedded in the fibres. She held the tray over the tank and spooned the melted chocolate into each heart. Scraped the excess back into the tank. Clattered plastic on marble.

With the bubbles popped, it was back to the tank, where she tipped most of the chocolate out of the mould and scraped the surface once more, leaving just a smooth thin coating inside each heart. She tipped the tray onto its side so the air would snap-dry the chocolate into shells, which she would fill tomorrow morning with strawberry liqueur ganache.

Abigail appeared, her dark fringe almost in her eyes. 'There's a guy out there asking for you. He was here the other day too, having lunch,' she said. 'I told him you were busy but he seems pretty keen to talk.'

Christmas considered her chocolate-covered pink pig apron, spattered arms and gently bubbling chocolate tank, drying at the edges. She clicked her tongue, irritated. 'Send him back here so I can keep going.' She didn't have time to stop.

She picked up a new shiny mould tray and dipped her ladle once more as the swing door puffed open and Lincoln walked in.

'Oh, hi.' All her irritation was gone. She was instantly pleased she'd invited him back here.

'Sorry to interrupt,' he said, then inhaled deeply. 'Wow, it smells fantastic in here.'

'You get used to it after a while,' she said. 'It's a bit sad really. There's nothing like that great rush of cocoa to the brain.'

He took a step towards her, a big, casual, easy-as-you-please step.

'Wait!' She held up her ladle.

He froze.

'You can't come over here near the chocolate with all that . . . hair.'

'Oh, of course. Sorry.' His eyes snapped up to the fetching snood currently plastering her hair to her scalp like a bathing cap.

He fished in the long pocket of his pants and retrieved a saggy leather wallet, flipped it open and pulled out a business card. She motioned that she couldn't take it as both hands were full and he took a single stride towards the bench, holding up his hands in a *I'm not going to hurt the chocolate* gesture, leaned forward gingerly and fully extended his arm, then placed the card on the edge of the bench where she could see it, before he retreated once more.

She peered down at it.

Lincoln van Luc
Botanist

'I thought I should give you that, offcially, so you know who I am rather than just thinking I'm a guy who hangs out in your store and eats loads of chocolate. I'm writing a book, actually, on cacao. And my editor, Jeremy, thinks my writing isn't particularly people-friendly. He says it's too scientific and dry. He wants me to find a co-author, someone who works on the other side of chocolate production. Someone like you.'

Christmas took a moment to understand what he was saying. 'You want me to work with you?'

'It seems ideal, doesn't it? I'm a scientist, you're a chocolatier—'

'I'm not, actually. A chocolatier is a professional, whereas I'm just an artisan . . .'

'—and I know you can sell chocolates and you used to be a PR manager. I read about you in the copy of the in-flight magazine you have in the shopfront, while I was eating here the other day after the expo. And I thought . . . well, in fact my grandmother suggested it, and I couldn't agree more, and I could kick myself for not thinking of it sooner, but you seem to be just the right person,' he finished in a rush, his posture stiffening slightly, betraying a degree of something like nervousness, or self-consciousness.

'I don't know what to say.'

'You've got to love the unexpected and random, don't you?' Lincoln said, with genuine enthusiasm.

Her mind whirred. She wasn't the person to write a chocolate book, was she? She'd only been in the business a few years and she was self-taught. Not exactly someone who should be claiming to be an expert on chocolate making and putting her name to a book.

On top of that, her career as a fairy godmother, which she pursued in her spare hours outside of the shop, was surprisingly time-consuming, and she was horribly behind on that right now too. She really didn't have time for any more commitments.

And then there was him: a shaggy yet somehow alluring man. *Lincoln van Luc—Just a Little Bit Cute.* He was far too tempting to work in close proximity with.

Absolutely NO romantic relationships. It said so clearly on the charter above the desk in her office, and she read it aloud several times a month, though of course she now knew it off by heart, having lived by it ever since the day she wrote it three years ago. Then again, that particular rule didn't specify how long it was to be enforced.

Why was she searching for loopholes?

'It's very flattering,' she admitted. 'And a wonderful opportunity. But I just don't think I have the time.' She turned towards the tempering tank and vigorously stirred, smoothing out lumps as she sought to settle the emotional ripples set off when Lincoln van Luc had loped easily into her kitchen.

'Look, I know this was totally out of the blue, and I can see you're working hard here,' he said, casting his eyes over the trolley racks stacked six-feet high with cooling chocolate moulds. 'How about I email you the synopsis and a bit of info and you can have a read and see how you feel? I'll be living nearby for a while, just ten minutes that way,' he pointed over his shoulder, 'so we're practically neighbours.'

'Okay,' she said, the word loaded with caution.

'Excellent.' He smiled, confidently, like it was a done deal.

The next thing, he was gone, leaving Christmas alone with her chocolate and her busy, busy hands.

A moment later, not yet recovered from the shock of Lincoln's proposition, she heard her mobile phone buzz with an email. And because she was looking for a distraction from thinking about Lincoln, she washed her hands and checked the message. It was from her old PR firm, McKenzie Jones, regretfully informing her that their friend and colleague, journalist Peter O'Donnell, had passed away from a heart attack at the age of sixty-nine.

•

'Emily!'

Emily turned around, a tube of eye cream in her hand,

to see Val walking through the cosmetics section of Myer in Launceston, loaded down with bags.

'Hi!' she said, putting down the cream and kissing Val on the cheek.

'What are you doing here?' Val asked, slightly breathless.

'I'm actually on an assignment. The station's been doing a series of segments on cooking, retro style. I've just been down in the mall at the CupCakery doing research on cupcakes through the ages. Have you been in there? It's really funky—lots of fifties posters, antique mixers and old recipe books, a bit like a museum to cake baking.'

'No, I don't bake,' Val said definitively. 'But I'm glad I ran into you. I've been meaning to call or text to say what a wonderful job you did getting that scholarship to France for Massy. That was so inspired! It will be so good for her.'

Emily bit her lip. She didn't want to break the unspoken codes of sister–friend–sister relationships, but as the nominated best friend in this triangle of women, she truly believed it was her duty to step up if she thought it was necessary. 'Actually, do you have time for a coffee?' she said.

'Sure. I don't have to pick up the kids for another hour.'

'Excellent. I was hoping we could have a chat about Christmas and this trip to France. I'm worried she's not going to make the most of the chance to do something about . . .' she searched for the appropriate phrase, '. . . healing her past.'

'You mean look for her father?'

'Yes.'

'I couldn't agree more,' Val said, and they wandered off to find a good brew.

•

Christmas had been to only a few funerals in her life, the most recent of which had been for Mr Tupper, Rosemary McCaw's twenty-year-old, arthritic, diabetic cat, who died last year in his sleep on Rosemary's lap while she was watching *Downton Abbey*. Mr Tupper was buried beneath a blossom tree in Rosemary's backyard, and she'd invited a handful of close or notable villagers to the service, which included readings (by Rosemary) from Shakespeare, and an opera singer—a friend from her days in the theatre. It had been surprisingly moving as Mr Tupper's ginger body was laid to rest in the grave.

Perhaps now, though, Christmas reflected morbidly, she was approaching the age when those around her started to shuffle off their mortal coils and this was just the beginning of an endless procession of sad farewells she'd have to endure until she too went to the big lavender field in the sky.

She swirled the red wine in her glass, sitting up in the queen ensemble in the bed and breakfast where she was staying for the night on Sydney's north shore. It wasn't far from where Peter's family were gathered in his home to comfort one another after the service. An empty Thai takeaway container sat on the bedside table and a pile of used tissues littered the sheets. She hadn't cried until tonight. She'd refused to let herself, forcing the tears back down inside her body. Let it hurt, she'd told herself. Because it wasn't hurting her anywhere near as much as it was hurting Peter's wife or children. What right did she have to cry? He wasn't her father.

His children all spoke so eloquently, reminiscing about child-hood games and recalling pieces of their father's wisdom that they'd carry to their own graves. They spoke of his insatiable thirst for knowledge and his intrepid enthusiasm for travel jour-nalism, which had taken him to places like Antarctica, Lebanon and Estonia and everywhere in between. He'd walked the Great Wall of China; unwittingly swum with a great white shark; trekked Kilimanjaro; been invited to Ethiopian family coffee rituals; walked on hot coals; been held up at gunpoint in Egypt; and cried in the refugee camps of Sudan.

But it was his eldest daughter's words that had reached deep into Christmas's heart. 'No matter what happened to Dad out in the field—dysentery, muggings, being detained on suspicion of spying, lost passports or cockroach-infested hotels—his enjoyment and love of travel, and of life, never waned. Dad always said, "Life's too short to live it behind a desk. Grab every opportunity that comes your way. Never say no."'

Christmas poured herself another glass of grenache and wondered. She wasn't living her life behind a desk; she'd at least extricated herself from that. But was she now hiding behind the four walls of her chocolate shop? If she was truly honest, as one could only be after more than half a bottle of fantastic Australian wine, she knew deep down that she was treading too carefully. She wasn't grabbing every opportunity that came her way.

Not even Peter could make her reassess her position on Gregoire Lachapelle. She just wasn't interested in going down that path. But Lincoln's book? It was a rare professional opportunity. And she'd been determined to turn it down because she didn't trust herself around an attractive man.

She cast her eyes to the ceiling. 'Oh, Peter, what a scolding you'd give me if you could see me like this.'

Years ago, when she was still at McKenzie Jones, she and Peter had gone on a junket to the Great Barrier Reef, staying in a five-star hotel that was the subject of one of Christmas's biggest-ever campaigns. They lay side by side on the beach under comically large straw hats, drinking piña coladas by the bucketful. As the day wore on and the sun got hotter they'd become quite hysterical, laughing at the silliest things, and then Peter had suddenly said, 'I'd trade all the trips in the world for just one more day with my mum and dad.'

Instantly stone-cold sober, Christmas had burst into tears.

Peter patted her arm. 'I'm sorry. I don't know what made me think of them just now.' He pulled himself up off the beach lounger with some difficulty and steadied himself on the back. He stared into his balloon glass and pulled out the glacé cherry and ate it. 'Alcohol, I suppose.' He had shrugged. 'Cuts right to the chase sometimes.'

Now, sitting in that bed-and-breakfast room in Sydney just five hours after Peter's funeral and his daughter's words, the thought slid into her mind that perhaps she should *just start saying yes*. She threw back the last of the red wine and decided that there was one thing she could say yes to right now.

Can we talk?

Lincoln van Luc
Who is this?

Christmas Livingstone
Oh sorry. It's Christmas Livingstone.
From the chocolate apocalypse
apoplexy
apagoge
Apothecary!!!
Are you still there?

Lincoln van Luc

Yes sorry. Just watching my neighbour over the fence. He's a retired sea captain and limps and smokes a pipe. As true as I stand here.

Lincoln van Luc

I probably shouldn't have said that. Now I sound like a weird peeping Tom or something. It's just that he's building something in his backyard.

Christmas Livingstone

What is it?

Lincoln van Luc

I don't know.

Christmas Livingstone

Can't you ask him?

Lincoln van Luc

No. He only talks in sign language.

Christmas Livingstone

He's deaf?

Lincoln van Luc

No. He actually writes stuff on a blackboard and leaves it on the footpath. Today it says, 'All governments are corrupt; you just need to pick the one less so.'

Christmas Livingstone

Huh. Cheery.

Lincoln van Luc

Yeah.

Anyway, did you want to talk?

Christmas Livingstone

Yes.

I think I'd like to write your book with you. I'm not sure what your time frame is—I'm leaving for France in seven weeks, and I'll be gone for a bit over three weeks. But I'd like to do it. I'd like to say yes.

Christmas Livingstone

If you're still interested.

Lincoln van Luc

I am.

8

It was Friday again—two whole weeks since Emily had delivered the news about the scholarship course, and Christmas still hadn't taken the first steps closer to France. If she was going to get herself overseas, she needed to start working through a long list of tasks to complete before she left. And at the top of that list were the two most recent godmother requests. She left Cheyenne in charge of the shop for a few hours to squeeze in a visit to Veronika Lambert.

It was a bit over an hour's drive from Evandale to Sheffield, and Christmas passed by seemingly endless yellow pastures that were occasionally interrupted by a stark, leafless gum reaching its bare branches to the moody grey sky like a bony hand. The paddocks resembled wheat fields; it was only the clusters of ebony Angus cattle and blotches of sooty grey sheep clumped like rocks on the ground that identified the stalks not as wheat but as tinder-dry grass.

The town of Sheffield sat flanked by Mount Roland to its south, and from the main street the view floated along rolling yellow hills down the highway towards Cradle Mountain.

The Lambert house was just one street away from the centre of town. Veronika answered the door with a baby on her hip and stains down her overalls, her hair in pigtails, making her look much younger than Christmas knew she was. Her bony frame and translucent skin gave her a fragile appearance, which wasn't helped by the red-rimmed eyes and her red-tipped nose, bright eyes and auburn hair, all of which made her look as though she might dissolve into tears at any moment.

Thankfully, she smiled with a burst of energy.

Christmas greeted her and handed over a box of chocolates tied with an aqua ribbon.

'Thank you!' Veronika said. 'Come in. The kids are going to love these. I'd better hide them away or I won't get any. I have a secret spot, in my underwear drawer. If I want to savour anything slowly, rather than having to fight the family for it like a pack of starving wolves, I have to hide it. And things just aren't as enjoyable when you're shoving them down your throat to get your fair share. You know?'

'Hey, your secret's safe with me,' Christmas said, wiping her feet on the mat and stepping inside as Veronika held the door open. The house was in desperate need of a makeover, with peach-coloured veneers and an outdated kitchen visible through a doorway, the standalone stove on a slight lean. Looking around, she glimpsed socks, shoes, a tricycle, a headless doll and a small television set. A mishmash of furniture that looked as though it had been picked up at garage sales or handed down from family members, some items with faded floral prints, others with seventies-style wood veneer. The greenish-grey carpet needed a good clean.

'Excuse the mess.' Veronika led the way to the dining table. She tapped it with her fingernail and it gave a hollow clang. 'Metal was the only surface they couldn't destroy.'

Christmas smiled sympathetically.

'Would you like a tea or coffee? Oh, wait. I think I've run out of coffee. But I can do tea. Teabag only, I'm afraid. No time for steeping leaves in a pot. I can barely finish a cup once I've made it. I'm forever finding half-drunk cups of tea around the house. Often with mould floating on top. That's awful, isn't it? I shouldn't have said that. Now you think I'm a disgusting slob.' Veronika moved the chubby baby to the other hip, swaying to keep him happy.

'No, I'm fine, thanks.' Christmas laughed. 'And you're certainly not alone with the half-drunk cups. My sister's exactly the same. She has three boys.'

'My condolences,' Veronika said.

'I really just wanted to come and say hello in person and bring you some chocolate. I have a meeting tomorrow with my friend Mary Hauser to see what we can do. She's a journalist and we often manage to swing some goodies for people who need them in return for publicity.'

'Oh, do you think you can help?' Veronika's eyes widened and a wisp of vulnerability floated across her face.

'Would you be open to sharing your story and being in a photo later on? With the washing machine or something like that? It helps if we can promise a store a feel-good news story promotion.'

Veronika nodded quickly. 'Yes, of course.'

'It would be tastefully done,' Christmas assured her, sensing a hint of embarrassment creeping in. 'I want to help you, not make you feel awkward or anything.'

Veronika placed the baby down in a wooden playpen in the corner and passed him a box of blocks. Then she pulled out a green vinyl chair and sat down across from Christmas. 'Of course I'd be happy to help. I'm just so grateful for any assistance at all. I can't keep up with taking the washing to the laundromat.' She covered her face with her long fingers. 'You don't want to open that door behind you. There'd be a landslide of footy jerseys and Taylor Swift pyjamas and you'd never be found again.'

Christmas reached out a hand and placed it on Veronika's thin arm. 'It's all okay. Believe me. You're not the first person to strike a rough patch, and you won't be the last. It's good you asked for help. I'm going to do the best I can to get this fixed for you straight away.'

As if that small touch of kindness had been a pinprick to a water balloon, a tear seeped slowly from the corner of Veronika's eye.

●

The Saturday lunch rush had passed and only a handful of customers were left in the shop, slowly savouring coffees and hot chocolates. Christmas was putting the finishing touches to another batch of flower-inspired chocolates. These pieces had been a hit at the garden expo and she'd completed many orders for them for Mother's Day. Now she was working on even more for Mary Hauser to give to her mother for her seventieth birthday. These particular pieces featured white and yellow daisies—Mary's mother's favourites. She'd made a batch of flat round Belgian chocolates about a centimetre thick and piped them with crème brûlée-flavoured ganache, then added a flat disc of chocolate to the bottom, wider than the first round, so each ganache was sitting on a chocolate plate.

She laid the tiny sugar flowers (ordered especially—she wasn't quite clever or patient enough to be able to make them herself) around the base and on top of the ganache so the whole thing looked like a perfect miniature chocolate cake. They were beautiful, even if she did say so herself. She must remember to take photos of them before she boxed them up for Mary to take with her today. They'd keep in the fridge till Mary saw her mother—as long as Mary could keep from eating them herself.

She wished she'd been able to send a selection out to her own mother for Mother's Day last week. Darla was a meat-and-three-veg or steak-and-chips sort of person and thought Christmas's obsession with gorgeous food and homewares was ridiculous and indulgent, but even she couldn't resist her daughter's handmade chocolates. Christmas would offer to do them for the wedding, too, next time she spoke to Val. She must find out what sort of flowers Val had picked for her bouquet so she could track down and order the appropriate sugar flowers to match.

She was just tying a sunny yellow ribbon around the white gift box when Mary opened the shop's front door. She was dressed in a military-inspired red dress with a double row of brass buttons and long black boots. Her lipstick and nails were a matching glossy red, as was the shiny studded harness on her schnauzer. Mary's ebony and ivory hair was strikingly similar to the colours in Ferdinand's coat. He'd been clipped recently, which made his pointy bat-like ears seem taller than normal.

'Hello!' Christmas said. 'Hi, Ferdy.' She scratched the dog's neck, and his tail thumped against Mary's ribs. His busy nose inspected as much of Christmas as he could, seeking out chocolate. She pulled a dog chocolate out of the tall glass jar she kept stocked full of canine tempters (made of carob, of course, chocolate being poisonous for dogs) and handed it to him, and he accepted it with glee, his tiny teeth chomping into the treat.

'Smells wonderful in here today,' Mary said, taking in the heady mingled aroma of brewing coffee, the pink roses in Cheyenne's displays, and the hot chocolate in the tempering tank. She raised a sculpted red nail in greeting to Abigail as she led her sleepy massage client out of the treatment room and into the cooler air at the front of the shop, sitting her down with a pot of lemongrass tea.

'I just finished your mum's daisy chocolates,' Christmas said, reaching for the box and placing it on the counter in front of Mary.

Mary peeked inside the box. 'Oh dear, I'm not sure she'll get them. They look far too good.' She bit her lip. 'I hope I can control myself.'

'Coffee?' Christmas offered.

'No thanks, darl. I just had one over at St Andrew's. I'm doing a story on their latest refurbishment project. If I have another right now I'll be too jittery to drive to my next appointment.'

'Actually, I wanted to talk to you about a godmother project, to see if you could help?' Christmas filled Mary in on Veronika's situation. 'I was wondering if you had any whitegoods suppliers up your sleeve who might like to help out in return for some publicity.'

'Great idea,' Mary said, moving her chin away as Ferdy's kissing got a bit too zealous. 'Try Phillip's Wonder Whitegoods, and maybe Eric's Electrical, let them know I'm looking for a feel-good story for the front page and I'd be keen to come and take lots of photos.'

Christmas enjoyed that familiar rush of excitement as another godmother project began to come together. 'That's wonderful. I'll do that this afternoon. It will mean so much to Veronika. I did tell her it would all be done tastefully. I think she felt a bit uncomfortable about the whole thing but I assured her you'd do a good job.'

'You can count on me.'

'Thanks.'

The ship's bell rang again. Christmas looked up to see Lincoln step over the threshold. Her stomach flipped. She said goodbye to Mary and stood solidly behind the counter, her fingers tightening around the marble.

Lincoln was smiling. He'd had a haircut, she realised. The back and sides were neat and straight, though he'd left some length through the top. His beard had been trimmed too, so he looked a little less Wild Man of the Forest and more Hollywood Actor, those piercing blue eyes enhanced today by an ocean-blue shirt with its top button distractingly undone.

'Hi.' He smiled, deep but gentle creases fanning out around his eyes. 'I hope I'm not late.'

'Hi,' she said, releasing her fingers from the bench. 'You're right on time. And you look good.' Instant regret. Sometimes her mouth said things from her brain that slipped past the censor.

He looked pleased. 'Thanks. I'm on my way out and decided it was time I let go of the jungle and cleaned myself up a bit.'

'Where are you off to?'

'To see my dad, actually.' His smile dropped. 'He's over at Oatlands. Well, a bit out of there, but close enough.'

'Near your grandmother, right?'

'Yes.' He sighed heavily. 'He's a difficult person and one of the reasons overseas travel suits me so much.' He put a hand to his face then and rubbed at his beard as though he'd said too much.

She decided not to pursue what was evidently a sore topic. Besides, she of all people was least qualified to comment on father issues. 'Let's go to the table in the corner,' she said, leading the way to the small round cafe table beside the window. Sitting down on one of the wooden chairs, she wiped her hands on today's apron—sage-green cotton with white and yellow daisies and dragonflies and bright yellow trim. She loved the feeling she got from wearing aprons, a kind of motherly protection from the outside world, and she was glad she had it on now as she sat under Lincoln's penetrating eyes. It felt like an added barrier between them.

He handed her some papers. 'I've brought you some preliminary paperwork, like a contract I guess, just outlining what we're doing and when our deadlines are—the first one's in September—and asking for your commitment of intention to work on the project. That will just cover us while the publishers get the formal contract set up for you to be my co-author.'

'Wow,' she said, thumbing through the pages but not really taking in any words. 'It's all happening so fast.'

'Are you having second thoughts?' he asked, anxiety lining his brow.

'Oh, no. Not at all. When would you like to start? Would next week suit? I shut the shop on Mondays so we could meet here then if you like.'

'That sounds good. Say, ten o'clock?'

'I'll lock it in.' She fished in the pocket of her apron and pulled out a pen and her slim Eiffel Tower diary and made a note. 'I have to write everything down,' she explained. 'I just can't keep track of all the different threads in my life otherwise.'

'I'm the opposite at the moment,' he said. 'I've found myself with all this space in my life a bit earlier than I was intending. I should still be in the Amazon right now.'

'Do you miss it?'

'Some things, like the constant movement of the jungle.

Nothing is ever still. Something is always growing—even if it's just fungus in the heat—or slithering, or dripping, or squawking. It suits me, the ever-changing unpredictability. I don't like to get bogged down.' He smiled then. 'Actually, maybe *bogged down* isn't the right word, since when it rains you get nothing *but* bogged down in the mud.'

She grimaced. 'Not for me, I'm afraid. I'm a bit of a princess, I think.'

'Life is easier here, in some ways. But you'd be surprised. You get into a rhythm. You find a way into all that movement and join it, like jumping into a flowing river and relaxing and letting it take you where it wants to go.'

'Do you think you'll go back?'

'Definitely.'

Christmas was shocked at how disappointed that one word made her feel.

'I'm applying for jobs all the time,' he went on, 'but I've no idea when one will come up.'

'Well,' she said, making herself smile supportively. 'I hope you get what you want soon.'

●

Lincoln reluctantly said goodbye to Christmas. He liked her. He admired someone whose heart was so open, so giving, and so passionate. Passion—that was something they had in common. She was easy to talk to and made him feel good, somehow. He'd much rather stay talking to her than go to see his father, but he couldn't put it off any longer.

He manoeuvred his long legs awkwardly into the small Honda and set off for Oatlands, watching the farmlands pass by in sweeping browns. So different from the green of the jungle.

Occasionally the tiny car rocked as it was buffeted by a squall of wind. So different from the still humidity of Napo.

Since arriving home just over two weeks ago he'd come up with all manner of excuses to avoid visiting his father. Jen was giving him a hard time about it, saying she was going crazy not knowing what was going on down there—Lincoln was only a short drive away whereas it was a plane flight for her, he didn't have a disabled son, and did she have to do everything herself? Irritation gnawed at him. He wondered why he was bothering to see Tom. It wasn't like it would make any difference to whatever crap he was pulling with Nan. Just like it had never made a difference to how much he'd ever thought of Lincoln. Or, more precisely, how *little* he'd ever thought of Lincoln.

Lincoln loved trees. Tom's longest-running job had been with the biggest logging company in Tasmania. And that pretty much summed up their relationship.

His father lived in a fibro shack that would have once been part of a busy sheep- and wheat-farming community. Now the town was desolate and virtually empty, the houses untended, with falling-down chain-wire fences and rusted letterboxes. Every house in Tom van Luc's street had likely not seen any sort of tradesperson for years.

Pulling up in the dirt driveway, Lincoln cast an eye over the open screen door on the verandah, the weathervane flipping and screeching in the wind, and the dark grey clouds above. It wasn't as though his father had ever been a ball of fun. He'd always been taciturn and rigid, a bit miserly. But sometime over the past decade he'd descended dramatically into a foul-tempered, unkempt hermit, the kind that frightened small children. The kind that became an almost legendary figure, encouraging adrenaline-seeking teenagers to egg each other on to sneak up onto the verandah, knock on the door and then run away, high on the thrill of fear.

Lincoln stepped carefully up the sagging steps and knocked once on the door, the peeling mustard-coloured paint flaking off under his knuckle.

Tom came to the door in his threadbare trousers and thin, holey jumper, peering warily out at his visitor.

'Where are the slippers I sent you?' Lincoln asked, immediately angry, pointing at the ancient pair on his father's feet.

'Waiting for these ones to wear out.' Tom put his hand to his mouth while a chesty cough shook his body.

Lincoln followed him into the kitchen, swept a pile of old newspapers off the stool by the stovetop and sat there in silence while Tom struck a match to light the gas. At least, Lincoln noted, he'd finally replaced the battered aluminium kettle with stainless steel.

He wanted to jump right to the point and ask Tom what on earth was going on with Nan, but he forced himself to be patient. His father didn't like to be pushed. Lincoln had learned at a young age not to rush him or risk an explosive outburst of criticism that wounded him inside and made him retreat up Nan's apple tree until the pain receded. She would let him stay up there, never telling him to come down, only ever setting up a picnic table beneath the tree and letting the scent of home-baked pie entice him from his branch. She knew not to push him either—Lincoln could be as sulky as Tom was explosive.

Tom pulled out two stained mugs from the cupboard over the sink and placed them on the bench, then poured boiling water over two teabags.

Lincoln took a breath. 'So. What's been happening?'

'Nothing new.'

Lincoln made himself bide his time. He looked at the piles of clothes, dishes and papers heaped around the room, then caught sight of his father's rod and reel in the corner behind the television. 'Caught anything lately?'

'The lake's got good stock again. Brook trout mostly. They had to restock it after the big drought. Caught a nice one last week and had it for dinner and lunch the next day.'

Lincoln wondered whether it was obscene indulgence or environmentally responsible to artificially restock the lake. He imagined a bunch of men paid to transport fat fish from a farm out to a lake so the locals and tourists could get a thrill hooking one. He couldn't help but think of the Ecuadorians swimming in the Napo River, wearing their gumboots and absurdly large eye masks to see the fish hiding under logs and rocks so they could pierce them with the poisonous *barbasco* root. How even a fish as small as your hand was worth celebrating as it was flung into the boat to be cooked over an open fire.

'I haven't been fishing for years,' Lincoln said, trying to think back. 'It must have been with you, out on the lake before the drought. So that's going back a bit.'

'Nineteen ninety-five,' Tom said. 'It was Father's Day. You and Jenny both came.'

'That's right,' Lincoln said, smiling at the memory. 'And Jen was in her vegetarian phase and kept banging the side of the tinny and shouting, "Run, fishies, run!"'

Tom shook his head in mock disgust. 'Bloody nuisance. Didn't catch a bloody thing. I banned her from the boat then, you know. Told her she couldn't come out ever again.'

'I do remember. She was relieved, actually. She said the only good use for a boat was to rock it, really hard, in any situation of too much seriousness or importance.'

Tom grunted a partial chuckle. Jen was safe ground. Lincoln wished she were here now. She'd always been the mediator in their family, bridging the awkwardness with deep philosophical lectures that left them with jaws dropping, alternated with random fluffy tabloid gossip that allowed the rest of them to brood in silence while she chatted on. In hindsight, it was probably her finally leaving home that had led to his parents' divorce, which was ten years too late by Lincoln and Jen's reckoning.

'Have you seen her lately?' Lincoln asked.

'Not for a while.' His father's eyes were focused on the back wall of the kitchen, his mind clearly elsewhere.

'She emailed me while I was in Ecuador,' Lincoln said, circling the issue, looking for a place to land that wouldn't get his father's back up. 'Nathan's going well, she said.'

Tom picked up a television guide and began flicking through it. Lincoln gritted his teeth. Tom had once made a remark within Jen's earshot, after her partner had walked out because he couldn't handle a child with disabilities, and after too many rums, that a child like Nathan, born with cerebral palsy, should have been knocked on the head at birth, that it would have been kinder to everyone. It was something Jen seemed to have somehow forgiven, or at least accepted, though Lincoln couldn't understand how and maintained the rage on her behalf. He took a deep breath and tackled the reason for his visit.

'She forwarded me an email from the nursing home.'

Tom's eyes shot up from the TV guide. *Guilty.*

Lincoln pressed on. 'It was from one of the nurses, who wanted to let us know that you hadn't been to see Nan for many weeks.'

'So?'

Lincoln tried to quell his rising anger. 'She suggested Nan was lonely, and she was worried she might be developing depression.'

'Was it that Sarah girl? She's a nosy cow.'

'Dad, you do realise you are the only member of this family who is able to visit Nan on a regular basis, don't you?'

'You're here.'

'Yes, but I had to cut my work trip short, just to come home and make sure she was okay.'

'Of course she's okay.'

'She needs more than being fed three times a day and assisted in the shower, Dad. She needs company. Love.'

Tom scoffed. 'Love? She doesn't know the meaning of the word.'

Lincoln stood up and paced. 'How can you say that? Nothing could be further from the truth.' Elsa had patiently taught Lincoln to pick and shell beans, and then how to salt and boil them. She'd let him collect the eggs from chickens and never once got angry when he accidentally dropped and broke them. She bought him books from fetes and markets and together they lay on the musty couch reading for hours. She let him turn up whenever he wanted, let him stay for as long as he cared, gave him space, hugs and apple pies as the situation necessitated. He'd never felt anything but love from her. Never felt criticised. Never judged. Only loved.

He stopped, suddenly, facing his father. It was something Sarah had said in her email. *I'm worried Tom might be, how should I put this, exerting pressure on Elsa.*

'You want something from her,' Lincoln said. And then, looking at the holes in his father's slippers, with shining clarity, 'It's money, isn't it?'

Tom flared, smacked the TV guide against the table. 'Don't you come here judging me. You don't live here. You don't know anything. She's an old woman who's never going to leave that place. She doesn't need all the money that's tied up in the house.'

Lincoln recoiled. 'You asked her to sell the house?'

'Why should she keep it? She doesn't need it. And you're plenty old enough to sort yourself out. You're not a teenager anymore who needs to stay with his grandmother when he can't hack it at home!'

Lincoln didn't even know where to start with that criticism. Forty years of never being good enough stood there in the room with him, gathered at his back like an army ready to charge forth.

But just then there was whining and scratching at the back door.

'Caesar! Shut up!' Tom shouted, his eyes flashing with anger.

'Who's Caesar?' Lincoln said, irritated that his moment to take on his father had been interrupted.

'A bloody dog.'

'So I gathered.' Lincoln opened the door to see a skinny old golden retriever staring up at him with liquid brown eyes and a worried brow. He knelt down. 'Hey there,' he said, reaching out a hand, trying to calm his bubbling fury so the dog wouldn't be frightened.

Caesar hesitated a second, clearly sensing the hostility in the room, but then burst into frenzied tail-wagging and tongue-licking. He knocked Lincoln to the floor and sat in his lap.

'Get out,' Tom growled. 'Out!' He waved the rolled-up TV guide at the dog's ears as if to hit him, but Lincoln shot him a stare so fierce his father actually pulled his hand back. Caesar dropped his head and leaned his body into Lincoln's chest.

'What's the story? Whose dog is this?'

'Bloody Mitchell, two doors up. Asked me to throw some food at the dog for a few days while he was in Hobart. Turns out he had no plan to come back.'

Lincoln rubbed Caesar's ears. 'So, he's yours now?'

Tom made an appalled noise in his throat.

'Are you feeding him? His ribs are sticking out!'

'He wanders.'

Lincoln rubbed Caesar's greying muzzle. 'No home, hey.' He felt a lurch in his chest. An old dog like this would have a hard time finding a new home. He thought of Elsa, waiting for her son to visit, and the anger hit him again. 'Why aren't you looking after him?' he demanded, still on the floor with Caesar's panting, bony body in his arms. 'Look at him.'

'Not my responsibility.'

'Well, whose is it? He's an old dog, Dad. It's nearly winter and it's freezing out there. It'll be snowing soon. How can you just sit by and watch him suffer?' He knew he was talking about more than this dog. He was talking about Elsa, Tom's own mother, stuck in a nursing home just six kilometres from Tom's house. And instead of visiting her and showing some sort of kindness, he was blackmailing her for money.

'It's got nothing to do with me,' Tom shouted, slamming down his mug. 'I'm not the bloody RSPCA.'

'But you are a son.'

Tom lifted his chin and examined Lincoln with calculating eyes. 'So this is why you came? Not to see me, as *my* son,' he thrust his pointer finger at his own chest, 'but to harp on at me about your grandmother.' He shook his head. 'You're a piece of work.'

Lincoln gently dislodged the dog and got to his feet. 'If that's true, Dad, then the apple doesn't fall far from the tree.' He strode to the front door, halted with his hand on the knob, turned back and called to the dog. 'Come on, Caesar. We're going home.'

The dog stood there for a second, looking nervously at Tom.

'Garn, get!' Tom threatened, and Caesar scrambled as fast as he could out of the house, sinking under a kick from Tom, and jumped into the Honda. Lincoln dropped the clutch and roared out of the driveway, tyres spitting up stones as he went.

He let out a growl of frustration. Just then, Caesar, refusing to stay in the back of the car, forced his way through the gap between the two front seats. He positioned himself across Lincoln's lap, his nose pressed to the driver's window. Lincoln had to arch and crane his neck over the dog's shoulders, the stench of unwashed canine filling his nostrils along with loose hairs; the dog desperately needed a bath and a good brush. No matter how many times he pushed Caesar across to the passenger seat, the dog wormed his way back again.

'I better not get a ticket, Caesar,' Lincoln said, reining in his anger and reducing his speed.

He passed through Oatlands and briefly thought about stopping in to show Elsa the dog, but quickly concluded that the nursing staff wouldn't be impressed to see a pooch of such appearance and fragrance. Besides, he wouldn't be able to talk to her right now without ranting and raving.

Eventually, Caesar settled across Lincoln's thighs with his head resting on his paws and his backside on the passenger seat and began breathing heavy, rhythmic breaths that suggested he'd found the most comfortable bed he'd had in years. And soon after, Lincoln found his left hand methodically stroking the dog's grimy ears, his own breathing slowing in time with his new companion's. Compassion wrapped itself warmly around Lincoln's heart and he found himself creeping around corners so as not to wake the dog.

About twenty minutes out from Western Junction, in Campbell Town, warm drool made its way through Lincoln's jeans and confirmed the dog's deep slumber. And it made Lincoln smile.

9

The day was stretching into that time of the afternoon when retired folk started thinking of napping before dinner. A gentle lull settled on The Chocolate Apothecary. Christmas put her newest chocolate creations on a polished silver plate in the glass display cabinet and picked up the phone to call Val. The jealousy she'd felt when she heard the news about the wedding had long gone. She was happy for Val and Archie, and excited about the wedding.

'Ahoy.'

'Hi, Archie, it's Christmas. How are you?'

'Well, my back's still playing up and the council is saying I need to move at least two of the cars in the front yard, but I'm fighting for my rights. Is a man's own yard not his kingdom?' he asked rhetorically.

'Yes, indeed. I wish you luck with that. Keep me posted, okay? Is Val around at all?'

'Val!' Archie roared, only inches from the phone. 'Christmas is on the line!'

There was the usual array of shouting and thumping noises in the background—the normal sounds of three mid-sized boys on a Saturday afternoon—and Val's screeching orders to them to *Get off your brother* and *Say you're sorry, now!*

'Hi, Massy,' Val said, her calmness at total odds with the shouting she'd been doing just a few seconds ago.

'Hi. How are things? How are the wedding plans going?'

'Good. The Leaning Church is booked for the ceremony, and Archie's mum is finishing up her cake-making course this weekend so she's bringing around some photos and we'll choose a design for her to do a test bake. Do you think Cheyenne could line me up with some flowers?'

'I'm sure she'd be thrilled. Leave it with me to organise. I'll find out what's best at that time of year.' Christmas wrote herself a note and slipped the diary back into her apron pocket. 'And just so you know, I'm working on some gorgeous wee wedding chocolates at the moment. I'd like to gift you bonbonnieres for everyone at the reception.'

'Oh, Massy, that would be great. Thanks!'

'And please, let me give you the flowers too. I'll work something out with Cheyenne once you've chosen what you'd like.'

'No, it's too much.'

'Don't be silly. My baby sister's only getting married once.'

'We hope.'

'Stop it,' Christmas said, though she knew Val was joking. Her sister was cheerful by nature, having inherited Joseph's robust mental strength. And she'd need it, living with all those boys.

'Dad was talking about you the other day,' Val said. 'He was saying how proud he was of everything you've done in your life and he said he remembered you as a seven-year-old making tea for Mum when she was having a bad day and how you would sprinkle hundreds-and-thousands in it and tell her it was magic healing dust.'

Christmas was stunned. 'I'd completely forgotten that.'

'He said he had too. But he read the article in the in-flight magazine and it all came back to him and he realised you were doing exactly what you'd wanted to do when you were young.'

A lump the size of a small country lodged in Christmas's throat and she blinked through blurry tears. Seven years old. The year Val was born. The year of her mother's worst episode that Christmas could remember. The year Darla stared blankly through her eldest daughter's eyes when Christmas tried to tell her about her day at school. The year Christmas had learned to pick out clothes every morning for her mother, rather than the other way around.

'What was he doing on a plane?' she said, needing to change the subject before emotion overwhelmed her. 'And are you allowed to keep those magazines? I'm never sure.'

'I'm not sure either. He'd been sent up to Melbourne for some sort of principals' conference. It was over a weekend. How mean is that? You couldn't pay me enough to be a teacher.'

'No, nor me. But that's Joseph, isn't it, always conscientious, always trying to do the right thing. You're a very lucky girl to have him,' Christmas said, barely a whisper, but still, Val heard.

'I'm sorry, Massy. I didn't mean to upset you.'

'Don't be silly. I've made peace with it. I'm happy for you. Now, has Mum RSVP'd?'

'Not yet,' said Val. 'I suppose she'll just turn up on the day wearing something outrageous.'

'Animal skins, probably, given her current occupation.'

'Don't even joke about it.'

The ship's bell over the shop door rang, heralding customers. Christmas smiled and gave them a wave. It was Cynthia Heather Who Liked to Wear Leather, with her two sons and daughter, all come for their weekly hot chocolate—Christmas's own recipe of melted Belgian chocolate and cream. It was so thick it had to be eaten. She served it in small, painted Turkish tea glasses with wooden spoons.

'Val, I've got to go. Give those boys a big hug for me. Love you.'

'Love you too.'

•

By the time he'd reached Western Junction and pulled into the driveway of Elsa's house, Lincoln realised he was definitely feeling a strong pull of affection and responsibility towards Caesar. The dog had been cast to the elements to fend for himself. The people who'd done this to him, including Tom, who had ignored his suffering, had decided he wasn't worthy of protection, love or commitment. Well, that ended, right now.

'Come on, boy,' Lincoln said, pulling on the handbrake with difficulty, wedged as it was underneath Caesar's long body. 'Wakey, wakey. Time to get up.'

Caesar lifted his head and the bags under his eyes drooped, making him look decidedly hung-over. He gazed out through the bug-spattered windscreen and gave a small whine as though realising, either for the first time or with finality, that he'd left his old home for good.

'You'll be right, mate,' Lincoln said, trying to cheer him up with more ear rubbing. 'Just wait till you see the size of the guest bedroom. There's a queen-sized bed in there that's got your name written all over it.'

Caesar perked up at that and voluntarily moved off Lincoln's lap. He shuffled to the passenger-side door, where he waited for his chauffeur to come and open it.

Inside the house, the dog trotted down the hallway, poking his head into every room, then came back to the lounge and lay down with a deep sigh in front of the fireplace.

'Okay, we'll make a fire, but first you need a bath,' Lincoln said, rubbing Caesar's belly with his foot. 'Now, what should we bath you in? I haven't had a dog since I was a kid, so you'll have to forgive me while I work this out, but I know I can't use human soap or shampoo on you.' He checked his watch. It was late but he just had time to nip down to the corner shop and grab some pet shampoo before it shut. Oh, and he'd need dog food too. And a collar. And probably a leash.

'Do you want to come for a walk?' he asked Caesar.

Caesar stayed put.

'Hmm. Okay. Rest up, old fellow, and I'll be back pronto.'

At the corner store, he found himself standing in front of the pet section, a little overwhelmed. A barrage of accessories implored him to buy them: food bowls, water bowls, collars, leashes, shampoos, conditioners, odour neutralisers, worming tablets, flea products, nail clippers, squeaky toys, rope toys, liver treats, brushes, combs, heartworm tablets. He bought them all, just to be sure.

Back home again, he burst through the door with his arms weighed down by several plastic bags. Caesar, apparently rejuvenated from his nap, jumped to his feet and rushed to greet him, his nose jammed into the bags sooner than Lincoln could get the door closed. He snatched out a rawhide bone, his eyes wide with ecstasy, and began running in circles, looking for a place to lie down and chew it.

Lincoln battled on with the bags and dumped them on the kitchen bench. Taking out the first bottle of shampoo (he'd bought two different types in case Caesar didn't like the smell of one), he considered his options. He'd never had to bath a dog this size before. The foxy they'd had when he was a small boy could be put into the laundry tub to be washed. That wouldn't work with Caesar.

He went outside to find the hose, but less than a minute wandering around in the gale-force wind convinced him he couldn't possibly put the old dog through that; he was skin and bone and the water would be ice-cold.

There was only one thing for it: he'd have to go in the bathtub.

He coaxed Caesar down the hallway and into the bathroom by taking the rawhide bone out of his mouth and getting him to follow it through the house. But as soon as Caesar saw the bathtub, he skidded to a halt and spun on his overgrown toenails.

'No you don't,' Lincoln said, throwing his arms around the dog's neck. With no collar, he was hard to get hold of, but somehow Lincoln pulled him back into the bathroom, then shut the door so he couldn't escape.

Caesar cowered in a corner of the room while Lincoln filled the bath with warm water and poured in copious amounts of shampoo to form froth and bubble. The smell of tea tree rose gently on the steam. He opened the linen cupboard next to the vanity and pulled out as many old towels as he could identify— ones with faded colours or tattered edges. He whistled while he laid them on the floor, and spoke in a cheery, spirits-bolstering tone to the miserable-looking dog.

Once the water was sufficiently deep, Lincoln turned off the taps. 'Okay, mate. Let's get this done.'

He tried to move Caesar by lifting up his front end and placing his paws ahead of his body, hoping the rest of him would follow. Instead, Caesar went as floppy as a ragdoll and dropped to the brown tiles.

'Caesar, come on, get up, buddy.' But Caesar was limp and unresponsive.

Lincoln tried sliding him across the tiles, pushing from behind, but the more pressure he applied the more the dog rolled and seemed to spread across the floor. Every time Lincoln stopped one part of his body from escaping, another part took off in another direction.

'Huh. Passive resistance. A remarkably effective tactic. Well played,' Lincoln said, amused. 'Perhaps I should rename you Gandhi.'

Puffing with exertion, he gave up and hauled the dog to the bath, then placed him gently in the water.

'There you go,' he soothed, sponging water over Caesar's back and legs. He poured more shampoo down his spine and tail, rubbing and rubbing while the water quickly turned brown. Pieces of grass and dead insects and leaves floated on the surface. Lincoln poured more shampoo down Caesar's legs, on his chest and the top of his head. The dog was soon covered in white foam.

Lincoln pulled the plug and let out the grimy water so he could start afresh. Seeing his opportunity, Caesar leapt out of the tub.

'Hold on!' Lincoln shouted as the dog shook himself violently, spraying foam over every surface and Lincoln too.

In spite of Caesar's vigorous efforts, white drifts still clung to him like snow, and soapy bubbles glistened on his coat. It was clear that the bathtub wasn't going to cut it. What Lincoln needed was a hose attached to the tap. He rummaged around in the vanity cupboard looking for such an item while Caesar ran in circles, wagging his long tail and flinging more filthy suds around the room. A big splodge whipped across the back of Lincoln's neck.

He wiped his brow. It was now quite warm in the bathroom. Steam condensed on the walls and mirror and the exertion of manhandling Caesar had made him sweat. He stripped off his shirt and stared at the empty, grubby bathtub, the muddy paw prints on the tiles, and the shower just behind where Caesar now stood, shaking himself from nose to tail.

'Let's try this again,' Lincoln said. He pulled off his boots and socks, undid his belt, took off his jeans and underwear and stood naked in front of his charge. 'You can't win, Caesar.'

The dog's ears flattened in defeat.

Lincoln turned on the shower, made sure the temperature was warm enough, picked up Caesar once more and placed him inside the glass cubicle. He let the water flow over them both, the skinny dog with his nose pressed against the glass, staring at the rawhide bone near the door. Lincoln sang as he worked, the sight of the water rushing down the drain filling him with an unexpected and energising sense of triumph.

It was only afterwards, when Caesar sat wet and shivering, his ribs poking out at sharp angles, that Lincoln realised he needed help. He couldn't leave Caesar like this to catch his death. He needed a hairdryer but didn't own one himself. But who could he call?

He checked the time. Six o'clock on a Saturday night. Would she be home?

•

Christmas was indeed home, and had finished a meal of chicken soup, one of her staple foods she liked to cook in batches and freeze for the end of working days when she was simply too tired to do anything more than light the gas, pop a saucepan of soup on to heat, and slice off some crusty bread and slather it with butter.

After two bowls of soup she felt revived enough to sit at her desk and check her godmother emails. Mary Hauser had sent a message saying Christmas didn't need to do anything because she'd managed to secure a washing machine for Veronika with just one phone call—Christmas's 'godmother fame' was spreading, she'd said—and she was working on the newspaper article right now. Christmas smiled. Whenever a godmother gift came together like this it was as though every bad thing in the world was healed just a fraction.

But she'd begun to fall behind on some of her other fairy godmother projects, and had regretfully decided that she'd have to temporarily stop taking on any new requests. She figured it was better to do a smaller number properly, and complete them before she left for France, than a larger number poorly.

She'd just responded to Dennis Chamberlain, giving advice on the choice of engagement ring (he'd emailed her pictures of *twelve* options to get her opinion), when her mobile phone rang. She checked the caller ID.

'Lincoln van Luc,' she murmured, and automatically responded to herself with 'Just a Little Bit Cute.' She was due to see him in a couple of days. What could he want?

'A hairdryer,' he said. 'Do you have one?'

'Yes.'

'Would I be able to borrow it?'

'Borrow it?'

'Yes. Right now, actually. I have a . . . well, is there any chance you might be able to pop over with it?'

'Now?'

'It's a hairdryer emergency, I'm afraid,' he said, a smile in his tone.

A hairdryer emergency. Christmas felt a flutter of excitement and the whiff of mirth. She couldn't resist seeing that for herself. 'I'll be right over.' She scribbled down the directions to his house.

A five-minute drive later, Lincoln greeted her at the door with evident relief. 'Thanks so much for coming,' he said, ushering her in out of the wind.

'What's going on?' she asked, glancing around.

'He's this way,' Lincoln said, leading her through the house.

He?

Lincoln's grandmother's house was a modest brick affair with a tiled roof, an ordinary (okay, somewhat scruffy) backyard and a plain but functional kitchen. It was typical of houses left behind by elderly owners, Christmas thought—solidly built, but untouched by any kind of facelift for at least twenty years. Floral-patterned furnishings throughout, dated green carpet, and framed photographs of family members from decades past: side-burns, flares, the muted colours of old photographic technology.

And then they were standing in a room with a green pastel synthetic bedspread covering a queen-sized bed, and lying on the carpet was a bedraggled, bony old golden retriever.

'Goodness, is he alright?' Christmas said, bending down to stroke his head. The dog looked up at her mournfully, his lower eyelids drooping down to show the pink insides. 'What happened?'

'This is Caesar. We only just met today. I found him at my father's place. Apparently he's been abandoned.'

Christmas gasped. 'That's awful!'

'Agreed.' Lincoln ran a hand through his own clipped mane. 'I couldn't leave him to starve out there in the cold so I brought him home.'

The dog gave a single lethargic thump of his tail as Christmas stroked his sides. 'Is he sick?'

'I think he's fine, just depressed.'

'Because he was abandoned?'

'No. Because I bathed him. He really didn't like that. I don't think he likes the smell of tea tree. I think he prefers his original smell of *eau de bouse de vache.*'

Christmas looked up from where she was kneeling next to Caesar. 'What's that?'

'Cow manure.'

'Oh.' She laughed. 'Do you speak French?'

He sat on the corner of the bed with a sheepish grin and a scratch at his ear. 'No. But I thought of it this afternoon and I just had to look up an online translator to find out how to say it in French.' He shrugged. 'I'm a bit of a geek, I guess.'

A totally gorgeous geek.

'I can't leave him all wet like this,' he went on. 'He might get pneumonia or something. Hence the emergency hairdryer.'

'Yes, I see. Let's get you dry, Caesar, and see if we can't lift your spirits a bit.'

She plugged the dryer into a nearby socket and set it to a low, warm level, using her fingers to fluff up Caesar's hair as she worked her way around his body. He twitched uneasily to begin with, then settled when he realised how lovely and warm it was, and started to relax. He had so much hair that it took a long time; Lincoln soon joined her on the ground and they passed the dryer back and forth to work each side of the dog, enjoying watching Caesar as he began to stretch and roll over onto his back so they could dry his belly.

At last his tail began to wag, his mouth split into a goofy grin and his droopy eyelids magically sprang upwards again. He half sat up, then threw himself into Christmas's lap, knocking her backwards onto the floor. She squealed as he snuffled around her ears and neck, licking her with his hot tongue. She tried to push him off but he was surprisingly heavy for such a scrawny specimen.

'You could help me,' she gasped at Lincoln, who was leaning back against the end of the bed and laughing at her.

'Not a chance. You're on your own. He loves you. He probably hasn't had so much joy in years.'

At last Christmas managed to pull herself back up to a sitting position and arrange Caesar so he was lying on the floor with just his shoulders and head in her lap, panting contentedly, his hair fluffed out so he looked at least twice the size. 'Phew,' she said, grinning at Lincoln. 'That was hard work.'

'You should see the bathroom.' He raised his eyebrows in mock horror and reached out a hand to rub Caesar's ears.

'What are you going to do with him now?' she asked.

'I don't know. I can't keep him.'

'Why not?'

'I travel all the time for work. I can't take on a commitment like that. It wouldn't be fair to him.'

Or me, she reminded herself, just in case some small part of her was being seduced by this whole knight-in-shining-armour thing.

He looked at her. 'What about you? Could you keep him?'

'Me?' She considered it for a moment as Caesar's lovely grey muzzle sniffed around her jeans, looking for treats. 'Unfortunately I can't have a dog in the chocolate shop. It's against health and safety rules.' She thought guiltily of Mary Hauser and her schnauzer and all the other folk she let bring in their dogs to get a doggie choc. She didn't let them stay inside for long, but she enjoyed their visits. It was a ridiculous rule, anyway. Heaps of places overseas allowed dogs in cafes. They couldn't be any more dirty than some people's children. That was a fact.

But her heart lurched for Caesar. 'Who'll take him?'

Lincoln shrugged. 'Something will turn up. It always does. Life's like that.'

'Hmm.' Christmas bit her lip. She didn't trust life to take care of all the details. *Rule number eight—Your destiny doesn't happen to you; you make your destiny.*

She was contemplating all the options that lay ahead for Caesar—the pound, euthanasia, a rescue organisation, a friend, a family . . . perhaps she could play fairy godmother and find him a home?—when she suddenly felt Lincoln watching her. She looked up and held his eyes with her own for a moment before turning away.

'Well, it looks like Caesar is all okay. I guess I should get going.'

Lincoln made a noise in the back of his throat. 'Yes. Thanks so much for bringing the hairdryer. I'm sure Caesar will get a much better night's sleep now.'

Christmas stood up and packed the hairdryer into her bag. 'So then, I guess I'll see you Monday for our first working session.' She affected a bright, professional air.

'Looking forward to it,' he said, leading her to the door, Caesar trotting happily behind them.

'Goodnight,' she said, patting Caesar, deliberately avoiding hovering in Lincoln's doorway for too long. She straightened quickly. 'See you Monday.'

'See you then.' He smiled, and her legs trembled.

10

On Monday, Christmas and Lincoln sat together at the long wooden table in the centre of the shop. The air was intoxicatingly thick with the sweet perfume of the bridal white *lutchuensis* camellias Cheyenne grew on her property and had wrapped in ribbons for sale. The flowers stood in metal buckets on wooden trestles and nodded gently on the current of the air-conditioning. Picked on Friday because Cheyenne said they couldn't wait another day, they'd kept quite well over the weekend, treated to filtered water and the constant temperature in the shop.

Christmas had just finished booking her flights to France online, the realisation that it was truly going to happen filling her with a rush of adrenaline, excitement and nerves, when Lincoln had tapped gently on the door, the morning sun on his shoulders.

'How's Caesar this morning?' she'd asked, letting him in.

'Great. We went for a wander around the streets. He has no manners and bowls into anyone and everyone to say hello. He sniffed three human crotches and one dog's bum, licked a cat's face, and stole a plastic gnome from a garden and crushed it before I could save it.'

'Did you knock on the owner's door?'

'No. Call me mean but I think the world's a better place without gnomes, don't you? They're creepy.'

Now, having poured Lincoln a cup of freshly brewed coffee, Christmas sat next to him clutching her cup of Piscean zodiac tea, with rose petals, orange peel, lavender and a dash of ginger, designed to complement the Piscean traits of compassionate femininity combined with a fiery disposition when provoked, or so the aqua box claimed. According to the description, Christmas should be a deeply romantic type, highly intuitive and emotional, but wearing an armour of wariness and independence to protect her from being hurt. She had to admit, it wasn't far off the mark. And it was really lovely tea.

As she sipped it, her mind drifted naturally to envisaging the types of recipes in which she could use the herbs in this tea. Medicinal herbs combined with medicinal chocolate.

She eyed the botanist in the room. It was so obvious, she'd nearly missed it. Lincoln was the perfect person to talk to about her hopes for developing healing uses for chocolate.

He passed her a sheaf of papers. 'This is a sample chapter that my editor—sorry, *our* editor—Jeremy has already seen and which he thinks is a bit dry. Maybe you could have a read and see what you think.'

Christmas replaced her teacup on its matching saucer and read the chapter, while Lincoln got up and wandered around the shop. He was awfully distracting with his long limbs moving about the space so freely. He didn't look like the kind of person who had any tension in his body at all. He stopped to pick up a bundle of antique French love letters from a display. Penned in the late 1800s, the paper yellow, the ink faded but readable (if you could speak French), they were tied together with tightly woven raffia string, a paper-thin pressed flower tucked under the knot.

'Where'd you get these?' he asked.

'I found them in an antiques shop. I thought they were so lovely. So intimate. Two people's lives captured forever there on the page. Although I can't read the words I think you can feel their passion on the page.'

'It's incredible,' Lincoln said, holding the papers carefully in his large hand. 'One day we won't have anything like this anymore. Everyone just texts or emails now and the messages get deleted willy-nilly.'

She snorted. 'Willy-nilly?'

He grinned and shrugged.

She returned her attention to the pages. When she'd finished reading he joined her once more at the table, swinging his legs over the bench seat. He held up a bar of imported Rococo Earl Grey dark chocolate. 'Does this have real tea in it?'

'Yes. They grind the tea leaves to a fine powder and add bergamot oil to it. I'd like to offer a lot more chocolates like that—ones that combine unusual elements like herbs. It's a small percentage of my overall chocolate stock but it's the part I love most.'

'You should always do what you love.' He pointed to the pages. 'What are your thoughts?'

'Well,' she said, pushing the manuscript to the side, 'I always think the key rule of writing is to deliver your message as simply and directly as possible and speak from the heart. There's a lot of passion here, I can tell, but it's a bit, I don't know, stuffy.'

'Stuffy?'

'Yes. Like a lecture.'

'That's no good at all. Do you think there's hope for it?' He fiddled with the pen in front of him, nervous.

'Absolutely! Why don't you tell me, right now, in your own words, some of the things you'd like to get across, and I'll see how I can help.'

Lincoln slipped his thumb under the wrapper of the Rococo bar and began to prise it open. He caught her watching him. 'Don't worry, I intend to buy it.' He smiled.

'Oh, no, I wasn't worried about that.' The truth was that she was thinking it was rather seductive watching him unwrapping that bar of chocolate, and a rush of heat had swept up her body from her toes. To distract herself, she jumped up and went to the iPod player sitting on the apothecary chest. She searched through the menu while Lincoln spoke.

He bit into the chocolate. 'The thing is,' he began, his words slightly muffled, 'sustainability is what it's all about. Oh my God, that's so good!' He licked his finger. 'I'm not normally into flavoured chocolate. I'm a bit of a puritan like that—I think in general you should simply appreciate the diversity of chocolate itself, getting the true rustic flavour of the cacao bean, whatever country, region, estate and tree it came from. I'm not a fan of uniform, mass-produced products where the true flavour is smothered by sugar and milk and vanilla. But this!' He shoved another chunk of chocolate in his mouth. 'Have you tried this?'

Christmas laughed. 'Of course I have. Rococo is one of my favourite suppliers. They inspire me.' She settled on *The Best of Edith Piaf*, and the charming lyrics of 'La Vie en Rose' came tumbling out into The Apothecary.

'What you just told me,' she said, sitting down again, her mind back on the job, 'that's great information and it's something I'm passionate about too.'

'Really?' He cast his eyes around the shop at all the marshmallows and jellies.

'Confectionary sells. But the real fire in my belly is for my consultations. Because I believe that chocolate can be a bona fide medicine. And I want to find out how far I can take that. As you would know, the rainforest is renowned for producing medicines and I'm sure it's no accident that cacao grows in the rainforest. And what you're talking about here,' she motioned over the manuscript, 'is the kernel of that truth. We just need to make it sexier.'

He raised an eyebrow. 'Sexier?'

Christmas felt her ears redden but ploughed on regardless. 'Tell me more about sustainability.'

'Sustainability of cacao production is the key to long-term economic benefit, but this is always in conflict with the short-term needs of corporations to make a profit. What I've seen is that so much of the sustainability concern around cacao is actually at a social level. A cacao farm is typically only a couple of acres in size, run by the family who owns it. They work really hard, for a handful of dollars a day, and it's all manual labour, every single step. Unlike other crops, no one's yet come up with reliable, effective ways to mechanise the farming, so the whole industry relies on paying wages to the workers on the ground, and it would simply cost too much to grow it in a developed nation with appropriate remuneration, even if one had the right climate.'

His eyes drifted off to the corner of the room as if he were recalling what he'd seen. 'In Ghana, the workers sit in a circle and chant to urge each other on to work harder while they split open the pods with machetes, pull out the beans, put them in a pile and cover them with banana leaves to ferment for five days or so.'

He looked back at her, enthusiasm animating his hands. 'Cacao's a cash crop, which means all their hard work doesn't even result in food they can eat, and the trade price for cacao is set by a global stockmarket thousands of miles away. The farmers receive paltry financial rewards for their efforts, and given this and the high labour investment necessary to grow cacao, the younger generations are turning away and leaving the farms. And fair enough. But that means the farmers are ageing and so too are the cacao trees.'

Christmas frowned. 'Sounds dire. Is it really possible we'd end up in a world without chocolate?'

'I think it's unlikely. But at the same time, I think we're going to see some big changes. Attempts have been made to create faster-growing types of cacao trees, but all that happens is that those trees take more nutrients from the soil and more water from the water table than can be replaced in time for new crops. And the newer, faster-growing varieties don't live as long as the traditional trees either. At the same time, if the farmer *can* actually produce more cacao with these new varieties, the world trade price actually falls. So they're forever chasing their tail.'

Christmas took a deep breath. 'Heavy stuff.'

'Yes, it is. Can I get another coffee?'

'Sure.' She led him to the coffee machine, which was her tool for providing fancy coffees for anyone who wanted more than the free plunger coffees on offer, and switched it on to heat up the water. They leaned with their backs on the apothecary chest and gazed at the rows of shiny chocolates lined up in the glass cabinet in front of them.

'Do you know, many of the farmers who grow cacao to supply the gigantic chocolate trade have never even tasted chocolate?' Lincoln said.

'You're kidding? That's outrageous. I just want to post them a box full right now!'

'Many of them say they just grow the beans for their broker but have no idea what the white people do with them after that,' he explained. 'Chocolate is one of the few gourmet foods where the ingredient is grown thousands of miles from where it's processed and consumed.'

Christmas considered her own part in chocolate's journey. Her beans certainly racked up a lot of frequent-flyer points on their travels, and hers was one of the smaller supply chains in the world. At least she didn't then export her chocolates again, like so many of the huge chocolate companies.

She mentally adjusted her PR hat and tapped her brain for ideas on how to convey this information in a way that would be easy for readers to grasp. 'I've got it,' she said, snapping her fingers.

'What?'

'A way to combine all this heavy, political but ultimately important stuff about cacao production with wonderful pictures and stories about chocolate.'

'Go on.'

'We can follow a bean, a single bean, from its life in the pod, on the branch on the tree, on the farm, region, country, et cetera, and onwards to market, the trader, the ship or plane or whatever it travels on, through processing and on and on until it's eaten.'

Lincoln rubbed his beard thoughtfully. 'I can see how that would work.'

'We could create a travel diary and postcards.' She smiled. 'Stamps in its passport. Send it to trade shows and chocolate-tasting competitions.'

'It could provide commentary about prejudice in the bean community between different countries of origin and different varieties,' Lincoln said, nodding as the ideas started to flow.

'It could look into its family history,' she said.

'It could build a family tree to follow the genetics of the bean families. There's been some amazing work in the past five years on rediscovering heirloom bean varieties and even three completely new strands of cacao in the Amazon. It's a fascinating field.'

'Could there be species we still don't know about?' Christmas asked, her attention arrested.

'Sure. Anything's possible.'

'And would it be possible for those species to have different chemical properties?'

'Of course.' He tilted his head. 'Why?'

'I'm holding out for the discovery of a super bean, one that has unrivalled health benefits.'

'Chocolate as medicine,' he said.

'Exactly.'

'I love that.'

She grinned at Lincoln. When he was excited his blue eyes blazed. She found herself wondering what his personal story was. Why someone who was obviously nice, intelligent and good looking was single.

She turned away and focused on making the coffee. They had a lot of work ahead of them and they'd need to get started quickly if they were going to get the manuscript up to scratch before she left for France.

Their plan was straightforward. They divided up the manuscript into botany-related areas for Lincoln, and created new sections for Christmas to write, focusing on the artisan techniques she used herself—such as sourcing, roasting and grinding cacao beans from scratch; creating raw chocolate from a few simple ingredients; tempering chocolate; and lashings of recipes from her own repertoire. They would swap sections and help each other, Lincoln concentrating on content and Christmas on improving his words to make them more friendly. They wanted the majority of a full draft put together before she left for France, and that would leave them about six weeks after her return to re-draft and edit it before their submission deadline in September.

Phew!

She felt lightheaded just at the thought of all this extra work. But perhaps it was a just what she needed right now to keep her mind free of distractions, because, she reminded herself firmly, there was no room for romantic dreams in her life.

Rule number ten.

11

When Christmas had discovered she was pregnant, she was thirty-five and living in Sydney. She was the senior PR rep for Simon Barton, an up-and-coming Australian tennis player with a brat-pack reputation. He was significantly younger than her and had longer hair too, which he wore piled on top of his head in a way that should have been feminine but actually just gave him an edgy appeal. Particularly when he had his shirt off. The guy was gorgeous. He should have been raking in the money from sponsors. Instead, his reputation as an arrogant player who was a bad loser, together with a couple of drink-driving convictions and rumours that he slept around, was pushing the fans and sponsorship money away.

Christmas had been given the assignment to turn it all around.

'I think we need to get you out doing some charity work,' she'd said the first day she met him in person. He was sitting across the desk from her, one ankle on his other knee, charcoal suit pants leg rising up to reveal no socks beneath the leather shoes. He was on his way to a photo shoot for a newspaper magazine feature, an article she'd worked hard to secure, and when he'd walked through the glass doors into her office she'd had to force herself to look only at his eyes. If she took in too much of his appearance she would lose her train of thought.

Kelly, the temp at the front desk, blushed noticeably and fluttered about him on his arrival, offering tea and coffee and magazines. Christmas had eyed him over the top of her laptop screen, deliberately making him wait. She knew he didn't want to be here but that his business manager had threatened to quit if he didn't turn up. At the thought of losing the person who looked after his money, Simon had conceded to the meeting.

'What sort of charity?' he asked now, suspicious.

Christmas tapped her pen against the leather cover of her diary. 'Something with children is always good. Sick kids, preferably.'

He sniffed and lifted his chin and she saw the muscles twitch in his neck. She could see the smooth rise of his pecs under his crisp white shirt, which he'd left artfully open at the top for just such an effect. Damn, the man had good fashion sense.

'It fosters goodwill and makes people feel better, brings joy and happiness,' she said, sensing his resistance.

He absently stroked the two-day growth on his chin, considering this.

Christmas leaned back in her chair and crossed her slim legs, and his eyes dropped to her knee. 'Look,' she said, smiling, 'the general public consider you heartless, and potential sponsors think you're unreliable. Visiting children in hospital, running a weekend tennis camp for underprivileged youth, flipping burgers for a charity barbecue in the park—all of these things will help build an identity of selfless giving.'

He studied her, a small smirk on his lips.

'I'm sure Trevor would agree,' she said, and at the mention of his manager's name, Simon evidently accepted defeat.

'Fine. Tee it up and I'll be there. On one condition.'

'What's that?'

'Have dinner with me tonight.'

'Sure. Why not?' Having dinner with a client was nothing out of the ordinary.

Kelly appeared at the door of the office, blushing. 'Taxi's here,' she said, simpering at Simon.

Christmas closed her laptop and stood up, grabbing her bag. 'Now, let's get to this photo shoot before we're late.'

Simon lived in an ultra-modern two-bedroom apartment in an exclusive building right on Bondi Beach. Floor-to-ceiling glass gave it expansive views straight over the ocean. It had wide oak floorboards, blond in colour, limestone features in the bathroom and kitchen, stone benchtops, squared-off basins and bathtubs, lots of mirrors, and minimalist furniture with straight lines and not a lot of comfort. It was beautiful, in a highly composed architectural way, but lacking in warmth. A lot like Simon.

They arrived there just on sunset, in time to share a drink on the balcony as the sky changed colours around them.

'You did well today,' Christmas said, clinking her wine glass to his highball of scotch. 'You answered the questions with real sincerity and humility, and the photos will look sensational. I think it'll be a great feature.'

She was genuinely proud of him. She'd coached him a bit in the taxi on the way to the shoot but hadn't really thought he would follow her advice. Yet when the journalist had asked him about a recent racquet-throwing tantrum on court, instead of scowling he'd lowered his eyes and spoken about how ashamed he was and how he was seeking help to learn how to process his emotions. He wanted the public to remember that he was still young, and sometimes he might stumble, but being a man was about acknowledging your faults and doing something about them. Listening, Christmas had been surprised and impressed.

Simon gazed out over the rolling waves. 'It was all true; I do need to grow up.'

Just then, a small ginger cat with a tinkling bell on its collar ran through the door to the balcony and rubbed itself against Simon's leg.

'Rosa! You shouldn't be out here.' He swooped down to pick her up and she threw herself backwards in his arms, exposing a white chest and chin, closing her eyes in rapture as he rubbed her, and purring like a chainsaw.

'I didn't know you had a cat,' Christmas said.

He smiled as Rosa reached up a paw and patted at his face. 'I got her from the pound.' He led Christmas back inside and closed the screen door behind them so Rosa couldn't escape.

'What were you doing at the pound?' Christmas sat down on his white leather couch, which she now noticed had claw marks in it.

'I featured in a commercial for dog food and, as a thank-you, they sent me a load of cans of the stuff. I didn't have a dog, so I went to drop it at the animal shelter. There was a row of cages with cats and dogs in them. The death row.' He stroked Rosa's back as she settled herself in his lap. 'They all had these expressions on their faces. You know?' He looked up at Christmas as though appealing to her for understanding, and his meadow-coloured eyes fastened on hers. 'They seemed to know it was over for them. The end of the line. Some paced. Some sat with their noses pressed to the wire. Some actually cried.' He paused for a moment and the sadness hung heavy in the room.

'Anyway,' he pulled himself up straighter, 'Rosa was in one of the cages. But she was sitting there serenely. Like, whatever was coming she was just going to take it.'

'Maybe she didn't know what was coming.'

'No.' Simon shook his head emphatically. 'She was brave. Really brave. I didn't think about it too hard. I just said, "I want that one," and they handed her to me.'

Rosa rolled over in his lap and bit the sleeve of his white shirt affectionately.

'So why the name Rosa?'

'After Rosa Parks, the black woman in America who refused to give up her seat on a bus to a white person. You know her?'

Christmas nodded, stunned. There was a lot more to Simon Barton than she'd first thought. Than anyone thought.

'I remembered reading about that in school and thinking how incredibly brave that was. Sometimes I think about that on court.'

'Simon, that is the most amazing story. Why doesn't everyone know this? We could really use it to our advantage for publicity.' Christmas leaned forward, her heart racing with excitement as her mind filled with ideas.

'People don't need to know everything,' he said. He put Rosa gently onto the couch next to him and stood up. 'Anyway, I'm starving. Let's eat.' He gave Christmas a thousand-kilowatt smile and held out his hand to help her to her feet. 'How does Italian sound?'

Really, it was no wonder so many women slept with Simon. Not only was he gorgeous, but he was actually very charming and funny when he stopped being a prat. Quickly, Christmas fell under his spell too. They began an intense relationship that seemed to go from zero to a hundred in a matter of days. At work, he became her all-consuming project, and because she could see all the wonderful things about him, it was easy to convince others of his good character with her enthusiasm.

Before long they were photographed together on the beach, where he liked to jog first thing in the morning, and she had taken to joining him. Not that she could keep up. But it wasn't hard to roll out of bed at his place at the crack of dawn, with the sun rising over the water, beckoning them to run and then eat bagels at a beach cafe. The photos appeared in women's magazines, with all sorts of speculative shoutlines splashed on the front cover.

Simon's older woman tames his wild ways!
Has Simon met his match?
Barton hits a love game.

The coverage did wonders for her PR firm's reputation too, and her supervisor, Kristy, winked at her over the magazine headlines and hummed a little ditty with every new client request that came through the inbox or over the phone. And their romance did wonders for Simon as well. Who wasn't cheerful and good-natured when they were in love? His public image began to improve.

A few months into their glorious love fest, Christmas fell pregnant. The baby had been the result of consuming a reckless amount of champagne at a race luncheon; afterwards, she'd left her huge, feathered hat on and Simon had left his tie on, and together they'd made a munchkin.

'What do you want me to say?' Simon had asked, his former surly self appearing once more. 'A baby's not exactly in my plans right now.' He was on the phone, away at an intensive training camp in the Bahamas after some time off for a minor shoulder injury. He was getting ready to hit the circuit again soon, intending to come bolting out of the gates a new and improved player with a new and improved image. His coach and sponsors were sure he would be dominating the sport next year.

'Well, it's not exactly in my plans either,' Christmas had cried. She was certainly of an age when it was deemed reasonable to have a baby. A little late, even. But it had never been a priority.

'I guess there's nothing we can do about it now.'

Christmas sniffed. 'Really? You don't want me to . . .' But she couldn't actually say the words. She wasn't going to end this pregnancy, no matter how inconvenient it might be. She was heading for a promotion and a huge pay rise and all of that would change once she announced the pregnancy. And this thing with Simon? Well, who knew where that was going. They'd been having a great time and she could honestly say she was in love. But that didn't mean they were going to be able to make it work forever.

The physical effects of pregnancy were shocking too. Her usual hectic working pace ground to a virtual halt and her productive afternoon meeting time was replaced by sitting at her desk with a glass of iced water pressed to the side of her neck and her forehead, sipping from it occasionally to relieve the nausea. And at two o'clock every afternoon, she had to shut the blinds of her office and lie down on the couch and sleep.

Although the munchkin wasn't planned, a few weeks after they'd found out, both Simon and Christmas had decided it was a boy. They would talk about him on the phone and sometimes Simon even sounded a little excited.

'I was thinking about when I should buy him his first racquet,' he said, smiling down the phone.

'I'm surprised you haven't already.'

Christmas had decided that at the age of four, the munchkin would be best friends with the dog. Because by then they'd have a dog, too. A beagle, named Snoopy, who would share a bed with Rosa at night.

And at seven, Simon insisted, the munchkin would be on his way to tennis stardom.

A baby. It was a miracle. Unexpected, but a miracle.

But the munchkin decided not to stay. He left without warning. One day he was there and the next he was gone, his little soul returned to wherever he came from, leaving Christmas feeling as though she was filled with nothing but wet sawdust. Her wide eyes were glued onto her face but there was nothing behind them. Her body had no substance and her legs could barely hold her up.

'These things happen,' Simon said. It was his interview voice.

She hated him for that.

He didn't know what to say to her on the phone in reply to her tears or her silence. She had no energy to talk. No patience for anything that was said. He sent flowers. But they spoke less and less. Emails stopped coming. And a month later, she saw a magazine with a photo of him out to dinner with a young platinum-haired fashion model.

She stopped going to work. She hated her job now. She didn't care about making other people's lives look better when hers was falling apart. Why couldn't a fairy godmother come into her life and fix everything? Take away the pain?

Days passed while she lay in bed with the curtains shut. She blamed herself for being reckless, for allowing herself to fall in love with Simon and with the munchkin. She was seared by the cruelty of the loss. Compounding it was the fact that they hadn't told anyone about the baby. Their little miracle, their little munchkin man, didn't even exist in any other sphere but her heart. And she couldn't tell anyone now. This huge surprise she had been only meant to keep for a few more weeks was now never to be shared. An announcement could never be made for something that wasn't there. *Oh, by the way, my baby died. Pass the cake?*

Except he wasn't a baby—only a *foetus*. The word the doctor had used. As though he wasn't real.

But he *was* real. She'd seen him. With a heartbeat and little balled fists at his side. And a tail. A tadpole munchkin.

She quit her job.

It was Val who came. She opened the curtains and pulled off her sister's rank pyjamas and put her in the shower and washed her hair.

'Come on, Massy,' she ordered, through Christmas's protests. 'You know what this is. It's not like we haven't seen it enough with Mum.' Christmas slapped weakly at her hands while Val used the shower hose to rinse the shampoo from her hair. 'You know the only way out of this is forwards. Yes, it's hard. Yes, it sucks. But you have to do it.'

Val stayed for a week. Drove her to the doctor. Drove her to the counsellor. Drove her to her office to pack up her belongings. Did her washing. Bought her food. Paid her bills.

Then Val had to go, back on a plane to Launceston and her family. And Christmas knew it was time to leave too. Sydney was no longer her home. She needed to change everything. So she booked a flight back to Launceston as well.

There was no room at Val's, so she spent a month moping around Emily's house. Emily didn't seem to mind the moping; she was just glad to have Christmas back on the island and she could be happy enough for both of them, she said. Christmas continued seeing a counsellor, Samantha, a tiny blonde woman whose long hair hung around her shoulders like a halo. Every time they talked, she sent Christmas away with the same homework—nurture the five senses, every day.

'We are traumatised through the senses,' Samantha explained, passing Christmas a box of tissues and a cup of peppermint tea. 'What we see, what we feel, what we hear, taste and smell. And the only way to heal from the trauma is to heal those senses through nurturing yourself. It's not a luxury; it's a necessity.'

Christmas agreed to follow her instructions. Emily's job as a television researcher was flexible and she often worked from home. Together she and Christmas picked flowers every few days from Emily's untended but prolific garden. They took an excursion down to Hobart and stayed overnight in a hotel so they could hit the Salamanca markets early the next morning, stocking up Emily's car with bounty. They bought passionfruit-scented candles and olive oil soaps that smelled of black raspberry and vanilla. They ate hot German sausages while listening to Peruvian street musicians. Christmas lay on a massage table in a tent while a reflexologist treated her feet. Emily helped her pick out a new set of soft sheets with embroidered details and a big fat doona with a matching cover. They took home chocolates, organic skincare products, silk scarves and new handbags, and returned to Emily's house in Launceston feeling light and revitalised.

Over the month, they continued the process, taking day trips up the Tamar Valley and wandering through the raspberry and lavender farms and the wineries (where they found the usual pinots and chardonnays, but also the unusual *gewürztraminers*), and passed apple orchards and strawberry farms, soaking up the frosty sunshine, and relaxing beside fireplaces in pubs and restaurants.

Gradually, smiling got easier. Laughter and silliness too. Christmas began to venture out on her own and took a pottery class one week, a dance class the next, and a one-day workshop in chocolate making the week after that, falling in love, instantly, with the aroma and sensuality of chocolate. She had experienced the power of self-healing and nurturing firsthand, and now she wanted to share it with others. She no longer wanted to help people *look* good, as had been her role in PR, but to help them *feel* good. One day, she picked up a copy of *O* magazine and found her idol: Oprah. Now there was a woman who'd overcome hardship and tragedy and gone on to make a bigger and better life not just for herself but for others too. She'd always loved Oprah, and now she wanted to be like her.

Christmas declared a day of decision-making. Fuelled by stories in *O* magazine about people who'd changed their lives, she resolved to do the same. She searched real estate sites for a new place to live and phoned several agents, making appointments for viewings. She decided to build a new life, one dedicated to nurturing and healing herself and others. She wrote a list of rules to live by.

That evening, she handed Emily a glass of pinot and a plate of chocolate-coated raspberries. 'My lovely friend,' she said, raising her glass, 'I'm moving out.'

12

A Tuesday morning seemed as good a time as any other to get the ball rolling, so Elsa met with Rita Blumberg in her room at the end of the corridor inside the main building of Green Hills Aged Care. She parked her wheelchair next to Rita's at the small table in the corner. The Chinese dragon lantern—a gift from Rita's grandchildren for Mother's Day—that covered the bulb above them cast a red glow across the metal safety rails of the narrow bed. It was one of the few cheerful things in that room, and Elsa was once again grateful that she didn't have to rely entirely on the government to sponsor her care as Rita did. Those Canberra administrators were certainly of the no-frills mentality.

Other spots of colour in the austere room came from the purple woolen blanket on top of the uniform white one they were all issued; children's drawings of people, cats and rockets; and one of Rita's own paintings, of a young girl in a sunflower field. The rest of Rita's unsold artwork, Elsa believed, was being held onto by family members, probably in the hope that its value would increase after Rita's passing, rather than selling it now to improve her care today. Then again, maybe Elsa was looking at Rita's circumstances through her own mud-coloured glasses, supplied by Tom's recent misbehaviour. After all, Rita's family did visit her regularly, often on a Friday night as was the Jewish custom.

'So you want to be *shadchan*,' Rita said, with a knowing smile. 'A m-matchmaker?'

Elsa suddenly felt foolish and began to pick at the knitted shawl around her shoulders. 'Well, I'd like to try. I'd like to see my grandson happy, and he seems to have some things in common with a local girl—Christmas Livingstone.'

Rita nodded as best she could through the tremors. 'What do you know about her?'

Although this was a perfectly reasonable question, Elsa felt herself prickle with irritation. She didn't really know anything about Christmas Livingstone. What on earth had made her want to get involved? Perhaps she *was* losing her marbles. 'I'm embarrassed to say, not much.'

Rita studied Elsa, her milky eyes blinking. 'The secret to good matchmaking is knowing the values and beliefs the coup-p-p-le share. Every person glows like a candle flame.' Rita held up each of her index fingers to represent two people. 'Bring them together,' she moved the tips of her fingers closer, 'and they should b-b-burn in one bigger, brighter flame. They should light up the room.' She dropped her hands and they quivered in her lap. 'A mismatched couple will not light up a room.'

Elsa's spirits lifted. 'Christmas is coming to visit us to lead us in a chocolate tasting.'

'We're all looking forward to that.'

'I'll make sure Lincoln is here too. That will give us something to go on, won't it?'

Rita nodded. 'Certainly.'

The tea trolley rattled down the hall and a pimply boy wearing a sticker on his polo shirt that said *Hello, my name's Kristof and I'm on work experience* bounded into the room proffering plastic cups with safety lids. 'Good morning, ladies,' he grinned. 'What a wonderful day. I've brought you tea.'

Rita raised her fair eyebrows above her huge glasses. She was hardly grey at all, lucky thing.

The boy's vigour was like sitting too close to a fire. Elsa felt the need to retreat. 'Goodness,' she said to him. 'Are you related to Tigger, by any chance?'

Kristof's smile waned slightly and he offered an uncertain chuckle before bidding them a good day and leaving again.

'Tsk,' Rita said. 'The poor lad's doing his best.'

'Ah, for the energy of the young,' Elsa said. 'They haven't a clue what to do with it.'

'Ah, for a proper teacup,' Rita muttered, tapping her plastic cup with her fingernail.

'Next time, come to my bungalow,' Elsa said. 'We'll have a proper tea party and I'll get my grandson to come along and you can meet him too.'

Rita's eyes lit up. 'Just let me know when and I'll get young Kristof to wheel me over.' She winked at Elsa and they tittered conspiratorially.

Elsa felt a bubble of joy rise up in her and was glad she'd made this trip to see Rita today. It was an odd thing about aged care, she often thought, that the people inside were often lonely but didn't necessarily want to connect with the others in the home. Perhaps it was because they all knew their time was limited. Or because they all needed to find their own personal space in the dormitory-like atmosphere. Either way, Elsa couldn't remember the last time she'd made a new friend. And she'd forgotten how good it felt.

She raised her plastic cup of lukewarm tea to Rita's. 'To new friends!'

•

Lincoln's morning had been frittered away via the wonder of technology. After walking and feeding Caesar, he'd sat down to catch up on emails and finalise his research for submission to the head scientist at Neptune, struggled with uploading a hundred photographs, thanks to a new version of Windows that had changed the way everything worked, and politely enquired if there might be another suitable contract in the near future that he could apply for. Before he knew it, lunchtime was upon him and he was running late to meet Rubble.

His friend had booked them both into a rented house in Swansea for the weekend, saying that he needed to get away for inspiration and that Lincoln needed to get out of his grandmother's stale house and away from his laptop and breathe in some fresh seaside air.

'You're working too hard,' Rubble had said down the phone, chewing something, his words indistinct. Evidently Lydia was still sulking.

'I think I'm working an appropriate amount, considering I'm technically unemployed right now,' Lincoln had replied. 'I'm finishing up my Ecuador research and working on chapters for the chocolate book.'

'How's that going, by the way?'

'Great, actually. We've been working together for ten days now and it's going better than I had expected. I think Christmas was a good choice for a co-author. She's really clever.'

'Stinkin' Lincoln! I can hear that tone in your voice. You fancy her.'

'I do not.'

'Do too.'

'Do not.'

'Do too.'

Lincoln gave up. When Rubble was in his gorging phase, not only did his girth expand but so too did his arrogance. He became immovable and inflexible, like the big heavy rock he resembled.

Lincoln's last line of defence had been that he needed to take care of Caesar.

'No problem,' Rubble said. He'd found a place that was pet friendly so Caesar could come too. There was some debate then over whose car to take, Lincoln's grandmother's minuscule but sturdy Honda or Rubble's unpredictable but larger BMW; they decided on the BMW, because although it might break down at any moment, at least there was more room for Caesar to stretch out in the back. Lincoln didn't really fancy driving two hours with Caesar sitting on his lap.

So now he threw some clothes into his backpack, turned off his laptop, considered whether to take it with him before deciding not to, and packed a bag of treats for Caesar. When Rubble tooted the car horn outside, Lincoln flicked off the switches and bundled the old fella into the BMW.

At Swansea, Lincoln took Caesar for a walk along the shoreline to stretch their legs and Rubble booked them a table for two at a seafood smorgasbord restaurant overlooking the water, then headed to the beach with his camera to photograph anything and everything, hoping that Lydia would start talking to him soon. While Rubble snapped away with increasing desperation, Lincoln indulged in a Bubble O'Bill, a childhood favourite ice cream, and let Caesar lick the stick clean.

That night at dinner, Rubble consumed lobsters and crayfish like some sort of large sea monster, miserable with failure.

'So, do you think the seaside is your next thing?' Lincoln asked, cracking open a crab claw.

Rubble shrugged. 'No idea.'

Lincoln considered his friend's sad and puffy face. 'Maybe you need to head overseas sooner rather than later? Maybe don't wait for me to find another position in the jungle. I think you need to get out of this rut now. Perhaps Lydia's moved her interest to Egypt, or Afghanistan, or Canada?'

Rubble licked his lips. 'Maybe.' He sat back from his plate, the frantic hoovering ceasing.

Lincoln was encouraged. 'When was the last time you headed OS?'

'I popped over to New Zealand a few years back for my cousin's wedding. But I haven't really done any significant international travel for almost seven years.' Rubble wiped his mouth with his napkin and let it fall back onto his lap. He tapped the table, his face taking on a grave, urgent look. 'You might be right. After you mentioned the jungle, I got cold feet thinking I didn't have enough money to spend on that sort of thing when I'm not producing anything and therefore not selling anything. And the longer that goes on the more precarious the finances become.'

'But you need to find the inspiration first. It's a catch-22.'

'Yes.'

'You don't have to do a massive trip to South America or Europe. You could do a week in Samoa, Tonga, Thailand, Bali.

Even outback Australia might be enough of a change to ignite some passion, don't you think?'

Rubble straightened, his eyes shining. 'The outback! The great red land that swallows backpackers and adventurers without a trace.' He whipped out his phone and began tapping away, presumably googling how to get to the outback.

A starched waiter appeared, offering another basket of bread. Rubble waved it away.

Lincoln suppressed his grin.

●

It was only the second day of winter and already the season had announced its arrival with pouring rain and single-digit temperatures. It was on days like these that Christmas wished terribly she could light a fire in her Georgian abode. This was the sort of weather a building like this was built for. Lien would be struggling today too, the cold making her joints much worse. Christmas made a mental note to pop a pair of the store's newly arrived bed socks into a bag to drop off to her when she visited next week.

On days like this, the best way to attract customers was to heavily promote her steaming hot coffee, hot chocolate, apple pies and hot fudge. Tourists still came to town over winter; she just had to be a bit savvier about her promotions. Sometimes, poor weather actually helped, with people happy to get out of the rain and sit inside with delicacies while they watched the droplets hit the pavement.

But today was slow in The Apothecary, as it was all along the street. The only real activity she could observe was an occasional forlorn visitor popping into the bakery up the road, no doubt hoping to get a seat by the fire and a hearty meal. She almost wished she could join them. She'd been thinking about the munchkin a lot today. Some days were like that. His ghost would appear from out of nowhere and she'd wonder what her life would be like now if he'd stayed around and she had a three-year-old at her side. Despite the loss she felt for him, she did know that she didn't want to have any children. But sometimes, the road not taken whispered to her. It was okay to feel like that, she told herself. It didn't mean anything had to change. She just had to acknowledge it when it did and look after herself.

She was alone in the shop. Abigail hadn't come in; massage appointments slowed during the cold months, and days like today guaranteed numerous cancellations. No one wanted to get their clothes off in this weather, even though the rooms were always heated to the point of making Abigail sweat. Clients just couldn't come to terms with heading out the door into the wind and rain to get to the warmth of the massage room. With the shop empty, Christmas took the opportunity to whip upstairs and grab her own new woollen socks, as her feet were a bit cool even inside her boots. There was something so nice about clean, new socks, with no pilling and no thinning. Just fluffy and ready to snuggle her toes into.

It was while she was upstairs that she heard the ship's bell. She skipped back down the internal staircase, buoyed by her new socks, and found Cheyenne at the counter holding an armful of roses. The florist was wearing a thick black windcheater with a faux-fur neck collar over a long white dress and knee-high boots. As usual she wore no makeup, but her full lips were a rich pink even without gloss. Christmas was struck by how Nordic she looked with her orange hair swept to the side.

'Hi!' Cheyenne said, a huge smile spreading across her face.

'Well, hello to you,' Christmas said. 'You look like the cat that got the cream.'

'My insurance company just sent me a cheque!' Cheyenne beamed. 'Apparently they'd overcharged me, so they sent me a refund for almost two years of excess payments. The girls and I will be having takeaway for dinner to celebrate.'

'An unsolicited refund! That's not something you hear every day. Good luck must be headed your way.'

A hiss of air brakes and the throb of a diesel engine outside signalled a tourist bus pulling up in the main street.

'And look,' Christmas said, rubbing her hands together, 'your good fortune's rubbing off on me. Can you stay to help out for a bit?'

'No problem,' Cheyenne said, reaching for an apron featuring a black cat with a white bow tie.

This time of year, tourist buses were often full of people over fifty who had money and time on their hands. Christmas hastened to get more coffee going and changed the music to Michael Bublé. Cheyenne's cheerful company and a busload of tourists were just what she needed to chase the creeping blues away.

But by that evening, the creeping blues had transformed into a nagging itch. The roads not taken in her past might be closed, but there were still new ones open now.

She lifted the valance and peered into the darkness under the bed, where she stored her wooden treasure chest. Made out of valuable Tasmanian Huon pine and engraved with her name and date of birth, it had been a gift for her on her twenty-first birthday from Joseph.

After he and Darla had divorced, Joseph had married again and had another daughter and son with his new wife, Gloria. Christmas had always felt a bit cheated by this, as though Paula and Sacha should have been her siblings too. She was Val's sibling and they were Val's siblings, so surely they should all be family? Then Joseph and Gloria had divorced and Gloria was now Val's ex-stepmother, and they didn't have a good relationship, and it had all become quite complicated. But regardless of these changes in his life, Joseph and Christmas had just carried on with their own odd but important relationship, something Christmas cherished. There were no set rules on how to conduct a relationship like theirs but she thought they were doing it rather well. Oprah would be proud.

She sat on the floor now, the heater going against the chill of the evening, and pulled out the chest. Over the years, she'd filled it with sentimental things. Birthday cards. Concert tickets. Ribbons won at sporting carnivals when she was younger. Notes. Photos. Gifts she didn't really like but didn't want to part with because they came from someone with love.

The ultrasound picture from the day she found out that her baby had no heartbeat. Evidence. The little blob there inside her. There but not alive. There but not here.

She touched it now, sadness shifting like a draught around her feet. Her hand had buried the ultrasound picture under a pile of birthday cards before she'd even consciously decided to do it.

There was something else she was looking for. She rooted around in the chest, pulling out piles of memorabilia, hovering for a moment here and there, with a smile or a flicker of sadness, but her hands kept moving until they found it. A letter. From Miriam Deschamps, her high-school pen pal.

She opened the envelope and pulled out the tissue-thin paper, then carefully unfolded the pages.

Bingo. The last-known address for Mim, from more than twenty years ago. But it was all she had to go by.

She wasn't going to try to find Gregoire, but it would be fun to catch up with Mim after all these years. And it would give her a sense of ownership of this trip to France, rather than just being the passive recipient of a gift kindly organised by Emily. She wanted to feel that she was taking charge of her fate, rather than just going where the wind took her.

She skimmed the letter. Mim described her studies, the boy she was interested in, her little dog, and talked about the latest music. Christmas smiled. Things seemed so much simpler back then. She wished she had copies of the letters she'd sent to Mim. She'd love to know what had been her biggest concern at fourteen.

Her socks slid on the floor as she hauled herself up, still holding the letter, and shoved the chest back under the bed. In the top drawer of her desk she found some cards with images of Provence on them; deciding that it was pathetic to send a picture of Provence to someone who actually lived in France, she settled on a card with a shot of Cradle Mountain instead.

Dear Mim,

I don't know if you'll remember me but we used to be pen pals when we were teenagers. I'm coming to France next month and I wondered if you might be interested in meeting up with me.

I don't know if you'll even get this card. I'm sure you don't live at the same address anymore, but I'm hoping that whoever lives there might still be related to you and can pass this on. My email address is at the bottom of this card if you'd like to drop me a line.

Christmas Livingstone

She considered signing off with 'love' but it didn't feel right so she added a smiley face instead. Tomorrow she'd take it to the post office and then wait to see what happened.

13

'Help me make chocolate,' Christmas said, handing Lincoln a plain white apron.

'I thought we were working,' he said, dropping his pile of books and papers on the table in the centre of the shop and following her into the kitchen.

'We are. But as this is our fourth week working together, I thought it was time I trusted you with the chocolate,' she said, smiling.

'Finally! My mouth waters uncontrollably every time you send through another recipe,' he said, tying on the apron.

'I think you've earned your stripes.'

They'd been meeting up at the shop every Monday to work together on the manuscript. Lincoln had found a cartoon image of a cacao bean and photoshopped a hat, hands and feet on it, and printed out maps of the world and cacao-producing countries. They'd been having a great time creating a travel itinerary for the bean and making up notes on his adventures. Christmas was enjoying writing her sections on the creative aspects of chocolate, and she enjoyed helping Lincoln with his text. They laughed a lot during their sessions and each of them took the other's criticism and suggestions well. Mostly, they ended the day together more excited about the book than when they'd started.

It felt significant now that she would invite him to make chocolate with her, as though they'd crossed an imaginary line, moving beyond colleagues to real friendship. Her chocolate-making world was a private sanctuary and only special people were allowed inside.

'You'll need this,' she said, passing him a hair snood.

He extracted the dishcloth type of shower cap and grinned. 'Sexy.'

Christmas smiled, thinking he'd look good in a sack. She put hers on too. 'You should really have a beard net as well, but I don't have any. I don't normally have men in here and thankfully I'm not old enough to have grown a granny beard yet. You'll just have to go without but do try not to shed over anything.'

'I promise not to rub my face in the chocolate—unless there's some kind of chocolate crisis, like an apocalypse or something. It would be such a shame for it to go to waste just because it was the end of the world.'

She really wished he'd stop being so damn charming.

'I think we should watch some episodes of Jamie Oliver's cooking shows,' Christmas said, organising the moulds on the kitchen bench and demonstrating how to polish them.

'He's not really my type,' Lincoln said, taking the cotton wool from her hands, his fingers brushing hers and sending a jolt up her arm.

'Ha ha. It's just that he's got this really fantastic way of educating people and celebrating food at the same time. Some of his documentaries are awesome. And he's ridiculously popular. I want our book to be just as popular.'

Lincoln had stopped polishing the moulds and was staring at her with a funny look in his eyes.

'What?' she said, suddenly self-conscious. She reached for her mouth. She'd been eating pancakes and syrup for breakfast just before he arrived. 'Is there something on my face?'

'No. You look perfect. It's just that when you said "our book", it made it all seem real. I know I've published a book before, but for such a different market. It's not like it got any mainstream publicity or anything. But the way you talk about the book, your vision for it, sometimes I can see us ending up on television talking about it. It's stupid, I know.'

'No, it's not stupid.' *It's adorable.*

'I spend a lot of time alone, in the forest, in the lab, or at computers,' he went on. 'It's not a particularly social existence. This is fun, working together.' His eyes lit up and she was struck by his incredibly long lashes. Any woman would kill for lashes like that.

'Yes, it is,' she admitted. She handed him the spoon to stir the brandy ganache. She stared indulgently at his wrist as it rolled and guided the spoon around the pot.

'So how is this helping us get our book done, exactly?' he asked, licking his finger.

'I figured you needed some creative practice,' she said. 'And in return, you're helping me get more scientific credibility.'

'With your medicinal chocolate?'

'If I get the chance to talk to Master Le Coutre about it when I'm in France it would be good to sound like I know at least a little bit about what I'm talking about. I know it seems like a pipedream.'

'No, it doesn't. I think it's entirely possible.'

'Really?'

'Absolutely.'

'I've told you about Lien Pham, haven't I?' she asked, filling a piping bag with ganache.

'Juvenile arthritis?'

'Yes. She's on all these horrible drugs with awful side effects and it would be wonderful to find something natural that could help her with the pain and inflammation. And imagine if it could be chocolate!'

'Potassium,' he said thoughtfully, his eyes turned up towards the ceiling. 'Cacao has high levels of potassium, and most of us, with processed foods and modern lifestyles, have a potassium imbalance.'

'What does potassium do?'

'It regulates neuro-muscular activity,' he said. 'Low potassium levels can lead to muscle weakness and tiredness.'

'What else?' she asked, excited.

'It's high in magnesium,' he said.

'And magnesium helps with muscle cramps, doesn't it!' she said, beginning to pace. 'Am I crazy? Am I totally off base here?'

'No, actually, I think it's quite plausible. It's not as far out there as you think. Like you said, heaps of medicines come from rainforest species. Why shouldn't chocolate be one of them? And maybe Master Le Coutre thinks so too. You might find that this is exactly why they chose you. Think about it. There are thousands of wannabe pastry chefs out there in the world. What they need is someone with a real edge. Something different, unique. Skills can be taught. Brilliance can't.'

Christmas froze. 'You think I'm brilliant?' The words were out before she could stop them.

'In my professional, studied, scientific analysis? Well, yeah.'

The space between them was immediately thick with desire, whether hers or his she wasn't sure. He held her gaze confidently and her heart hammered madly within her breast. He reached out a hand towards her neck as though to draw her to him.

But just then, the thermostat on the tempering tank clicked off, breaking the trance.

She tore her eyes away from his and brushed some imaginary fluff from her arm.

He hurried to fill the awkwardness. 'You'll be fine in France,' he said. 'Who knows where it will lead? Anything could happen.'

•

Val asked Christmas if she wanted to meet her and her brood at the Clarendon Arms for dinner mid-week. Christmas had happily agreed and told Val she'd ask Emily along too, thinking it might help them both to move into a more normal state of being and wipe away any remaining unease between them.

While Christmas was at the bar ordering another round of drinks before their meals arrived, Val leaned over to Emily, talking quietly so Archie and the boys couldn't hear—which was unlikely, actually, given the commotion they were all making, ravenous and overexcited about eating something other than tinned spaghetti on toast for dinner.

'Have you told Christmas we've been talking?' she asked.

'No, have you?' Emily said.

'No.' Val paused. 'It would seem like we're ganging up on her, wouldn't it?'

'Hmm. Are we?' Emily asked, appearing anxious and watching Christmas out of the corner of her eye.

'I don't know.'

Val sipped her white wine thoughtfully while Emily began a tournament of thumb wrestling with Nate; Willis and Archie shouted with glee as Archie's Keno numbers came out; and Braxton played a game on her mobile phone.

The thing was that her own boys loved their dad and she couldn't even begin to imagine Archie not being in their life. And she had such a close relationship with Joseph that the thought of not having her dad now, let alone when she was growing up, was inconceivable. She simply wanted what was best for Christmas, and if that meant putting a bit of pressure on her to find Gregoire than that's what she'd keep on doing. Surely it was better to have a chance of something rather than a guarantee of nothing?

She resolved to keep trying, for Christmas's sake.

•

Dennis Chamberlain had declined to meet Christmas prior to the night of the wedding proposal, claiming that he was simply too busy. He was an accountant with more work than he could handle, and the sole reason he'd asked for her help was that he was too busy to organise a satisfactory proposal and, besides, he was no good at love. She'd spoken to him once on the phone and he'd sounded exactly the way she thought he would after his taciturn emails.

'Do you have a specific date in mind to propose?' she'd asked.

'Sunday, in the evening.'

'Do you have a preferred location?'

'At her house. She wouldn't like a bunch of strangers watching.'

Christmas remembered that he'd said she hated crowds. He'd also said she loved jazz, spicy food, cooking, foreign films, good chocolate, and cats. Juliette sounded like someone Christmas might actually like very much. Someone who appreciated sensual experiences. And she sounded very different to Dennis, who seemed to possess no sense of joy or spontaneity, or appreciation for luxury.

She could just picture Dennis sitting in his chrome and glass office with his synthetic tie and ten-dollar business shirts, which he probably threw away after a few wears rather than investing time into taking care of more expensive ones. He would have a receding hairline and boofy waves to counteract it, and pasty white skin. By contrast, the photos he'd sent her of Juliette showed a pretty, well-groomed woman with simple but stylish clothes, minimal jewellery and makeup, and smooth, shiny hair.

Christmas had begun to feel a little uneasy about this relationship and her role in it, with a sinking feeling in the pit of her stomach. If Dennis hadn't been a paying client, and hadn't already transferred over the godmother fee, and Christmas hadn't gladly spent it on travel insurance, she might have thought about calling the whole thing off.

'Will anyone else be there for the proposal?'

'Just her mother.'

Her mother?

'They're very close, and at the same time as proposing to Juliette I intend to ask Virginia if she'd like to live with us after we're married.'

Christmas wasn't sure if she thought this was sweet, or kind of twisted.

But Christmas's vision of Dennis Chamberlain couldn't have been further from the reality. Dennis met her at the end of the leafy street in which Juliette lived so they could make their surprise appearance together. Christmas had kept hounding Dennis to tease out ideas so there would be some chance of getting this proposal right. They'd eventually come up with a plan that Dennis had said was 'good'. She hoped what he really meant was 'fantastic' or 'perfect', but she accepted 'good' and proceeded to make the preparations. It was fortunate that Juliette liked chocolate. That was safe territory for Christmas.

Nerves had been plaguing her before he got out of his car. Then she saw him and stared in disbelief. This man must have been a model. Or a personal trainer. Or perhaps a health-conscious chef.

He was tall. Broad. Buff, in fact. His clothes were impeccable. Actually, he looked like a motivational speaker and had the intense eye contact and engaging smile of one. He had hair. Lots of it. Dark, neat, brushed. He shook her hand firmly and with confidence. His hand was dry and warm. He was lovely. How could this friendly, charismatic man possibly have been 'no good at love'? Where was the dour man she'd been dealing with up till now?

'Juliette's house is up this way,' he said, tilting his head to indicate the direction. 'Shall we go?'

At Juliette's front door—a pot of cheery orange flowers on each side—Dennis knocked once and called out, then opened the door without waiting for an answer.

Juliette was sitting at her kitchen counter, a bunch of take-away menus spread out in front of her. She didn't look up. 'Hi. Do you fancy Vietnamese or Indian?'

'Neither,' he said.

She looked up. And noticed Christmas. 'Oh, hi.' Her wary expression turned to Dennis as he stooped to kiss her lightly on the lips.

'This is Christmas Livingstone,' he said. 'She's the owner of The Chocolate Apothecary.'

Juliette's eyes widened. 'Oh, I love your chocolates!'

'I'm glad to hear it.' Christmas smiled, now abuzz with excitement. These two were so comfortable and looked so good together.

Juliette stood and pointed to the vintage mint-green suitcase Christmas was holding. 'What's in the suitcase?'

'I wanted to surprise you,' Dennis said. 'I thought we could do something different tonight and learn how to make chocolate.'

'Really?' Juliette did a bit of a jig that made Christmas laugh.

'And I've invited your mum, too,' he said. 'I know she's been a bit lonely and I thought she'd enjoy it. But she's going to join us a bit later because I wanted some time alone with you first.'

Juliette kissed him.

Again, Christmas marvelled at how well they seemed to fit together. They lit up the room when they looked at each other. People could be very surprising.

She couldn't help but smile as she unpacked the tools from her suitcase. Her plan was to set them up with everything they needed, offer some basic directions and leave them to it. She also had a small white box, trussed up with pink and red ribbons, containing one perfect double-layered 'wedding cake' chocolate, with rose petals on top and the engagement ring nestled into a drop of frosting to keep it secure at the pinnacle. Dennis was going to bring it out at the end of the evening and present it to Juliette.

Christmas slipped some champagne into the fridge unnoticed, then lined up her ingredients on the bench. A brown paper bag with white chunks of cocoa butter, a tin of fine cocoa powder, a bottle of agave syrup, a small bottle of her handmade vanilla essence (with the vanilla beans still in the bottle), and a tiny thimble of sea salt. She also left three chocolate mould trays, in the shapes of half eggs, hearts and birds. And she had included a small number of additional ingredients—roasted hazelnut pieces, dried cranberries and raisins.

Juliette picked up the brown bag of cocoa butter and inhaled. 'It smells like chocolate,' she said. 'Just a bit, I don't know, thinner somehow.'

'Smell the cocoa,' Christmas said, opening the tin and holding it to Juliette's nose.

Juliette breathed in, looked puzzled, and breathed again. 'It doesn't actually smell very strong at all.'

'I know. Odd, isn't it? You'd think the cocoa was the main ingredient contributing to that gorgeous chocolate smell, but it's the butter, which is why white chocolate still smells like chocolate, even though there's no cocoa in it.'

'It's just fat!'

'Sadly, yes.' Christmas could see Juliette was hooked on the process already. She opened the agave syrup now and commented on its molasses-like aroma, despite its thinner-than-honey consistency.

Dennis rolled up the sleeves of his blue shirt and pulled out a saucepan for boiling water and a steel bowl for melting the ingredients. Christmas handed Juliette a brand-new French linen apron with images of dried lavender and rosemary around the hem, and a navy apron for Dennis—gifts for them to keep.

The last things she had to do were hide the box with the engagement ring in the pantry as planned, and give them some basic instructions on how to proceed.

'Melt the cocoa butter, add the agave syrup, sift the cocoa and whisk it in, add a pinch of salt and vanilla and away you go,' she summarised.

Dennis's arms wound their way around Juliette's waist and she leaned into his body.

Christmas took a moment to enjoy the thrill of a successful godmother wish. Then she left them alone to make chocolate, make love, and make a new life together.

The next day was Monday, which was dedicated to working with Lincoln on their book. But today was also the day of the chocolate tasting at Green Hills Aged Care in Oatlands. Christmas had made plans to meet with Lincoln afterwards, late in the afternoon, grab some takeaway together, and work into the evening. But Lincoln texted her early in the morning to ask if she'd like to share a ride to Green Hills. He explained that his grandmother had asked him to come and he thought it was a good idea, since Christmas was educating him for chocolate credibility and all.

Christmas's heart did a skip and a jump, like a child leaping over puddles for fun. She swiftly rebuked herself for being so silly. She was just swept up in the romance of the night before with Dennis and Juliette and her feeling of triumph when she'd received Dennis's text message saying it was 'all systems go'. He'd even managed to thank her and add a smiley face. Love was well and truly in the air.

But she must stop any kind of fantasising about Lincoln, she told herself firmly. She replied to his text, explaining that she had to take her own car because she had errands to do on the way there and she needed space to transport large boxes. Then she spontaneously texted Emily to invite her along to dilute the intensity of the attraction. Because, she realised with a shock, there was no denying it: there was definitely a mutual attraction going on. Or at least a mutual flirting. With Emily there she could ensure that she wasn't alone with Lincoln.

But once she'd picked up Emily, she almost regretted inviting her.

'Have you thought any more about finding your father?' Emily said, almost the moment she'd buckled up in the front seat.

'Oh, not again, Em. I told you, I'm not interested.'

'You know you don't actually have to do anything with the information if you *did* happen to stumble onto something, right? It's just all about options.'

'Maybe I don't want to open that can of worms in the first place. And besides, I'm busy enough as it is just organising myself an itinerary—spending hours online researching what I might want to do in my week in Paris and where I'm going to go in the week after the course, organising credit cards and euros and all that, let alone writing half a book, without wasting time looking for a man who mightn't even exist.'

'I'm sure they have people who can help you do that now,' Emily persisted. 'Genealogy people and, I don't know, social services and such.'

'Again, it all takes time I don't have,' Christmas said, teeth gritted.

'But what about—'

'Please! Can we just drop it? I need to get my head into the right space for this chocolate tasting.'

'Fine,' Emily huffed. 'I was just trying to help.'

Christmas tried to be patient. She flicked the radio station to find one playing some lazy jazz to break up the dense mood in the car. She didn't know why Emily was being so dogged about this, and it was irritating in the extreme, but she'd done a lot to help Christmas over the years and for that she was grateful. Their friendship seemed to be chugging through some choppy waters right now, but it would pass, like all things do. In the meantime, they just needed not to lose sight of what was important.

•

Elsa gripped the rubber wheels of her chair. This was not going the way it was supposed to. It had seemed so promising last week when they'd discussed *Chocolat*. Everyone had loved the book, even Lulu, and likewise for the movie. It was charming, magical and delicious. There was consensus that the chocolate tasting this week could only be a resounding hit. And it should be.

On the surface, it looked wonderful. The common room of Green Hills was alive with voices and colour and laughter. Lincoln was at her side, enthusiastically writing notes. Her chocolate-tasting event had generated much excitement among the residents, their families and the staff. The residents were seated behind tables, which had been laid out in a U-shape so they could see the guest of honour as she guided them through their activity. Residents' daughters, sons and grandchildren sat with them, chatting, tasting and laughing.

Robert Graham's wife's shoulders were relaxed, her hair was loose, and she smiled as she helped him participate, guiding his hand to each chocolate and then writing down his remarks on a clipboard. Yvonne Murphy, without family, was assisted by lovely Sarah, who'd recently dyed her hair a cherry red. She was helping Yvonne navigate her way through the colourful flavour wheels that Christmas Livingstone had printed out for them all, encouraging their struggling minds to label flavours as buttery, floral or spicy, and then more specifically as egg, rose or cinnamon.

Doris Laherty was there too, occasionally interrupting her snoring to eat a piece of chocolate fed into her mouth by the fat hands of her four-year-old great-grandson, who was perched on her lap. Her eldest daughter, Mavis, was gently massaging her shoulders and chatting with the work experience boy, Kristof, who was a permanent volunteer now as a placement for some kind of course he was doing, and was still as bouncy as ever, rushing around to assist wherever needed.

Even Lulu Divine had stopped whinging for once and was instead passionately competing to win the quiz prize, a large basket of goodies from The Chocolate Apothecary. Elsa would very much like to win that basket too. Her mouth had watered the moment Christmas unpacked it from her suitcase for today's session.

The music of Edith Piaf filled the room, courtesy of Christmas's iPhone. Technology these days was so small and portable. Elsa's mind was momentarily taken back to the farm, one night when Ebe had come home singing a song in Dutch, celebrating the sale of a bull, pushing wads of pound notes into her hand and then spinning her around the kitchen in front of the Aga.

'Ebe!' she'd laughed, pushing him away. 'The copper's boiling and I need to get the washing done before the storm hits. It'll take days to dry as it is.'

He'd let her go, turning away to put a record on the turntable. Dropping the needle onto the vinyl with that exquisite bump and scratch you never heard anymore. Such a loss.

Still, it was nice to hear Edith singing now.

To anyone else, this event would appear a success. But at least she knew that Rita Blumberg, sitting to her right, understood completely. She'd raised a sympathetic eyebrow at Elsa the moment Christmas had walked in the door with that other woman in tow.

Lincoln, who had arrived a few minutes before, had introduced Christmas to Elsa as his co-author on the book he was writing, his hand on the back of her shoulder, which had pleased Elsa no end. Christmas shook Elsa's hand warmly and said how lovely it was to meet her, and thanked her for organising the event. She laughed with Lincoln and touched her hair. All good signs.

And this Christmas girl was pretty. Not overly tall and not too thin. Shapely. Short fair hair. Elsa preferred long hair on women and had kept her own hair long her whole life. But it didn't do Christmas any harm. She had large eyes the shape of teardrops lying on their sides. A rosy mouth that shone with some sort of lip gloss.

Christmas had then introduced the other woman as her friend, Emily Bathurst, who worked from home and was therefore lucky enough to have flexible hours to attend events such as these. And that was the problem. This Emily girl had a nice face and open, friendly eyes. She beamed a warm smile at Lincoln and then held his hand in greeting for just bit too long, in Elsa's opinion.

No, this wouldn't do at all. Elsa had her heart set on Christmas, and Emily's presence was muddying the waters.

'It's lovely to finally meet you,' Emily had said to him. 'I've heard a lot about the work you're doing with Christmas. Here . . .' She dug out a business card, slightly creased, from the bottom of her handbag. 'I'm a television researcher for a lifestyle program and we've been doing regular features on food. It's my job to come up with new ideas. If you're interested in chatting to us about the origins of chocolate, just give me a call.'

'Thanks,' Lincoln said, studying her card for a moment before pocketing it.

Elsa ground her plastic teeth. 'Lincoln,' she said quickly. 'Could you please run back to my bungalow and get a rug for my lap? The air conditioning is a little cool in here today.'

'Absolutely,' Lincoln had said, and disappeared out the side door.

'Round two,' Christmas said now, pulling out her quiz cards. 'Ready? Okay. True or false: the Cadbury company was founded by two brothers who were Quakers.'

'True!' Elsa called, getting in first. She had no idea, but it was a true-or-false question; she had a fifty per cent chance of getting it right. Lulu screwed up her lips.

'Correct.' Christmas nodded to Emily, who was keeping score on a clipboard. 'Next question: chocolate contains chemicals from the alkaloid group. Name a medication that is a type of alkaloid.'

Silence. Shuffling.

Lincoln put up his hand. 'I know, I know.' But Lincoln was banned from answering questions.

Robert Graham's voice: 'Morphine?'

'Yes, well done, Robert. That was a tricky question. Caffeine, nicotine, cocaine and quinine are also alkaloids.' Christmas applauded and there were impressed murmurs from many in the group.

'What part of the cacao tree do the cacao beans come from?'

'The pods!' Lulu would have jumped out of her wheelchair if she could have.

'Correct. The pods are actually a fruit and the beans are the seeds of the fruit,' Christmas said. 'What sort of climate do cacao trees grow in?'

'Rainforest,' Rita said, at the same time as Lulu said, 'Warm and wet.'

'You're both correct. It's actually a very narrow strip either side of the equator and the trees do like a steady temperature and rainfall.' Christmas gestured to Lincoln. 'Our resident botanist, Elsa's grandson Lincoln, can give you lots of information on that.'

Lincoln blushed, Elsa was sure of it, though all that facial hair was an effective mask. Blushing was a good sign. She started to feel hopeful again about her matchmaking. Still, she hadn't seen 'the light' Rita had gone on about.

Emily wrote down a point each for Lulu and Rita.

'Last question for this round. True or false: chocolate contains the same chemical that's produced in our brains when we're in love.'

'True!' Multiple voices and multiple hands in the air. Lulu even slapped the table in front of her.

'Yes,' Christmas said. 'It is true.' And her eyes drifted to Lincoln. Elsa smirked at Rita.

From there they proceeded to try more chocolate, cleansing their palates between samples with warm green tea; Christmas explained that the tannins in the tea sucked the fat of the chocolate from the mouth. 'Warm polenta soup is actually the best palate cleanser,' she added, 'but not so pleasant. Green tea is good. We just need to follow it with some room-temperature water to wash away the taste of the tea.'

Elsa even managed to forget about the problem of the Emily woman for a while, enjoying comparing tasting notes with Lincoln and studying the flavour wheel together. They had a considerable debate over whether a particular piece of chocolate had hints of mint or fresh-cut grass.

'How do you know what fresh-cut grass tastes like?' Lincoln asked, amused.

'Most of taste is smell,' Elsa said. 'I worked a dairy farm most of my life. If I thought about it long enough I could probably tell you what species of grass it is.'

'Impressive, Nan.'

It was amazing what some people could detect in a flavour. Many couldn't get past a general label of citrus or floral or woody. Doris's great-grandson could only say 'yum' or 'yuck'. But others could detect pineapple, sauerkraut, dust, plastic, sherry or aniseed.

Christmas wrapped up the session by revealing the identities of all the chocolates, some of which were common supermarket brands while others were more exotic, from Trinidad, the Ivory Coast, Ghana or Indonesia. Robert Graham had won the quiz prize and Christmas handed it to him to group applause. Lulu applauded but then ran over Robert's wife's toes with her wheelchair in her hurry to get going.

Residents slowly dispersed back to their rooms and the Kristof boy flexed his muscles moving tables. Elsa and Rita lingered, watching as Lincoln jumped up to help the girls gather the laminated flavour wheels, click lids onto containers of chocolate pieces, and collect tasting notes.

Then, right in front of them, Lincoln and Emily both reached for the same flavour wheel. Their hands touched, and it was plain as day where the light in the room shone—exactly where they stood.

Rita put her hand on Elsa's age-spotted arm. 'Sorry, dear.'

•

If the discussion in the car on the way to the home had been all about Christmas's father, heading back, it was all about Lincoln.

'You're absolutely crazy!' Emily said. 'Lincoln's a total catch. How often do great men like that end up in Evandale?'

'I'm not saying he's not great; he is,' Christmas admitted.

Emily gave her an exasperated look. 'Well, if I was you, I'd be grabbing that opportunity as fast as you can, because a man that great isn't going to be on the shelf for long.'

14

Emily was playing Go Fish with her nieces. She was wearing a plastic Viking helmet with long yellow wool plaits attached; Imogen wore a bonnet that did up under her chin with a fat pink ribbon; and Rose wore a tiara.

'Emily, have you got a six?' Imogen asked, narrowing her eyes at her. Since she'd turned ten, Imogen had decided she would drop the 'Aunty' and just call her 'Emily' in her most mature voice.

'Why yes, I do,' Emily said, handing it over. Rose groaned and pouted her perfect little lips. Obviously she'd been looking for a six too.

Imogen's face broke into a grin and she smoothed her messy fringe out of her eyes as though that had been a very hard decision to make and she was relieved she'd got it right. She collected Emily's six and put it together with her own in a very neat pile, then lined it up with all the other very neat piles she was building.

'Girls,' Tony called from the kitchen. 'Dinner's nearly ready. Help Aunty Emily up off the carpet and then go wash your hands.'

'I'm not quite a granny yet,' Emily said, piling up the cards and holding out her hands for her nieces to tug her into a standing position.

'You're not exactly a fresh chicken either.'

'Spring, not fresh. And why are you being so mean?' She turned to the girls and pulled a face. 'Your daddy's being a big meanie.'

They squealed and jumped up and down, excited at the idea of an impending fight between their father and their aunt. Imogen spanked Tony's backside as he passed by with a platter of salad for the table. 'Naughty, Daddy!'

'Meanie, meanie,' both girls chanted.

'Now go to your room and think about what you've done!' Rose demanded, hands on hips and an expression on her face that was so intently cross Emily couldn't help but laugh.

'Good one, Em,' grumbled Tony. 'Now look what you've done. It's already hard enough being the only man in the house.'

Emily directed the girls down the hall towards the bathroom, then went to help cut up and serve the lasagne. It was a pre-made one from the supermarket and had been baking in the oven for an eternity, the aromas of melting cheese and bubbling tomato sauce torturing her rumbling stomach.

'Should I put some aside for Britney?' she asked.

Emily had never really got over her sister-in-law's name. *Britney* was so Britney Spears. So bubble gum, peroxide and flirting in bars. 'She'll have to change her name once she graduates, you do realise,' Emily had said once to Tony. 'She'll never be taken seriously as a solicitor with a name like that.'

Now Tony pulled the garlic bread out of the oven. 'Yes, thanks. Her last lecture doesn't finish till nine. She always rummages through the fridge afterwards like a cranky bear trying to find honey at the end of a long winter. You don't want to be in the firing line when Brit's blood sugar's low.'

This happy little domestic scene awakened a yearning in Emily. Unlike Christmas, she *did* want a partner and a family. Sometimes she had the distinct impression that once she'd passed the age of thirty-five or so, people had silently marked her as a spinster. No one asked about her love life anymore, probably because they didn't want to offend her, and possibly because they thought she'd made a deliberate choice. But she hadn't; it had just been the way the cards fell. Sometimes, these days, she even forgot herself that she wanted these things. So when she'd met Lincoln it was a shock to realise that she felt an immediate interest in him.

But Lincoln was off-limits, because Christmas was clearly smitten with him, even though she was stubbornly refusing to do anything about it. As Emily knew all too well, Christmas had a set of rules that told her not to go there, rules she seemed set on following, just as she'd fiercely shut down any discussion about finding her father.

But Emily didn't have any rules. Quite the opposite.

'I met someone the other day,' she said as casually as she could, setting placemats.

'What? A bloke?'

'Yes. And you don't need to sound so surprised . He's a botanist and living locally.'

'A science man,' Tony said, noisily gathering cutlery from the drawer. 'How old?'

'Forty-two, according to Christmas. He's her co-author on a book they're writing together on chocolate. I met him on Monday at a tasting she was doing at the nursing home in Oatlands.'

'Divorced?'

'I don't think so.'

'Kids?'

'Nope.'

'Gay?'

'Doesn't seem to be.'

'Drunk? Gambler? Criminal?'

'Not that I'm aware of.'

'Then what's wrong with him?' Tony threw a few things into the dishwasher and yelled out to the girls to hurry up. 'I don't like it when they go quiet,' he muttered.

'Why do you think there's something wrong with him?' Emily asked, trying not to sound defensive because hadn't she asked the very same thing of Christmas? She wondered if this cynicism they seemed to share was a genetic thing.

Tony shrugged. 'Just seems weird, that's all.'

She was suddenly furious. 'But *I'm* not married. And I'm nearly forty. Is there something wrong with me?'

'Of course not. You just haven't found the right person.'

'Then what's the difference?' Her voice was regrettably a bit shrill.

Tony, a veteran of life with fiery females, took a deep breath and stopped what he was doing to think before he next spoke. 'You know, you're right.'

Emily laughed. 'You're well trained, you know that?'

He smiled. 'Maybe. But now that I think about it, no one ever asks "What's wrong with her?" when they're talking about a single woman. It's all pity and sympathy for the dearth of good men out there. But as soon as we hear about a single man over the age of, I don't know, thirty, we think there must be something wrong with him. It's terribly sexist, isn't it?' His eyes twinkled. 'I really don't know how you put up with these double standards. You think we've come so far and then a Neanderthal like me opens his mouth and you realise you're basically still in the fifties.'

Emily flicked him with the tea towel.

There was a thunder of feet down the hallway and some incoherent screeching and two small girls exploded into the dining room.

'What have you two been doing?' Tony asked suspiciously. Then, catching sight of Rose, 'What on earth is on your face?'

Imogen giggled. 'She wanted to dress up for dinner.'

Rose batted her eyelids and fluffed her hair, which had been combed and sprayed into rock-star frizz. And they'd had a very good time in their mother's makeup bag by the looks of it, with blue eye shadow and red lipstick and orange blush applied all over, apparently at random.

'Isn't she lovely?' Imogen said, with such warmth and genuine pride that it shot straight through Emily's heart, as it did Tony's, if his misty face was anything to go by.

'Yes, she is,' he said gravely. 'Rose, you look just like your mother.'

They took their places at the table and Tony poured the grown-ups wine while the girls had Ribena. He raised his glass. 'Here's to good men and great women.'

'I'll drink to that,' Emily said.

'Go get the botanist, Em. What've you got to lose?'

Hmm. Well, possibly my best friend.

●

Lincoln's attention span for writing this chapter was being challenged by both Caesar's pacing and his own thoughts of Christmas, who was waiting for the file so she could edit and rewrite and *enflourish* it, a word she'd made up to describe her role. The word made him laugh, but he loved it. It sounded racy, somehow.

Their work together had taken on a new, assured rhythm. Their ideas came together easily now, any early hesitation gone, their words and thoughts merging and flowing in a natural dance, like the drummers and dancers of Ghana, where he'd spent time on a research station a couple of years ago. For them, there was only one word for both drumming and dancing; it was simply one action. He'd thought of this at lunchtime, having a bacon sandwich and a beer in the back garden with Caesar as they monitored the neighbour carrying his wooden planks around, measuring and sawing and sanding.

But Christmas was avoiding him, he was sure. He'd felt her cooling off after their 'almost moment' in the shop kitchen. Since then, she'd brushed off his attempts to catch up for coffee, and suggested they work separately for now, and send through chapters over email, because she was too busy in the lead up to France. There was the shop, with supplies and rosters to organise, she'd said. There were bills to pay before she went away and there was her work as a fairy godmother, not to mention organising the hundred little things you needed to do before going overseas—copies of your passport, locks for your bag, travel pillows and eye masks, credit cards, new shoes, a medicine kit, she should really get a flu shot, and surely she didn't need vaccinations to go to France, did she? No, it was a first-world country. But perhaps she should check with her doctor?

It was all smoke, he knew. It was a polite and reasonable way of keeping him at a distance. Of keeping him included, keeping their conversation going, but efficiently avoiding intimacy or awkwardness. She didn't want to jeopardise the book. That was all. She needed him, but only for his mind.

Caesar whined at the back door again.

'You just came back in. I promise you nothing major's happened out there in the last five minutes.' But Lincoln got up to let the old boy out anyway. Caesar was obsessed with watching the sea captain's activity. It was as though he didn't trust him. And really why would you, when the latest message on his blackboard on the footpath was *Keep calm and carry guns.*

Each time Lincoln let him out, Caesar would trot up and down the fence line between the properties, decide it was safe for now, return to the door and whine to be let back into the house. A few minutes later, the captain would drop a plank or pick up a hammer and Caesar was back on his feet, worrying about what was going on.

This time, Lincoln decided to just wait by the back door for the dog to finish his latest inspection. As he stood there he surveyed the backyard and realised he needed to do some work. There was an overhanging branch that should be cut back, weeds growing between the pavers leading to the rotary clothesline, and paint flaking off the wooden toolshed by the back fence. He didn't mind doing it; he was grateful to be able to stay in his nan's place rent free. But it was all so domestic and he'd already started to feel the drag of unwelcome responsibility.

He shoved his hands into his pockets, a comfortable gesture, and the fingers of his right hand touched the corner of a card. He pulled it out: Emily Bathurst's mobile phone number. Call me, she'd said, under the guise of a professional meeting, but he'd felt it might have been a bit more than that.

But Emily was Christmas's best friend. If there was a skerrick of a chance left with Christmas it would be blown to smithereens if he called Emily. He folded the card in his palm.

Caesar's attention was diverted from the neighbour's activities by leaves floating along and he leapt towards them, his jaws snapping, though there wasn't a lot of determination in it. More like a preprogrammed gesture—leaves, snap, leaves, snap. Lincoln smiled. He really did like the dog. He had such gusto for each day. It was a shame he couldn't keep him.

But Lincoln's life wasn't like that. He wasn't the suburban type with a wife, two kids and a dog in the backyard. He was a botanist who travelled the world on research grants and lived off an inconsistent cash flow, and he liked that just fine. He liked being able to pack up his bag and leave at a minute's notice. The world was a fantastically rich and diverse place and he had only one life to live. He wanted to take any opportunity that came his way. No regrets.

He smoothed out Emily's business card once more. Here was an opportunity in the palm of his hand right now.

The only problem was that he'd already fallen for Christmas.

•

To: Christmas Livingstone
From: Miriam Deschamps
Subject: Bonjour mon amie!

Dear Christmas,

I can't believe it! I was so delighted to receive your card. My parents moved out of their house but my brother bought it off them as an investment and rented it out for years but has recently started his own family and decided to move back there.

He passed your letter on to me.

How are you? What do you do now? Are you married? Kids?

I can't tell you how excited I am that you're coming to Paris!!! When? How long will you be here? You must give me all the details. And you must come stay with us if you haven't already booked a hotel. I'm married to Hank Banks. Seriously, can you believe his parents named him 'Hank Banks'??? What were they thinking? He's American, of course, no one else in the world is called Hank, surely? We have one daughter, Margot. She's fifteen and awfully scary but I'll try to protect you from her. She was born in America, actually. I blame that for everything. I worked in the States for a few years and my last job was as Hank's receptionist. He's a dentist. Now I'm his practice manager here in Neuilly-sur-Seine. We set up a new clinic a short walk from our place and go back to see Hank's family once a year. We're going this year in July. Which is great timing because I'll just get to see you before we go.

I can't wait to catch up. Tell me everything!!!

Gros bisous!
Mim

●

'My spirit is vexed.'

Poor Rosemary McCaw's spirit was more vexed than a diabetes educator at an all-you-can-eat chocolate buffet.

'Oh dear,' Christmas said, ushering her to the stool at the counter and taking her bulky handbag, out of which poked the tip of what looked to be a metal piccolo and the brim of a straw hat. Rosemary did look a little off, actually. One pencilled eyebrow was a little awry and the clasp of her brooch was hanging open. Christmas reached across and gently fixed it for her.

'Oh, thank you, dear.'

'Would you like a coffee?' Christmas asked, moving towards the espresso machine.

'Very much.'

When Christmas returned with the coffee, Rosemary had reached under the glass dome on the counter next to her and helped herself to some rosewater coconut ice. Her heart must be hurting for her to be drawn to rose.

'What's happened?' Christmas said, placing the coffee in front of her. She took her place on her consulting stool opposite and opened her notebook, pulling a pen from the pocket of her cherry-patterned apron.

'It's too horrible to speak of.'

'Is it your family? Is everyone alright?'

'It's me.'

'Have you had some bad news?' Christmas asked carefully.

To her horror, tears sprang to Rosemary's eyes. But she sniffed them back valiantly. Raised her chin and set her jaw. 'I've been insulted in the most grievous way.'

'Insulted? By who?'

'By whom,' Rosemary corrected her automatically. 'By a hack from Melbourne.'

Christmas shook her head to indicate that she didn't know who he was.

'It's almost too awful to say out loud.'

'Rosemary, please tell me what's happened before I die from anticipation.' There was something about Rosemary that brought out the correspondingly dramatic in Christmas.

Rosemary's eyes darkened. 'He rejected me. It was a foolish, foolish idea, I see that now. I don't know what I was thinking to subject myself to such humiliation.'

'You fancied him?'

'Heavens, no. I auditioned for a role in *Cat on a Hot Tin Roof* at the community theatre. That man, barely out of nappies, what, he must be all of twelve years old, said thank you so very much but he envisioned someone not quite so mature for the role.'

'Oh, Rosemary.'

'*Old*. That's what he meant to say. Old. Haggard. No place for an old broiler like me.'

'What did you do?'

'I fled. I should have told him he was a pathetic pimply dimwit who'd die a virgin clutching his pretentious visions in his cold and lonely hand and walked out with my head held high, smiling with relief that I'd escaped the colossal disaster that sham of a play would become.' She grimaced. 'But instead I scurried out of there like a frightened mouse.'

Christmas poured thick vanilla-laced cream into Rosemary's mug. She hurt for her. It was outrageous that a professional actress of her calibre and generosity would be turned down so callously. That director had no idea what he'd let slip through his fingers or of how much he'd hurt Rosemary's feelings.

'Youth is wasted on the young,' Christmas said.

Rosemary gave a deep hearty laugh. 'Oh, my dear, you're hardly over the hill.'

Christmas raised an eyebrow. 'Nearly forty.'

'Piffle. That's nothing. You're in the prime of your life.' Rosemary sipped at the creamy coffee and murmured in appreciation. Her shoulders were already relaxing, her face softening. 'When I was forty I took up hip hop.'

Christmas laughed. 'Maybe you could teach me.'

'When are you off to France?'

Christmas's heart fluttered and she reached for a piece of the rosewater coconut ice. 'Tuesday.'

'Are you ready?'

'Nearly. Abigail is on holiday from uni and will be looking after the shop while I'm away, and because I won't be here to make handmade pieces I've just got to make sure all the extra orders and supplies are sorted so she doesn't have to do any of that and can just concentrate on customer care. Lots of fiddly things like that. I want it to be really easy for her. Three weeks is a long time.'

'Indeed. Are you sure Abigail is the right person?' Rosemary said doubtfully. 'She's not overly, how shall we say, inspiring.'

'I don't have a lot of options; Cheyenne has another job and two children to look after. I could close the shop entirely, of course, but it's so important in a small town to keep the doors open or people start to not bother coming at all. And all the businesses in town rely on each other to create a bit of bustle. I do trust Abigail to do an efficient job.' *If not an overly enthusiastic one.* 'We'll cut down the days and hours so she's not overwhelmed. And Cheyenne will help out, of course. I have to make temporary signs for the door, change the website, email reply, phone message, all those sorts of things.'

'Is there anything I can do?' Rosemary asked hopefully, wanting to be useful and needed.

'You know, it would be great if you could email me while I'm away, let me know how things are going here?'

Rosemary's eyes sparkled with intrigue. 'Spy on the Abigail girl?'

'No! Nothing like that. But you're a good friend and you know the shop well. You'd notice if something was amiss, and it would make me feel better knowing there's another set of eyes and ears keeping watch.'

'It would be my honour.' Rosemary sipped her mocha then asked, 'And how are things going with the lovely botanist?'

Christmas was shocked. She had no idea Rosemary even knew who Lincoln was. Was her attraction to him so obvious that the whole town was talking about it?

'There's no need to blush,' Rosemary said. 'It's plain as day.'

'Is it?'

'Oh yes. Your eyes light up when he's in the room and you have an extra bounce in your step.'

'Gosh.' Christmas took a deep breath. 'Well, it's complicated.'

Rosemary cast her eye around the shop. Bert and Ernie were the only other customers at the moment, seated at the distant end of the long wooden table, companionably engaged in completing a crossword together. 'We have time.'

Suddenly, Rosemary seemed like the perfect person to confide in. Christmas made herself comfortable and talked about the rules, about her considered approach to risking her heart, and about the crazy feelings she had when she was with Lincoln, the ones that told her to abandon all caution and just follow her desire.

By the time she'd finished, she and Rosemary had consumed two coffees each and enough coconut ice to give them that sickly over-sugared feeling. In the meantime, Bert and Ernie had packed up their crossword and waved a farewell, Abigail had arrived and taken in her first massage client, and Cynthia Heather had popped in to buy a birthday gift of macarons for one of her kids' teachers.

Rosemary said little until Christmas was spent, with no more words to be spoken.

'May I offer some advice, from an *old* woman?'

'Stop it. You're not old.'

'You cannot control when or with whom you fall in love—and that applies to a man, a new friend, an Italian cheese, or a puppy. Your only job is to embrace each opportunity as it arises. Go and kiss this Lincoln van Luc.'

Christmas recoiled. 'No, no . . .'

Rosemary held up her hand. 'Go and kiss him. That is my prescription for you. Then you will know whether there is anything more to it than a passing attraction. If not, you can go on your merry way to France without giving him another thought. It will free your mind.'

Christmas leaned across the table and spoke quietly. 'And what if there *is* something there?'

'Let us cross that bridge when we come to it.'

'Us?'

'Yes. I think maybe you need a fairy godmother of your own.'

'You may be right on that count,' Christmas said. 'But I'm definitely not kissing him.'

15

It was Sunday and there were only two days to go until she left for Paris, so Christmas organised to have dinner with Val and the boys, leaving her half-filled suitcase and baskets of clothes in various states of laundering lined up in the kitchenette in her loft. She arrived at the Kennedy–Bowen household bearing a basket of ingredients, much to everyone's delight. Mealtimes were a bit of a sore point in the house. Val really was a dreadful cook and had only mastered spaghetti bolognaise and pasta with pre-prepared sauce; Archie wasn't much better, and relied on throwing frozen fish fingers, pizzas and potato gems into the oven.

Poor Nate was actually very keen to learn to cook and had aspirations of making it onto *Junior MasterChef*. But Christmas feared that with his parents he was truly behind the eight ball. As she was gathering the ingredients she had realised with a stab of guilt that she should have taken him under her wing by now and started coaching him. She spent all this time helping children and adults realise their dreams through her fairy godmother work yet here was a sensitive, anxious child—her own nephew, no less—right under her nose whose dreams she could help with right now. She resolved to begin tutoring him at her shop as soon as she came back from France. She'd find him an apprentice's apron and hat.

Nate's whoops when she unpacked her basket weren't solely elicited by the thought of helping her in the kitchen, however. And it wasn't just that she was making BLTs, either, though bacon was a huge favourite with all three boys and with Archie regardless of how it was served. (Val appreciated that this way the boys would at least get some lettuce and tomato in for the day, and Christmas whispered that she'd sneak in some avocado slices too.) And the whoops of joy weren't for her presence, though all three boys threw their arms around her and leaned in to allow her to kiss their grubby cheeks. No, the excitement was because she'd brought a one-litre jar filled with chocolate balsamic glaze that would be poured onto the BLTs and, she assured Val, could be used on almost any vegetable, making it instantly appealing to her children who, Val feared, must surely be about to fall victim to scurvy.

'I pour orange juice into them each morning to cling to the vague notion that I'm succeeding as a mother,' she admitted to Christmas. Hopefully the chocolate sauce—made with only dark chocolate, so it really was reasonably good for them—would help ease Val's guilt and encourage the boys to expand their idea of vegetables past potato chips.

The BLTs were a big hit, and Christmas, along with her special helper, Nate, was busy in the kitchen slicing and toasting and frying multiple servings for each person. Plates were licked clean. Val enjoyed an extra glass of wine since she didn't have to be in charge of the stovetop. Archie declared it a triumph of modern cookery. Willis, at nine years of age an exact replica of his father, right down to the dark blue trousers and steel-capped boots, pronounced bacon the best food in the world. And six-year-old Braxton asked for an extra BLT to feed to his toy dinosaurs.

At that, Willis rolled his eyes at Braxton and leaned back in his chair with his hands behind his head, just like Archie. And lovely Nate, the eight-year-old wise man of the house, said that of course he would make the dinosaurs a BLT, and then went outside and picked some grass to add to the plate so the herbi-vores in the group could have something to eat too.

For dessert, Christmas had brought over chocolate roulade with strawberry mousse filling. Afterwards the adults groaned and patted their stomachs while the boys sprang out of their seats, high on sugar.

'I've got them,' Archie said, easing out of his chair and herding the boys to the lounge for a game of sponge ball soccer.

Christmas and Val sat at the table, surrounded by the detritus of the feast, and sipped wine. 'Don't touch a thing,' Val said. 'It's outrageous you even brought your own farewell dinner.'

'Don't be silly. I don't have a family to look after.'

It was meant to be a light-hearted comment but they both paused a moment, catching the other's eye.

'Are you sure it's not something you want?' Val asked. 'It's not too late.'

'I think it's too late for me.'

'No, no, lots of women have babies up into their forties these days.'

Christmas shrugged. 'Then I guess that's not really the issue. Before I got pregnant, kids really hadn't been on the cards anyway. Yes, I would have loved that child and my life would be totally different today. But I'm not unhappy.'

'You work hard not to be.'

'What does that mean?'

'Nothing,' Val said, backpedalling, her hand across her heart. 'I just worry about you, that's all. It's my right as your sister.'

They sat in silence for a minute or so while yells erupted from the lounge room over the validity of a goal.

Christmas had her legs crossed and swung the top one back and forth, thinking. 'Did I tell you I heard from Miriam Deschamps? My pen pal from high school.'

Val's eyes widened. 'Seriously? How?'

Christmas filled her in.

'Are you going to visit her?' Val asked.

'Of course. I'm going to spend a week with her and her husband and teenage daughter when I first get to Paris, though Mim's warned me they'll all be crazy busy and I'll hardly see them.'

'Do you think she could help you find Gregoire?'

'Oh God, not you too!' Christmas let her head fall back in frustration. 'Emily's been on at me about this since Easter. I think I've made it pretty clear that I'm not interested.'

'But . . .'

'Maybe I would have been in the past. But not now.'

Val pursed her lips.

'Oh, go on,' Christmas said. 'Say it.'

'Look, I'm not a psychologist or anything,' Val began. 'But do you think it's possible that you're in denial?'

'Denial of what?'

'That this really is a big deal and you're just too afraid to see it for what it is?'

Christmas stood up to get another bottle of red from the wine rack on the dresser and held it up questioningly to Val, who nodded her head in affirmation and sculled the last of her glass. Christmas thought about the question while she peeled off the foil and twisted in the corkscrew. It was so much more satisfying to pull out a cork with that pleasant *pop* at the end. She'd never got used to the idea of twisting off a top, the snapping metal sound that was no different to removing a soft-drink cap. There was no ceremony in that. Nothing special about it at all. She braced her hand on the bottle and extracted the cork, pausing to inhale the fermented aromas wafting from the neck, before glug-glug-glugging wine into both of their glasses.

'Why do you think that?' she said at last, turning the tables back on Tiny Val. 'That I'm afraid.'

Val held up a hand. 'I'm not trying to be difficult,' she said. 'I was just wondering.' Val, with the practical, patient, negotiating mind of her father the school principal, wasn't taking the bait. She took another tack. 'How do you feel about France, then, in general? Because like it or not, it *is* France—the home of your father.' She raised her shoulders. 'Some people might think that was a big deal.'

She sipped at her wine, turned in the direction of the lounge and shouted, 'Willis, I can hear you from here. Stop being the boss of everyone. Daddy makes the rules, not you. Give the others a chance to play too!' Then she turned back to Christmas, her face mellow once more, waiting for her to answer.

Christmas was hit with a numbing wave of alcohol, her body feeling pleasantly heavy. 'Look, I'm not saying that France itself doesn't stir something in me. Of course it does. What I am saying, though, is that I can't afford to let thoughts of my father take over my mind. I accept that France is where Gregoire comes from. That is all. It will be nice to see some of the country, but it doesn't mean I need to go any further.'

'But supposing you *could* find him, would you actually want to?'

'Honestly, I'm not sure. I mean, yes, if it was the happy-ever-after tale, but so much could go wrong, couldn't it? He could be horrible. He could be an axe murderer. He could be filthy and slobby, in jail, homeless, or just plain mean and nasty.'

'He could be the President of France.'

'Or Louis Vuitton.'

'And you could get free couture clothes for the rest of your life!'

'Exactly. But that's the point, isn't it? I have no idea what I'll get. The risks are really high and the whole thing could be so devastating that I might never recover. I could end up back in the foetal position in bed and you'd have to come and get me again.'

'Hey, I wouldn't mind a trip to France. Once I got you out of your pyjamas we could go to the Champs-Élysées and buy handbags.'

'It's similar to the question of having kids,' Christmas said. 'The rewards are tremendous but the risks are just as high. I could lose a baby before it was even born. Again. It could be stillborn. It could die due to complications at birth. It could have a serious illness or major disability. It could live five years and then I could lose it. And I *know* I'd never recover.'

'Oh, Massy.'

Christmas wiped at her eyes. 'Sometimes it's the braver choice to know your limits and stick to them. I'm happy right now. Why would I risk that?'

Suddenly, there was a nasty, human-sized thump from the living room, followed by a shriek and tears and shouting. Val gripped the table and took a shaky breath. 'Is everything okay?' she called.

'It's okay,' Archie said. 'It's under control.'

Val shuddered.

'Huge risks,' Christmas said, gesturing towards the lounge room.

'Yes,' Val said. 'And huge rewards when it works out.'

'It's the unknown that's the problem,' Christmas said. 'If only we were fortune tellers.'

'There's always Jaelle,' Val said.

'I can't believe I went to her.' Christmas slapped her hand to her forehead at the memory of visiting gypsy Jaelle in her wooden wagon in a field.

'She seemed to help at the time. She said you have a gift for helping others. That seems to be true.'

'I was just feeling lost after coming back from Sydney. Probably anyone could have helped me at the time. I shouldn't have gone. It broke rule number eight—*Your destiny doesn't happen to you; you make your destiny.*'

'Do you ever break the rules?'

'Apparently only when my life's a shipwreck and I want advice from gypsies who appear mysteriously overnight and read tea leaves by oil lanterns and catch rabbits to cook on open fires.'

'Well,' Val said, 'here's to a fabulous three weeks in France!'

●

'So tomorrow's the day,' Lincoln said, here with her once more on a Monday. 'Is everything set to go?'

Christmas bit her lip. 'I think so. I've got to empty my fridge upstairs and take out rubbish and turn off appliances and all that, leave extra keys for Abigail, book the taxi to the airport. I have a list but it just keeps getting longer.'

Butterflies had set into her belly, chasing each other around in circles as she tried to get on top of everything. It was silly, really. She'd be back in three weeks and life would carry on as normal.

Now she kept her hands busy while they discussed the book and their plans and timetables for its completion. It would be the end of her if she had to sit still and stare into Lincoln's eyes and be taunted by his new aftershave. Something citrusy and salty. It was like sitting by the ocean and squeezing lemon on fish and chips under the warm sun. She'd rushed him to the chocolate immediately, smothering the smell in comforting cocoa instead.

They were making chocolate cigars. The truffle ganache was infused with Lapsang Souchong tea leaves and the cigars were rolled in powder-soft cocoa. Together, they were now wrapping the ends with thin strips of tissue paper and dipping the tips into a crushed cornflake and tea mixture to imitate the glow of fire, then lining them up in mock cigar boxes. It was fiddly and they had to concentrate, which suited her just fine.

She used a knife to neatly score small indentations across the cigars for added texture and effect. Beside her, she could feel the heat coming from Lincoln's body as he worked. He seemed to sense her mood, and once they'd finished discussing the book he maintained a companionable silence, not even needing to ask many questions.

They'd dealt with the business discussion efficiently enough. Lincoln had work to go on with and would make sure it was completed for her to *enflourish* on her return. And she gave him a copy of her itinerary—a week in Paris with Mim, a week in Aix-en-Provence at the chocolate course, and a week in Provence at the end, staying at a chateau—so if he had any chocolate emergencies he could contact her. He wouldn't, of course, it was really just to make herself feel that she'd ticked off every last box on her checklist so she could leave with a clean conscience.

She'd called her mother last night to say goodbye, and just because Emily and Val had been on at her so much, she decided to ask Darla one more time about Gregoire, if only to prove to them that it was pointless.

'Why would you want to dredge up all of that?' Darla snapped, the sound of a hooting owl in the background. She was camping in a dry creek bed somewhere in Victoria.

'Well, I don't actually—'

'It's in the past and has nothing to do with your life now. Even if I wanted to help you, I can't. You know everything I know. We didn't keep in contact. I've no idea where he is. And you're only interested because it's France, you know. If he'd come from some war-torn hellhole or deathly poor, filthy, disease-ridden country you wouldn't be so keen.'

Despite having to endure the harangue from her mother, Christmas was glad she'd asked one more time, just to make absolutely sure. She said she'd email at some point from France and ended the conversation.

So that was that.

But Rosemary's advice about Lincoln was a different matter. Ever since the older woman had told her to kiss him it was all she could think about. It had been years since she'd kissed a man; there had been no one since Simon. She didn't even know if she still remembered how to do it. Besides, Lincoln was forbidden. And yet that just made him more attractive. She clenched her jaw. It was a good thing she was getting out of the country tomorrow. This could only end in tears.

'What are you thinking about?' Lincoln asked.

'Hmm?'

'Just now. Your face went all kind of red and grumpy.'

'Really?'

'Really.'

'Oh.' She forced her eyebrows up towards her hairline to smooth out the crease she knew would have pinched between her brows and moved her jaw around to release the tension. 'Sorry. I guess I'm not very talkative today. Got a lot on my mind.'

'France?' he said, passing her the scissors and some raffia.

'I guess.' She forced a laugh. 'You're probably relieved not to have to listen to me prattling on as usual.'

Lincoln reached for the scissors as she passed them back. But instead of taking the scissors he clasped his big warm hand around hers and held it, his eyes locked onto hers, the muscles in his neck twitching as though with the effort of self-restraint. 'I like talking to you,' he said. 'You're addictive. Like chocolate.'

She didn't move. She didn't take her eyes off him. She didn't breathe.

It will free your mind, Rosemary had said.

Her mind could sure use some freedom right now.

Would there be anything between them? She had to know. For her own sanity. To free her mind. To be able to go on her way without giving him another thought.

She looked down at his hand on hers, cocoa powder adding a smooth layer of sensation between their skins, like silk sheets she just wanted to dive into. Everything stopped except her heart, which beat like a drum. Aromas rushed to her nose—Lincoln's aftershave, that alluring combination of lemon and salt; the cocoa powder; the tank of chocolate; the Lapsang Souchong tea leaves; the sickly sweet cornflakes; the linen starch on her poodle-print apron. She could hear the ticking of the thermostat and the small moist parting of Lincoln's lips. His pupils were fixed on her lips.

He increased the pressure on her hand, capturing her in his grip, a slow but inexorable pull, drawing her to him.

She let him.

She wanted him.

Her eyes closed, blocking out the world, as she felt herself falling into him.

The last sensible thought she had before her lips met his was that she had to kiss him for the greater good. Was there anything between them? With just one kiss she could prove there was nothing there and free them both to go on their ways.

Their lips connected for her first kiss in four years and it was like falling into a meadow of soft grass on a warm day. And Rosemary was right. Christmas knew straight away that she could never be with Lincoln van Luc. Anything that could feel that wonderful, take you to such heights of joy, could also cast you into the very pits of despair.

She pulled away from him, her hand across her mouth, instantly saddened by the shock and confusion in his eyes but determined to protect herself, and then hurried him out the door.

16

'Where are you?' Emily asked.

'On my way to the airport,' Christmas said, her voice raised over the taxi's radio.

'Is everything okay?'

'I just had to call you before I leave. I want you to know that I'm not interested in Lincoln.'

'What do you mean?'

'I'm not interested in him. At all. But I thought maybe you were, because you gave him your card at the chocolate tasting—'

'That was just business.'

'—and all those things you said about him in the car on the way home . . . I want you to know it's okay if you want to see him. You know, date him.'

Emily was confused. 'Why are you saying this?'

Christmas sighed. 'I think Lincoln is a really great guy. And you're right, it would be a terrible shame to waste a good man in

Tasmania. So if there's any chance you like him, I just don't want you to hesitate because of me. That's all.'

'I don't know what to say. You sound upset.'

'No, no, no. It's just the stress of getting out the door on time. Anyway, that's all I wanted to say,' Christmas repeated, sounding slightly unhinged. 'So I'll see you in three weeks, okay?'

'Okay. Take care of yourself and have fun.' Emily hung up, stunned.

●

Caesar burst in through the front door of Elsa's bungalow and greeted her with a huge, slobbery nosing around her knees, leaving wet patches on her purple track pants. As he thoroughly licked any traces of an apple tea cake from her hands his long tail efficiently cleared her side table of photographs, the television remote control and her mobile phone.

'Caesar!' Lincoln growled, reaching for his collar to halt the wild circling that had now brought down a three-legged stool.

Elsa laughed. 'Oh, leave him.' It was rare to see anyone with such bounce in a place like this. Then again, there was the Kristof boy, she realised with some regret for treading on his spirit.

Lincoln let go of Caesar to pick up the stool.

'Why do I have that thing anyway?' she said. 'It's not like I ever sit on it. I'd topple off it in less than a second. I can't even get myself in and out of the lounge chair very often these days.' She stared at the soft blue couch in front of the television. Caesar followed her gaze and evidently liked what he saw. He trotted over and pulled himself up onto the couch, not without some stiffness in his back legs, she noticed sympathetically, and settled himself down with his big head resting on a cushion. He let out a heavy, satisfied sigh and thumped his tail a few times to indicate that all was well in his world.

'He's looking so much better,' Elsa said, admiring his shiny coat and plumper appearance. 'You're obviously feeding him well.'

'Do you think it's too late to teach him manners?'

'I like his manners. He's honest and straightforward. Something few of us achieve in our whole life.' She tapped her teeth together. 'You might as well take that stool with you. I'll never use it again. Your father was the only one who ever sat on it.' She suddenly felt cold and reached for the mohair rug on the floor beside her wheelchair. Lincoln picked it up for her, and she slapped his hand away as he tried to place it on her knees. 'I can do it.'

Lincoln held his hands in the air in dramatic surrender, just as he'd done as a boy on the rare occasions she spoke crossly to him. He never fought back, just calmly backed away. That irritated her now.

Lincoln observed her quietly. They held each other's gaze, each considering the other.

He broke first. 'We need to talk about Dad. I know we've been ignoring it ever since I got back, pretending everything's okay now I'm here, but we need to try to resolve this.'

This wouldn't be coming from Lincoln, she knew. It wasn't his style. 'You've spoken to Jenny?' she guessed.

Lincoln sat down, stretching his arms above his head and sighing. She wondered if he did yoga. All the celebrities did yoga these days. Even the men. She almost burst out laughing, imagining her Ebe doing yoga out in the paddocks in the forties.

'Yes,' he confessed. 'Why are you laughing?'

'Oh, was I? Nothing. Just thinking.'

'Tell me if I've got this right: Dad wants you to sell the house and give him his inheritance now.'

'Correct.'

'And you said no, so he's stopped visiting.'

'Correct.'

'He's emotionally blackmailing you?'

She shuffled in her chair, shifting her weight off her right hip. It had been more painful than usual this week. She should really tell the physio-terrorist, but that would only lead to more poking and prodding. At this stage of life, she might just like some more drugs. Surely they could do that. Didn't they do that all the time with cancer patients and the like? Just keep giving them morphine and more and more of it until they died?

She shocked herself with that thought. She didn't actually want to die. Not yet. She wasn't done yet. True, some days it was hard to know why, but she still just felt she had something to do here.

'Nan?'

'Blackmail.' She considered this. 'I suppose it is. Yes.'

Lincoln nodded. 'I did accuse him of that.'

'Did you?' She was genuinely surprised, and touched. 'And what did he say?' she asked, feeling a bit misty.

He seemed to struggle to know how to answer.

'Just say it. I'm too old for beating around the bush.'

'He said you don't need the house and he does, so it's a waste for it to be sitting there waiting for me, someone who's old enough to look after himself and who doesn't need to flee to his grandmother's protection anymore.'

'That was mean and unfair.'

'Yes.'

'He's a piece of work, your father.'

'Yeah.'

'I'm sorry. I'm not sure what I did wrong.' She thought of brave, funny, music-loving first-born Matthew, blown to bits in Vietnam. And studious Jake, with no skill with cattle but endless patience for boring details and numbers, now on the other side of the world in England, with three grown children and enjoying Sunday roast each week with his wife's mother. And then Tom, the last born, always whinging, always looking for shortcuts and handouts. As a boy, Tom would steal food from the dogs' plates, not because he needed or wanted it, just because he felt more entitled to it.

It must be at least partly her fault. Third-child syndrome. Left to his own devices because she was too tired and distracted to pay him attention. It was probably karma that she'd been left with him now, reaping what she'd failed to sow.

How had Tom's own two children, lovely Lincoln and Jenny, turned out so well? Their mother, no doubt. Sweet young Katherine hadn't known what she was getting herself into when she'd accepted Tom's proposal. At least she finally saw sense before she lost all her joy and softness; after the divorce she'd gone to north Queensland, the other end of the country, married herself a cane farmer and now happily played bingo each Monday night.

'You know you don't have to hold onto the house for me, don't you?' Lincoln said. 'I *am* old enough to take care of myself, and if you need the money or would like the money . . .'

'I don't need the money. Not now. But that's the point. Your grandfather and I worked hard our whole lives and we—actually *I*—carefully put aside savings.' She'd been the money manager. Ebe was naive at best, volatile at worst. But somehow she'd managed to steer their ship through the rough waters to safe harbour, tucking pound notes into books she knew he never read, burying tins of notes in the chook yards. 'All you need to know is that I'm fine. Your father might not come and see me anymore, but life's rarely neat. Truth be told, I never really enjoyed his company anyway.'

Lincoln grunted.

'I don't need his miserable company,' she said.

'But you know . . . you know I won't be here all the time,' he said carefully.

She knew—hence the attempted matchmaking. But she nodded in answer to his question, not wanting to let on that she held hopes that he would end his wandering.

'There's just no real opportunities for me here,' he explained.

'Tasmania's an island. You need to go where you can. That's reality.'

A large white delivery van rumbled over the pebbles outside and pulled up at the back of the main building. The driver's door clicked open, he stepped out and sang a friendly hello to a passing nurse, and the van's side door slid back in a metallic whoosh.

'I'm worried about you,' Lincoln said. 'I'm worried you'll be lonely. Depressed.'

She scoffed. 'I'm made of tougher stuff than that.'

He smiled tightly and she knew he was thinking of her mortality.

'The best gift you can give me is to live your life with joy,' she said. 'That will make me happy.'

He smiled, relieved.

'But if you'd like to get married and give me a tribe of fat great-grandchildren, that would be wonderful.'

'I'm sorry to say it doesn't look like there's anything on the horizon,' he said.

'What about Christmas Livingstone?'

'No,' he said, and he looked sad.

Elsa's heart leapt. Ah! So it wasn't straightforward. That was good. 'It seemed like you two had something,' she pressed him. 'I thought, maybe, since you were working on the book together there might have been shared interests, common goals, that sort of thing.'

'I thought so too, for a while.'

Interesting. 'Well, did you make it clear how you felt?'

'I thought I did.' He lifted a heavy shoulder, weighed down by a bit of a chip by the looks of it, his masculine pride battered. 'She turned me down.' He moved to the couch and shoved Caesar over so he could fit on the edge. Caesar snuffled and rearranged his head for optimal proximity to Lincoln's lap so his ears could be rubbed.

'What happened?' she asked, trying not to sound too interested.

He focused on the carpet, thinking, but no words came. She knew she wasn't going to get much more out of him today. But she had enough to go on. There was a chink in the wall. Light could still get through. There was still hope. She couldn't wait to go back and tell Rita!

Then she tapped her nail on the rubber wheel of her chair as a thought struck her. Perhaps she needed more than Rita. This was a mission that might call for strategy, determination and fierce commitment to winning.

And there was only one person in this place who fitted that description.

•

Miriam Deschamps had finished her fourth coffee since picking Christmas up at Charles de Gaulle airport. Thanks to Mim's repeated request for *un café* for herself and *un café au lait* for her Tasmanian pen pal, Christmas already felt confident she'd be able to negotiate her own caffeine needs in Paris from tomorrow. Now, as they walked into the lobby of an elegant apartment building, it looked as though Mim was hearing the call for her fifth. In the few hours they'd been together, Christmas had noticed that Mim's nose and left eye began to twitch when her caffeine levels fell.

'Nearly there.' She smiled, with perfect white teeth, much improved from how they looked in photos of her as a teenager, Christmas noticed—the benefits of being married to a dentist.

In the elevator, Mim entered the passcode into the security panel and pressed the button for the fourth floor and they whizzed silently upwards, then gently slid to a halt.

The doors opened directly into the apartment and Christmas could have cried with relief. After more hours in the air than she could add up, serious leg, neck and back pains from the cramped seat, dehydration, anxiety about what lay before her in the coming weeks, and the relentless mind games she'd been playing with herself over Lincoln van Luc and the awful, rotten way she'd said goodbye to him, she now found herself entering a place of total calm and aesthetic order.

Mim stepped out into the open-plan home, her killer heels tick-tacking their way across the polished boards. Sunlight streamed in through the large windows, reflecting off the white panelled walls and illuminating Mim's shiny black ponytail and slightly sparkly makeup. She slung her handbag over the back of a chair and held out her arms. '*Bienvenue à la maison!* Our home is yours for the next week.'

'This is such a beautiful place. Thank you so much for having me. *Merci.*'

'It is our pleasure. Well, it's my pleasure, and Hank's pleasure. It's probably not Margot's pleasure.' Mim folded her thin arms across the front of her tightly buttoned blouse, a line appearing between her perfectly shaped brows, and tapped her foot, a gesture Christmas suspected the Margot in question saw plenty of.

Then Mim shrugged off her annoyance and clapped her hands. 'We have a few hours before the others get home, so would you like to have some rest? Can I get you a tisane of verbena to settle you?'

'Yes, thanks. I think I might have a heart attack if I have one more coffee.'

Mim snorted. 'It makes no difference to me. I could have twelve cups a day and still sleep peacefully.'

Christmas wandered across to the window seat and drank in the view. Spreading out in all directions in Neuilly-sur-Seine was block after block of the classic Haussmann-style buildings, just like the one she was in right now. It was surprising that something so ordered, neat and repetitive could be so beautiful. Big wide boulevards lined with cafes and leafy green trees lay at the feet of six-storey buildings currently bathed in golden light. The identical buildings, each with the same tall, slender windows and narrow wrought-iron balconies, were stately and grand. They were a light-filled cream colour and reminded her of formal wedding cakes. Or miniature castles.

'How old are these buildings?' she called to Mim.

'Mid eighteen hundreds,' Mim called back, cups clattering onto the stone benchtop in the kitchen.

There was nothing like these buildings in Australia, let alone Tasmania. Christmas loved the history of Tasmania and her lovely Georgian Apothecary and the early colonial buildings that made the state so beautiful. But it was almost impossible to fathom that at the same time as convicts were still being transported to Tasmania in horrendous conditions on ships, to be worked in freezing conditions in chains, lashed to the bone by the cat o' nine tails, starved and kept in coffin-sized isolation, bustling Paris was undergoing a major urban redevelopment to create the magnificent city it was today.

A week in Paris was going to go by much too fast. She couldn't even begin to scratch the surface of its history. She took a deep breath, the rest of the world forgotten for the moment as she relished the bliss of simply being here. She had to hand it to Emily. She was right, Christmas *had* always been obsessed with France, but she'd never realised just how much she needed to be here until now. She pulled her mobile phone out of her pocket, snapped an image of the view from the window and sent it to Emily with a heartfelt message of thanks for making all this happen. It had been an inspired thing to do.

The sounds of the espresso machine whirring in the narrow galley kitchen and Mim muttering to herself were like comforting mind chatter, the kind that takes up space and stops you thinking about anything too serious. There'd be lots of time in the months ahead to think serious thoughts. Right now, she just wanted to absorb everything.

She wasn't aware of how long she'd been grinning until her cheeks began to ache.

Christmas's guest room was as immaculately styled as the rest of the Neuilly apartment—minimalist, modern, with muted tones. The stone-tiled ensuite had glass basins, and warm lighting that made her face look a lot better than she felt even after a night's sleep.

She had met the stocky, effusive Hank last night when he came home late after an emergency extraction, smelling of some sort of chemical and speaking in a mixture of French and English with a confident American accent, kissing his wife and nuzzling her neck in a way that made Christmas uncomfortable: she had to keep shifting her eyes away.

She'd also met the terrifying Margot, who came home in time for dinner. She was completely different from how Christmas had pictured her. She'd expected the girl to be dressed in black, festooned with piercings, with dreadfully dyed hair, sullen eyes and a sour expression. But she was devastatingly beautiful, with California beach-girl looks, French chic and soft, gentle curls to die for. Blue eyes. A slim figure. She wore a pastel-pink dress and cardigan and pink lip gloss. She was terribly sweet and interested in Christmas, and it was several hours into listening to her talking to Mim and to her friends on her phone—a device nearly continuously jammed to her ear—that Christmas started to get a sense of Margot's game.

Margot Banks was a sugar spider. Someone who wove sugary sweet webs of charm and deceit and then wrapped you up in a sticky prison and kept you alive in the corner till she sank her fangs into you when she could be bothered. She was the girl who would come home one day engaged to a fifty-year-old. The girl who said she was studying when she was really snorting coke at the back of a club. The girl who'd take her clothes off for photographers, swearing to them she was eighteen. The girl who could lie as easily as she could smile. And all the while she'd be getting straight As and going to confession. Christmas had to agree with Mim—she was terrifying.

She fished in her toiletries bag for some anti-frizz serum to smooth down her hair, feeling guilty that she'd overslept.

The house was quiet and she knew everyone had left for the day.

Last night Mim had helped her plan out her first day's activities. 'I have everything done,' she'd said, presenting Christmas with an elegant black leather journal. She snapped it open and went through the pages of information, all clearly colour-coded. There was a Metro map and instructions on how to buy tickets and find the right stops; a highlighted city map; lists of phone numbers to call if she got lost or needed help; the address of the apartment and directions on how to get there so she could hand it to a taxi driver if necessary, and the same for the dental surgery; and notes on how to tip in France, something Christmas was particularly grateful for. She'd also given Christmas a set of keys to the building and a few useful phrases written on cards.

Christmas felt prepared and confident as she adjusted a silk scarf so that the V of the material hung down to her chest, tied in front with a classy knot, one that suggested she was an expert at wrangling scarves. She wasn't. But it would be a perfect match with her new dark blue jeans. She felt different. Parisian. And ready for adventure.

With Mim's encouragement, she'd decided to have a leisurely day. 'You cannot possibly see all of Paris in a week,' Mim had lamented. 'But never mind. You'll be back, *oui*?'

'How do you say *absolutely*?' Christmas had asked, still high on enough caffeine to raise an elephant from the dead, and on the magical view of the lights of Paris turning on like a perfectly orchestrated symphony as the sun went down. Right now, she might agree to never going home at all.

'*Absolument!*'

'*Absolument*,' Christmas had repeated, practising her accent.

'Then don't do her badly this time. *Elle est belle*—she is beautiful. She deserves undivided attention. Go at leisure. Eat. Drink.'

'Sounds like wonderful advice,' Christmas had said, sipping her first glass of French wine on French soil.

So today she'd decided to follow Mim's advice and take it easy. She hit the boulevard at nine thirty under a bright blue sky, and at Les Sablons Metro station she headed underground and boarded the sleek silver train, pungent with the smell of rubber, and zoomed through the dark tunnels towards Charles de Gaulle–Etoile, where she swapped lines in a confused rush of platforms, escalators, old chewing gum, and dim lighting to head to Louvre–Rivoli station.

Back on the surface, she was greeted by more Haussmann-style buildings flanking each side of the wide street. She headed towards the Seine, along with hordes of other tourists, with cameras, backpacks and guide maps, doing exactly as she was: heading to the magnificent sights of the Louvre. However, she'd decided not to go inside on this trip.

'It is mammoth,' Mim had said, holding out both hands as though measuring an enormous fish. 'You'll be exhausted. Your poor feet will be dead before you start. And the Mona Lisa? *Pft!* Is tiny! So tiny and so many people crowded in front of her, you won't even see.'

Christmas hadn't needed much convincing. The inside of museums had never done much for her. She'd far rather be out in the fresh air, watching life.

So she deliberately set her walking pace to half that of the tourists around her, all marching earnestly towards the Louvre. She also took the opportunity to sip a *café au lait* under the pale orange awning that spanned the stone archways of Le Fumoir, and added a croissant in observance of rule number two: *Never let yourself get hungry.* Around her, dogs sat beneath tables, their narrow muzzles resting on pointed toes, and a white-haired man hid behind the open pages of *Le Monde* while his youthful female companion polished her sunglasses. A taxi sounded its horn at a pedestrian in the middle of the road. Cigarette smoke drifted through the air. High heels clacked on the flagstones.

She found people-watching such a pleasant pastime, one that relaxed her surprisingly well, that she began to welcome thoughts of Lincoln rather than batting them away. She let the memories of their time together in the shop hover around her like a lovely dream, conveniently ignoring the way she'd treated him after the kiss, and just remembering the feel of his skin, and the intense way he'd looked at her.

When she felt ready, she set off on foot again. She took her time walking along the street to enter the archway of La Cour Carrée, the courtyard of the Louvre, though its open square surrounded by three storeys of Renaissance stonework felt more like standing inside castle grounds. She passed the fountains and the modern glass pyramid entrance to the former palace and kept going, glad she'd worn her most comfortable boots.

On the other side of the museum's boundaries she found herself in the Tuileries—the vast royal gardens: expansive emerald-green lawns you weren't allowed to walk on, interspersed with beds of purple and pink flowers; the towering white ferris wheel so tourists could take in the view from on high; the huge shade trees sheltering small tables and chairs beneath their protective limbs; and the seemingly endless supply of marble sculptures standing in the sunshine as though it was totally normal to populate a public garden with authentic historical artworks. As though, *Hey, this is Paris, we have thousands of these things just lying around in the back of the wardrobe.*

Christmas was relieved she'd decided not to go into the

Louvre. Just taking in the grounds was a considerable undertaking. She didn't know how large the area was in acres, but it certainly felt extensive. Like a decent-sized farm.

In fact, everything seemed big. If there was one thing she'd been feeling all morning, it was small. And provincial. She'd lived in Sydney, sure. But other than going to Peter's funeral she hadn't left the small isle of Tasmania for years. Her world had shrunk to the tiny village of Evandale and her chocolate shop. And other than on trips to Launceston and Hobart, she seldom saw a building over two storeys high. Paris was monumental. Surely no one in the world built structures this large anymore? It was grand. Opulent. Decadent in the most awe-inspiring way.

It was incredible to think that anyone could build something so large that would last so many hundreds of years. She doubted the skyscrapers of Sydney would still be there in five or more centuries. Everything in the world was getting smaller. The world's largest species were disappearing—elephants, tigers, polar bears, whales. Technology was getting smaller all the time. The phones, computers and music systems of the past were shrinking to a single palm-sized device. Weapons of war could be shrunk to a single button, a virus or a change in DNA.

Paris was different. The city was full of giants.

And then there was the river. The mighty Seine with its green-grey water muscling along, a steady, unstoppable force. Open-topped tourist boats chugging white water. Wooden rowboats, their oars rising and falling like the large wings of birds. Stone bridges arched to allow the passage of vessels below. And the majestic Musée d'Orsay flanking the left bank opposite. The whole city seemed to be made of stone and marble and waiting for the arrival of royalty.

Mim was right about Paris. *Elle est belle.*

17

Emily was at the television station for a team meeting when a call came through to her mobile. She was bored. Most of the morning's discussions of program ideas had nothing to do with her and had instigated a lot of macho hooting and revelry and scribbles on the whiteboard—car racing and triathlons or something equally dull. She was just doodling a picture of a cupcake on her notebook when she felt her handbag vibrate against her leg.

She cast a furtive glance at Rod and Eddie, who were all but ignoring the three women at the table, and at Alice and Rupna, who looked as bored as Emily felt. Alice was studying her chipped nails. Rupna was on her laptop, and from the movement of her eyes and the lazy tapping of her scroll key, Emily was pretty sure she was reading a blog post of some sort.

Certain no one would notice, she slid her hand down and slipped the phone out of the front pocket of her bag. She didn't recognise the number. A mystery number was far more inter-esting than anything else going on in this room.

Rising, she waved her apologies, mouthed that she'd be *back in a tick*, and stepped out into the dank-smelling hallway.

'Hello?'

'Emily?' The man's voice was vaguely familiar, a little unsure of himself, but friendly nonetheless.

'Yes,' she said brightly. 'How can I help?'

'Hi, this is Lincoln. Lincoln van Luc. We met at the chocolate tasting at Green Hills Aged Care a couple of weeks ago.'

Emily stopped picking at the peeling paint on the wall next to her. 'Oh, hi.' She tried to sound casual and confident, the vocal equivalent of a saunter.

'How are you?' he asked.

'Great! How are you?'

'Good.'

She shouldn't have said she was great. No one said *great* in answer to that obligatory, routine question. It made her sound hyperactive, bouncy, too keen. Or desperate.

Or snooty—like her being *great* was far superior to his being *good. La, la, la, look at me; my life's great! What about yours, sucker? How are you doing over there in your good life? You should try my great life. It's GREAT!*

Or one of those annoyingly positive people who saw the *blessing* in every tragedy and were so *grateful* for the lesson when their husband abandoned them, they broke their arm, their child contracted rabies and their house burned down while they were out shopping. It didn't matter because *it was a great lesson* and they were *so grateful* for the experience! It was GREAT!

Oh, shit. He was still talking . . .

'. . . so I was wondering if you wanted to catch up for a coffee?'

Coffee? As in a date? But what about Christmas? Christmas, who had sent her a lovely text to say how very lucky she was to have Emily as her friend?

But Christmas was the very same friend who had explicitly told Emily that she wasn't interested in Lincoln and not to waste a good man in Tasmania. And while her best friend might choose to find happiness by cutting things out of her life, Emily liked to bring new things in. So why shouldn't she go out with him?

'Yes,' she said, returning to the sauntering pace. 'That sounds good.' But then a surge of excitement rushed through her body and she couldn't help adding, '*Really* good.'

•

Lincoln couldn't remember how long it had been since he'd dated someone in Australia. When he was overseas, with other workers or travellers, people were different. There were fewer rules. There were fewer expectations of a future together, fewer people you were answerable to—like interfering mothers, nosy neighbours or ex-partners—and fewer social obligations. Everybody knew that impermanence and transience lay beneath all their decisions.

So he hadn't expected his skin to prickle with heat beneath his jacket on such a cold day when he saw Emily walking towards him along the edge of the mangroves in front of Rosevears Tavern, dressed in tight jeans and some sort of knitted wrap, but that's what happened.

And then she was in front of him and she went for the hug and he went for the kiss on the cheek and he kissed her arm instead and there was a flailing of limbs and apologies and flushed cheeks and snorts from her (who doesn't like a girl who snorts?) and then she accidentally stood on his foot and her ankle rolled and she fell to the ground with her foot in the air and her face contorted and she yelped with pain and dropped her handbag and the contents spilled across the footpath and he swore over and over and tried to stop her lipstick from rolling into the gutter and patted her shoulder while she writhed and clutched at her calf to hold her foot up in the air and he went looking for his mobile phone but couldn't find it and didn't know who to call anyway until a man stepped across the road from the beer garden and said, 'Can I help? I'm a doctor.'

*

Emily shifted her weight across the squeaking plastic-covered bed in the back room of the doctor's surgery and sucked in her breath sharply through her teeth as Lincoln placed a fresh icepack on her ankle. Wordlessly, he took another pillow and gently raised her leg to elevate it a bit more. Then he passed her a plastic cup of water from the dispenser in the waiting room.

'Thanks,' she said, and sipped carefully on it. It was too cold. The air conditioning was too cold. She shivered.

'I think I saw a pile of blankets in the room next door,' Lincoln said, already rising again. He disappeared around the corner, leaving her to study the growth chart on the wall and the archaic-looking set of weight scales in the corner, the ones with the thingummybobs that slid from side to side.

He returned with a pale blue cotton blanket and covered her up. He sat down again in the chair by the bed.

'You don't have to wait here,' she said for the hundredth time. 'It's truly okay. It's no problem to catch a cab home. It's just a sprain.'

'I've already told you I'm not leaving you here,' he said. 'I'm so sorry. I feel awful.'

They'd been going round and round like this for the past hour, him apologising and self-flagellating, and her brushing it off and trying to send him home, when of course she didn't really want him to leave but she didn't want to seem needy either.

'Let's change the subject,' she said, wedging her right arm under the mountain of pillows behind her head. She stared into his beautiful but worried eyes. 'Why aren't you married?' She gave him a cheeky grin. 'My brother thinks you must be a criminal. Or crazy. Or divorced.'

'I like your brother. I think we should meet.'

'So what should I tell him?'

'Tell him he's a very good brother. Older? Of course he is. And you can tell him I'm not most of those things.'

'Most?' she said.

'But wait,' he said. '*You're* not married. Are you a criminal? Am I sitting here with a fugitive?' He looked over his shoulder.

'Touché. Okay. Let's do this. You go first.'

'I was married once.'

'When?'

'I was twenty-two. It was silly and it only lasted eight months. Her name was—still is—Benita. I met her at uni. It turned out she was more into her soccer-loving friend Giuseppe than me.'

'Sorry to hear that.'

'It's okay. Now, your turn.'

'Well, surely you're aware there's a man drought in Tasmania.'

'What do you mean? Dr Birtle looks like a fine catch.'

Emily rippled with giggles while shushing him. Dr Birtle, who'd been half cut on rum and Coke when he crossed the road outside the pub to help her, had long greasy hair, wore thongs and reeked of cigarette smoke.

'I'm still thinking you should get a second opinion on that, by the way,' Lincoln said, pointing to her ankle. 'I don't know that you should take the word of someone who carries a hip flask.'

'I think it's fine. He seems to have bandaged it quite well. And he gave me Panadol.'

'So, what else then, besides the man drought?'

'Well, let's see.' She took a moment to think back on her failed relationships. There was the workaholic, the unemployed lay-about, the one more into cyber people than real people, the one who used her as a rebound relationship, the one who used her for a one-night stand when she'd reasonably thought it was going to go further, the heartbreaking five-year relationship with a man who turned out to be just-not-that-into-her. 'Gosh, this is rather depressing.'

'In summary?'

'I simply haven't found Mr Right.'

'Hmm.'

'What?'

'Well, it sounds perfectly reasonable,' he said. 'You're attractive. Have a job. Only one head that I can see. You seem like a nice, normal person—shocking clumsiness and disastrous first dates aside.'

'Yes, there is that.' He was flirting with her! While she was in bandages on a doctor's bed! Well, this was all very *General Hospital*.

'So I see no reason why we shouldn't do this again,' he said definitively.

She couldn't stop the smile that spread across her face.

'But maybe we should meet sitting down next time,' he added.

'Or on horseback,' she said, and clasped her hands together melodramatically.

Lincoln squinted. 'Horses. Yes. They seem like sane, rational and safe animals. It seems completely sensible and statistically sound to balance on top of a half-tonne animal that can gallop at, what, a hundred kilometres an hour?'

'Something like that.'

'Then we should do that.'

'Okay.'

'It's a date.'

Lulu Divine was wearing a red and black woollen poncho and matching knitted beret and sat at the tiny table in Elsa's bungalow looking for all the world like some sort of dangerous animal. A red-bellied black snake perhaps. No, that was too harsh. But perhaps a wasp. Yes. One that was sharpening its stinging tail right now.

'What's in it for me?' she said.

Rita wheezed through the oxygen mask on her face, the little rolling trolley standing by her side. It was unnerving, the mask. And it was only because she'd had a cough for a while and the weather had turned very cold, a thick layer of snow descending over much of Tasmania in the past two days, and the nurses had decided to give her lungs a bit of support. But the sight of it made Elsa uneasy, as though it were the hand of death clamped down over Rita's nose and mouth to snuff her out. She shuddered. This was crazy. Where were all these morbid thoughts coming from? This wasn't like her at all.

'Have you n-no heart?' Rita ticced and wheezed, her hand shaking in what was probably a Parkinson's movement but did look a little like she was threatening with her fist.

'I gave up on heart a long time ago,' Lulu said quietly. 'I never found it to be a reliable companion.'

'That must be a lonely way to live,' Elsa said.

'I get by.'

'Love is the gr-greatest gift you can give someone else,' Rita said. 'It is a huge honour and privilege to match a couple and wat-t-t-ch them grow through life. I've successfully matched four couples in my time. Four weddings. Thirteen children.' Her voice filled with pride.

'So why do you need me?' Lulu asked.

Elsa stretched her stiff knee. 'We've hit a stumbling block. Christmas has turned Lincoln down.'

'So?'

'I thought of you, with your great success in competitions. I thought you might have some advice.'

'Elsa,' Rita ventured, 'are you positive that Lincoln should be with Christmas? There was no light.'

'I know,' Elsa said, 'but I think something was wrong. I believe Christmas is the one.'

'What light?' Lulu asked, narrowing her eyes and folding her hands in her lap.

Elsa gestured to Rita to explain the theory of the light, and she wheezily complied. 'Unfortunately, the light was not there between Lin-Lincoln and Christmas,' she finished. 'It was with Emily.'

Lulu thought about this. 'That doesn't mean anything,' she said finally.

Elsa's mouth watered, hungry for another opinion to match her own. 'Go on.'

'All that means is that Emily is the show queen, someone who can turn it on when she needs to. Someone who can use her charm to influence the judges.'

'You sound as though you've done this yourself,' Elsa said.

216

'I've had my time in the spotlight. But not everyone can sustain that brightness. I could. And I did. I was at the top of my game for as long as the competitions kept rolling round. But not everyone's like me.'

'No, they're not,' Elsa agreed.

'Most people are shooting stars. They flare and then fizzle. Like reality television identities. They start strong, confident, arrogant even. They can fake it well. But they get the wobbles. It's just a matter of time. True champions are rare.'

Elsa suddenly felt something like affection for Lulu, and reached for the pot of tea, adjusted the bright yellow cosy, and topped up her teacup for her.

'In my experience, you can always see it,' Rita said, as forcefully as the oxygen mask would allow. 'You walk a dangerous line thinking you know better than the light.'

'So what do we do?' Elsa said, ignoring Rita.

Lulu scoffed. Elsa recoiled, surprised.

'It's not all about her. To win a buckjumping competition you need a horse as well as the rider. The first thing you need to know is whether *your grandson* is a shooting star or a true champion.'

Rita remained silent, though Elsa was sure she felt a wave of smugness shoot from her—retribution for being ignored and replaced by this younger ring-in from the bungalow next door.

'What do you mean? Lincoln's wonderful.'

'Then why hasn't he settled down yet?' Lulu asked, a small smirk tugging at one corner of her sun-spotted lips. 'Why is he still galloping the world on a whim?'

Elsa felt her hackles prickle against her thermal underwear. 'Didn't you do that too?' she shot back.

'Exactly.' Lulu smiled thinly and Elsa wondered if there was some regret in the acknowledgement. 'I never wanted to be tamed. Perhaps Lincoln is the same. From where I sit, it looks like he has no intention of settling down at all. I think you need to face up to the fact that you're wasting your time.'

●

To: Lincoln van Luc
From: Barney Jones
Subject: Get your arse out here!

Mate u have got to get out here!! The outback will blow your mind!

U have to see it. I can't believe we live in this country and really know nothing about it. You think it's vast and empty but it's teeming with mind-blowing sights. Just yesterday I came across a fossil dig that uncovered so many gigantic dinosaur bones they couldn't move them. They're 98 MILLION years old!! There are rib bones TWO METRES long!! Leg bones so big they don't even fit on the back of a ute! They're so big I could lie down on them like a bed. And these blokes, you know, real outback blokes, just standing around swatting flies like this is just an ordinary day in the dirt and I'm thinking, shit, shouldn't you be getting some sort of security guard for these things? And they're just laughing their arses off at me and saying, well what's anyone gunna do with 'em? Feed 'em to the dog?

I've got more sculpture ideas than I know what to do with— dinosaur-bone furniture design! My sketchpad is full and I'm drawing on bits of bark.

Hey, and there's a job going here right up your alley. Something about researching fossilised ferns that are coming to the surface and also fossilised plankton from some inland sea.

Get out here, man.
Rubble

●

The day after her first big day out alone, Christmas was thankful to have Mim take her in hand and lead the way confidently through the streets, to a taxi, and to a restaurant for Saturday brunch. It was more like lunch, since the doors opened at midday, but she'd done as Mim had suggested and fasted all morning until they got there. An array of bicycles and motor-cycles lined the parking bays at the entrance to the building and a large chalkboard hung on the dark grey wall outside. It was just the two of them, Mim having sent Hank and Margot out on chores related to their upcoming trip to America, and Christmas was pleased. She was so grateful to be staying with Mim and her family, but she craved some time alone with her old friend.

Mim ushered her through the sombre front of the restaurant to the back, which was brightly lit. At a table for two, Mim sat in the chair and Christmas sat opposite on the bench seat along the wall, with huge white cushions at her back. Patrons filled the spaces either side of Christmas and she smiled good-naturedly at the woman next to her as they jostled their handbags into the small gap between their hips.

'You must always book ahead here,' Mim said, signalling a waiter, who appeared a moment later, briskly speaking to Mim while she nodded. She halted him a moment to address

Christmas. 'You choose your drink—coffee, tea, juice—and then the platters will start. Many types of food. You will find something you like.'

'Orange juice, thanks.'

Mim ordered the juice and a coffee for herself and the waiter disappeared. What seemed like only seconds later, the first platter arrived—a huge white square with an eclectic mix of cake, salmon, cucumber, eggs and salad. Christmas began on the salmon and salad; Mim started with the cucumber in a white cheese sauce.

'I still can't quite believe I'm here,' Christmas said, 'with you, I mean. After all that time of writing letters to each other, like you were some sort of imaginary friend, and now here we are, in the flesh. It's a bit like having brunch with a storybook character or something.'

'You are exactly how I imagined you would be,' Mim said, accepting the coffee from the waiter and directing the juice to Christmas's side of the table.

'Really? How so?' Christmas asked, amazed. To her eyes, Mim was similar, certainly, but she seemed to have lost the softness of girlhood and the romantic indulges she'd loved reading in her poetry. Now, she seemed so practical, so business-like and efficient.

Mim progressed onto the cake and closed her eyes with pleasure as she moved it around her mouth. Then, 'You are genuine.'

'Genuine?'

'Not pretentious. Not, ah, I don't know the word I'm looking for . . . maybe, plastic?'

'Plastic?'

Her friend giggled then, and Christmas suddenly saw that teenager she'd seen in the photos all those years ago. 'You have heart,' Mim said, affectionately.

'Thank you. That's a really lovely thing to say.'

'As for me, I am a stressed-out mum with an unnerving daughter and no idea what to do about it. There is something going on with her but she won't confide in me.' Mim's face scrunched in sadness and Christmas's heart lurched.

A waiter hovered, wanting to take the first platter and move them onto the next. Clearly, seat space was at a premium. But Christmas refused to be intimidated. She'd waited more than half her life to have this meal with Mim.

'I can't say I know what it's like to be a mum, but my sister has three boys and she worries all the time that she's not doing enough. I think all mothers beat themselves up when the truth is they're doing a superb job.'

'You think?'

'Absolutely. And, hey, you can cook! My sister just opens a can here and there and pops some toast on,' she said, cheekily— she was only joking . . . kind of—and was pleased to see Mim's face relax again. 'Margot will be fine. Being a teenager is tough, remember?'

Mim nodded, thoughtful.

'But we got through it,' Christmas assured her. 'And so will Margot. Don't underestimate yourself. You're a woman with a career and a loving relationship. I'm sure you're a much more powerful role model than you think.' She hoped her words had reassured Mim, at least a little, and given her back just some of the kindness she'd shared with Christmas so far.

'Okay,' Mim said, smoothing her brow with the back of her hand. 'Enough about me. Tell me all about your life, everything you've done for the past twenty years.'

They stayed in the restaurant for as much time as they could tease out of the anxious waiters, who eventually delivered all three huge platters of food (Christmas had had to loosen her trouser buttons to go on after the second). And when they finally wobbled out the door, they linked arms, swung their handbags happily, and strolled the nearby shops, and Christmas felt as though she belonged here in this beautiful city, at least for the day, with her friend at her side.

A couple of days later, left to her own devices once more, Christmas found herself drawn back to the river, emerging from the Metro at Pont Neuf under the bright and hot summer sun and heading west towards the seven arches of the Pont des Arts. On the way she lingered at the *bouquinistes*, the book dealers with their numbered metal pop-open stalls and hundreds of secondhand books, posters, postcards and magazines laid out under the green leaves of the overhanging trees.

'*Bonjour, madame,*' the dealers called, proffering books with yellowed pages; aged books with faded ink and fraying edges wrapped in protective plastic; hardbacks, leather-bounds, paperbacks; copies of French *Vogue*; and packs of ten postcards of cafe scenes, which she found hard to resist, handing over some notes before putting them in her satchel. She also bought a novel in French, even though she couldn't read it, because it had a stunning cover with a picture of sunlit wheat fields. The men shouted at her and waved her towards prints of the Mona Lisa and the Eiffel Tower, certain now they'd found an easy target.

'*Non, merci,*' she said, over and over, smiling and waving them gently away until they shuffled off in their sneakers and money belts towards the next set of tourists coming along the path.

Traffic rumbled past as she continued on her way to the Pont des Arts. At the pedestrian bridge, she stepped onto the wide wooden boards and took a deep breath. Far off in the distance, rearing many times as high as the highest building in view, was the real Eiffel Tower, standing dark and strong against the smoggy air, commanding the skyline.

The bridge was crowded and she couldn't hear her footsteps above the ceaseless rush of traffic on the road on the other side and the gushing of the river below as it charged into the pylons. A busker played the saxophone, his case open at his feet, sending out soulful notes to the crowd gathered around him, many sitting on the bridge. Christmas stopped too, listening to him play as she took in the sights around her.

She watched couples with their arms around each other, their faces beaming as they touched the thousands of padlocks chained to the railing as symbols of eternal love. Some took photos as they clipped their own padlocks to the metal grille or shared a picnic on a blanket, right there on the bridge under the mellow sunshine, a glass of wine in hand, feeding each other crusty bread dipped in olive oil. A man sat cross-legged against the padlock railing, a scarf around his neck, a notebook and pen in one hand and a cigarette in the other. Further along the bridge, another busker played an accordion. Someone cut into an orange and the sharp citrus tang hit her nostrils, propelling her back to The Apothecary, standing there with Lincoln and the smell of his aftershave. And her body rocked, hit with an invisible force.

Her breath caught in her chest. All she could think of was Lincoln and that kiss—the perfect kiss of truth, telling her it had to be over.

But why? Because she had some rule that said so?

Standing here now, the beauty of Paris flooding every one of her senses, optimism made her feel dizzy with possibility.

She'd been stupid. So stupid. Lincoln was lovely. Funny. Warm. Yummy to look at. They got on well. They worked together well. They both loved chocolate. They were creating a book together. He was single. She was single. And he liked her. He'd kissed her.

And she'd hurt him.

Why oh why had she pushed him away?

The saxophone busker finished his tune and the gathered crowd applauded and toasted him with wine and threw money into his case while he bowed.

Christmas began to jog to the left bank, across this bridge redolent with passion and amorous intoxication, which seemed to vibrate and urge her on. The stories in each and every one of those padlocks called to her. *Go find love, Christmas.*

She had to find a cafe with wi-fi. She had to contact Lincoln. Right now. Before it was too late.

•

Lincoln was just finishing up for the day. He'd been working on the book. For the past half hour he'd been writing about alkaloids. Theobromine was the alkaloid found in *Theobroma cacao*, and was part of the methylxanthine class of chemical compounds. He was trying to discuss the way certain medicines, such as analgesics and anaesthetics and recreational drugs like cocaine, were derived from alkaloids, and explain why dark chocolate makes us feel good. But it had all got very scientific. Very dull. There was far too much discussion of atomic structure. He needed to include more information on the interesting things. Like the way plants used alkaloids to kill or repel insects, for example.

Then again, most people would probably think that was dull too. He held down the backspace button on his keyboard.

Then he clicked undo. Maybe they *wouldn't* think it was dull. *He* didn't think it was dull, but then he was a botanist. He really didn't know what the average person thought. But then wasn't the point of a book like this to give people information they didn't know before?

He needed Christmas, and that thought made him instantly angry because he'd felt guilty after going out with Emily and that was stupid because Christmas had made it clear that she thought kissing him was a mistake, uttering those exact words as she pushed him out the door. It was humiliating, frankly. And that made him even crankier about the fact that he was still hung up on her. Worse, he'd been *hurt*, something that was not easy to admit, even to himself.

She was making him crazy.

He rubbed his hand over his chin. Maybe it was the beard. There was too much hair on his head and face, messing up his thoughts. Like tree roots growing into pipes and clogging them up. And it was winter. Everything slowed and shut down and froze up in winter. Except at the equator. The Amazon just kept going, like a twenty-four-hour marketplace. The jungle that never slept. But maybe here in Tasmania his brain had gone into hibernation.

He cast an eye at Caesar, lying on his back with his paws in the air, his long belly hair just begging to be rubbed. He thought about his grandmother. And he felt the walls closing in around him. He was starting to feel an uneasy sense of permanence towards this dog. When he checked for job prospects overseas he immediately wondered what would happen to Caesar. And then he wondered how he could leave his nan all alone with no one to visit her.

He got up and paced the room.

His phone beeped with a text message. It was from Christmas.

Hi. Just wanted to say how sorry I was about the way we said goodbye.

Lincoln read it twice. What should he say to that? It was okay? Well, it wasn't okay. He understood? But he didn't.

Still, just getting that text from her made him soften a little, let go of some of the anger. Then hot on the tail of that came burning questions.

Finally he typed, *Why did you push me away?*

He waited a long time for a response. For several agonising minutes he even thought she might not reply at all. Then his phone beeped.

It's complicated. But I'd like to see you again when I get back, apart from working on the book. Would that be okay? I'd like to make it up to you.

Now it was his turn to take his time. Part of him wanted to say that of course they could see each other, that nothing would make him happier. But another part thought that maybe it was a good thing she'd pushed him away when she did, because he'd become far too invested. And now he'd asked out Emily, again, and why shouldn't he see her? She was nice, funny, clumsy, and she didn't make his heart gallop like a racehorse, and that meant he could keep his head when he was around her.

At the same time, he couldn't bring himself to totally smash down Christmas's efforts. He wasn't a complete prick.

He decided to keep it simple.

Maybe.

●

Maybe?

On the other side of the world, Christmas read his message and her heart plummeted. But what did she expect? She'd shot

226

him down hard. She deserved to be on the back foot now. And at least he hadn't outright turned her down. There was still a chance. She'd created this and would have to be happy with a small, partial opening in the window of opportunity. But she didn't dare to ask for further clarification.

It was simply best not to ask.

18

Before she knew it, Christmas's week in Paris had flown by in a whirl of walking (she had blisters), feasting (the weight gain fortunately offset by the walking), photography (it would take her days to upload the pictures when she got home), window-shopping and sightseeing, balanced with joyful non-touristy hours spent in Mim's home as an extended member of their family. She'd offered to be on kitchen clean-up duty each night alongside Margot and had become quite fond of the girl. Her English was excellent and she regaled Christmas with stories of her school life and friends as they packed the dishwasher and scraped food into the sink's disposal system. Christmas had no doubt that Margot had a secret life she was carefully protecting, but she also saw her natural sweetness and warmth during those nightly discussions.

When Margot then retreated to her room for homework and study, and Hank disappeared onto his laptop or mobile phone— with many last-minute things to organise for the dental surgery before they left for America—Christmas and Mim spent hours sitting on the balcony, overlooking the Haussmann buildings glowing brightly in the extended evening sunlight, drinking wine and talking about life.

Christmas had avoided the museums and galleries, but had taken a boat ride down the Seine, which was simply magical, and climbed the Eiffel Tower, which was packed with tourists and not as much fun as she'd hoped, but she'd spent many hours on the lawns surrounding the construction, eating her packed lunch, just sitting quietly and absorbing the atmosphere and gorgeous weather. And now it was her last evening with Mim, Hank and Margot; she would be flying to Marseille tomorrow afternoon.

She reclined against the leather seats of the family's shiny black car as it sailed through the yellow-lit streets of Paris towards the left bank, where they were taking her for her farewell dinner. Beside her, Margot's earphones emitted scratchy music sounds and she gazed out her own window, her pretty face looking tired.

Christmas felt for her. The final years of high school were difficult, with enormous peer pressure, and the French culture set high expectations of its young people. How could it not? Look what lay on every street! Beauty and craftsmanship and grandeur. Inside every French person must lie some sort of molecular connection to the masters of art and design who built this city into what must surely be the most beautiful in the world.

Suddenly, she realised that all of this must be part of her too. The very genes that made up half her body had come from someone who breathed this country's air, drank its water, lay in its sun, ate its food and grew up surrounded by its extraordinary beauty. It was all in her too.

Did it matter that instead of visiting the Louvre she'd spent afternoons when she was young visiting her grandparents' red-brick home in Hobart and eating fish and chips by the water, throwing batter to the seagulls? She was French. How had she reached nearly forty years of age and never really believed it? Or felt it, more to the point.

But she *had* felt it, wandering through the royal bedrooms of Versailles palace, picturing the people who'd lived there, imagining waking up in a bed in a room the size of a ballroom, absorbing the history as though she was part of it, because she *was* part of it. The French history was her history too.

And she'd felt it in the Latin Quarter, watching old men playing chess while sitting on wooden crates and smoking cigars. Watching men and women in business suits ordering coffee and food and talking on their phones just as they would down near the docks in Hobart. Getting lost in the twisty, winding laneways. Finding herself unexpectedly alone in deserted, quiet streets and wondering where all the people had gone. Then finding them again a few minutes later, swarming outside bakeries and fresh food markets as though they'd never seen or smelled anything so wonderful as the baguettes that left the stores wrapped in paper, or the soft figs that sat piled on wooden barrows on the footpath.

It was all part of her.

And that made her feel special. And capable. Maybe it was only when we compared ourselves to others that we truly saw who we were. It was like chocolate tasting: it could be difficult to identify flavours in a piece of chocolate until you compared it with a different piece. Only then could you pick out and appreciate the uniqueness of each.

She loved The Chocolate Apothecary. Adored it. But now she wondered what more might lie beyond the walls of her store. Her ten rules for happiness kept her safe and content and steady. And that was important. But they also set limits. It was entirely possible that she'd stalled; her life was sitting comfortably in neutral. What if she changed the rules? What could she do then?

'You will love this place,' Mim said, turning around in her seat to grin at Christmas as Hank manoeuvred a reverse park. 'Have you ever tried *l'andouillette*?'

'No, I haven't,' Christmas said, unbuckling her belt and peering out at a small stone two-storey building with a tiny Juliet balcony on the upper floor, and a couple dining by candlelight, with vines clambering up the iron railing.

'It's the best in Paris,' Hank boomed happily. She could almost hear him salivating. Even Margot had brightened, and she removed her earphones, straining to see the elegant crowd gathered at the entrance, with its red ropes and a bouncer, as though waiting to enter an exclusive club.

'We made a reservation as soon as we knew you were coming,' Margot said now, smiling at her.

'Thanks. That was really thoughtful. What is *l'andouillette*, exactly?' Christmas asked.

Hank grinned and Mim chuckled. 'Warm stomach sausage,' Hank said.

'Oh.'

'You game to try something new?'

Christmas took a deep breath of Parisian air. 'You know, I think I am. How bad could it be?' And as she stepped out onto the lamp-lit footpath, she made the decision right then to say goodbye to the ten rules of happiness.

•

Darla Livingstone pulled her sleeping bag more tightly around her inside the back of her Kombi van. It was stiffly cold tonight. The sky above the sclerophyll forest was a dome of black and indigo, with diamond-white stars sprinkled as liberally as the hundreds-and-thousands on the fairy bread she used to make for Christmas on Sunday mornings for breakfast.

Darla was angry. But she wasn't totally sure why, and that made her all the angrier. It irked her, this idea of Christmas being in Paris. Her daughter's parting questions about Gregoire had left her feeling scratched, the implication that she was a bad mother leaving marks the way koalas' claws cut into the eucalypt trunks as they fought for a footing.

It had been the seventies. Back then unwed mothers in Australia were still being forced into giving up their children for adoption. Christmas was lucky she even knew who her mother was.

Darla rolled over and punched the pillow into a different shape just as her mobile phone lit up and buzzed against the torch. She hesitated when she saw the name on the screen, then picked it up anyway. 'Joseph? I was asleep.'

A pause. 'It's only six o'clock.'

'And winter. The bush goes to bed at five o'clock these days. It's not like I can just pop out for dinner and a movie.'

'Mmm.'

'What's up?'

He continued, as he'd always done. Patiently. His calm principal attitude to everything had always driven her nuts. No matter how outrageous she became, no matter what she tried to provoke him, he just looked at her like she was a social project to be dealt with.

'. . . so I thought we should talk about the wedding. See if we can come to a place of mutual support. For Valerie's sake.'

Darla rolled her eyes in the dark. 'Not her too. Is there some sort of campaign going to find me Worst Mother of the Year or something?'

'Sorry?'

'Never mind,' she muttered. 'Just Christmas asking questions about her father again. Hello? Joseph, you're breaking up. The signal out here is terrible. Hello? Can you hear me?'

'. . . her father . . .'

'Her bloody father! That's all I hear about these days. Not a phone call to talk to me about my work, how many animals I've found, how the research is going, or if I've hooked up with a drover or anything, no, it's all about weddings and Gregoire Lachapelle, the man who made goat cheese. No one cares what I'm doing . . . hello? Joseph?'

She switched off the phone, tossed it on top of her hiking boots and pulled her beanie down furiously.

●

Val blew her nose loudly and opened her jaw wide to pop her ears. 'Ugh. I'm sick of the green stuff,' she said miserably.

Joseph winced. Decades of teaching children and he'd never got used to snot. It was the one thing he couldn't stomach. He'd once held a boy on his lap for over an hour applying pressure to the gushing wound on his head where it had hit the concrete. He'd applied a first-aid bandage to an arm that was clearly broken in two places. And he'd mopped up vomit more times than he could count. But the snot? He shuddered.

'Here.' He handed her a cup of tea and directed her to the kitchen table to sit down.

'Thanks.'

'I spoke to your mother on the way over tonight,' he said, focusing on chopping the carrots and celery for the fried rice. Nate sat perched on a tall stool beside him, his collection of sauce bottles in front of him, waiting for the right time to add them to the pan.

Willis swaggered by, a wrench in his hand, smacking it against his palm, his eyes focused out the window. Joseph eyed his eldest grandson. If Willis were one of his students, he'd be directing him into a specialised stream for boys. Some kind of manhood development program. He was just the right age for it and was exactly the type that would do well with mentor-directed activities. He knew he should speak to Val about it, but it was hard to know when to step in with advice. No parent liked to think they were missing something. But it did take a village to raise a child. It was the eternal balancing act of knowing that a parent always knew best, except when they didn't.

'I wanted to talk to her about the wedding,' he went on, dropping the carrots and celery into the hot oil. 'Here, mate, stir that,' he said, passing the wooden spoon to Nate.

'What about it?' Val said, sipping her tea.

'I just hoped I could encourage her to be a bit more supportive.'

'Yeah, well. That's just Mum, isn't it?'

'But I know it hurts when she's so dismissive.'

Val's eyes went bright and she looked quickly at the floor. 'Yeah. I guess.'

Joseph waited for more. Silence always encouraged the other person to open up. This time was no exception.

'I know Archie and I have been together forever. But it's still . . .'

'Special?'

'Exactly.'

'Of course it is,' he said.

'I'm lucky I've got my dad,' she said.

'It's odd, I was talking to her about the wedding, and I wanted to ask her how she might like to be involved, you know, maybe see if we can get a bit more spirit from her, when out of the blue she mentioned Christmas and said something about Gregoire.' As he spoke he wished, yet again, that he'd been able to play a more active role in Christmas's life when she was young, but grateful they were still close. 'It was a bad line so I didn't catch everything, but she said that no one cared about her and they only wanted to know about the man who studied goat diseases.'

Val straightened. 'Really? That's more than she's ever told Christmas. How exciting. A scientist! That's kind of ironic, given she's working with Lincoln the botanist now. Come to think of it, Mum's kind of a scientist too. In a mad, decapitating-animals way.'

'And I teach science. Not big on the decapitating though.'

'Yes! That's true! How did Christmas and I turn out so *not* sciency?'

'Cooking's a science,' Nate said gravely, pouring in the oyster sauce.

Joseph rubbed the back of Nate's neck. 'Good job, mate.' He looked around. 'Where's Braxton?'

'In his room. A new pack of dinosaur books arrived so we won't see him for a week now.'

'I better go get him, then.'

'Oh, this is great. I must email Christmas with the news about Gregoire.'

●

The teapot sitting on the coffee table in Emily's lounge was covered with a knitted tea cosy in the shape and colours of a bright red strawberry, with the green leaves and stalk forming the handle.

'You really didn't have to bring me food,' Emily said, putting a tray with teacups, a sugar bowl and a tiny milk jug down in front of Val. 'You look like you need food deliveries more than I do right now. You look terrible, frankly.' She limped back to the couch to sit down and propped up her foot on the footstool.

'Thanks. Just what a girl always loves to hear,' Val said, simultaneously wiping her nose and reaching for the teapot. Perhaps she should have washed her hair before she came, she thought. Emily still looked nice, despite having been off her feet for days. Maybe Val was getting too fat and comfortable in her almost-married state. 'Nice cosy, by the way.'

'My colleague, Rupna, gave it to me. She's a mad knitter and needs to offload some of her work from the house before her boyfriend divorces her. Apparently he's more of a modern-design, clean-freak type.'

'Oh well, it sounds like they're a match made in heaven.' Val laughed. 'And don't worry about the food. Dad came over last night and made a mountain of fried rice to help me while I'm sick. Anyway, I've been meaning all week to come over and drop off some food to help you with your sprained ankle, but then the flu got hold of me and everything turned to crap. So I'm sorry I'm late. The thought was there days ago.'

'Much appreciated,' Emily said.

'Hang on a minute. Why are you drinking tea? Aren't you a coffee addict?'

Emily twisted her lower lip. 'Yes. But my migraines have been a bit out of control lately. I seem to have them if I don't have coffee and if I do. I'm not sure which is worse though, so I'm still experimenting.' She took a sip and screwed up her freckled nose. 'I've been trying hard, but I really haven't found any teas I like, despite all the recommendations Christmas has given me.'

'Oh no!' Val slapped her forehead. 'I meant to email Christmas last night to tell her that Dad found out from Darla that Christmas's dad was a scientist who studied diseases on farms.'

'Really?'

'Isn't that amazing?'

'Yes, it is. This is perfect! It might finally be the thing that convinces her to try to make contact with Gregoire! But you didn't email her?' Emily said.

'No. My head was so full of mucus I couldn't think straight. I've got so much sinus pain it's hard to look at a computer screen right now. All I want to do is lie down in bed with a bottle of brandy and not get up again until this horrible lurgy is gone.'

'I can email her,' Emily said. 'I've got a heap of work to do online tomorrow so I'll do it then. Take it as a small thanks for the food. I'm on the mend and you look like you could use another week off.'

'I fear you're right. The house is falling apart. It's complete chaos in every room.'

'So, same as usual then?' Emily smiled.

'Yep. Same as usual.'

●

Emily reached down to the floor beside the couch where she'd been lying for the past hour, ever since Val had left, with an ice pack over her eyes and the curtains and blinds closed. Her fingers groped around on the carpet seeking her mobile phone, as much to shut off the shrill noise as to answer it. She tried not to shift her position on the couch. Any small movement of her neck sent wild throbbing pain shooting through every part of her head. Even her teeth hurt.

At last she found the cool metal of the phone. She brought it to her chest, used one finger to lift the ice pack just enough for an eye to see the green button, pressed it and immediately dropped the ice pack back into place.

'Hello,' she whispered. Even the sound of her own voice was too much.

'Hi. I got your text,' Lincoln said, sounding concerned.

'I'm so sorry,' she said, her words still soft. 'I seem to be a disaster when it comes to dating you.'

'It's okay. It's not your fault. And I didn't really want to drink award-winning wine and eat four courses of gourmet food and sit by a roaring fire in a stone manor overlooking rolling green hills and mist and ducks on a pond, with good company and charming and funny anecdotes that I may have spent a week preparing and which are guaranteed to win over the pretty girl I'm with. I mean, who in their right mind would want to do that?'

'Don't make me laugh; it hurts.'

'Sorry. Is there anything I can do?'

'Sadly, no. Not unless you have some sort of black-market migraine-strength pain relief.'

'If we were in Ecuador, maybe. But here? Not so much. Is there anything else?'

'No. Oh, wait. Yes. I was supposed to email Christmas to give her some news about her father. Apparently, her mother says he's some sort of microbiologist who studies farm crops. Could you tell her?'

'Er . . . wouldn't that be better coming from you?'

A pause.

'Emily? Are you still there?'

'Uh. Yeah. Um, I think I'm about to vomit. Look, could you just email her? I've really got to go.'

19

The first night of the scholarship course in Provence wasn't going anything like Christmas had thought it might. She was currently sitting on the floor in front of Master Le Coutre's shoes. They were very nice shoes, made of some kind of soft forest-green leather with neat rows of stitching around the soles and on the upper. They had the air of handcrafted pieces. The hem of his dark trousers brushed his fine woollen socks as he swayed back and forth in front of the group, waltzing by himself. His silver hair, the suggestion of white whiskers, and leathery tanned skin conveyed his years. The tops of his ears wilted gently outwards, as though they were tired of standing upright. But his eyes burned with a fierce youthful confidence and zest for life. Whenever he spoke, his eyes widened and his brows and forehead raised, and he held an expression of perpetual questioning, as though waiting for answers he might not have even asked. Right now, though, his eyes were closed as he hummed the Blue Danube.

This was how they would learn to make chocolate, he'd said. First, you learned to dance. Then to make love. Then chocolate. 'You cannot dance without balance,' he explained. 'You cannot dance without a partner. Nor can you craft chocolate without these things. The flavours are your balance. The ingredients, your partner. You must have mutual respect and support for each other for a winning performance, an event that will leave no one unmoved.' He paused here for so long that Christmas wondered if they were supposed to respond. But it seemed that no one was brave enough to speak or ask questions.

'You probably think you already know how to make love,' he said. 'You think because you can fit all the pieces together and get some sort of enjoyment out of it that you have succeeded. *Non*! It is rubbish! What does it mean to make love?'

Christmas very much hoped that was a rhetorical question, and sighed with relief when he continued without waiting for a reply.

'Attention to detail. Intimate knowledge, exploration and experimentation. Tender, gentle caresses. At times, robust activity. All the senses. Softening. Consuming. Taking another into your mouth. Becoming one.'

Oh boy. Christmas lowered her eyes to the floor.

'Making love and making chocolate, they are not so different, *non*?'

'Right on!' Philomena cheered.

The toes of his soft shoes made little sound on the flagstones of the private room in the Aix-en-Provence restaurant. Christmas shifted her weight. The hardness of the stone was beginning to make her lower back ache, unsurprising since she, and the four other scholarship winners, had been sitting here for what felt like an inordinate length of time while Master Le Coutre shared his offbeat wisdom.

They were supposed to be enjoying a first-night get-to-know-you meal with their teacher, but Christmas hadn't had a chance to speak to any of the others properly yet. Master Le Coutre had entered the room just as the first glasses of wine were being poured and whisked them away from the dinner table. He'd taken them to the open space near the unlit fireplace, where he'd given a speech to welcome them, surveying them with his deep grey eyes, then announced that he would rather 'demonstrate than ruminate' on what the magic of chocolate making was all about.

To Christmas's right, Philomena Sarah (a Martha Stewart lookalike 'from Denver, Colorado, U-S-AAAA!') was scribbling notes in the back of her well-worn and food-stained recipe book— Master Le Coutre's *The Art and Genius of Chocolate*, which she'd brought for him to sign.

On the other side of Philomena was Henry Jacobs, a greying gentleman from Gloucestershire in the south of England, who wore tweed, smelled of cigars, walked with a cane and had been given a chair to sit on, rather than directed to the floor like the others.

To Christmas's left was Tibbie Tottie Taylor, from California, who looked like a cheerleader and chewed gum.

And beside Tibbie Tottie was Jackson Kent from Johannesburg. He had briefly introduced himself as a police officer wanting a career change. Fair enough, too. Christmas's mind had flicked momentarily to what life must be like for a policeman in South Africa and she had quickly decided that a career with chocolate won hands down.

While Master Le Coutre continued to dance, an impatient waiter hovered in the background, twisting a napkin, obviously keen to get on with serving dinner. The flickering candles around the room gave the man's thin face a dramatic gothic appearance.

Christmas's stomach growled. She hadn't eaten anything since some pretzels from the minibar in her hotel room this afternoon. Her plane into Aéroport Marseille Provence had been delayed and she'd not had time to grab anything before meeting the courtesy shuttle bus for the forty-minute trip to the city of Aix-en-Provence and the hotel. Once there, she'd had a bit of time to relax and settle into her room. She'd flicked through the room service menu and considered ordering something, but the description of the dinner in the scholarship's welcome letter sounded wonderful, and there were five courses of it, so she wanted to save herself and be able to enjoy every mouthful. Right now she really wouldn't mind tucking into the promised red bell pepper soup with crab mayonnaise, wild mushroom and summer truffle omelette, and spit-roasted lamb leg with herbs of Provence. Hell, she'd even try the squab if it was hot and available. But the way Master Le Coutre was going, it didn't look like she'd be eating any time soon.

He folded himself down to the ground, not fluidly as a young person might, but nonetheless with grace and dignity, and began patting one of the arms of his cable-knit jumper as though stroking the long hair of a woman, and cooing gently to it in French poetry. Or maybe it wasn't poetry. Practically everything said in French sounded like poetry to her ears.

But, oh boy. If this was what dance lessons would be like, what on earth would the lessons on lovemaking involve?

Unsurprisingly, her thoughts turned to Lincoln. And that kiss.

She trembled. But whether it was from the thought of lessons in lovemaking, or simply a lack of food, she wasn't sure.

•

It was time for some truth telling.

Elsa heard Lincoln's car pull up outside and straightened her spine. She had to motivate him into action. He'd always needed a push here and there. He had been a dreamy, thoughtful child who often spent his days perched up in the apple tree. He was happy to help out with chores and liked to feel useful. But he was, unfortunately, rather passive. He took life as it came and had never really planned too far ahead. Look at that disastrous pseudo-marriage in his twenties: he clearly hadn't thought too much about that, just agreed to go along with the idea when the girl had suggested it. Gosh, what was her name? Elsa rubbed at her temple.

So now, with Lincoln here, she laid it out for him. 'Lincoln, you are a lovely, sweet and kind boy. And I know I'm not supposed to have favourites, but you are my favourite grandchild.'

He twisted his foot on the floor then, like an awkward teenager under a gush of unwanted emotion, and reached for the dog's ears for something to do with his hands.

'But you're a bit lazy.'

His head jerked up, his jaw a little loose. 'What?'

'You're forty-two years old and you're still cruising through life. Do you know what you're doing next year?' Elsa raised her eyebrows.

'No,' he said, with a note of resentment in his voice.

'Do you know what you're doing next month?'

'No.' Firmly this time. Challenging.

'How about next week?'

'Nan, what is this about?' Crossing his arms now.

'I want you to stay here.' The words were out, finally. They'd been sitting in her chest since the moment he'd arrived back from Ecuador—hairy, delivering chocolate, wearing that relaxed smile he always had when he came back from a trip.

Her eyeballs stung. She had no right in the world to say it. But she didn't care if things could be fixed with Tom. Not really. She was pragmatic enough to know that she and her son were so very different and there was so much water under the bridge that things between them would never be okay. Lincoln was the one she wanted. She'd transferred her affection from her son to her grandson long ago. The reality was that Tom never stood a chance in her heart once Lincoln lay in her arms.

Was that so bad?

Yes. It was.

But could she help it?

Apparently not.

Lincoln's eyes held hers gently. Too gently. She looked away in disgust and tried to slow the beating of her heart.

'And what else?' he said. 'What else do you want?'

In for a penny, in for a pound, Ebe always said.

'Alright, then. I want you to get married. Have children. Stay here in Tasmania. Bring them to visit me after school.' Then she realised she probably wouldn't be around when they were at school. She rubbed her slippered toe against Caesar's chest. 'I think I might even want this dog to visit me.'

Lincoln took a deep breath and whistled slowly through his teeth. 'So a chocolate basket won't do?'

'Well, I *would* like some more of Christmas Livingstone's chocolates.' She smacked her lips. 'But I need more than that.'

He scratched absently at his head till his hair stuck up like a cockatoo's tuft at the back. She wanted to lick her hand and smooth it down the way she had when he was a boy and had just woken up, sitting at the kitchen table and waiting for his boiled eggs and toast soldiers.

It was like it was yesterday. How could time spin around like that? Time wasn't linear as everyone assumed. It couldn't be. It must twist like a tornado and you sat inside the funnel and every now and then you could catch a gust as it came rushing past and ride it for a bit before dropping back into the funnel.

'You've always supported my work and travel plans,' he said, sounding slightly aggrieved. 'What's changed?'

'I'm old now.'

'No you're not,' he said automatically, though she saw the fear in his eyes. 'You've got plenty of time.'

'No. I don't. And neither do you. You're halfway through your life and you've never really committed to anything.'

Benita! That was his ex-wife's name.

'That's not fair.'

'Perhaps. But I'm too old for fair. At times in my life I've been fair when I shouldn't have been. Now I want to be unreasonable and selfish. Let someone else have a turn at being fair. It's time for you to grow up, Lincoln. It's the way the world works and you're no exception to the billions of other people who share it.'

'I'm committed to my job.'

'You're committed to short-term contracts.'

'And as for marriage and kids, I just haven't found the right person. Would you have me marry just for the sake of it?'

'Of course not, don't be daft. But I don't believe there is only one right person out there for us. It's more about *you* being in the *right* frame of mind.'

Lincoln got up and started to pace the room, then stopped to look out the cheap louvres at the driveway, where Rita Blumberg's daughter and her two children had just pulled up and were racing into the main building, so excited to see their gran.

Elsa was on a roll now. 'What about Christmas Livingstone?'

He grunted under his bearded breath. 'I told you, she's not interested.' The audible sting in his voice wounded her heart a little. Love was such a complicated beast. Perhaps Rita had been right and Christmas wasn't the one after all. But Elsa had been so sure.

She sighed, resigned. 'Well then, what about her friend, Emily?'

'She's been sick,' he muttered grumpily.

'And?'

'And what?'

'And have you been around with chicken soup?'

He laughed and scrunched his fists against his eyes in frustration. 'I'm not a housewife who calls on the neighbours.'

'That's very narrow-minded of you, Lincoln. Aren't you a new age yoga type?'

'What?'

'I just mean don't underestimate the power of chicken soup, dear. Didn't someone write a book about that?'

'You can be very pushy sometimes, Nan.'

'Good.'

They eyed each other until the sound of an ambulance's siren diverted their attention. They watched out the window for a bit until they realised what had happened and Elsa reached for Lincoln's arm.

Rita's family had been rushing not because they were so excited to see her but because it was an emergency. Now, Elsa's new and treasured friend, Rita, was being packed into the ambulance before her very eyes.

It was early in the morning and Christmas sat in the corner of her hotel room, a modern affair with luxe furnishings and two separate balconies that were drenched in morning sunlight and overlooked the city of Aix. Here, closest to one of the balconies with its round cafe table and climbing vine up the wall, she could access the complimentary wi-fi. It was a beautiful room. One thing people couldn't say about Master Le Coutre was that he was cheap.

Her stomach was rumbling again, anticipating a big breakfast of croissants and berry yoghurt, but she wanted to see if Val was logged onto Skype so she could tell her about the mad Master Le Coutre and his plans for dancing and lovemaking lessons. It was almost time for school pick-up, but she might just catch her.

She opened Skype. Val's photo appeared with a green tick to show she was online. Christmas was just about to type her a message when another online contact popped up: Lincoln.

Her fingers froze over the keyboard. Her nerves quickstepped.

After Master Le Coutre's dancing last night, and the memory of that kiss, she'd been unable to sleep for a long while. Her mind had kept imagining things, things about Lincoln. She'd tried to push the thoughts away but they kept coming back. She'd tossed and turned but her imagination was an obstinate mule refusing to think of anything else except what life might be like with Lincoln in it.

And now a chat message had arrived.

Hi. You online?

Was she online? Well, clearly her Skype status said she was. But did she want to be online for him? She typed tentatively, wondering where this would go after his last, cryptic message. *Maybe.* But she wanted to talk to him.

Yes. Hi. What are you up to?

Caesar and I are having afternoon tea and a chat about philosophy.

That's cute.

Also, it's been a bit of a rough day.

What happened?

My nan and I had a 'chat' and she told me what she thought about a few things.

What do you mean? What about?

It doesn't matter. But I saw you were online and I wanted to touch base with you. The last couple of times we've spoken have been kind of messy.

It's my fault.

Well, let's just say we're friends again, okay?

Absolutely ☺

But enough of that. How's the land of frogs?

Paris was great. Amazing great! I'm in Provence now and have met the other winners of the scholarship and the famous Master Le Coutre, who is a little eccentric to say the least!

There was a long pause, then:

That sounds great.

And then, nothing.

It was impossible to read tone and emotion properly through cyberspace, but she was certain she could feel some sort of sadness. She typed quickly.

Are you okay? You seem a bit down.

Another long pause.

I guess.

Now it was her turn to hesitate. What could she say in a chat box that would possibly cheer him up? She suddenly wished she was with him so she could pat him on the arm, or make him a coffee, or feed him some of her Kahlua-laced hot chocolate. Or hold his hand and kiss him till he smiled again.

But she couldn't do any of that from the other side of the world.

Do you want to play a game?

She stalled for a moment before hitting the enter key, then sent it off into the ether and held her breath for several painful moments before he replied.

Okay.

She smiled, relieved.

This is a game Val and Emily and I play when we've had a few drinks. It's called Twisted Title. You take a movie or book title and change it around so it sounds like the original but has a new meaning. So, I'll start with 'Schindler's Wrist', the story of a brave physiotherapist who saved people from carpal tunnel syndrome. Get it? Your turn.

A very long pause in which Christmas got the giggles just waiting to see what he'd come back with. Finally, the little pen symbol popped up to show that Lincoln was typing at his end. A warm summer breeze blew in the doorway from her balcony.

'Legally Frond', a happy but ditzy fern overcomes prejudice in the rainforest community.

Christmas hooted with laughter.

Hey, you're a natural! And bonus points for making it botanically related. Okay, my turn . . . umm . . . . Oh! 'Love Practically', the touching story of ten tradesmen who find love on the work site.

Good one! Alright . . . 'Gnarly and Me', the story of a guy and his surfboard.

'Madame Ovary'—memoirs of an ageing hen.

'Silence of the Clams'.

Just an underwater shot of a bunch of clams sitting around
doing nothing. Admittedly, it didn't do very well at the box
office, but it was a cult hit among insomniacs.

Christmas was having so much fun and found herself
laughing so hard she ignored a notification about a message from
her sister. This was too good to stop now.

Her turn again.

'101 Palpitations'—the agony and ecstasy of being in love.

And she'd hit enter before she could think twice about it.

•

The agony and ecstasy of being in love.

Lincoln leaned back in his computer chair. Why would she
write that? Was it a coded message? A slip of the typing fingers?

He tapped the keys, wondering what to say in return. He
didn't want to stuff it up now that they'd just begun to get back
to how good things were before the kiss. And if she was admit-
ting her true feelings for him then that was brave and he wanted
to be equally brave in return. Suddenly, the whole sidestep he'd
taken towards Emily reeked of childishness. Christmas had hurt
him so he'd wanted to hurt her back.

But now he wanted nothing more than to be with her again.

I can't top that, he wrote. *But I know exactly what you mean.*

20

Later that morning, Christmas found herself dancing in Jackson Kent's strong arms. Clearly a stickler for the rules, the policeman was taking the lesson very seriously. Philomena was dancing with Henry, who had cast off his cane for the moment and was waltzing slowly and smoothly, as though he'd been doing it for decades. Tibbie Tottie was waltzing with Master Le Coutre.

'Hand on my shoulder,' Jackson said, shrugging his deltoid to indicate that Christmas had let her hand slip.

'Sorry.' Then, 'Oops!' She trod on his foot again. Rather incongruously, they were waltzing to Céline Dion's 'Only One Road'. Céline was singing in French, but Christmas knew the lyrics well. 'It's like the whole of France has set out to torture me with love songs and poetry,' she said, her heart still aflutter from Lincoln's declaration.

'What's that?' Jackson said, sweating now as he guided her

once more around the room, the same space at the back of the restaurant where they'd met the night before.

'Nothing.' She smiled brightly, puffing a little herself.

Master Le Coutre addressed them over Tibbie Tottie's shoulder. 'Remember why you are dancing,' he commanded. 'You are looking for synchronicity, the blending of bodies and minds to move as one, for one purpose and one connection. Effortless communication. Spiritual union. Sumptuous delight.'

Christmas rolled her eyes and Jackson broke rank for a moment.

'Did you just laugh?' she whispered.

'Certainly not.' But his eyes flashed glee.

As his dance partner, gazing into his eyes was something she was supposed to be doing a lot of but she'd felt far too self-conscious to do so. Now their eyes locked and she got a fit of giggles, waves and waves of them, which quickly spread to Jackson, who made small puffing noises from his wide nostrils that she could recognise as giggles because the corners of his eyes had crinkled. For a few moments, they sailed around the room in unison, awkwardness and tension gone, somehow having reached a perfect point of connection.

A hot gust of wind blew in through the open shutter, bringing with it the sound of a bicycle bell and a waft of bread baking in the wood-fired oven in the kitchen. Christmas had to admit that it was quite nice being held in the steady arms of a man who wasn't bad looking. That scar on his nose actually added a good deal of mystery and character. His square chin was more like a boxer's than she would normally go for. But it was nice to move around the room in his arms. If she didn't count that one embrace with Lincoln, it had been years since she'd been held by a man. By Simon, to be exact. A man with a weak chin, she thought now, upon reflection.

Thinking of Simon made her lose concentration and she tripped and fell against Jackson's chest. He caught her effortlessly. 'Never mind,' he said kindly, helping her regain balance.

She smoothed the hem of her shirt, which attracted Jackson's gaze for a second before he resumed his impenetrable expression.

'Thanks. Sorry.'

'It's no concern,' he said, taking her hand.

As they continued to dance, Céline Dion's voice filled her mind, urging her on to feel more than she'd permitted herself to for a long time. After she'd lost the baby, after she'd grieved messily and unexpectedly deeply, after she'd said goodbye to Simon and a relationship she'd known was never right but which had still been important, she'd carefully packed her heart in bubble wrap, trussed it with rope and clicked a padlock into place.

Her feet moved. *One, two, three, one, two, three, one, two, three* . . . She tried to concentrate on counting the waltz steps, but Céline wouldn't shut up. Love found and lost. Paths chosen. Lives connected. A thunderbolt of passion. A sensuous love affair.

Shut up!

But it was too late. Between the beat of the music and the steps of the waltz, Christmas heard the tiniest ping of a lock clicking open beneath her breastbone.

And the idea that Lincoln just might feel the same way scared and excited her in equal measure.

●

To: Christmas Livingstone
From: Abigail Hurst
Subject: Shop Update

Hi Christmas—I hope you're going well and having a great time in Paris. I just wanted to give you an update on the shop. One week down, two to go. So far, so good. Massages have dropped off but that's pretty typical for winter. Hot chocolate is doing a roaring trade. People have missed your handmade pieces but a few have ventured into trying imported bars, nothing exotic though. Thanks to some snowfalls, sales of throw rugs, knitted socks and scarves have increased. I haven't seen Cheyenne this week so the flower stand is bare. I tried calling her yesterday but got no answer. Would you like me to try to find some flowers somewhere else?

Abigail

————

To: Abigail Hurst
From: Christmas Livingstone
Re: Shop Update

Hi Abigail, thanks for the update. I'm in Provence now and we're off on farm tours tomorrow.

Glad to hear all is going well but it's a bit strange about Cheyenne. Do you think you should pop around to her place and make sure she's okay? Maybe hold off on flowers until you've spoken to her. For now, try arranging some vertical products in the silver flower buckets, maybe dried lavender bunches, those little heart-shaped blackboards on sticks, and some soap pyramids in between.

Thanks, Christmas

P.S. Could you let me know as soon as you know that Cheyenne's okay? That's a bit worrying.

———

To: Christmas Livingstone
From: Rosemary McCaw
Subject: You

Dearest Christmas Angel,

I hope this letter finds you calm of spirit. I have been keeping a watchful eye on The Chocolate Apothecary. Your vibrancy is sorely missed. The place feels empty and bereft of ambience. The Abigail girl is doing her best, but she has no charm or enviable attributes as far as I can see. Don't get me wrong; transactions are happening and customers seem content. But the intangible gift of your ageless wisdom and guiding hand— your very breath that is part of every square of this abode—is noticeable to anyone who is of that persuasion. Still, the shop is in no immediate danger. And you are doing exactly as you should.

But you have not told me. Did you kiss him?

Your confidante,

Rosemary

•

'There are only two things in life that involve all five senses,' Master Le Coutre declared from the front of the minibus. They were alternately speeding along flat, straight stretches of road and then slowing to ascend the hills of the Luberon, an easy drive from Aix. Although on the first night they'd been told that today would be spent in the kitchen, the very next day Master Le Coutre had changed the plan. Again. He seemed not to care much for organisation, itineraries or actual chocolate making. Christmas had begun to wonder if he might be a Wizard of Oz–type figure and not really make chocolate at all but simply hide behind pomp and smokescreens. It probably should have irritated her, but since no promises were made in advance as to what they'd be doing when they got to France, and she was having a delightful time, it seemed churlish to be annoyed. She was just going to enjoy whatever came her way. There had to be some sort of method in the man's madness.

'The first is food,' he said, pinching his fingers in a cluster and miming eating. 'You've heard it said that you eat with your eyes first. The look of the food is as crucial as the actual taste. So too the aroma, the sharp citrus smell, the sweet caramel, the spicy bursts, the herbaceous warmth. You hear the food sizzling, crunching, snapping, opening. And touch—eating with your fingers is so much more sensual. Why do babies eat with their hands? It is natural. It is fun. It is stimulating. You're connected to your food. And you feel it on your lips, over your tongue, as you swallow and it descends your throat, and even when it's in your stomach. Sight, smell, sound, taste and touch. It is all there.' He paused for a second. '*Oui?*'

'*Oui*,' the group responded.

'And what is the other?' he asked, grabbing onto the back of a seat as the minibus lurched around a particularly sharp corner.

Christmas was pretty sure she knew the answer to this, but she wasn't going to say it out loud.

Tibbie Tottie put up her hand and waved it around excitedly, her silver bangles jangling. Master Le Coutre raised an eyebrow in her direction.

'Tequila slammers in a noisy bar.'

Philomena smiled at Tibbie and patted her tanned knee. 'No, darlin'. He means making sweet love.'

'Ah! Making love!' Master Le Coutre closed his eyes and hummed a tune to himself, rocking backwards and forwards on his feet until the bus driver slammed on the brakes for a herd of small brown and white goats crossing the road and Master Le Coutre fell back against the dashboard.

Jackson Kent leapt to his assistance and steadied him before resuming his seat. They all rushed to take pictures through the window of the bleating and tail-wagging goats while the driver unleashed some swiftly executed hand gestures at the goat keeper, accompanied by a spray of rapid French.

The animals passed and they set off again, Master Le Coutre leaning back on the dashboard for added safety as he returned to his theme. 'Making love. The feel of another's body. Their scent. Their voice in your ear, the murmurs from their throat. The way they look by candlelight as they slowly undress. The taste of their salty skin. Other than eating, and making love, is there anything that fully employs all five senses at once? *Non.*'

'Are we going to make chocolate today?' Henry Jacobs asked, his tweed jacket removed, revealing a short-sleeved cotton shirt, on account of the heat.

Master Le Coutre stared at him for so long that Christmas began to feel sorry for Henry. It was, after all, what they were all thinking. Except perhaps for Tibbie Tottie, who seemed not to care about cooking as much as she did about tweeting.

Christmas wondered just why Tibbie Tottie had been selected for this course.

Finally, Master Le Coutre spoke, ignoring Henry and addressing the rest of them. 'Today, we are visiting our flavour ingredients—our partners in the chocolate dance. For a true partnership, a perfect match, you must know your partner's origins. You must know their history. Where and how they grew up. This is what we're here to do. Uncover the birthplaces of our most important significant others.'

Master Le Coutre sat for the last half of the journey and Christmas stared in wonder at the passing scenery—the blue-grey Luberon ranges in the distance behind ochre fields of grapevines tethered in straight rows under the blazing sun; the seas of purple lavender that seemed to greet them around every second bend; the dry-stone borie huts with their pointed roofs and their ancient origins as shelters for shepherds and wanderers; the obscenely bright yellow sunflowers nodding in the summer breeze and smiling at everyone who passed by. It felt like another world, yet one somehow anchored into her bones.

Master Le Coutre's words had stirred something in her. *For a true partnership, a perfect match, you must know your partner's origins.* But what if she didn't really know her own origins?

Since arriving in France, she'd once or twice found herself staring at men she thought would be around Gregoire Lachapelle's age and wondering if she could see any resemblance to herself, or whether she could sense any sort of connection to them. Because surely she would feel it, wouldn't she, the same way she was feeling this pull towards Provence? But she'd brushed the thoughts aside almost as fast as they arose because it simply wasn't relevant to this trip.

Eventually the group tumbled out of the minibus at a rolling lavender farm drenched in mauve in all directions, with a stone farmhouse standing tall above the flowers. Dozens of small wooden boxes chequered the landscape, housing beehives. It was late morning and Christmas wasn't sure whether she was imagining it but a purple haze seemed to hang over the fields, as though the atmosphere was reflecting the intensity of the flowers.

The lavender farmer, Paul, kissed Master Le Coutre on each cheek and welcomed them all to his *champs de fleurs*, then invited them to wander the fields at leisure. 'Come back when I start the tractor,' he said, mopping his forehead with a red handkerchief from around his neck. 'Then we'll work.' He grinned and shooed them on their way.

The five of them moved off as one, mobile phones and cameras at the ready to capture the beauty of the scene, leaving Master Le Coutre to catch up with his friend. Their own chatter soon faded away and they spread out, each walking alone, except for Philomena and Henry, who walked in easy silence.

Christmas waded into the ocean of flowers and let it swallow her whole. The scent of the lavender was overwhelming. The drone of the bees, enchanting. She let the tall stems brush against her legs and waist, reached out to rub the flowers between her fingers, surprised yet again that the oil wasn't oily at all, but kind of sticky. She'd done this before, of course; Tasmania was famous for its lavender fields too. It was different here though. It was the difference between visiting an exotic animal in a very nice zoo and seeing it in its homeland. *This* was where lavender belonged.

She kept walking, wading deeper into the ocean of purple beneath the wide open blue skies, hearing the church bells tolling in a nearby town. A lone eagle hovered high in the air above her.

She felt each footstep on the soil, brushed her palms against the waving flowers, and listened to the hum of bees drunk on lavender perfume.

Then Paul started his tractor in the distance and she turned around to head back to shore.

She had read before that it took a hundred kilos of lavender to produce just a couple of litres of the essential oil, or thereabouts, but until Christmas saw it for herself these were only numbers. Paul set them to work dragging the harvested lavender plants off the trailer and laying them out on cotton sheets on the ground. They all pitched in, even Henry and, remarkably, Tibbie Tottie, who must have been high on the aroma because she couldn't stop smiling the whole time and didn't tweet anything once. Soon the harvest was all spread out on the sheets, standing tall over their heads in rows of fabulous-smelling and colourful haystacks. Master Le Coutre had lavender pieces in his hair and caught on his shirt and he kept rubbing his hands together and placing them over his nose and inhaling like an addict.

Paul ushered them into the stone barn, where they stuffed lavender down into the huge metal still, big enough for them to climb in barefoot and help to stamp down the cuttings, which they all did, even Jackson Kent, who Christmas thought would have been too uptight to take off his shoes in public. But he must have been high on the oils too, because he looked genuinely relaxed and happy as he respectfully squashed down the lavender.

When the still was as full as they could possibly get it, the enormous lid was put on top and clamped down and Paul disappeared downstairs to set the controls and begin the steam distillation process. They watched in fascination as the steam, having built up inside the still, began to make its way out through the glass tubes, the heavier oil separating and dripping into a beaker as it went. The pale yellow oil collected in the bottom of the beaker and the process continued at length until no more oil came out.

'There it is!' Paul shouted, holding the beaker up to the light, then closing his eyes and sniffing from the opening at the top, swirling the contents and moaning and murmuring like a passionate wine lover. Next he strained the oil through coffee paper to remove any stray particles, and at the end they had just half a litre of oil from the mountain of lavender they had dragged off the trailer.

'Unbelievable,' Christmas said. 'Here I was just casually adding a drop of lavender oil here and there to my chocolate work, and look how many plants were needed for my one tiny bottle.'

'So much harder for rose oil.' Paul grimaced. 'You need tonnes of petals. Tonnes!'

'What happens to the rest?' Jackson asked, pointing to the still.

'Ah!' Paul held up a finger. 'Watch.' He unclamped the lid of the still and then hoisted up the contents with chains and a pulley, and a wet, matted mass of hot vegetation rose into the air, shooting steam around the room and giving Christmas an instant facial. 'We use it as mulch, feed it back to the lavender plants, and what we can't use we burn.'

He picked a glass pipette out of a tub of clean implements, drew up some oil from the beaker and placed a single drop on each person's fingertip. 'Try it!' he said.

Master Le Coutre wasted not a second, putting his finger to his mouth and licking off the oil. 'Bravo,' he said, applauding Paul. 'Another perfect drop.'

Christmas licked the tiny bead of oil on her fingertip and it instantly felt as though her whole head, from her chin to the roots of her hair, had been gassed with lavender. It was impossible to understand how one teeny drop could have that much punch.

If Paris was a place of giants and grandeur and thoughts as big as the cosmos, then Provence, Christmas thought now, was the land of single grains of sand, just as William Blake had put it hundreds of years before: *To see a world in a grain of sand; And a heaven in a wildflower; Hold infinity in the palm of your hand; And eternity in an hour.*

Their next stop was a dairy that specialised in goat cheeses. They took a guided tour and then the farmer tied up one of his nannies for Master Le Coutre to milk.

Their fearless leader got down on a stool and hand-milked the soft-eyed brown and white nanny goat, her yellowish creamy milk squirting into a metal pail with a ting and a froth while he sang to her. Her small tail flicked from side to side and her bell jangled on its leather collar as she shook away the flies. Master Le Coutre finished, wiping his brow with his surprisingly muscly forearm, bare where he'd rolled up the sleeve, then dipped a cup into the milk and drank from it.

'Ahh,' he exhaled, smiling, wiping his lips. 'Try it!' He offered the pail and cup to Tibbie Tottie, who vehemently refused; to Philomena, who happily accepted, commented on its unique flavour and made notes in her book; to Jackson, who drank without expression as though it was just one more task he needed to complete; and to Henry, whose eyes lit up and who talked about life as a young boy back in England, drinking milk straight from their cow.

Christmas was last, and even though others had already commented on this, she was shocked at its warmth. 'It's different,' she said, smiling politely at Master Le Coutre and handing back the cup. In truth, it felt weird drinking something that was just a moment ago sitting inside a hairy goat's udder. It felt disconcertingly as though the milk was still alive, like the goat herself, rather than the way she normally experienced milk, as something sterile and cold, sitting in a cardboard carton, a composition from many faceless cows.

This experience felt almost like eating a piece of the goat herself while it was still alive and watching her. She suppressed an urge to apologise to the nanny. Instead, she bent down and patted her neck and rubbed her ears. The nanny turned her nose to Christmas, and its downy lips snuffled into her outstretched hand. The goat herder came to stand at her side, beaming down at her and his goat.

'She's beautiful,' Christmas said, though she didn't know if he spoke English, and he didn't respond. But his pride in his animal and his work was palpable. She stood straight again and gave the goat a final scratch between the shoulder blades.

In that moment, she was acutely aware of the modern disconnect between the way food was produced and the way it was consumed. The thought suddenly struck her that Master Le Coutre was a genius after all. How could you make chocolate— or anything at all—if you had no true knowledge of it? If you didn't even know where it came from?

The goat let out a shaky bleat and pulled at the rope tying her to the post. She wanted to be on her way, back to her friends in the green meadow beyond the straw-filled yard. The farmer, tanned by fifty summers, let her go with a gentle slap on her rump.

And if Christmas had let herself, she would have heard a tiny, soft voice inside her wondering what it might be like to know where *she* came from too. But she wasn't listening.

21

Lincoln checked the caller ID on his phone.

'Well, if it isn't the dinosaur artist gone walkabout. How's it going?'

'What's that sawing sound? Where are you?'

'The butcher, getting bones and meat for Caesar.'

'Well, grab two pieces of rump steak and a bottle of the finest red wine you can find. I'm on my way back and we need to celebrate.'

Lincoln pointed through the glass at the rump steaks and then held up two fingers to the butcher's expectant face. 'What are we celebrating?'

'I'm getting married.'

'What? To who? You don't even have a girlfriend.'

'I'll tell you all about it tomorrow night. I'm in Sydney now and I'm about to board the plane home.'

'I'm confused. This is big news.'

'You're right, it is. Better make it two bottles of red. And buy the dog a rump steak too. My shout.'

●

It was early morning in Aix and the streets were mostly deserted. Christmas had woken when it was still dark with that clear sense that dawn was fast approaching. She'd always been an early riser, so that wasn't unusual, and after a few moments of checking in with herself to see if she was likely to go back to sleep, she'd got up, pulled her hair back into a low ponytail and put on casual clothes and sneakers to wander outside. She found the northern hemisphere with its lengthy daylight hours in the height of summer both exhilarating and exhausting. But she wasn't here for long so she might as well make the most of it.

She found herself in a silent cobblestoned alley, flanked by rows of tall weathered stone buildings. A lone cat wandered at leisure, its sleek black coat a deep contrast to the greys of the cobblestones and walls, the archways and their iron gates, and the light greens and flushing reds of the leafy foliage climbing up the walls, window eaves and rooftops. The feline flicked an ear in her direction but continued unconcerned, its lithe shoulders assured of its claim on this alley and its soft pads evidently treading a well-worn path. It was completely oblivious to the obscene beauty of the morning sun filtering down through the gables of the buildings. The alley just begged to be filled with wagons of colourful produce and serenading minstrels.

Suddenly, the cat veered to the right, jumped up two steps and disappeared through a hole between a pair of rustic wooden doors, as though the hole was made just for the cat to come and go as it pleased. Christmas mused for a moment on the self-sufficiency of cats, their determination not to need anyone else;

they were content to carve out their own lives and live them to the best of their ability, which was what she'd done, certainly since she'd left Sydney, but maybe before that too. Growing up with her mother's lack of attention to things like clean school uniforms or sports days and awards nights meant she'd had to.

But now she couldn't help thinking that it would be nice to walk up the alleyway with someone else instead of by herself.

The scholarship class didn't start making chocolate until just before midday and didn't finish until almost midnight. They were squashed into a small commercial kitchen at the back of a vineyard, with stainless-steel benches and appliances and Tuscan orange tiles. For light, there was just a row of small windows above the workbenches, and hanging bulbs that swayed in the breeze.

Master Le Coutre had changed from a poetry-quoting, dancing philosopher to a marching, barking commandant. This was boot camp. There would be no breaks, he informed them, handing out blue-and-white-striped aprons. There would be no chairs, other than for Henry, on account of his seniority. There would be espresso shots from the vintage copper machine in the corner, which looked like a domed rocket ship with appendages of hanging scales, pressure dials, levers and crested taps, but they would need no food, he told them, because tasting their products was an essential part of the job and they would receive enough sustenance from that. Was he understood?

They all nodded in shocked silence. Philomena slipped her notebook into her back pocket and folded her hands in front of her. Tibbie Tottie struggled to do up the strings of her apron. Henry looked around, presumably for his chair, as there was none to be seen. Jackson Kent stood to attention beside Christmas, and his calm strength and broad chest (she could see the man's pecs and eight-pack through his T-shirt, for goodness' sake) slightly eased her anxiety about what lay before them.

Master Le Coutre split them into two groups. Henry, Tibbie Tottie and Philomena were in one, and Jackson and Christmas were in the other. The day would be divided into two six-hour shifts, one focusing on savoury chocolate creations and the other on sweets, the groups swapping halfway through.

Christmas and Jackson were to begin with the savoury tasks. They started out simply, melting dark chocolate to make sauces, then moved on to a chocolate tapenade, featuring olives, anchovies, garlic, chilli and rum. Jackson's scarred nose twitched as he poured the oily anchovies into the food processor.

'Not a fan of the little fish?' Christmas asked.

'They smell like cat food,' he said.

They tasted it with celery sticks and crackers. It had a good texture, firm and smooth. But Christmas had to agree that the smell was off-putting.

They both loved the milk chocolate glaze for roasted pumpkin pieces.

'I made something similar for my sister and her husband and three boys. It's fantastic for kids who won't eat vegetables,' Christmas said, wiping up the sauce with her last piece of pumpkin.

'You could put it on pretty much anything, I should think. We might have just solved the problems of parents everywhere who despair about their children's diets.'

It was an odd conversation, considering that neither of them had children. Christmas leaned back against the bench, her feet hurting already, only three hours into the first shift. 'Do you want kids one day?' she said.

Jackson slid his empty plate into the dishwasher and took Christmas's from her to do the same. He closed the door and faced her. 'Johannesburg is not an easy place to have children,' he said.

'No, I imagine it's not. Do you have a partner in your life?'

He rested his eyes on her and she had the feeling that he was skilled at seeing right through people. 'My duty is intense. It is one reason I am looking for a new career.'

'I get that. You want to be happy.'

He tilted his head slightly, the light cast by the bulb above him shining through the small stumps of his close-cut hair. 'Yes,' he said.

'I get that too.' She smiled and put her hand on his elbow. 'Come on, let's get some coffee from that old rattler over there. We've still got chocolate oysters, rabbit, goat cheese and fennel to get through.'

It was a good thing the sun didn't set in France until ten o'clock in summer. The extra daylight helped them all to keep going when the fatigue began to hit. Only Jackson, so used to being on his feet for lengthy periods, was still looking reasonably fresh when the teams switched over.

'Time!' Master Le Coutre shouted, as if this was a sporting event. Each group finished cleaning their workstations to pass to the other. Tibbie Tottie looked fragile, her eyes bloodshot. Master Le Coutre had shouted and clapped at her for her slowness, and when she'd dropped a pile of cocoa butter transfer papers he had launched into a lengthy diatribe in French, the tone of which, combined with his flailing arm gestures, was unmistakable to everyone in the group.

Christmas and Jackson had also borne the brunt of his wrath when they burned white chocolate and then butchered some oysters while extricating them from their shells.

'What does he expect? We're not chefs,' Christmas grumbled under her breath to Jackson.

'He seeks excellence. That's not so bad,' Jackson said.

'I suppose.'

Her mood improved when they started their sweets shift with raspberry champagne truffles. They were divine, no other word for it. They began with the champagne and vodka ganache, sneaking sips of the champagne as they went, which went a long way to lifting flagging spirits, then whizzed together dried raspberries and icing sugar to coat the ganache cube. The dish was a revelation, and Christmas knew she'd be adding it to her shop products and to her life. The smell of the raspberries and chocolate was intoxicating enough in itself, even without the kick of the champagne. The colour was gorgeous, a pale pink, and the soft, powdery texture of the coating tickled the tongue before the silky ganache spilled out into the mouth and filled the nostrils with its piercing aroma.

'I could die right now and be happy,' Christmas said, swallowing another piece and closing her eyes in pleasure.

They made chocolate sponge and cut it into slices, as though it were bread, to assemble chocolate club sandwiches. They tempered chocolate into slabs and made triangles and shards, easy enough for Christmas because she did it all the time. They decorated moulded cat-shaped chocolates with paintbrushes, using coloured white chocolate as paint—definitely not one of Christmas's strengths, though she was pleased to see that her pieces were finer than anyone else's. They wrote with tempered white chocolate in tiny paper piping bags.

They moulded chocolate teddy bears that could stand upright on their feet and then sprayed them with melted chocolate and cocoa butter to give them a flocked finish.

'They look too cute to eat,' Jackson remarked, his face softening as he gazed at the little bears, giving Christmas a small glimpse into a man who might just have been as soft on the inside as the whipped chocolate mousse they were making concurrently with the bears.

When the sun had finally disappeared below the horizon, Christmas and Jackson had whipped, stirred, crumbled, cooled, heated, spread, shattered, hammered, glazed, filled and decorated their way through Master Le Coutre's list of tasks.

Christmas stopped to look at her hands. They were trembling from fatigue, sugar, alcohol and caffeine. 'I need some real food,' she said, gobsmacked that Jackson was still motoring through the cleaning. She'd let go of any pretence of wanting to help him and was simply grateful he could work like a machine to get it all done.

Tibbie Tottie was now curled up in a corner of the kitchen, glassy-eyed with weariness, her mobile phone clutched to her chest, while Philomena and Henry finished cleaning their workstation.

Master Le Coutre was beaming around the room, a wild look in his eye as he surveyed the bounty spread out on the central bench. It looked like a full banquet table in a medieval castle. 'Marvellous, marvellous!' he shouted.

Christmas went to retrieve her phone from her handbag to take photos. Her body was charged with a new burst of energy, somewhat akin to the rush of finishing a marathon, she imagined, and she suddenly felt wonderful.

Jackson smiled at her. 'You made it through the pain barrier,' he said.

'Seems like it.'

Finally, Master Le Coutre dismissed them. 'Go now,' he said. 'Find yourself dinner. I will put all of this away and tomorrow the vineyard will serve it to customers, and your love, your dancing, your creativity will be shared with others through your beautiful creations.'

Even Tibbie Tottie managed to pull herself up to standing and look pleased with the colours and sights laid out before them.

Christmas wanted to stay longer, to soak up the achievement, but her stomach growled loudly and she didn't want to get dragged into another mad scheme of Master Le Coutre's. So she said goodnight, kissing him on each cheek, thanking him for his guidance, forgetting his admonishments and fiery temper.

'Come on,' Jackson said. 'There's an open-air restaurant not far from here. Let's get something to eat. I'm starved.'

'You'd never find a restaurant in Tasmania that served food at this time of night,' Christmas said, enjoying the beef cassoulet. It was far too hearty for a warm summer evening, but she was ravenous. There were many delicious salads on offer but she needed more than green leaves and goat's cheese. The heavy, hot meal made her sweat, but it was fantastic, fortifying her from the inside, distracting her from the throbbing in her feet.

'We used to have curfews in Johannesburg,' Jackson said.

Christmas stopped chewing. 'Jackson, your life is so scary.'

He grunted. 'Maybe I should come to Australia. I hear it's quiet.'

'A lot of it is. A lot of it's empty.'

'Empty is good. Silence is good.'

Christmas poured water from the carafe on the table, wondering what Jackson had seen in his time but too afraid to ask. He was hoeing into a *carpaccio de boeuf*—a wide plate of paper-thin slices of raw beef, which looked a lot like salami, with a topping of spinach leaves, cherry tomatoes and a mountain of freshly shaved parmesan, drizzled with olive oil and lemon juice. A bowl of hot chips sat beside him. Between them sat two glasses of white wine served *bien frais*—extra cold—the outdoor lights reflected and sparkling in them.

'I can't believe tomorrow morning is our final farewell,' Christmas said. 'Mind you, I'm not sure I could take another day of work like that. I work hard at home and twelve-hour days aren't unusual, but that was brutal. Speaking of which, what have you thought of this strange course we've been on?'

Jackson wiped his mouth with his serviette. 'For me I think it's actually been less about the technical side of working with chocolate and more about discovering passion I didn't know I had.'

'So you're happy you came?'

'Definitely. I feel much more alive now than I did before. And I'm sitting here in the peace and quiet, with the stars above, enjoying this fabulous meal with you, and there's nowhere else I need to be. It's perfect.'

'Naw, that's so sweet. What are you doing next?'

'I'm staying at the language institute just outside of Sauveterre. It has a residential course for intensive French instruction.'

'You do set the bar high!' she said, leaning back in her chair, putting her hands on her distended belly. 'I'm heading to Sauveterre too—we should share a taxi.'

'That's a good idea, thanks,' he said.

'I decided to treat myself with a week in a chateau so I can explore Provence. But my plan is indulgent relaxation, not straining my brain on learning French. There's no way I could conjugate verbs. I don't even know what conjugation is.'

'In grammar, it is just about producing different forms of a verb. But it also means to couple, or to connect.'

'This is starting to sound like one of Master Le Coutre's lectures on making love as a metaphor for working with chocolate,' she said.

'The French language is very sexy.' Jackson's eyes held hers, unwavering, unflinching.

'It's really late,' she said, her voice weakening. 'We'd better get back to the hotel. This has been a marathon day already.'

•

A man just two-thirds the size of his former incarnation came up the driveway and knocked on Lincoln's door.

As soon as Rubble stepped inside, Caesar threw himself on the newcomer, then turned around so Rubble could scratch at the itchy spot on top of his rump, at which Caesar made small ruffing noises in appreciation.

'Maybe you two should get a room,' Lincoln said, opening the bottle of red with a satisfying pluck of the cork.

'I don't know how Eleisha would feel about that,' Rubble said, accepting a balloon glass of wine.

Lincoln smiled. 'Pretty name.'

Rubble burst into a huge grin, lines now appearing on his face where flesh once plumped them smooth. 'The prettiest.'

'You look great, by the way,' Lincoln said, leading Rubble out into the backyard, where they sat in plastic reclining chairs and looked at the grass he still hadn't mown, while Caesar stalked the fence line.

His friend patted his much-reduced gut. 'Lydia isn't just talking; I can't shut her up.'

'How does Eleisha feel about you hiding away and working?'

'She isn't missing out, trust me. I've got so much energy since meeting her that there seem to be twice as many hours in the day as usual.'

They sipped in silence for a few moments while the sea captain next door began to hammer and saw in the fading light. Caesar barked at him half-heartedly.

'What's he doing over there?' Rubble said, getting to his feet to peer over the tall wooden fence.

'He's been building something for ages. It's big but I'm not sure what it is.'

Rubble walked closer to the fence to have a good long unashamed look. He turned back, grinning. 'It's a boat.'

'Really?' Lincoln got up and surveyed the scene for himself. 'It is too.' He could see it now, the spine, the ribs, the hull. 'Why the hell would he want a boat in his backyard?'

'Everyone needs to be the captain of his own ship,' Rubble said sagely, putting a paw on Lincoln's shoulder. 'That's what Eleisha and I are doing. That's what the sea captain is doing.' He looked at Lincoln meaningfully.

'And you think I need to do the same.'

'Maybe it's time to chart some new waters.'

•

'Have you heard anything back from Christmas about the new information on her father?' On the phone, Val sounded breathless, as though she was walking through the house and picking up toys and clothes as she spoke.

'Nope,' Emily said sending a document to the printer in her home office.

'So I guess she's ignoring us then? She really isn't interested in looking for Gregoire?' Val sounded disappointed.

'It's a shame, I agree. But I think I should just stay out of it now. I've already made my opinions very clear and I think I'd be ruining our friendship if I continued to push. If she changes her mind in the future and wants to talk about it, she'll know where I am.'

'Yes, you're right. We don't want her to stop talking to us. So we'll just let it go?' Val clarified.

'I think it's for the best.'

•

To: Christmas Livingstone
From: Abigail Hurst
Subject: Cheyenne

Hi,

Cheyenne's fine. She's just having some personal time off. Nothing to worry about. I'm sure she'll tell you about it when you get back.

Abigail

•

The scholarship group was farewelled in a private function room of their hotel the next morning over *pains au chocolat* and raspberry mousse, all whipped up by Master Le Coutre after a dawn visit to the street market. They broke fresh bread and grazed on the last of the season's plump figs, as well as preserved walnuts, rabbit salad, stuffed artichokes, capers and a sinful number of pastries. Afterwards they hugged and exchanged email addresses, though of course Christmas knew she wouldn't be in contact with any of them. Except, perhaps, Jackson.

But before she left the building, she took Master Le Coutre aside, nerves making her hands unsteady as she fiddled with a bouquet of field flowers on the bench next to her. He raised his bushy brows expectantly at her, his white chef's shirt still buttoned up tightly at the neck.

'I want to ask you about chocolate,' she said, her voice barely a whisper, and he leaned in to hear her over the laughter and jovial banging and scraping of chairs as the group members prepared to leave. She couldn't believe how nervous she was. It wasn't as though Master Le Coutre hadn't read the application Emily had submitted on her behalf. Disappointingly, he'd not said a word about it, and neither had she. But she couldn't leave without asking him.

'Well, you know I want to find and make medicinal chocolate—chocolate with special health benefits,' she said, steeling herself for potential ridicule.

'*Oui.*'

'Um, well, I'm just wondering, do you have any advice for me, or ideas? Is it just a dream or do you think it's possible?'

He held up a hypnotic finger, lowered his voice and intoned slowly and seriously. 'There is a legend that speaks of a cacao tree. She is so revered by the people who tend her, and so valuable in the way of dollars to the people who "own" her, that very few know of her location. She is somewhere in South America, though almost no one knows exactly where, and she is heavily guarded.'

All background noise faded away as Christmas strained every cell to focus on what he was saying.

'This tree is very old. At the same time each year, when she produces a crop of pods, an official makes his way through the jungle to count the number. She is known as The Compass for every cacao plantation everywhere. The biggest chocolate maker in the world forecasts its entire year's profit based on her bounty. All chocolate in the world is tied to this tree.' He spread his hands wide and his eyes turned to saucers, taking in the imagined globe.

Then he leaned in further and Christmas did the same, so that their cheeks were nearly touching. 'She is never wrong,' he hissed. He straightened again. 'But! There are others who revere her differently. They know she nurtures exceptionally powerful cacao beans, far superior to those from other trees. They are waiting for the day when her true value—as the provider of life-saving medicines—is recognised. To them, she is known as the Cacao Queen, the one whose gentle benevolence is needed by many who suffer all manner of illnesses.'

Master Le Coutre folded his hands behind his back and nodded solemnly to Christmas, and she offered some kind of clumsy bow of thanks in return. Then he kissed her on each cheek and was gone.

What the hell?

She had no idea what to make of that story. But she had no time to think about it now; Jackson was calling to her because the taxi they were sharing had arrived.

Christmas put on her seatbelt with some degree of trepidation, concerned that the new level of intimacy they had developed yesterday and last night might be gone in the cold light of day and they'd be back to the hesitant, slightly awkward vibe that had been there when they'd first paired up to dance. But she needn't have worried. The journey to Château de Fagan in Sauveterre was over an hour long but it flew by in easy, entertaining conversation. All too soon, she had to part with her new friend. The taxi pulled up on the sweeping driveway beside the central fountain in front of the castle, and the driver went around to retrieve her bags from the boot.

'Well, goodbye.' She smiled at Jackson, opening the door and letting in the pleasant sounds of water sprinkling into the stone pond. 'Thank you for being such a great dance and chocolate-making partner.'

'You too,' he said, his voice gravelly this morning, as though he'd been up late drinking whiskey, though it was likely just fatigue from their long day yesterday.

She turned to step out but he put a hand on her wrist. 'Here,' he said, passing her a chocolate wrapper. On it was a mobile phone number. 'If you need anything at all while you're in France, just call. No matter what time or where you are. I don't sleep much anyway.'

No, she couldn't imagine he did. She pictured him as the eternal sentry, standing guard.

'I look after my friends,' he said.

Touched, she took the paper and put it in the pocket of her handbag. She bent forward quickly and pecked him on the cheek. He didn't move. But she caught the scents of shaving cream and coffee. '*Au revoir.* Good luck with your French,' she said, and climbed out of the taxi. She closed the door and it drove away, Jackson Kent staring straight ahead.

*

There was a knock at Elsa's door, followed by the direct, clear voice of Lulu Divine. 'You in there?'

Elsa considered ignoring her; she wasn't in the mood for cantankerous old ladies right now. She was fulfilling that role quite well all by herself.

'I can see you through the louvres,' Lulu said.

'Of course you can,' Elsa muttered, and navigated herself to the door. The two women gazed at each other, their wheels facing across the threshold.

'Hi,' Lulu said.

'This is a surprise.'

'How's Rita?'

'Sarah tells me she's doing fairly well. The hospital's looking after her but it's a bad strain of the flu so she'll be there for a while yet.'

'Still, it's good to know it's not worse,' Lulu said, and Elsa thought she almost sounded sincere. 'I'm off to hospital next week, too,' she continued, her hair shifting in the winter wind. Elsa really should invite her inside.

'You got the call, then?'

'Finally going to get these old legs up and working again.'

'Well, that's great,' Elsa said politely, trying to muster some sort of genuine feeling. It must be a relief for Lulu to know that her time in the wheelchair was almost at an end and she'd be independent once more. 'You'll be back on a horse before you know it.'

Lulu smiled slightly and her gaze drifted dreamily to the top of the bungalow roof. 'That would be wonderful.' Her eyes dropped again, sharp and pragmatic once more. 'I think my riding days are well and truly over. But it will be great to be on my way, after the arduous rehab.'

'Yes. Such freedom.'

'Mmm.'

Elsa felt weird, as though a big empty space was yawning in her chest. She didn't even like Lulu, yet the news of her departure had thrown her. 'What will you do afterwards?' she asked. 'Do you have somewhere to go? People to see?'

'I've rented a house in Launceston for a few months while I do my rehab. After that, who knows?' Lulu thought for a moment, her head turned away to look down the driveway and out to the town of Oatlands. 'I think maybe I'd like to tidy up some stuff. Finish unfinished things. Do you know what I mean?' She looked at Elsa sideways.

Elsa let her imagination jump to some of the things Lulu might need to attend to—broken hearts, abandoned children, lies, estranged family members, long-held grievances, perhaps even retribution and payback. She could imagine Lulu having ties to all of those things. 'Yes. I think I do.'

'There's some people I'd like to see before . . . you know.'

'Yes.'

Lulu sniffed and straightened as though only just realising she'd let her normally impenetrable guard fall. 'Anyway, I just wanted to tell someone. You're my neighbour and all.' She smiled and shivered. 'I better get out of the cold. They won't let me have the operation if I get sick now.'

'Certainly.'

Lulu reversed, the rubber wheels hissing over the concrete.

'Thank you for telling me,' Elsa said.

Lulu nodded and encouraged her chair along, cursing at the *mongrel thing* to go faster.

Elsa rubbed her shoulders against the chill and closed the door.

22

A day lazing in the French sunshine was well deserved, by Christmas's reckoning, after the work Master Le Coutre had put them through. And ever since her last, strange conversation with him, she'd been replaying his words in her mind.

The Cacao Queen. The Compass. Life-saving medicines. Heavily guarded. What was she supposed to do with that information? She felt like she was in some sort of spy movie. And let's face it, the master was more than a little eccentric. There was some genius there, sure. But he was also a good deal in his own world.

Right now, though, there was a lot to see and enjoy here in the grounds of the chateau—expansive, immaculate green lawns that led out into woodlands, with a trail that bordered the farm land of neighbouring properties, and with topiaries, pencil pines and two huge oak trees whose limbs stretched gracefully across the lake.

She spread out a complimentary picnic blanket under the oaks and took off her shoes, then sat down to watch the ducks on the water as they bobbed their heads under the surface, their neat tails to the sky and their feet paddling the air. On the far side of the bank, two large white geese wandered companionably together, pecking through the grass, the sun on their backs. Christmas inhaled a deep breath of warm, fragrant air and wriggled her toes. It was so beautiful here, an oasis of serenity.

Her plan for today was very simple—to relax under these trees, alone with her thoughts, allowing herself space to unwind, recoup, and be present in the moment. Then, she would explore the woodland, and later the rest of the chateau. This afternoon she would take a stroll down the road, past a neighbouring vineyard and a dairy farm, pick some wildflowers and press them inside the novel she'd picked up in Paris.

Giselle, the chateau's young red setter, trotted over towards the lake. Spotting the birds, she dived eagerly into the water, chasing the ducks and the black water fowl through the lily pads, sending them into frantic take-offs and landings until they all decided to take off for good. Undeterred, she spied a large stick—a branch, really—floating in the shady waters beneath an overhanging tree and snatched it in her jaws. Dog paddling expertly, her tail swinging behind her like a rudder, she made her way back to the grassy bank and pulled herself up before shaking vigorously, sending bullets of water shooting in all directions.

Christmas sighed happily and leaned back against the trunk of the oak, folded her hands together in her lap, and closed her eyes. She should probably check in with everyone back home today. And maybe she should try to contact Lincoln again? No, she quickly decided. The less said the better right now. She didn't want to mess it up again. Instead she allowed herself to daydream of him, even daring to consider what it might be like to have him permanently in her life.

What would a future with Lincoln look like? Would he settle in Tasmania for her, or would she have to find a way to follow him around the world, or would each of them pursue their own careers in their own city or country, overcoming the difficulties of distance, then coming together again as circumstance allowed?

And then there was the matter of children. She couldn't imagine that having kids was high on his list of priorities, being so in love with travel as he was, but what if it *was* on his agenda? She allowed herself to sit with the idea, testing out the feelings it conjured, mentally experimenting with the notion of children. She'd only recently told Val she didn't want kids. But since then she'd thrown away the rules. She was free to make up a new plan if she wanted to. So would she consider it if Lincoln was interested?

She opened her eyes again, blinking into the contrasts of shade and light, and took in the pretty red flowers lining the front entrance to the circular driveway. One or two other guests wandered the gardens, picking flowers and enjoying the sunshine.

One of the guests, a tall man, walked purposefully towards her. She raised her hand to shield her eyes from the glare and he smiled and raised a hand to wave. She frowned, trying to work out where she'd seen him before. And then he reached her blanket and it hit her like a clap of thunder.

Standing in front of her—smiling, shaven, his hair trimmed and neatly brushed, an ironed shirt open at the neck, looking so completely different that she first thought she must be mistaken, then that she was hallucinating—was Lincoln van Luc . . . looking *spectacularly* cute.

'Hi.' Lincoln was smiling, but he was looking at her a bit off-centre, as though about to turn and leave if she objected to his arrival.

'Oh my God. What are you doing here?'

Lincoln helped her to her feet and she brushed a leaf from her pants, grateful that, inspired by the elegance and beauty around her, she'd taken care with her appearance this morning. Now was not the moment to be caught at her worst.

'I wanted to surprise you,' he said, and she couldn't take her eyes off his face and lips, entirely smooth, utterly transforming him. 'You look great.'

'Thanks. You do too,' she said, and he looked pleased with the compliment. 'And the surprise worked,' she said, before being hit by a huge wave of embarrassment that the last time they'd been together they'd kissed, and it had been beyond perfect, and then she'd pushed him away. He was scratching the back of his neck, likewise embarrassed, she assumed, and suddenly she desperately wanted to ask him to give her another chance.

She was standing here, with him, with his full attention. And they were in Provence, of all places, and she looked good, and he looked scrumptious, and the sun was shining. If there was ever a moment to put her best self forward and win him over, it was now.

'I hope you don't mind that I've just turned up announced like this,' he said, his voice hesitant.

'No! Not at all! It's wonderful to see you,' she said, gushing. 'I mean, it's weird, completely surreal. But wonderful! Why *are* you here?' she asked, touching his arm in a way she hoped was both charming and assuring.

'Well . . .' He stretched the word out and took a breath. 'That's a good question.' He looked down at his hands then, as though suddenly nervous.

'Before you say anything else,' she said, 'I need to apologise, properly, for what happened at The Apothecary.'

'No, no, don't,' he said, shaking his head. 'It's okay, I think that . . .'

But just then, Giselle the red setter noticed the arrival of a new person, dropped her stick and galloped over, covering the distance in seconds. She jumped up on Lincoln, who gently pushed her away; still excited, she leapt at Christmas.

'No!' Christmas backed away from the big wet dog, not wanting muddy pawprints on her clean pants, but tripped on the edge of the picnic blanket and fell to the ground. As she tried to struggle to her feet, and Lincoln reached out to help, Giselle was on her in a flash. The dog hopped, bounced and leapt like a triple jumper at the Olympics and tackled Christmas to the ground. Barking rapturously she pinned Christmas down on the grass, her paws scrabbling on the white cotton shirt and expensive soft bamboo pants.

'Off!' Lincoln said, trying to get his arms around the dog's chest and pull her away. But Giselle was wet and slippery and Lincoln lost his grip, stumbling backwards.

Christmas was horrified. If ever there was a time to be thrown to the ground and snogged by a saturated dog, it was *not* now. She managed to flip herself over onto her belly and cover the back of her head with her arms as the overgrown puppy embraced her, reeking of swamp water and algae.

'Giselle!' screamed Lisbet, the mistress of the chateau, running across the lawn and clapping and growling at the dog as though it would do any good. Christmas yelled out in pain as one of the dog's sharp claws pierced her trousers and punctured the back of her thigh.

'She doesn't have a collar,' Lincoln puffed, pushing the dog off with his knee. Hysterical with enthusiasm at this grand romp, Giselle spun back around and landed on Christmas again.

The setter tightened her grip around Christmas's waist with her front paws and gyrated and . . .

Oh. My. God! The dog was *humping* her!

To her horror, Lincoln laughed helplessly as he attempted to wrangle the wet mutt.

'Giselle!' Christmas screeched. 'This is wrong on so many levels! Wrong species! Wrong sex!'

Lisbet arrived, and between her and Lincoln, Giselle was dragged off, coughing as someone's efforts pushed on her throat. Christmas flipped over and Lincoln helped her to her feet.

'I'm so sorry,' he said, through barely suppressed laughter.

Lisbet spewed mortified French and Giselle finally quietened, her face dropping in shame as she was likely called every bad word in the French vocabulary. Her tail lowered and she slunk behind her mistress.

'I'm so sorry, I'm so sorry,' Lisbet repeated, herding the canine swamp monster backwards. 'You will send us your drycleaning bill, of course, and we will discount your hotel bill, and oh, look at your pants! And your leg!'

Christmas craned her head around as best she could to see a long rip in her pants and a thick scratch down her leg, with tiny spots of blood popping up along the ridge of the swelling wound.

'It's fine, really,' she said, burning with humiliation.

Lisbet made a hasty exit with Giselle, leaving her alone with Lincoln.

'Are you okay?' he said sympathetically.

'I think so.' She wasn't entirely sure, awash as she was with mortification and shock.

'I'm so sorry for laughing,' he said. 'I wasn't laughing at you, truly, it was just so absurd and . . .'

'It's okay. I would be laughing too if I wasn't so embarrassed.' She'd lost her moment to make a perfect first impression on Lincoln in Provence.

He smiled, the left-hand corner of his lips—*lips! He had lips under all that hair!*—rising. 'Come on, how about we get you inside and cleaned up and then I can catch you up on why I'm here.' He held out his hand for hers.

She took it, feeling a current travel right down to her toes, and walked silently beside him, peeking across at him from time to time, not quite believing he was really here. Across the driveway, up the two stone steps and through the tall double doors into the ground-floor foyer, down the hall, and she fumbled in the pocket of her now-ruined pants for the key. Then she unlocked the door and they stepped inside.

'Nice room,' he said, taking in the heavy curtains drawn back on either side of the open shuttered doors, the rich toile wallpaper, oval gold-framed mirrors, thick textured bed linen and the chandelier hanging from the ceiling.

She was still speechless from shock.

'How about you have a shower and then I'll help you with that scratch, if you like,' Lincoln said, pointing at her leg. She didn't move. He looked quickly behind him, then back at her. 'Why are you staring at me?'

'Your face.'

He reached up a hand and ran his fingers down his smooth olive-skinned cheek, then grinned. 'You like?'

'Oh, yeah. Obviously. I mean, not that I didn't before . . . You just look so . . .' Several words came to mind. Smouldering. Sexy. Masculine. Dark and brooding, even—not in a scary way, but

in a *you're-a-deep-lake-I-want-to-dive-into* way. She settled on
'. . . different.'

She'd been attracted to him from the first moment she'd met
him on the footpath outside The Apothecary, no question. But
there had always been a touch of woodsy *Folk of the Faraway Tree*
about him too. Now, suddenly, his lips had definition. They were
full, and the top one was a true bow shape with a dark shadow
of regrowth over it. He'd left small strips of sideburns that drew
attention to his cheekbones. And his hair was now short, though
still with some height at the front and even a bit of attitude.

He smothered a grin, betraying a hint of self-consciousness.
'Take your time in the shower,' he said. 'Don't worry about me;
I'll just make myself at home.'

She stood in the claw-foot bath and let the hot water run over her,
wincing as it hit the scratch on the back of her thigh, then sham-
pooed her hair thoroughly and scrubbed her fingernails. She let
the aroma of lavender and patchouli soap calm her nerves.

Lincoln was *here*, in Provence, and sitting on the other side
of the wall.

What was he doing here? Had he told her? She couldn't
remember now with all the kerfuffle. She stepped out of the bath,
took the fluffy white robe from behind the door and put it on,
knotting the tie at her waist, and finger-combed her hair to let it
fall around her face. She checked herself in the mirror—so much
for being dressed to impress.

She straightened her shoulders and stepped out into the
bedroom.

Lincoln was sitting in a wingback chair by the window,
sunshine falling onto one side of his face. He jumped to his feet
when he saw her. 'Feel better?'

'Yes, thanks. More Lily-of-the-Valley and less Swamp-of-Provence. Always good.'

Two long strides and he was close enough to touch her. 'Can I have a look at the scratch? Put something on it for you?'

She bit her lip. The scrape *was* stinging. And she didn't want it to get infected. But the thought of lifting her robe for Lincoln to see the back of her thigh was ... well, it was hugely erotic.

'I promise I won't bite,' he said, a small smile struggling to emerge.

'That's a shame,' she said, smirking.

'Is it?' He raised an eyebrow.

'There's some antiseptic ointment in the first-aid kit in my suitcase.' She moved to her purple case on the luggage rack and ferreted around inside, careful not to let any underwear items escape and flutter to the ground, excruciatingly aware that he was watching her every move.

Stop it. Keep your head, Livingstone.

At last she found the small box and pulled out the tube of ointment, then slammed the case shut again. 'So, where would you like me to be? To see my leg.'

Lincoln squared his shoulders and set his face to a professional, detached expression. 'Why don't you just stand here by the window, in the light, and hold your robe just above the wound so I can see it properly.'

'Okay.' She stood stoically at the window, her head turned to look out at the trees, pretending that Lincoln wasn't positioned directly behind her on one knee, peering at her leg.

He whistled through his teeth. 'A bit of a war wound, but nothing you won't recover from.'

'Ow!'

'Sorry.' He applied the ointment gently, with the tip of a warm finger, smoothing it evenly down the scratch. The ointment stung; the burning grew more intense until she was gritting her teeth, and then began to subside. But his finger continued its rhythm and gradually pleasurable sensations took over from the stinging. Her mind strayed to all sorts of places it shouldn't go. To thoughts of the beautiful room they were in and the warm, gentle breeze shifting the white curtains around them. The long day ahead of her with nothing planned. The new dashing Lincoln, kneeling behind her, his careful fingers tending to her skin as though it were a precious object.

'That should do it,' he said, his voice nearly a whisper. He took his hand away but didn't rise from where he knelt.

She dropped the bottom of her robe and turned around slowly, looking down into his upturned face and serious, captivating blue eyes. As though of its own accord, her hand reached out and touched his hair, running her fingers through it. 'So short,' she murmured.

'Yes.' He extended a hand towards her and laid it on the side of her thigh.

'Yes,' she said softly, remembering with glee that she had decided back in Paris to throw away the rules. She could do whatever her heart desired.

His free hand wrapped around her other thigh, carefully avoiding the dog scratch. Her fingers kept running through his hair, moving down now to the back of his neck. He leaned his head into her hand and she ran a finger down his beautiful throat. His hands moved in circles on her legs, slowly ascending under the robe, pulling her gently towards him.

There was a final flicker of mental resistance but it was extinguished just as fast as it flared. Who was she kidding? This was exactly what she wanted.

This was exactly why she'd thrown away the rules.

She took one, two, three baby steps and then her knees buckled and she dropped to the floor with him. They both froze for a moment, eyes locked, chests rising and falling. And then their lips met and they tumbled to the carpet and before she knew it the waist tie of her robe had come undone and his strong hands were on her bare back, their legs entwined, and her hands were pulling at his shirt and fumbling with his buttons and he was tearing at them, saying, *I don't care, just rip it off.* So she did. And buttons flew across the room, pinging off furniture, and they both giggled and kissed some more and she nipped his shoulder and he let out a growl of desire that was totally manly and not the slightest bit like a wood elf.

Lincoln's fingers traced delicious patterns on Christmas's shoulder and slid lazily down her ribs towards her hip.

'You'll have to stop that or I won't be able to get up off this floor,' she said. 'I'll melt into a puddle.'

'Mmm.' He kissed her neck and a wickedly fast shudder ran down her body.

'You still haven't told me why you're here,' she breathed, reaching for his lower back to pull herself further into his embrace. 'Not that I'm complaining. You're like Mary Poppins turning up to make everything better.'

His fingers stilled. 'I'm not sure that analogy works.'

'No. You're right. Not Mary Poppins. You're Johnny Depp.'

'Which version: Edward Scissorhands, *21 Jump Street*, or Captain Jack Sparrow?'

'Jack Sparrow, obviously.'

'Savvy.' He sounded pleased with that.

'Although I don't know if any of that makes sense. I think my brain is just offering up rambling thoughts because it's lost all ability to think straight.'

'That works for me. Shall we just keep searching for lost treasure?'

'Yes please.'

'Savvy.'

•

They were ravenous, then, and gorged on bread and cheese in bed, still tangled in the sheets.

God help him, she was gorgeous.

She'd put on a pair of knickers and a singlet. Sexy and natural, her body relaxed and moving freely as though she hadn't a care in the world. It was all he could do to leave her alone for half an hour while she refuelled.

'What?' she said through a mouthful of bread, following it with a black coffee chaser.

'Nothing. You just look so different.'

She paused in her chewing and considered him. 'France has been good for me. I do feel different here. I think back in Evandale maybe I'd got a bit stuck.'

'I always feel different when I'm overseas,' he agreed. 'There's something very liberating about it. Like all the old definitions of yourself don't apply anymore because there's no one around to insist on their own version of who you are.'

'Exactly.' She licked her fingers clean. 'Now tell me what you're doing here.' She reclined against the huge white pillows, her hair fantastically messy.

He was reluctant to allow in any thoughts of the world outside this room. But he couldn't keep ravaging her without some sort of explanation.

'And where's Caesar?' she said suddenly.

'He's with Nan. I got permission from the home for him to stay with her in her bungalow until I get back.'

'They were okay with that?'

'Not really, but the young nurse, Sarah, she seems to be a good advocate for the residents and she got her way in the end, guaranteeing that if there were problems she'd take Caesar home with her. I hope it's okay. I think Nan could use the company, though she'd never admit it.'

'You said you and your nan had a "chat". What was that about?'

He lay back on the bed and exhaled. 'She gave me a bit of a lecture about growing up.'

'What do you mean?'

'She thinks I need to settle down—job, wife, kids. The lot.'

'So you ran away to France?'

'Good plan, hey? No, not really. It was Rubble who made me think the most.'

'Your friend the artist?'

'He's back from the desert and he's getting married next month to a woman he met in a pub up there. He says he fell in love with her instantly and he doesn't want to waste another second of his life. Life's too short and all that. I tried to tell him he could be making a big mistake but he just shook his head and patted me on the arm like I was a child and said that a wise man knows there are no such things as mistakes in the universal trip of life.'

'Had he been smoking something at the time, by any chance?'

Lincoln laughed. 'Quite possibly.'

'It's rather brave, really,' she said.

He reached out a hand to run his fingers through her hair and she leaned into his palm. 'That's what I thought too.'

He wanted to say more but he was still blown away that she'd been so pleased to see him and hadn't pushed him away again like she'd done at the shop. When had everything changed? The last time he'd seen her she was shoving him out the door and leaving the country. But somewhere between his grandmother's lecture and Rubble's news, and the thought of making Emily soup . . .

Bugger.

He'd forgotten about Emily. He should have said goodbye and closed that chapter properly. That was poor form. And now, here with Christmas, he very much regretted leading Emily on.

Emily was nice. He'd convinced himself that it was okay to ask her out because it wasn't anything to do with Christmas but instead about him and his freedom to see whomever he wanted, when, really, it had been *all* about Christmas.

'What's the matter?' she said.

'Oh, I just remembered something I forgot to do before I left.' He put a smile on his face. 'But it doesn't matter. I'm here with you now.'

'I'm still a bit confused about that, actually. Why are you here? In France? In my bed?'

'Ah.' He entwined his fingers with hers. 'Well. I guess there are a few practical explanations, like that I don't have any work commitments right now and I had a heap of frequent flyer points I could cash in and I was feeling a bit claustrophobic in Evandale. And then I guess there are the crazier reasons.'

'Like?' She stroked his fingers, which was intensely distracting and arousing.

'Believe it or not, I didn't come here planning to rescue you from a love-crazed canine, and I didn't plan to spend the day in your bed. My only thought was that the time we spent together . . . well, you made me feel a way I've never felt before.'

'Oh.'

'Yes. But then you turned me away, and then I was petty when you said you wanted to see me again, and I felt bad about that, and I didn't want to die not knowing why you pushed me away, because it seemed like a really good kiss to me, so I was wondering if there was any chance at all for us to see where it could go. I'm not saying we should follow Rubble's lead. Or Nan's advice, for that matter. But I think they might have had a point about seizing the day and all.'

'I see.'

'I knew where you were because you left me your itinerary, and I knew your course finished yesterday. So I jumped on the first plane I could get and came here intending to ask you why you sent me away and then maybe see if I could change your mind. And just maybe I thought you'd like to spend some time with me in Provence. Or not. I don't know. I have no plans. I have no return ticket date yet. I just wanted to know. You know?'

●

Why *had* she pushed him away? Christmas twisted the sheet between her fingers.

Because the kiss was terrifyingly good? Because her rules of happiness said she couldn't have a relationship right now? Because she wanted to protect the happiness she'd built up and not put it at risk, because she knew what true heartache felt like and she never wanted to go there again? Because, sometimes, the risks *did* actually outweigh the potential benefits. And at some points in life you had to choose what you were willing to risk. Movies and fairytales would have you believe that love was always worth the chance, but reality could prove otherwise. Real life was unpredictable and could be cruel and crushing.

But these reasons all sounded quite nutty now she thought about it.

'Well, I was leaving the next day and I didn't want to cause any confusion.'

Sure, that was simple.

Instead, that confused him more. 'But you were only going for three weeks. It's not like you weren't coming back.'

'That's true.' She paused, stuck for words, the silence edging towards awkward while she racked her brain for something to say.

'Look, I'm sorry,' he said. 'This is all very sudden. I just show up here unannounced, and then . . . well, I think you know what happened next. This is a bit of a shock, really, for both of us. We don't have to talk about this now.' He looked hurt. She felt mean.

Oh, what the hell. She might as well tell him about the ten rules of happiness. So she did. And he listened, increasingly amused, as she had known he would be.

'And the kiss was out of this world, by the way,' she added. 'So it seemed like I was destined to break rule number ten.'

'You turned me down because we might actually be happy?' he said. 'I'm not following.'

'Great happiness can lead to great devastation, so I reasoned I should cut my losses before it was too late.'

And then, mustering courage, she told him about Sydney, about Simon and the baby, the darkness that had followed, and returning to Tasmania. She explained how she had carefully crafted a life to bring hope to herself and others, because she knew what it felt like to be in a dark place. And she told him that love was the greatest risk of all.

He listened, stroking her arm. 'I'm sorry that happened,' he said when she'd finished.

'Thanks.'

'I can see why you'd create the rules. A broken heart can take a long time to mend.'

'You speak from experience?'

'I was married once,' he said.

'Really?'

'You don't have to sound so surprised,' he said, with mock offence.

'No, of course. Sorry. You're a total catch. Why wouldn't you have been married?'

'A catch, hey? That's nice.' He filled her in on his brief marriage to Benita. 'It was difficult when it ended. Even though it made total sense, like there'd always been something missing, it was still a shock and I felt like a bit of a failure for a while. So I can understand why you'd want to avoid that.'

It *had* seemed perfectly reasonable. But now, after Paris, in Provence, with Lincoln here in her bed, those fears didn't seem to matter so much anymore. She'd been wrong. She was a different person now from the one she had been back in Sydney. Heck, she felt like a different person than she'd been two weeks ago.

She reached for him. 'I'm clearly very glad you came.'

'It has seemed like you've enjoyed yourself.'

'Perhaps we could continue this?' she said, swallowing a final gust of nerves. 'You could come and explore Provence with me, if you have no other plans.'

He smiled a delectable, handsome, totally kissable smile. 'If you're sure.'

'Yes. I shouldn't have pushed you away. Please come with me.'

'I'm all yours.'

23

On Saturday, their first full day together, Christmas and Lincoln bounced out of bed, keen to get out and explore Provence. Lisbet, still mortified by her dog's behaviour, had offered them her spare car by way of an apology. After briefly demurring, Christmas and Lincoln looked at each other and agreed in spontaneous unison that yes, actually, that would be great.

They decided to combine some random pottering about with a few rigorously executed plans. Lisbet recommended Les Halles d'Avignon as a sensational food market in the famous city. 'The traffic is terrible,' she said, grimacing. 'Parking, a nightmare. But still you must go.'

Driving on the right-hand side of the road was terrifying for both of them, but they managed, albeit slowly and attracting several abusive gestures from local drivers. But it was worth it. They ate food straight from the stalls, eating slices of melon, *pains au chocolat*, tomatoes exploding in the mouth with sweetness, and sampled plenty of local wines.

Between mouthfuls, Christmas told him about the legend of the Cacao Queen, as shared by Master Le Coutre.

Lincoln nodded knowingly, throwing back a small glass of wine and licking his lips. 'I've heard that story. I work for the biggest chocolate company in the world; they turn over billions of dollars annually. Wouldn't surprise me in the slightest.'

'But you've never asked about it? Never tried to find out where this tree is?'

'Not really. From a scientific perspective, it's not possible that one tree could predict a whole year's crop around the world, particularly one that's as old as the legend says it is.'

'So where did the story come from? I tend to think that legends are often based on something factual.'

Lincoln sidestepped a large family of children and waved away apologies from the parents trying to shepherd their brood through the throng. 'Where there's smoke there's fire?' He raised an eyebrow. 'Not exactly scientific.'

'But fascinating!' she said, linking her arm through his. The market was hot and crowded but it was a great excuse to bump into each other pleasurably and hold hands so they didn't get separated.

'I agree that it's an enticing notion,' he said.

'Would you ask around for me? Just casually. I don't want to get you knocked off by the chocolate mafia or anything if you're getting too close to their secrets!' She was only half joking.

'Sure. Anything for you.' He kissed her under the intense sun and she hummed with deep satisfaction.

Lincoln pulled out his phone and asked a man passing by if he would take a photo of them together, each eating a *pain au chocolat*.

'Maybe we can use it for an author photo,' he said to Christmas, pulling her into him tightly and kissing her lips as the bored-looking man took photos.

'I don't think that one will be appropriate,' she said.

So they posed together properly, holding their sweet treats, while the man muttered and took more shots.

'*Merci*,' Lincoln said with exaggerated enthusiasm, taking back his phone, and the man shrugged and walked away. 'Cheerful soul,' Lincoln observed, and she laughed some more because, well, why not? She was so glad at that moment that she'd thrown away the rules. Look what she'd been missing out on!

Leaving the market, they strolled the cobbled streets of Avignon, watching artists painting under the canopies of trees and listening to buskers playing near the cafe tables, and wandered at leisure until a small Italian restaurant opened for dinner at around eight o'clock. They shared wine and pizza and then drove back to the chateau, where they fell into bed for joyous sex and, finally, deep sleep.

The next morning, Christmas woke feeling lighter, freer and more content and beautiful than she'd ever felt before. She was headily, gloriously happy. She nestled into Lincoln's chest and traced her fingertips slowly from the tip of his thumb, all the way up his muscular arm to the point of his shoulder. His eyes stayed closed but his lips smiled.

'Morning,' he rumbled, pulling her closer to him and nuzzling her hair and neck.

'Good morning to you.'

They kissed indulgently and basked in the rapturous glow of desire and made love slowly—and in her opinion quite brilliantly.

They were the perfect partners in the dance of love. It seemed Master Le Coutre did actually know what he was talking about after all.

Afterwards, they lay wrapped in each other's arms, grinning and laughing.

'Would it be totally terrible to ignore Provence and stay in bed all day instead?' she asked. They had planned to go to Arles, to the square mile of the old town that was largely built during the Roman empire, to visit the ancient amphitheatre, to wander the narrow streets of tall, smooth buildings with recessed doors and windows and blue shutters, and to find van Gogh's cafe from the famous painting. It had seemed like a good plan, yesterday.

'You'd get no arguments from me,' Lincoln said, rolling her over to kiss her chest, his eyes dark with lust. They kissed for some time until a growl from Christmas's belly made him sit up.

'Are you hungry?'

'Starving! But we've missed breakfast, I'm afraid.' The buffet noises had ended some time ago.

'What should we do?' he said.

'Steal some food from the kitchen?' she suggested, not quite seriously.

'Excellent idea!' He jumped up and found some pants.

'Where are you going?' she laughed.

'To hunt and gather. Back soon.' And he was gone out the door, shirtless and barefoot, in search of breakfast.

Christmas stretched across the sheets and then got up to have a shower, enjoying the steam rising in the bathroom and the feel of the water as she splashed it with her feet. She felt so alive, so connected!

Lincoln returned with a thud of the door and some clattering of plates before he appeared in the shower with her, naked. She soaped his arms and back while he kissed her neck. She watched him wash his hair and ran her hand over his chest. Then her stomach growled again.

'I'd really better get some food,' she said, hopping out and wrapping a towel around herself, leaving him to finish his shower.

On the small table by the tall window, she found bread rolls and slices of cheese and cold meats, some orange juice, coffee and a disc of yellow butter. She wasted no time in dipping a knife into it and slathering it on a roll. Lincoln joined her, put his hands around her waist and bit into her bread roll, making growling animal noises.

Taking the other chair, he gulped down some juice, one hand still on her. 'I just can't seem to stop touching you.'

'Then don't. I like it.'

They stared at each other, smiling like goofs, and shuffled the wingback chairs closer together so their feet could touch while their hands were busy with the food. They ate for a while, gradually slowing their pace.

'When we get back to Tasmania,' he said, his voice deep and serious, 'do you think we can keep doing this? Having breakfast together?'

'Definitely.' She could think of nothing she would love more than waking up each day with Lincoln beside her and eating bread rolls sitting next to him. She remembered something. 'My sister's getting married the weekend after I get back. Will you come with me?'

'Just try and stop me.' He leaned forward, taking her hands in his. 'You do something to me,' he said. 'I know this is sudden, me turning up like this, but we were getting close, I think, working together in Tasmania.'

She nodded.

'You see, the thing is . . .' he paused and took a deep breath '. . . I think I might have fallen in love with you.'

The sun seemed to have taken up residence in her chest. She felt intensely cherished, and instead of being scared, she felt safe and totally at peace, with the promise of a hundred new beginnings. 'I think I might have fallen in love with you too,' she said, unable to keep the smile off her face. And it was a huge relief to finally admit it to herself, and to him, and to just . . . let . . . go.

'I'm really glad I came to France,' he said.

'I'm really glad you did too.'

And so they gave up any idea of travelling to Arles and stayed in bed all day long.

That evening, as they were getting dressed to leave their love nest and find some food for dinner, Christmas let herself daydream about Lincoln in her life in Tasmania. For real this time. It was actually happening. They both wanted this. Yes, there'd be things to work out, but for now it was simply a precious new phase of her life just finding its feet. She changed her earrings from sensible studs to dangling dinner jewels, smiling as she imagined dancing with him next weekend at the reception.

'I'm sorry you won't really know anyone at Val's wedding,' she called to him. He was shaving at the bathroom sink, a towel around his waist.

'I only need you,' he said, his voice muffled as the razor ran over his chin.

'Oh, but Emily will be there,' she realised. 'That's at least one other familiar face.'

'Ah.' He dropped his razor to the sink and tapped it on the edge, then ran it under the water.

'What?'

He wiped his face on a towel and turned and leaned against the bench. 'You should probably know that Emily and I . . .' He paused and cleared his throat.

Christmas felt ill. 'You've dated?'

He squinted one eye and looked with the other at the ceiling. 'Not exactly.'

'I can't believe this,' she squeaked. But then, of course, she *could* believe it. Because she had done this to herself. She'd told Emily explicitly that she was free to pursue Lincoln because Christmas herself wasn't interested.

Stupid, stupid Christmas.

'Did you sleep with her?' she asked, her heart racing.

Lincoln looked horrified. 'No! Absolutely not. Not even a kiss!' He was smiling now, and came to her, putting his hands around her waist. She let him.

'We just met at the pub, but we didn't even get to have a drink because she twisted her ankle and had to go to the doctor's. That's it.'

'That's it?'

'Yes.'

But then he hesitated.

'What?' she asked again, almost afraid to hear the answer.

He rocked his head from side to side. 'We did try to go out again. But she had a migraine and had to cancel. The whole thing was stupid of me. I'm so sorry. It's just that after you rejected me at the shop . . .'

She dropped her head, pained. 'Yes, I know. I'm sorry.'

'And she'd handed me her card and told me to call her, and I was very immature and thought, well, why not?'

She nodded. It hurt. But she'd pushed him away and then pushed Emily towards him. She could hardly get on her high horse now, could she? The man had just flown around the world to be with her.

His eyes were watching hers, pleading for her to understand. She took a deep breath. 'Okay, look. I'm not going to say I'm happy about it, but I can understand how it happened and I'm going to acknowledge the role I played in the situation and just choose to move on,' she said decisively, trying to convince herself as much as him.

'You might be the most perfect woman in the world.'

'Well, the fact that you're standing here in my hotel room in Provence is pretty good evidence for me that you meant what you said.'

He looked coy. 'What did I say?'

'You know!'

He kissed her. 'That I love you?'

She melted under his fingers. 'Yes, that.'

'And you love me too,' he said, his lips moving over hers.

'Yes. But no more surprises, promise?'

'Done.'

•

What's that noise?

Elsa was suddenly aware of a hard surface against her back and legs and, disturbingly, the back of her head. Something was wrong.

There was a noise. A very loud, repetitive noise, and her head seemed to thump in time with it.

She'd been doing the crossword. Seven down. It was an irritating question, one that really wasn't worded very clearly and was in the wrong tense, asking for something in the present tense that *goes* when the answer, she was sure, ended in *ed*. It was highly frustrating. Did nobody learn grammar these days?

A pain shot through her lower back and she moaned involuntarily. She was on the floor, she realised. That was the problem.

She tried to open her eyes but they seemed firmly resolved to stay closed. Her head spun, not entirely unpleasantly. It was as though she was about to drift off to sleep.

But she should get up. She took a breath and braced herself for the effort, but nothing happened. Where had all her strength gone? It was a pesky business, this getting-old malarkey. Just when you needed a bit of oomph it was nowhere to be found.

And her throat felt very tight and stiff.

Lucifer, what *was* that noise?

•

The sun rose in Provence the next day behind wisps of teased cottonwool clouds.

'We should really leave our room today and go sightsee,' Lincoln said, though from the sound of his voice, his heart wasn't in it. He was drinking coffee by the window and looking out at the majestic oak trees on the green lawns.

Christmas rolled onto her side in bed and lifted her head, cupping it in the palm of her hand. 'That seems a little ambitious. Maybe we could just walk around the grounds. Or borrow the chateau's bicycles and ride to a cafe for lunch?'

The rest of the world had melted away, leaving just her and Lincoln in their gorgeous, exclusive bubble of love, which actually felt even stronger today after Lincoln's revelation about Emily. The past had been confronted and the slate wiped clean and they were free to move forward in their life together. Down the hallway, someone had started to play a piece of French folk music featuring the piano accordian, and instantly causing Christmas's chest to swell with contentment..

'I could actually die right now and be totally happy,' she said, closing her eyes and absorbing the bliss.

'Please don't do that,' Lincoln said, sipping his coffee. 'I'd miss you too much.'

Just then her phone buzzed inside her bag and she jumped. She'd completely forgotten she even had a phone.

'Man, that scared me.' She laughed, her hand on her chest. She reached across the bed and down into her bag on the floor to retrieve it.

Did you get my message on Skype?

Christmas frowned. Then she remembered that a message alert had popped up when she'd been playing the movie title game with Lincoln. She'd forgotten all about it.

'What is it?' Lincoln said.

'Val. She wants to know if I got her Skype message.'

Christmas replied to the text, asking what the message was about. She only had to wait a moment before Val responded.

About your father?

'That's weird,' Christmas said. 'Val says it was something to do with my father.'

Lincoln lowered his coffee cup to the table and stared at her, his eyes wide. 'Oh shit.'

'What?'

'I'm so sorry. I forgot to tell you.'

'Tell me what?'

'About your father. Apparently he was a microbiologist who studied farm crops.'

Christmas laughed, not comprehending. 'What do you mean?'

Lincoln hesitated. 'Emily told me.'

Christmas sat up in bed, pulling the sheets up to her chest. 'Emily? I don't understand.'

'She asked me to tell you and I just . . . forgot.' His shoulders rounded forward and his face became pinched.

The music Christmas had been enjoying a moment ago disappeared beneath the rushing sound in her ears. Emily? He and Emily had not only dated but had also shared information about her—something deeply personal and important—but they hadn't told her.

'What's going on?'

He came to the bed and sat on the edge. 'There's nothing going on between me and Emily,' he said evenly. 'She had one of her migraines . . .' He went on, shooting out words quickly. But all Christmas heard was that first phrase. *She had one of her migraines.* Like he *knew* her. Like they were an old married couple. She stared at him and waited for his words to dry up like a slow-running tap that was taking too long to stop ·dripping.

Lincoln rubbed his forehead. 'I'm so sorry, I just forgot. It's a lame excuse, I know, but it's true.'

'But we said no more surprises,' she said childishly. 'You promised.' And the pain of potentially missing out on something to do with her biological father smashed together with the pain of Emily and Lincoln's careless handling of her heart.

All this time she'd been telling herself that she had packed away any idea of finding Gregoire Lachapelle and that it simply didn't matter. The fact that she didn't have anything to go on other than his name made it easy to convince herself that it was true. She'd ignored the small voice inside that had been trying to get her attention. But now, with this new piece of information in her hands, suddenly it did matter, very much.

She jumped out of bed, adrenaline charging through her. The room was too small. Her chest was hurting. It was all too much to process.

Was this new love really what it seemed to be? She'd trusted Lincoln. She'd trusted him with her most fragile emotions and with the belief that this time it could all be different. But now she wasn't sure of anything.

Gregoire existed. He was real. He had a job, a specialisation. He worked in the world, here in France, perhaps even walked the same soils that she had walked just the other day out in the fields with her scholarship group. She could have been just metres from him. He could have been the goat farmer.

'I think you should sit down,' Lincoln said, moving to her, trying to guide her to a chair. 'You need to take some deep, slow breaths. You're going to hyperventilate.'

She shook her head. 'No.' She pulled her arm away. 'I need some space,' she said. 'I need you to leave the room.'

'Christmas, wait . . .'

'No. Just . . . give me some space, please. I need to think.'

Lincoln stepped back, grabbed a T-shirt and pulled it over his head. 'Okay. I'll just go and sit by the lake for a while,' he said, hovering in case she changed her mind. 'Take your time.' And he left the room reluctantly, closing the door quietly behind him.

The room spun. Christmas sat down and concentrated on breathing.

Val texted again.

Gregoire Lachapelle was a scientist who studied diseases on farms.

Christmas stared at the screen. Something wasn't right: Lincoln said that Emily had said Gregoire was a microbiologist. It was a subtle difference, but it made her wonder. Where had this information come from? She ran the bath while tapping out another text to Val, hit send, then tipped the entire bottle of bubble bath into the tub and submerged herself in soothing, fragrant foam.

●

Lincoln sat on the edge of the lake, his feet buried in the soft damp earth of the bank, and thought about fish. Specifically, about gutting fish. About the way you placed the knife behind the gills while their fins waved at you and they gasped for breath, pleading for that final chance, before you sliced down through the resistance of the body and bones and crunched off their head before tossing it to the nearest waiting pelican. About the way you ripped off the scales with the back of the knife, spraying them like ghoulish confetti while the seagulls screeched in grisly pleasure. The way you took the tip of the blade and sliced it down the centre of the white belly flesh and pulled out the guts.

He hated fishing. He always had. But he'd persisted with it longer than he should have because his father loved it and he'd wanted there to be at least one thing they shared. As a teenager, he'd learned to ignore the bleeding still-alive worms and the bewildered glassy eyes of the hooked fish. The ones that swallowed the hooks were the worst; they had absolutely no chance of reprieve.

He was thinking of fish because right now he felt just like a gutted fish. Sliced right down the centre. He'd had something so wonderful in his hands and because he'd been stupid, forgetful and—what was it his nan had said? . . . oh yes, *lazy*—he might have lost it all.

Christmas had been generous in forgiving him for dating Emily. But he wasn't sure she'd forgive him for this.

And then a message arrived on his phone. He reached for it in his pocket, hoping it might be Christmas asking him to come back. But it was Jen.

Nan in hospital. Fainted in bungalow. Doing tests. Might be serious. Like, really serious. I'm flying down tomorrow. When u back? x

Lincoln dropped his head back and looked up at the branches of the tree above, his hands clenched. A thousand emotions hit him at once. He was ten years old and sobbing inside because his nan might die. He was forty-two years old and excited that Nan might see him settle down with Christmas Livingstone. He was here now, on the grass, fretting about what Christmas was thinking back in the room. He was cranky because, as timing went, a family crisis like this was awful. And he felt guilty because how could he even think something like that when his nan might be about to die and he was on the other side of the world?

The most important thing to do, the only thing to do, was to go home right now.

Will get on plane today x

•

Val

I asked Emily to tell you. I thought it was all straightforward. Dad told me when he came over to make dinner when I had the flu. I'd just been so sick. ☹ But it's no excuse.

Joseph

I didn't say he was a scientist but that he studied goat diseases. Your mother told me. I thought you'd want to know. Val said she'd tell you. It might help you find him. Are you having a good time?

Darla

I never said that, I said he made goat cheese. It's not my fault if Joseph can't hear. Why are you being so stroppy about this?

Darla

I can read your tone in your text messages, Christmas. You don't have to shout at me.

Darla

Look. I did my best. You've been on about this for thirty years and I've had enough. This conversation is over.

●

'I hope everything will be okay,' Christmas said, wringing her hands while Lincoln darted around the room collecting his scattered clothes.

'So do I.'

'I know how much your nan means to you,' she said, feeling tears spring to her eyes, overwhelmed by all the emotions of the past hour, including the idea of Lincoln losing Elsa.

He didn't say anything to that. She wanted to go to him and hold him, but it had been such a tumultuous morning that she didn't know if it was the right thing to do.

At last he stood, dressed in jeans and a loose cotton shirt, his suitcase zipped, casting his eyes around the room one last time.

'I have to go,' he said, just as the taxi's tyres rolled onto the gravel driveway.

'I know.'

'I'm sorry about everything this morning,' he said, his eyes filled with unhappiness.

'Me too.'

'I didn't mean to cause you any pain,' he said.

'I know.'

'But it's weird now between us, isn't it?'

'A bit.' She tried to smile. 'But we don't have to talk about any of that now. All you need to do is concentrate on getting home to Elsa. We can talk when I get back. Okay?'

'Okay,' he said, and then looked off into the distance, his face awash with worry.

She went to him then and hugged him tightly and he wrapped his arms around her and kissed the top of her head. She hoped, fervently, that everything would be okay, for all of them, but she simply didn't know.

24

Darla shoved the potoroo head into the hessian bag and tied the rope tightly before flinging it into the cool box with some vigour. She tossed the hacksaw onto the spindly grass on the side of the highway and took a moment to catch her breath and survey her surroundings.

Last night's text conversation with Christmas had rattled her, if she was honest. And she did like to call things as she saw them. Christmas was out of line.

A mob of grey kangaroos dotted the fields as far as she could see. There must be two hundred of them at least, poking around in the last pink light of dusk, their joeys loping about on unsteady legs while they experimented with chewing on long blades of grass and tree shoots. The younger ones that were still in pouches hung their faces out and sniffed and blinked, secure in their mother's care.

She did admire wallabies and kangaroos. They were such

tough, formidable breeders and survivors. A mother kangaroo would spy a predator approaching and call to her joey, twitching anxiously while it stuffed itself back into her pouch, and then speed away with her baby tucked safely inside.

But in truth, not all kangaroos were good mothers. She'd watched enough mobs in her time doing this work to see that not all macropod mums were created equal. There were the ones who simply left their babies out in the cold after dark and they froze and starved to death. The ones who would flee to save themselves from the approaching dingo and leave their baby to be taken. And the ones who were clumsy—who smacked their pouches into rocks or tangled their young in barbed-wire fences as they zoomed through.

The fact was that some kangaroos were just bad mums.

Darla retrieved the hacksaw, picked up the cool box, slid it into the back of the Kombi and shut the door. That would be her last collection for the day. It was far too cold now to keep going, and night was falling. Tomorrow she'd complete all the paperwork and statistics that were outstanding and find a post office to fax it to her supervisor, who was intensively analysing her research.

She stepped into the van, snapped the seatbelt buckle into place and wondered. Was *she* a bad mother?

She cast her mind back to the dark days of fear and uncertainty as a pregnant eighteen-year-old, having moved back home to be with her parents. The long months leading up to the birth, subjected to looks, sniggers and judgement from strangers.

And then the birth itself, a now-almost-forgotten endurance of pain that ended with a squirming red, goopy baby landing in her arms. And that moment when the baby's miniature fingers grabbed tightly onto hers and Darla had cried and cried, unable to believe that she could create something so utterly perfect and complete. *She* had done that. It was astonishing to her that this happened every minute of every day all around the world. It seemed impossible—a true miracle.

Like her very own Christmas miracle, right there in her arms in the month of March.

Her parents quizzed her on the name, probably thinking she'd been high on painkillers or something. But Darla had just laughed and laughed, ecstatic with her little baby, and said, 'Look at her! She's the best present I've ever received. She's like every Christmas morning everywhere in the world, from now until forever, here in one precious baby.'

Now Darla shook her head, shoved the van into gear, and eased off the clutch. Of course she wasn't a bad mother.

●

Christmas lay under a mountain of pillows. A large and heavy goose-feather one lay across her face, shielding her from the day outside the drawn curtains. The sounds of breakfast came from down the hallway once more. Of cutlery and crockery and whistling kettles. Laughter and loud discussions of the best way to travel the motorways to avoid expensive tolls. The smell of burning toast crept in under the door. It made her feel sick. It was so offensive it might as well have been the smell of burning hair.

She and Lincoln had planned to go to Gordes today—if they could finally tear themselves out of bed—to explore the vine-yards, and she'd allowed herself to imagine sipping wine with him, overlooking the valley of picture-perfect farming land, talking and laughing and kissing. Instead she ached with the humiliating knowledge that she'd ruined all of this for herself. She'd pushed Emily towards Lincoln. She'd convinced herself that finding her father wasn't important. But it did matter, much more than she'd allowed herself to admit. And then she'd lost the plot, spectacularly, in front of Lincoln, who'd said he'd fallen in love with her and genuinely seemed to mean it. The very thing she loved about him—his easygoing nature and natural optimism—had been the complete opposite of what he'd seen in her. He'd seen her freaking out. And now he was gone.

She only had herself to blame, because she'd thrown away the rules.

She'd been going along just fine before she met Lincoln van Luc. She'd been happy. Ecstatic? No. But who really was? Even those who claimed to be happy were only going through the motions half the time. Most people, she'd come to realise, defined happiness more as the absence of unhappiness rather than any sort of actual bliss. Everyone said they wanted to be happy, of course, but few people seemed to be so. They were always moaning about the weather, about politicians, the price of petrol or their aching bones. Or the person who served them at the supermarket yesterday who wouldn't stop whinging.

There'd been nothing wrong with her carefully devised system of happiness. It had been working for her. And she'd slipped up, like an alcoholic who momentarily thought they had it under control. And now here she was, in one of the most beautiful places on earth, hiding under a pillow.

Well, it wasn't good enough. She needed to get herself up and moving. Stop wasting the last days of her time here.

Yes, that was all she needed to do. Just get up out of bed.

Ready? Come on. One, two, three . . . and . . . up!

But her limbs didn't budge. She couldn't get up.

•

Lincoln arrived at the hospital straight from the airport and ran into his sister in the corridor. She was returning to Nan's room with hot chocolate in a paper cup.

'Missing Link!' She beamed, putting her cup down on a wooden bench directly beneath an excessively large and jaunty poster for bowel screening, which showed lots of laughing middle-aged people playing croquet and, rather inappropriately, slapping each other on the backside.

'It's good to see you,' he said, hugging her tightly. 'How's Nan?'

'Doing better. I'm sorry you've had to race home. It's the flu—the true flu, not a cold or the man flu, but the one that can kill oldies—so it was serious, but luckily she's on the mend. I think hospital was the best place for her to be.'

'That's a relief,' he said, releasing a breath he wasn't even aware he'd been holding.

Jen cocked her head to one side. 'You're rocking the two-day growth thing,' she said, tapping him on the jaw. 'Suits you.'

'Thanks.'

'You tired? Of course you are, you just got off the flight from hell.'

'Not too bad.'

'Then why the long face?'

'Because I'm a horse that walked into a bar.'

'What?'

'You know that joke. A horse walks into a bar and the bartender says, "Why the long face?"'

'Oh.'

'Never mind. Nathan would get it.'

She smiled with maternal pride. 'You'll have to call him and tell him later.'

Elsa's room was overly warm and her face looked flushed. She smiled weakly at him. 'No more yeti, I see.' A nasty-looking cannula was taped into a blue vein in her age-spotted hand, and a large area of bruising seeped from beneath the white tape holding it in place. A saline bag dripped away into the line.

He kissed her forehead and his lips sizzled on her skin. 'Are you hot?' he asked, putting a hand on her forehead. 'You feel hot.'

'She's had a lot of fevers,' Jen answered for her, making herself at home in a vinyl armchair as though she'd been sitting there for two days, which she likely had been.

'Lot of fuss for nothing,' Elsa said.

'What are they doing for you?' Lincoln said, towering awkwardly over her as there wasn't another chair to sit in.

'Trying to rush me to my grave with horrible mushy food you wouldn't feed a dog,' she said.

'Painkillers and fluids mostly,' Jen added.

'Speaking of dogs, where's Caesar?' Lincoln asked.

'He's with Sarah. Do you know it was him that raised the alarm?' Elsa said, before descending into a long and hacking coughing fit that was uncomfortable to listen to. Jen caught his eye and wrinkled her nose.

At last the phlegmy noises ceased. 'He barked and howled and whined until someone came to find me on the floor. I couldn't work out what the dreadful noise was, but it was him.'

Lincoln's chest swelled with deep gratitude. And a little pride, too.

'Now Sarah's taking him in every day she goes to work and she's got him a little red cape to wear because he's a rescue dog. He's sleeping his way around the nursing home, the rogue.'

'I bet he's being spoilt rotten. He won't want to come home again.'

Elsa chuckled, coughed some more, then yawned. Jen drained the last of her hot chocolate and stood up. 'Nan, I'm going to take Lincoln home and get him cleaned up and then we'll be back later, okay?'

'Fine,' Elsa said, before closing her eyes.

Lincoln sat in the passenger seat of his grandmother's tiny Honda while Jen drove.

'Jeez, Jen, do you think you might want to slow down a bit?'

'I've never had a speeding fine,' she said, slamming in the clutch and revving up another gear as she careened around a bend through the wheat fields.

'I don't think that's the point.'

'Hey, how was France? Tell me what happened with the girl.' She turned fully to grin at him, waiting for him to answer. In that split second, he took in her dark hair—freshly dyed by the look of it, with some sort of slightly purple tinge to it—and her sun-weathered face. She looked good, actually. Like one of those super mums who always seemed to be cheerfully busy and hugely efficient. Not manic, but capable and sturdy. Like you'd expect a nurse to be. Or a special needs teacher. And she was both, really. But that observation was quickly swept away by mortal terror as another long bend approached.

'Eyes on the road, Jen!' His hand clenched on his seatbelt. 'Shit! Do you drive like this with Nathan in the car?'

'He loves it. He laughs and laughs and makes engine noises and gear-change noises at all the right times.'

'Again, I don't think that's really the point.'

'Stop changing the subject. What happened with the girl?'

'It's messy.'

'Do you want to talk about it?'

'Nope.'

'Do you want ice cream?'

'I'm not a woman.'

'How about a beer, then?'

'Now you're talking.'

•

'This is a terrible idea,' Lincoln said, gripping the dash, Jen once again behind the wheel. At some stage over multiple beers last night at the Clarendon Arms, Jen had convinced him to go with her to their father's place to try to sort things out.

'Well, it can't go on as it is,' she said. 'Oh, look at that cow, isn't it gorgeous? It's licking the other one like it's a long-lost friend.'

'Eyes on the road, Jen,' he said again, teeth gritted. But nothing he said made any difference to the way she drove. They barrelled onwards through the bleak countryside, narrowly missing an ambling echidna, and jolted to a stop in their father's driveway.

Their footsteps creaked over the sloping verandah. Jen opened the screen door, calling out as she went.

Tom was just coming into the kitchen from the backyard, carrying three large muddy lumps.

'Hi, Dad,' Jen said. 'Still growing weird-shaped potatoes, I see.' She hugged him, and it was only as her robust arms wrapped around Tom's frame that Lincoln noticed just how scrawny he'd become.

Tom accepted the hug and patted her lightly on the arm. 'Doesn't matter what they look like. Cheaper than the outrageous prices you pay in the shop.' He nodded at Lincoln, warily.

'Hi, Dad.'

Jen looked from one to the other. 'It's going to be like that, is it? Just like it always was whenever you had a blue?'

'It's hardly just a blue, Jen. He's been blackmailing Nan.'

'Yes, Dad. What's with that?' Jen said, her gaze direct, motherly hands on hips.

Tom dropped his grimy potatoes into the dull sink. 'Don't get above yourselves with me. This has nothing to do with the two of you.'

'Of course it does,' Jen said. 'We love Nan. She's doing better, by the way, in case you were wondering.'

Tom looked out the window. 'That's good.'

'And Caesar's doing well too, in case you were wondering,' Lincoln said.

'You still got that old mutt?'

'He might have saved Nan's life, actually,' Jen said.

Tom looked at her, fleeting appreciation crossing his face before he set his jaw again.

'Can we all sit down?' Jen said. She herded Tom to the old green sofa, currently hidden under piles of newspapers, and beckoned to Lincoln to join them. He sat reluctantly in the single chair opposite.

'I don't have much time in Tasmania,' she said briskly. 'I've got a boy at home who needs me, and Mum can't be expected to look after him on her own for long. I love him to bits, but gosh he's hard work.' It was a rare, brief admission of her daily struggles. 'And I'm going to skip the pleasantries because there doesn't seem any point to that.'

Tom folded his arms and looked to the ceiling. Lincoln stared at his father, daring him to make eye contact.

Jen spoke firmly. 'So, Dad, you have to realise that what you've been doing to Nan, bullying her, is not okay.'

Still, Tom said nothing.

'Even if you don't feel you can love her—'

Tom jerked his eyes to his daughter and went to say something but Jen halted him with a stern hand and continued. 'Even if you don't feel you can act like a son and treasure every last day you have with your mother here on earth, I'd like to ask you to please consider acting like a polite stranger. Actually, maybe a touch more than that. Maybe a concerned neighbour.'

She waited, allowing Tom to absorb that.

'I want to visit Tasmania under pleasant circumstances,' she went on. 'Not because Nan might be critically ill and her son won't look after her, and not because my father and my brother aren't talking to each other. You are not individuals in this family. A family is a system of which each of us is a part. Do you get that?'

Lincoln got it. He was a botanist. Nothing in the jungle could exist without everything else. Every living organism had to do its part in order for the whole system to work properly. Everything depended on everything else. Sickness in one area led to sickness elsewhere.

'Yes,' he said, 'I get it.'

Jen gave him a grateful smile. 'Dad? Do you get it?'

'What is it exactly you're asking me to do?' Tom said.

'Well, first tell us this. Why are you so hung up on getting Nan's money now?' She looked around the room. 'I mean, it's pretty clear you're not flush with cash. Are you broke? Do you have debts? Have you got a gambling problem?'

Tom dismissed her questions with a wave of his hand.

'Well, what then? Because we don't understand. Please, let us help you.'

Their father worked his jaw. 'You can't help. And if you must know, I stuffed up.' Bitterness edged his voice. 'I got done in a deal, okay? I know that will come as a huge shock to you,' he said to Lincoln.

'What sort of deal?' Jen asked gently.

'Real estate. House flipping.'

'What's that?' Lincoln asked.

'Mitchell, two doors up, who took off and dumped that dog on me, invited me into a group of investors who buy houses for a low price, hit them with a team of renovators, and then put them back on the market to sell them again in less than a month. They reckoned they do it all the time and make big profits fast.'

Lincoln bit back words, not wanting to stop his father from talking.

'They had lots of brochures and videos of their previous successes. So I borrowed against the equity in this house to invest, but it didn't work. I was screwed over. Now my money's tied up in a bad investment and the bank wants the repayments for the loan and I can't make them.' Tom looked angry, embarrassed. He glared at Lincoln as if daring him to criticise.

'So why don't you just tell Nan that?' Lincoln said instead.

'She'd love that,' Tom muttered. 'She'd just love to hear how I proved yet again to be a disappointment, how I could never live up to her first-born saint, Matthew, or successful Jake.'

Lincoln felt a tug in his chest. 'Nothing you ever did was good enough,' he said. 'Painful, isn't it?'

Tom stared at him but didn't say anything.

'You need to tell her,' Jen said.

'No.' Tom tapped his finger on the wooden arm of the couch. 'It's the principle of the thing.'

'The principle?'

'She took my money.'

'What do you mean?' Jen said, shaking her head in confusion.

'Back when I was eighteen. I'd been working my guts out on the farm for years, earning a pretty good wage back then, milking and cutting hay and mucking out yards and stalls. Backbreaking work. It wasn't all machines like it is these days. I was saving up to get off this island and go to America. I'd missed the call-up to Vietnam and I was disappointed, to be honest.'

Lincoln felt the shock of his father's confession through his whole body. He couldn't imagine anyone being anything other than hugely relieved to miss out on being forced to go to war.

Jen just nodded, listening.

'So I decided to get out another way. I had my money all stashed in a tin in the milking shed. I was going to pay for my airfare to America. And then Pa got in trouble, again.' He screwed up his nose.

'What sort of trouble?' Lincoln asked. His grandfather had been a bit of a menace. He'd swap his milk urns for his neighbours' if they had richer, creamier tops on them. Perhaps he went too far, ended up on the wrong side of the law.

'Money trouble. Same as always. Debts he couldn't pay. So Mum took my money. Just took it. Stole it!' Tom's face had turned an ugly purple.

'But that doesn't make sense,' Lincoln said. 'Nan's got a good amount of money to her name now and she says they made it dairying.'

'Yes, interesting, isn't it? She always knew what Pa was like and she used to hide money all over the place. I don't think she even realised how much she'd hidden till after he died and she went and found it all. And her parents knew what Pa was like, so they left all their money—which they'd made from their own dairy farm—to just her, as well as the land.

'So you think she owes you?' Jen said.

'She *does* owe me!'

'I see.' Jen twirled a vine of hair, something she'd always done when she was thinking.

Tom thrust a finger at Lincoln. 'You think she is a perfect grandmother. But she was far from a perfect mother.'

25

A midnight bird squawked through the darkness outside Christmas's window. And now that the whole of the chateau was sleeping, she had energy roaring through her like an express train. It was Wednesday night. She would be back in Tasmania on Saturday and she could be metres away from her father right now. Or she could be on the wrong side of the country.

Lincoln had sent her a short text soon after arriving home to say Elsa would be okay, but he hadn't made contact since, and she was swinging between feeling cold with dread that she'd ruined everything and sick with shame that she'd brought all of this on herself. Well, almost all of it.

What she needed right now was to be making chocolate, harnessing her wild mind into constructive activity. But there was no such distraction to be found here.

Then she thought of something and rushed to her handbag. She had a bottle of lavender oil she'd purchased at the farm last week. She could rub some on her temples to ease the anxiety. But while rummaging through the contents of the bag, she found something else—the chocolate wrapper with Jackson Kent's number on it. His language school wasn't far away. And he did say to call any time. She didn't let herself think about it for too long before she picked up the phone and called him and, bless him, he answered almost straight away.

He arrived at the chateau not long after in a utility vehicle he said he'd borrowed from a fellow campus inmate.

'Inmate?' Christmas said.

'It's a pretty fair description.' He was joking. She hoped.

He asked her no questions as they drove along the darkened roads to his language school, and Christmas felt increasingly silly for calling him, fearing that she was imposing. But she needn't have worried, she realised when they arrived, because the campus was lit up like a jolly school camp with a carnival atmosphere. Midnight feasts were going on at candlelit wooden tables beneath leafy trees with fairy lights wound around the branches. Cigarette smoke waded heavily through the still air. All around was the sound of corks popping from wine bottles and glasses clinking.

'What's that sweet smell?' Christmas asked as they picked their way across the damp grass, passing a few rows of grape vines that harboured at least two romantic entanglements that she could see.

'Some sort of flower, I think,' Jackson said. 'It's strongest at night and makes me dream of travels I'm yet to have.'

'Careful, Jackson, I think the French language has released the poet in you.'

He smiled and opened the weathered wooden door to his cabin. 'There are worse things, I suppose.'

The room was spartan, but pleasant enough. Two single beds, blue quilts pulled up, a bedside table and lamp between them, an ancient writing desk and chair, and a small bar fridge humming in the corner. French dictionaries, books, maps, shopping catalogues and transport timetables lay scattered around. Outside, someone picked up a guitar and began a Spanish-sounding tune, accompanied by a chorus of whoops, claps and table slapping.

Jackson picked up a half-drunk bottle of red wine off the fridgetop and plucked out the cork. 'Would you like some wine?' he asked, reaching for glasses on a small shelf above the fridge.

'Yes, thanks.'

He poured them each a glass and she gratefully took hers, if only to give her hands something to do while his eyes studied hers.

'It seems as though you're all having a great time here,' she said, sitting on the chair at the desk. Jackson sat on the end of one of the beds and put his glass on the bedside table. She felt better already just for being out of her room away from her own thoughts and with a friendly face to talk to.

'I'm enjoying myself,' he said, flexing his fingers and then stretching his arms over his head and loosening his neck. 'My brain hurts all the time, though. Immersion language schools are tough but I feel like I've come a long way in a few days. We aren't supposed to speak anything other than French while we're here and it can be really exhausting.' He rubbed his eyes.

'I'll bet.' Christmas reflected guiltily that she still only had a few simple words and phrases. 'I'm sorry for keeping you up,' she said sipping the wine. It was thick and warming.

'*Non, non.*' He gestured towards the window. 'As you can see there is little rest to be had. I think it's part of the torture method of breaking you down and then building you back up again.'

'Like a cult?'

He laughed. 'A bit.'

'Lucky you're so strong then,' she said, genuinely admiring him. His eyes connected with hers and a jolt went through her. She put down her near-empty glass.

'Thank you.' He waited a moment and then said, 'So, why are you here, Christmas? Really? I'm sure it's not to make chocolate—as much as I enjoyed our time together doing that.'

'Well, I do actually like to make chocolate when I'm stressed. It's what I do at home. It soothes me.'

'What are you stressed about?'

It was a long list. She'd fallen in love, been loved in return, and then it had all come into doubt and been turned upside down. The information about her father. Elsa's illness. Her mini breakdown in front of Lincoln at the chateau.

She suddenly felt hot and stood up, looking for a window to open. There was one above the bed where Jackson was sitting; she reached over him, her shirt lifting and the skin of her abdomen finding the air. She shoved the window open as hard and fast as she could and stepped back out of Jackson's personal space, but his eyes were focused military-style, straight ahead. A wave of affection for him made her want to reach out and stroke his cheek. But she held back.

She sat on the bed opposite him, their eyes level. Most of all right now, she needed a friend. 'It's a long story,' she said.

'I don't have anywhere else to be.'

'That's good, because I've been feeling really bad the last couple of days. Bad in a way I haven't felt for several years. I started to worry myself.'

Jackson waited for her to go on.

'I got some information and it was quite a shock.'

'Is everything okay back home?'

'Yes. I guess. I'm not sure.' She paused, wondering where to start, and fiddled with the bedspread near her knee.

'I hear it helps to start at the very beginning,' he said.

'Like a Julie Andrews song?' She grinned.

'Huh?'

'"Do, re, mi"? You know, *The Sound of Music*?'

'Never seen it.'

'Oh, come on. You must have.'

'I haven't.'

'But you *have* to,' she said. 'Everyone needs to see it. It's such a lovely film. Too long, granted. I've probably watched it twenty times and only made it to the end twice. But, still! You *have* to see it. I'm going to send you the DVD as soon as I get home.'

Jackson laughed, his neck muscles flexing as his head tilted back. Seriously, the man only had to breathe and muscle would flex.

'Here, give me your address.' She fished in her bag for paper and a pen and passed them to him to write it down, which he did, amused, resting the paper on his knee. He wrote carefully.

'Excellent,' she said, putting the paper back in her bag. Outside, the music sped up and more instruments joined the guitar. It sounded like a gypsy festival out there and Christmas's mood soared.

'Okay, so now that we have my movie viewing sorted, let's get to the reason you're really here,' Jackson said.

'Oh, yeah.' She paused again. Maybe talking about this wasn't such a good idea. Maybe it would just make her mind focus on it more. Perhaps, in the absence of chocolate making, she needed another form of physical outlet. 'You know what? I think you've helped me already. How about we just go outside and drink wine and dance?'

'Fine with me,' he said. 'I'm better with action than talking.'

'Then let's just dance instead of talking, or making chocolate,' she said, excited.

'Master Le Coutre says it's the same thing anyway.'

'He might just be a genius,' she said solemnly.

'Or mad as a hatter,' Jackson said.

'Oh, so you've seen *Alice in Wonderland* then?'

'No. Why?'

'Oh, Jackson!'

'Maybe we should dance?' he suggested.

'Amen to that.'

And so they danced, barefoot on the damp grass, overly warm in each other's arms, the smell of wine on their breath as they laughed, surrounded by people from all around the world, singing in different languages, live music effortlessly directing their steps, until at three am they finally began to droop with fatigue and Jackson drove her home, their conversation slowing naturally as their eyelids began to close.

'You should stay,' she said when he pulled up outside the chateau. 'You're too tired to drive. There's a foldout couch in my room. It's probably not very comfortable, sorry, but maybe no worse than the compound you're already in. And at least it's quiet.'

He shook his head.

'Okay, I'll sleep on the foldout and you can have my bed,' she said cheerily.

'It's not that,' he said, looking straight ahead. 'It would be too difficult to be there with you and not be with you.'

Christmas's heart lurched. 'I'm sorry, Jackson. I really like you. I just think my heart is, kind of regrettably, somewhere else.'

He looked at her then and butterflies stirred around her navel. 'Why "regrettably"?' he asked.

She shrugged. 'It's always such a big risk, isn't it?'

He nodded. 'I live in Jo'burg. I understand something of living with risk.'

'Yes, I suppose you do.'

'But there is one thing I know for sure,' he said, reaching out to brush some hair from the side of her face. 'Being alive is a risk. You risk dying every single day. But you can't let it stop you living. And nothing . . . *nothing* . . . you can do will stop death from coming eventually. So the only choice you have is to live.'

Christmas swallowed past the tightness in her throat and took a deep breath. 'Well, that's sobering.'

'I'm sorry,' he said. 'I didn't mean to upset you.'

'No, you haven't. I think you're right. Maybe the trick is just to keep on dancing.'

He gave a small smile and she hopped out and closed the door gently.

Christmas watched Jackson's borrowed ute until the taillights disappeared around a bend. She hoped very, very much that she would see him again one day. For now, she blew him a kiss goodbye.

For her final two days in Provence, Christmas decisively made herself three temporary rules, just to help her get to the other side: she would make peace with the fact that she wouldn't find Gregoire Lachapelle on this trip but know that the door was still open for the future; she would allow no more angst over Lincoln—that situation would be sorted soon enough, one way or another; and she would devote herself to drinking in the stunning beauty of Provence, savouring every taste, sight, sound and smell, filling her inner well before she got back on the plane.

So that was what she did.

She arrived back in Tasmania after dark on Saturday evening

and slipped into her loft above The Chocolate Apothecary. She dropped her luggage just inside the door, set the heaters to a fierce level to warm the frosty air, pulled on a fresh pair of fluffy paisley pyjamas from her armoire and climbed under her doona, falling into a deep, dreamless sleep.

Her first day back in the shop was a Sunday, so there wasn't a lot of time to indulge in jetlag, with the expected weekend visitors coming as usual. But she'd woken feeling better than she'd thought she'd might, and enjoyed reading through Abigail's notes on everything that had happened on the days the shop had been open; she also flicked through the collection of letters and bills that had accrued. Unexpectedly, and touchingly, there was an invitation from Dennis and Juliette to their nuptials in a few months' time. They'd set the date on the same night as the chocolate-inspired proposal, they said, and would love her to come. She was honoured that they would acknowledge her for the very small role she'd played in securing their happiness.

But she'd have to leave all communications and paperwork until tomorrow when the shop was closed. Today, she needed all her mental power to concentrate on making coffees and serving treats without burning or spilling anything. Throughout her time on the floor, she noticed that the store was slightly changed with the movement and rearrangement of stock; coming home was like reacquainting herself with a good friend who had adventures of her own to share. She was also enjoying the creative, entre-preneurial thoughts that kept floating to the surface—inspired by her trip—such as hosting farm tours to local producers, connecting people with the origins of their food, and running chocolate-making workshops—though she'd be a lot kinder to her clients than Master Le Coutre's boot camp had been to her cohort.

Christmas wasn't surprised that Rosemary McCaw was the first visitor on her doorstep. What *was* surprising, however, was how she was dressed—in head-to-toe hot-pink lycra and carrying a black bicycle helmet under her arm.

'Christmas Angel, it's so wonderful to have you back at the helm of this ship,' Rosemary said, tip-tapping her way across the floor to embrace her.

'It's wonderful to see you, Rosemary,' Christmas said, hugging her. 'And why are you dressed like that?'

Rosemary stepped back and pointed her foot to one side to show Christmas. 'My new shoes.' They were cycling shoes, which explained the noise they made on the wooden floor. 'Gordon Harding has been instructing me in the fine art of penny farthing transportation. We're training for next year's seniors races.'

'Oh.' That also explained the skin-tight pink outfit. '*Oh!* You and Gordon, hey?' Christmas winked at Rosemary and raised her eyebrows. It was so heart-warming to see two senior residents find new life with each other. Especially since Rosemary had seemed down before Christmas left for France.

'Yes, we're an item. He's my beau. We have regular sleepovers at each other's houses.'

'Ah, that's . . . nice.'

Just then, Gordon Harding, Who Was Riding His Penny Farthing, rolled to a stop outside the shop, perched high on the big wheel and flicking the lever of the metal bell to make it click and clack.

'That's my call,' Rosemary said. 'After this morning's ride we're going to look up videos on YouTube for race tactics.'

'That sounds like great fun,' Christmas said. 'But with all this training, will you no longer be coming in for chocolate consultations?'

Rosemary placed her hand on her heart. 'My dear, I simply could not live without your chocolate. There is nothing on earth that would make me stop coming.' She positioned the bicycle helmet on her head, wobbling it from side to side to find the best fit, then did up the chinstrap with some difficulty under that rather wide jaw. 'At any rate, I'll be back soon, as I need to hear all about your adventures and your own love story.'

'I'm not sure what the ending to that story is yet,' Christmas said pensively.

'Then you can still choose the final scene,' Rosemary called over her shoulder, heading to the door. 'I'll be back for the encore.'

Around midday, Bert and Ernie arrived, a cold gust of wind following them in the door. They welcomed Christmas home with smiles and a tip of their caps before moving to the coffee station for their free coffee of the day.

'Off to canasta?' she called to the back of the men's trademark baseball caps as they sorted out their brews.

'Yes,' Bert said. 'And those Henderson boys are going down today.'

'They only won last time because of those four red threes. Can't beat luck like that. But the stats would suggest they won't get that lucky again today,' Ernie said.

'And that red canasta of aces.' Bert shook his head. 'I'd swear they were cheating.'

Bert and Ernie took their places at the long table and ordered chocolate toast, and Christmas placed the bread, fresh from Jane's bakery, under the cafe grill.

Then, just as she delivered the plates to the men, a text message arrived from Emily, asking if she'd like to catch up for dinner, but Christmas didn't have time to think about how to respond before Cheyenne came in carrying a bunch of sunflowers so large they almost dwarfed her short stature.

'Hello!' she called from behind the yellow heads and long green stems.

Christmas rushed to help her get them onto the counter. 'It's great to see you,' she said. 'Abigail was a bit worried about you while I was away. What happened?'

Cheyenne shot her left hand up into the air, the back of her hand facing Christmas, her fingers straight. A white gold and diamond ring sparkled under the lights.

'Oh my God!' Christmas took her hand and gazed at the beautiful ring, shiny with freshness and new beginnings. 'How did this happen?' Cheyenne wasn't even seeing anyone as far as she knew.

'His name's Wilbur,' Cheyenne said. 'He lives in Melbourne and we've known each other since we were kids but we'd lost track for a decade or so. Then he looked me up on Facebook and we began chatting and it was as if we were best friends and always had been and should never have lost contact. He came to stay for a couple of weeks while you were away and I guess we fell into a bit of a . . . well, a consumed state of affairs.'

'You've gone red to the tips of your ears!' Christmas laughed.

'The rest of the world just fell away, including, I'm afraid to say, your shop and my flower commitments. I'm very sorry.'

Christmas waved a hand. 'It doesn't matter.'

'Abigail came knocking on the door eventually. She didn't look very pleased. You know how she gets that horseshoe-shaped wrinkle between her brows when she's grumpy.'

'Yes, I do. She must be grumpy a lot, come to think of it, because I see it often.'

'She told me off and said I'd let you down and you'd be so disappointed.' Cheyenne tucked her left hand behind her back then, as though suddenly ashamed.

Christmas pulled it back around to the front. 'Not at all. I'm delighted for you.'

'Really? Because I'd love you to be a bridesmaid. I mean, I know we're too mature for that sort of thing, but I don't really have another word for it. I can't call you a flower girl. Or maybe I can!' Cheyenne laughed—loud, joyous laughter that simply couldn't be contained.

'Well, of course I'll be your person, whatever you want to call me.' They hugged.

'I've got to run,' Cheyenne said. 'We're off to look at venues together while the kids are at school. But I wanted to get these flowers to you and say how sorry I am for falling off the radar. I promise I'll get my head together soon.'

'Go on. Have fun.'

Cheyenne practically bounced out the door.

Christmas took a deep breath and a moment to absorb Cheyenne's wonderful change of luck and the new direction her life was taking. Life was full of surprises. It seemed as though the whole world was in love or getting married: Val and Archie; Lincoln's friend Rubble; Dennis and Juliette; Rosemary and Gordon; and Cheyenne.

Val appeared in the afternoon carrying a bag with the wedding shoes she'd just picked up for next weekend. She held them aloft and smiled sheepishly. Christmas was still annoyed with her, but Tiny Val was her sister. It was par for the course of sisterhood that you got annoyed, got hurt, but still kept going. It was the unwritten universal pact. And besides, Val was getting married in a week. Softening, Christmas held out her hands for the box to inspect them.

'Have you come to see me here so I can't make a scene in front of my customers?' she asked.

'Of course not,' Val said, taking a freshly baked gingerbread man from the jar in front of her stool at the counter.

'Because I'm still cranky,' Christmas said, setting out cups to make tea. She'd had quite enough caffeine for one day. Despite the promising start to the day her stamina hadn't lasted, and for the past few hours she'd been fighting off random waves of jetlag, which felt like she was being dumped in the surf and smothered by the weight of the ocean as she scrambled for air. She'd changed the music in the shop to an up-tempo Beatles compilation to keep her going. But she was very much looking forward to the shop being closed tomorrow so she could catch up.

'Oh, Val, these are gorgeous,' she added, touching the soft white fabric flowers on the toe of the shoe.

'And they're actually comfortable too! And half price! I'm a lucky girl,' Val said, biting the foot off the gingerbread man. 'Here, I brought you this,' she went on, handing over her offering.

Christmas eyed the object uncertainly. 'You brought me a rock?'

'Yes.'

'Why?'

Val shrugged. 'We'd run out of packet mixes for any sort of cake, so I chose a rock from the garden. Count yourself lucky— the rock's probably more edible than a cake would have been anyway.'

Christmas looked at her. 'You're a bit odd.'

'I know. Look, I really am sorry. It was an awful blunder of miscommunication and bad timing. You said so many times that you didn't care about finding Gregoire, so when I didn't hear back from you I assumed you were just ignoring me, but then later thought I should check just in case . . . But I'm still sorry.'

Christmas turned the rock over in her hand. On the back, Val had painted a red love heart in nail polish.

'We're family, Massy, and always will be,' Val continued. 'Families are the foundations of life, just like rocks are the foundation of the earth, which is of course why it hurts you so much that you might have missed your chance to find your father.'

Christmas lifted one shoulder—a partial relenting. 'I think I'm old enough to know that there are many chances in life. They keep coming, like buses. If you miss one, you just take the next one.'

As Val took her hand, Christmas thought that her little sister might be right: family was the base of life and it was also the bedrock of happiness. If yours was a bit wonky to begin with, then you had to work harder to make it strong.

'Okay, so I suppose I forgive you.' She turned away to get the tea.

'Hurrah.' Val clapped.

'Now, shall we follow the rules of making up after a fight and stuff ourselves silly with chocolate?' Christmas said.

'Pass me that bag of salted caramel drops there.'

'This one?'

'Yes. And get the slab of rocky road too.'

'Sure. And while we're on family, I want to start cooking classes with Nate. I should have done it before now. He's been right under my nose.'

'He'll love that,' Val said, biting into the rocky road. 'Make sure you teach him how to make this first, though, because I plan on eating all of it.'

By the late afternoon, Christmas had also caught up with Mary Hauser and her schnauzer (who came in for doggy chocolate); Abigail (who came to let Christmas know she'd be reducing her working days to just Saturdays because she was taking on more study); and Tu and Lien. The last pair had popped in on their way to hydrotherapy for Lien, and Christmas had told them to wait in the shop while she raced upstairs, tipped out the contents of her suitcase and skipped back down the stairs with the novel she'd bought in Paris. She handed it to Lien.

'It's in French,' the girl said, puzzled.

'I picked it up at a book stall beside the Seine. At the rate you read, I was worried you might get through everything ever written in the English language, and I wondered if maybe you might like to start taking French lessons with me, and then you could start on the French books?'

Lien looked up, her eyes wide under the red woollen beanie on top of her long hair. 'Together?'

'Yes. I think it's time I learned, but I hear it's a difficult language and I reckon it would be much more fun with a friend. What do you say?'

Lien looked at Tu, who smiled and nodded. A bright smile flashed across Lien's face, quickly replaced by an attempt at teenage nonchalance. 'Okay, sure. I could do that.'

'Wonderful!'

Tu had mouthed a silent *thank you* to Christmas while Lien was busy flipping through the book's pages.

Now, Christmas turned her thoughts to Emily, who was waiting for an answer about having dinner tonight. The problem was, though, that she'd pushed Lincoln and Emily together, and then Lincoln had up and left Tasmania and followed her to France. She couldn't be sure until she spoke to Emily, but perhaps her friend might be—justifiably—upset about this. And since she didn't yet know where she stood with Lincoln, it would make their conversation rather awkward. She felt guilt about Lincoln, but at the same time she was still hurt that Emily hadn't told her about Gregoire herself. It was all a bit much for her tired and foggy mind to handle. So she sent a message in reply to Emily, saying she was horribly jetlagged and would get back to her when she felt better.

26

Elsa was still in hospital, much to her own disdain. She had improved but the doctors were very fussy with old people. She guessed it would look quite bad on their records if they discharged elderly people only for them to cark it. But it was tedious in the extreme. It was one thing to be old and unable to walk around by yourself but quite another to have people asking the same boring questions about food and bowels and breathing over and over again. And she detested these modern pulse clips they put on the end of your finger. It was far more human for someone to press their warm fingers against your papery skin rather than hook you up like a robot.

Even worse, people kept asking her questions that were clearly designed to see if she still had all her faculties. Like this girl, with her ponytail swishing around her shoulders like some sort of hair commercial.

'What did you eat for breakfast, Mrs van Luc?' the ponytail asked. The girl knew the answer, of course; it was written on Elsa's chart, clasped in the girl's purple-painted nails.

'Can you tell me which year the charts changed from wood to plastic?' Elsa said.

'Sorry?' The girl was confused now, probably slightly anxious. Elsa could see a finger wandering towards the pen to make a note.

'The piece of plastic you're holding,' Elsa said patiently. 'Those charts used to be made of wood.'

'No, they've always been plastic.'

'You're so young,' Elsa said, a criticism, not an observation.

The girl left, frowning, passing Elsa's youngest son in the doorway.

'Well, don't hover over me,' the old woman ordered, refusing to show surprise. 'Sit down.'

Tom half sat on the edge of the visitor's chair. Elsa found it difficult to read his expression. Defensiveness, certainly. But maybe a hint of contrition? Or perhaps that was just what she wanted to see.

'I'm taking it this visit is because your children have been to see you,' Elsa said. 'Probably got your hopes up I was about to die.'

He had the decency to at least look a tiny bit ashamed at that.

'Stop fretting,' she said. 'I know why you're here. They told me about your investment issues.'

Tom muttered under his breath and wiped his hand across his mouth. She looked at his rumpled shirt. Gracious, did the man never iron? She waited to hear what he would say, though she doubted it would make any difference to her decision. Mr Nettle from the solicitor's practice down the road was on his way so she could change her will.

'Then you know why I need the money,' Tom said.

'And why should I bail you out?' she said.

'Because you owe me. You ruined me,' he said, and the words struggled to emerge from beneath years of resentment.

'Ruined you?' That was surprising. 'What on earth do you mean?'

'I had plans and dreams. I'd worked hard to save that money to go to America and you just'—he puffed a few times—'just took it!'

Elsa looked down at the white cotton blanket pulled up to her armpits, frowning, casting her mind back to pluck at the memory Tom had stirred. In due course she found it. That was one benefit of getting older. The distant memories came back again, because just as you were finishing your lap around the circle of life you met up again with the parts at the start.

'To pay the creditors?' she clarified, remembering now that she'd counted out her son's notes and been impressed he'd saved so much.

'Yes, to pay the creditors,' Tom said, his voice heavy and slow, laden with decades of contempt.

'But we were going to lose the house,' she said, incredulous that her quick thinking that day could be so ungratefully condemned.

'That wasn't my problem. I was out of there anyway. I was on my way to America and a new life.'

She shook her head sadly, wondering how Tom had turned out so dense. 'But that wasn't the end of your life, Tom. You've lived a long time since then. You've had plenty of opportunities to get whatever life you wanted. Bad things happen to people all the time. People lose their homes, their livelihoods, their families. People lose their children!' She choked up then, unexpectedly, and looked away. *She'd* lost a child. A grown man

349

by then, but still her child, always. And out on the terrifying battlefields where she couldn't even say goodbye.

'Money is seasonal, Tom. It comes in like the tide and it goes out again and then it comes back. To lose a bit of money . . . it's nothing. *Nothing*,' she said fiercely.

'But you betrayed me,' he said.

'Ah, I see. Now a sense of betrayal is a powerful emotion. I don't believe it's justified here. Your father was in trouble and that put all of us in danger. I did the only thing I could do to save us as a family. You were a part of that family and you had the resources in that moment to help. That's what families do.'

'But you didn't even ask.'

Elsa opened her mouth to say that she didn't have time, it was their only chance, that that was what she'd had to do time and again throughout their lives but Tom had mostly never seen it, and sometimes she'd had to make choices and sacrifices she didn't like. Ebe made their life hard. But you didn't get divorced back then; you just got on with it.

But something made her stop. There was a slow-moving feeling of heaviness travelling through her body. There was something wrong with her recollection of that event. She felt herself automatically try to resist it, to defend her actions. Instead, she closed her eyes to search inside for whatever was trying to surface.

And there it was.

The truth of the matter was that she did have enough money tucked away to pay the creditors that day. But if she'd taken it, they'd be left with no reserves, and she didn't ever want to be without reserves. Ebe's erratic choices meant she never felt truly safe and secure. The rug could be ripped out from beneath her at any moment. So she couldn't just have enough for one financial catastrophe; she needed more. And in keeping her focus on the big picture, in ensuring they could meet the next inevitable crisis, she'd overlooked her son's smaller picture—his dream, his plans.

Now here he was telling her she'd ruined his life. Whether or not she agreed with that belief, or thought it was reasonable, she did accept that she'd acted that day without thinking it through. She'd acted without considering Tom's feelings. And now? Well, she was certainly old enough to admit her mistakes.

'You're right, I didn't ask and that wasn't fair. I'm sorry.'

Tom stared at her, his lips twitching, his fingers worrying at the seam of his pants. Her words had affected him.

'And now I might lose *my* house,' he said. 'I'm in the same predicament you were in.'

She raised her chin and looked at the ceiling. Ah, she hadn't really considered it like that. She supposed her little speech about families still applied, then, and she should take heed of her own self-righteousness. 'Why didn't you just tell me about the investment and why you needed the money instead of trying to bully me into selling the house?'

He was struggling to come up with words, shuffling his feet and looking all around the room, ashamed, she realised, and that touched her deeply. She'd failed him as a mother if at his age he was still ashamed to tell her the truth. But perhaps she could ease his discomfort a little; it would be a kind thing to do.

'It doesn't matter now,' she said gently. 'We all know the truth. And, Tom, you did what you thought was right. Sometimes bad luck comes our way no matter how hard we try.'

There was a moment's silence.

'So will you help me?' he asked evenly. Her words had calmed him.

She licked her dry lips. 'Yes, I will help you. I won't be selling the house, but I have a bit of money I can give you that will buy you some time, give you a chance to work something out for the long term.'

'Thank you.'

'My solicitor is on his way. I'll get him to send you some money to tide you over for a bit. But that will be it, do you understand? There'll be no more. It's up to you now.'

He nodded and scratched at the back of his ear. 'Yes. Thank you.'

She couldn't quite bring herself to reach for his hand, but she wanted to leave him with something kind, something that might at least make up for a little bit of what she did all those years ago. 'I hope you can move forward from this and be happy. You deserve that. Everyone does.'

Tom's nostrils flared, whether from unspoken words or suppressed emotion she wasn't sure. 'I'd better get going,' he said.

'Okay.'

He scraped back his chair and rose, passing the solicitor in the doorway on his way out, and Elsa watched him go, feeling the load she'd been carrying for some time—the weight of having to pretend her son's anger didn't hurt—begin to lift.

•

Monday had passed for Christmas in a blur of catnapping and zombie-like wandering, of laundry and unpacking, a touch of paperwork and bill paying, and chicken soup. She didn't have anywhere near enough mental clarity to speak to Lincoln—not when everything was so fragile—so she concentrated instead on tending to her domestic needs, and being gentle with herself while her body adjusted to being in Tasmania and in the middle of winter once more, rather than the deliciously hot French summer. Before she knew it, Tuesday was upon her and she was back in The Apothecary, tempering chocolate and grinding coffee beans, serving and chatting to many locals who popped in to ask about her trip. She made a mental note to get some photos printed to display as soon as possible.

Lincoln had sent her an email with the last draft of their book attached and a short message saying he hoped she was well and giving her an update on Elsa—who was still in hospital, poor dear. He told her he was busy for the rest of the week with his sister, who was here to visit Elsa, and asked Christmas if they could catch up on Friday. Christmas was shutting the shop on Friday so she could help Val prepare for the wedding on Saturday. Inside her chest, her heart had thumped loudly.

The wedding. She'd been so looking forward to enjoying the wedding with Lincoln. Dancing with him. Kissing him. What would happen now? She didn't want to ask him via email so she agreed to see him on Friday and would just have to wait to find out.

Now, it was Tuesday evening and she sat cross-legged on her bed with the manuscript pages spread out before her, a red pen in hand. Jetlag still had her wide awake at inconvenient times. It was nearly midnight. The night outside was quiet and dark. So it was surprising when her phone lit up with a message.

R u up? I was just passing and saw your light on.

Emily didn't live anywhere that would require her to just pass by Christmas's door. She froze and considered ignoring the message; later she could always claim that she'd been asleep. But she had to speak to Emily at some point.

Come up. You know where the key is.

She got off the bed and automatically turned on the kettle. She heard Emily fish out the key from under the brick at the back of the building, open the door and climb the stairs.

'Welcome home,' Emily gushed, puffing slightly from the stairs, and hugged her. 'I've been dying to see you and hear how everything was. I'm starting to get the feeling you're avoiding me!'

'I'm glad you came by. Coffee?' Christmas said, hoping Emily would say yes so it would give her something to do.

'No, thanks. It's a bit late.'

'Yes. Tea?'

'No, thanks.'

'I could do you a hot chocolate?'

Emily relented. 'Okay.'

She sat down on the couch, pulled off her woollen scarf and ran her fingers through her curls to unknot them while Christmas took some chocolate ganache she'd made fresh today and heated it gently, then added milk and a swig of butterscotch sauce—Emily's favourite twist—and topped it with a dollop of vanilla cream.

She presented it to her in a tall glass mug. 'Sorry there aren't any embellishments today,' she said, thinking of the flaked chocolate downstairs that would go so well on top.

'Oh, please. At home I'd be making it out of a tin from the supermarket.' Emily took a sip. 'Ah. That is truly fabulous.'

'I'm glad you like it.'

Christmas took a seat in the lounge on the other side of the coffee table. Emily eyed her over the top of her glass. 'Is everything okay? You seem a bit edgy,' she said, licking the spoon.

Christmas buried her face in her hands for a moment then looked up and grimaced. 'Everything seems like such a mess.'

'What do you mean?'

'I know that you dated Lincoln.'

Emily looked wary. 'I . . . yes, kind of. But how do you know that?'

'And I found out about Gregoire, about the information you told Lincoln to pass on.'

Her friend looked confused. 'Isn't that a good thing? You've always wanted to know about your father.'

'Yes, but *you* didn't tell me,' Christmas said.

'But I thought I had. I was too sick to look at a computer screen, so I asked Lincoln to do it.'

The deep inhalation from Christmas was loud in the silence between them. 'It's just that . . .' She paused, looking for the right words. What she wanted to say was that Emily was her best friend and if anyone should have been motivated enough to ensure she got the information about Gregoire it should have been her. She felt injured that Emily seemed to have carelessly delegated the information. and it seemed especially surprising given how much she and Val had been hassling her to look for her father.

Emily waited, looking hurt.

Christmas exhaled.

Really, it was all just water under the bridge. It had been a calamity of errors and circumstance. And right now, Christmas herself had something to confess here. Emily might have hurt her, but she might well have hurt Emily too.

'You're right. It's okay. It's just one of those things that happened.' She waved her hand and leaned back against a cushion.

Across the table, Emily put her glass and spoon down and bit her lip. 'No. I'm the best friend. I was the last person to handle the information, other than Lincoln. I'm sorry. I can understand why it would upset you.'

'Thanks,' Christmas smiled, and Emily's shoulders relaxed.

'Did Lincoln tell you that we'd dated? When he emailed you the information?' she asked, curious.

'He didn't email, actually.' Christmas braced herself. 'He came to visit me—in France.'

Emily leapt off the couch. 'In *France*? Why? How?'

'He turned up on my first day off after the scholarship course. Surprised me.'

'But why?' Emily's knees slowly bent as she lowered herself back down.

'Evidently because we had more of a mutual attraction than I'd first wanted to believe. He wanted to give us a shot, as a couple.' She waited, wanting to reach over and take Emily's hand.

But Emily's hand had gone to her chest. 'I can't believe this.'

'I know. I'm sorry. I know I pushed you two together. I panicked after Lincoln and I kissed in The Apothecary and I had such strong feelings for him and it wasn't *in the rules*. But then once I was in France, it was all so beautiful and everything felt different. I realised we could have something really special and I wanted more. And at the same time, apparently, he was thinking the same thing back here and made a snap decision to jump on a plane.'

'I wondered why he didn't return my last text. I knew he was busy working on the book and . . .' Her voice faltered. Then she swallowed whatever emotion was trying to come to the surface. 'He's so lovely,' she said.

'Yeah, he is.'

'I really liked him and I thought he liked me too.'

A stab of guilt pierced through Christmas's heart. 'There's no reason he wouldn't like you, Em. You're wonderful.'

'I should have known it was too good to be true.'

'It's not your fault, Em,' Christmas said. 'I can't speak for Lincoln; I've no idea what was going through his mind but he's a good guy so I'm sure he'll explain it to you soon.' She paused. 'Then again, things got a bit messy between him and me so I'm not entirely sure about anything right now.'

'What happened?' Emily asked. 'Please tell me. You two obviously have something serious here and nothing like whatever he and I had.' She scoffed. 'We never even got a real date. Did he tell you that?' She smiled wanly.

Christmas returned her smile, sympathetic. 'Yes, he did.'

Emily waved her hands at her face, as if drying tears. 'So just forget about him and me. It obviously meant nothing. You two clearly have a lot more going on than any of us first thought. That's a huge deal for him to fly to France. So tell me, what happened?'

Christmas breathed a sigh of relief that they'd made it through that conversation with their friendship still intact. It had been a bumpy few months for them; but they'd made it. They both settled into the couch with blankets and Emily kicked off her shoes. Christmas started with the kiss in The Apothecary; moved to the text message to apologise and his vague response; their Skype game and their 'almost' declarations; his arrival on the lawn of the chateau; Giselle's humping (which made Emily hoot with laughter); her wonderful days with Lincoln; and then the revelations about his dates with Emily and the news about Gregoire; and, finally, her panic attack that coincided with Elsa's collapse.

'Oh God, that's terrible,' Emily gasped.

'Elsa's going to be okay, but I don't know about Lincoln and me. I'm worried I might have frightened him off for good.'

'I'm sure that's not true.'

'He said he'd fallen in love with me,' Christmas said, feeling herself flush at the memory.

'Ohhh.' Emily clasped her hands together and her face went misty. 'And how do you feel?'

'The same.'

'Then what's the problem?' Emily asked, excited now. 'It's all coming together.'

'Except for me behaving like a lunatic,' Christmas said, picking at threads of the blanket on her lap.

'So tell him you had temporary insanity! Tell him you love him and want to spend the rest of your life with him!' Emily said, bouncing up and down on the couch. 'I can see it written all over your face—he's The One! The man flew to other side of the world for you. Who does that? You clearly have a big cosmic thing going on and nothing and no one, especially not me, can keep you apart. Don't die wondering. Make it right! Do it now!'

Emily's enthusiasm was infectious and Christmas suddenly felt light and buoyed by hope. She laughed. 'Alright, alright, I will. But not now; it's after midnight. He's coming over on Friday morning to talk about our book. I'll tell him then.' She felt resolve set inside her like steel despite the nerves.

'Thank you for being so understanding,' she said to Emily. 'I'm sorry for pushing you towards Lincoln when I didn't really mean it deep down. I hope you're not too hurt.'

Emily waved a hand. 'I'm already over it. The important thing now is that we get you two back together and you live happily ever after.'

Christmas shook her head in wonder. 'Imagine that.'

Emily paused, and then said, 'I have news of my own, actually.'

Christmas grimaced. 'Sorry, it's been all about me so far. Please—tell me your news.'

'I'm moving to Melbourne in a couple of weeks.'

'What?'

'A research job came up for a production house making a new children's television program and I applied online one day at work because I was bored and thought, well, why not? I didn't think much about it again, but then they offered me a Skype interview while you were away, and today they phoned to say I got the job. So, I'm going.'

Christmas felt winded. 'Wow.'

'I know.' Emily sounded like she couldn't believe it herself.

'Congratulations,' Christmas said. 'That's great, and of course I'm really happy for you.' But she was numb. All she could think was that her friend was leaving her. She wanted to take hold of her and beg her not to go. 'How long do you think you'll be gone?'

'I don't know. It's a full-time position, but you know what television's like. It could all change next week.'

Christmas moved across to Emily on the couch and hugged her. 'That's really great, Em, a fantastic opportunity. It'll be wonderful and open all sorts of new doors. But I'll miss you.'

'Oh, don't start!' Emily wailed, and burst into tears.

27

Lincoln pulled the postcard out of the letterbox. It was a hand-drawn cartoon of Rubble, now thin as a rake, and his dreadlocked fiancée standing on a surfboard on a large wave, dressed in Hawaiian shirts. The wedding invitation details were on the back: Bondi Beach, next month. Lincoln smiled and shoved the card into his pocket.

He was genuinely happy for Rubble and Eleisha. They were embarking on an exciting new adventure. As for him, he was anxious to see Christmas tomorrow morning. He'd been so busy for the past few days alongside Jen, on their secret mission, that he'd not been able to go to see her. And he needed to see her. Especially now that things had turned out differently from what he'd expected. The path had definitely taken a sudden and unexpected turn.

'Come on, Caesar,' he said, opening the car door and trying to hurry the old man up in his never-ending search for the perfect place to pee. 'We've got somewhere to be.'

Caesar lifted his head, smiled, wagged his tail. Then he cast his eyes over at the neighbour's place. Today the blackboard outside the front fence said, *Want a marriage that will make you rich? Marry a divorce lawyer.*

Lincoln shook his head. 'Miserable old bugger. What happened to captaining your own ship?' he asked to the wind in the trees.

Caesar trotted over to the board and lifted his leg, letting his opinion be known.

'Good boy, Caesar,' Lincoln said. 'Now, let's go.'

•

Elsa, without too much fuss, allowed Lincoln to pick her up out of the passenger seat and place her in the wheelchair on the driveway at Green Hills. The dog was in the back seat; he'd stood up most of the way from the hospital with his head hanging over her shoulder, an occasional drip of drool running down her arm. She was glad he was here. She felt a bit deflated after her stay in hospital and the upset with Tom.

Lincoln wheeled her across the gravel towards her bungalow. The shades were down over the windows. The sky was dark grey and a cold wind tore across the yellow farmland around the home.

Home—such a strange idea.

Lincoln opened the door into the darkened bungalow. So this was it, then. This was going to be her last home.

He closed the door behind them and turned on the lights.

'Surprise!'

Elsa jumped. Her room was crowded with a welcome-home party. There was Sarah, blowing on a hooter, a neon-pink feather boa thrown over her nurse's uniform. Rita sat in her own wheelchair, looking much better after her bout of the flu, a crumpled tissue in her hand and a big lopsided smile on her face. Elsa gave her a small wave, pleased to see her dear friend recovered. The rest of the book club was there too, Robert Graham and his wife smiling as always, Yvonne Murphy, and Doris Laherty actually awake for once. Everyone, of course, except Lulu. They were all holding a copy of the book Elsa had chosen for their August meeting before she got sick (*James Herriot's Vet Stories*), which she'd picked because it was set in the pre-war era so was of interest to many of them, and because it featured a lot of farm animals, and most of them came from rural backgrounds. She'd thought she might organise a visit from a mobile animal farm, the sort that went around to schools.

And the bungalow! She could scarcely take it in.

As Caesar worked the room to greet everyone and steal a sandwich off the table, Lincoln knelt beside her. 'Jen suggested it might be a good idea to give your place a makeover,' he said. 'What do you think?'

Think? She could barely breathe. The drab mauve walls had been painted a fresh but soothing antique white. There were new curtains, crisp white with a sprig of lavender embroidered in the corners. A new blue toile bedspread and French linen cushions. Vases of bright flowers everywhere. New Tiffany-blue lampshades on the side tables and light shades hanging from the ceiling. A new flat-screen television set and, best of all, her very own computer and workstation so she could Skype her family in peace whenever she wanted, rather than having to go to the common room. A scented candle burned on the dresser and the smell of vanilla floated in the air.

Her hands were at her mouth, she realised, and she dropped them to speak. But a large, painful lump was in the way, wedged in her throat. She sucked in her lips and nodded quickly. Lincoln put his hand on her shoulder and she reached up her own hand to pat his.

Then, through the sudden blurriness in her eyes, she saw the last, best surprise.

Out from the bathroom came Jenny and her son, Nathan, in his wheelchair, his head resting back against the lambswool cover behind him, and wearing a huge smile. Behind them was Jenny and Lincoln's mother, Katherine. Elsa's ex-daughter-in-law had been more of a daughter to her than Tom had been a son.

Elsa began to cry.

They all rushed at her, shushing and clucking. Sarah quietly brought over a cup of tea on a matching saucer and placed it in Elsa's hands. All the while Elsa stared in disbelief at the three from north Queensland.

'How did you all get here?' she asked shakily.

Jenny smiled and shrugged as if it had been no big deal, but of course it would have been a major logistical feat with Nathan in his chair. 'I stayed on to do the makeover with Lincoln, which we did over the past few days, and Mum and Nathan wanted to see you too, so they hopped on a plane and arrived this morning.'

Katherine gave Elsa a hug, careful not to knock the tea, and Elsa leaned into her round, squishy body. It was tiring being the mother all the time, and it was such a joy to be held and rocked by another.

'I should have come much sooner,' Katherine said plainly.

'No, no. You have Jenny and Nathan to look after,' Elsa said. She reached out to Nathan as their wheelchairs met. She was pierced with sadness for him. He was far too young to be in one of these contraptions. 'And how are you?' she said to him.

'I like flying,' he said, and jerked his skinny arms out to the sides to pretend to fly.

'Maybe you could be a pilot,' Elsa said. 'I'll send you some books on planes.'

It was incredible that Nathan was here now. She'd hardly seen him since he and Jenny left Tasmania. And seeing him made her that much happier that she'd instructed the solicitor to draw up the papers as she had, with all of her estate going into trust for Nathan's care. She patted him on the knee, and he laughed as Caesar came to lick his hand.

Someone had turned on some music, some kind of happy big band song, and Sarah was cutting a lemon meringue pie—Elsa's favourite—and passing around plates.

'We all want you to know how much we love you,' Lincoln said.

'And Tom's a fool,' Katherine said, shaking her head.

'He lacks foresight,' Elsa agreed, her strength returning a little. 'But I feel I know him better now, after all this. And myself, too. Perhaps there's some good to come out of it after all.'

'That's generous of you,' Katherine said, accepting a slice of pie. 'You were the one I was most heartbroken about leaving at the end of the marriage. I'm so glad we've stayed in touch.'

'Speaking of which,' Lincoln said, checking the time on his phone, 'Uncle Jake and his family will be calling soon on Skype. They stayed up late in London to join the party. We'd better get you over to the computer and logged on.'

He wheeled her over to the workstation and showed her where all the bits and pieces were on the new machine, though he needn't have bothered. She was quite technically proficient, but he was clearly feeling good about helping so she didn't interrupt, just busied herself sipping on her tea. Good old Sarah. She knew exactly how she liked it, strong and hot.

Someone popped a champagne cork—goodness, this was a real party—and Caesar chased it across the room.

Then she noticed that amid all the clamour Lincoln had gone quiet and was staring at the floor. 'What's up, my boy?'

He inhaled, struggling with whatever it was he wanted to say. 'I want you to know that I thought very hard about the idea of taking you home to your place and being your carer.'

'Oh, no, no!' She waved him away. 'You can't!'

'And I agree with you. It wouldn't work.'

Even though Elsa knew it was true and right, there was still a burst of disappointment inside her. This was absolutely her life now, for good.

'But I promise you this. I will make your life so much better than it's been lately, and together we will squeeze every last bit of fun out of this world that we can.' His voice was determined and uncompromising.

'Okay,' she said quietly.

He kissed her on the forehead just as a noise started up on the computer, signalling that Jake was calling, and Elsa plastered a smile on her face and clicked the accept button. She had a lot to tell Jake, and then she had a party to get on with. After all, this was the first day of the rest of her life.

·

Christmas had a lot to do on her day off to help Val get organised for the wedding, but of course she'd made time for Lincoln. She ushered him in, jittery with nerves, and sat opposite him at the long table. He was friendly, but looked guarded, which she could understand, and it only made her more eager to get in with what she needed to tell him. So when he put the manuscript on the table and began to speak she quickly interrupted him.

'I need to say something first,' she said, smiling, but below the table her hands gripped the material of her trousers.

'Sure,' he said, leaning back.

She took a moment to take him in, his endless blue eyes, his dark hair, his lips. That body beneath his clothes that she'd savoured and wanted to hold onto for the rest of her life.

'I'm sorry,' she began. 'For losing the plot the way I did at the chateau. It was a bit over the top. I was shocked. And spun out. And I just needed some time to process all of that.'

'It's completely understandable,' he said, earnestly. 'I totally screwed up by forgetting the information about your father. And as for Emily . . .'

Christmas flinched.

'I shouldn't have started anything with her. It was easy to ask her out but only because I knew I wasn't going to fall for her. And I sound like a right bastard for saying that, but it's true. I didn't have any real feelings for her, not like I did for you. You knocked it out of the park.'

Christmas was almost afraid to breathe.

'My nan told me I'm lazy, and I think she's right. You might have pushed me away—twice—but I shouldn't have let you, either time. I should have come back and knocked down your door and told you I loved you.'

A shaky breath hiccupped through Christmas's chest. She reached across the table and took his hand. It was strong and warm and she adored it.

'I love you,' she said firmly, decisively. 'And I don't want to waste another moment with either of us being stupid or overreacting. I can't wait to take you to the wedding tomorrow and start a whole new adventure with you.'

But then she noticed that instead of looking joyous, the way she felt inside, Lincoln looked distressed. 'What's the matter?'

He cleared his throat, and her heart turned cold.

'I've been offered another job,' he said.

'Where?'

'Back in Ecuador, pretty much doing the same thing I was doing before, except I'll be a team leader this time, with more responsibility, more money, more freedom. They didn't give me much time to think about it, and they need me there quickly.'

'You're leaving?' She pulled her hand away and pressed the heels of her palms against her eyes, wanting to block out the world and the words he was about to say.

'Tomorrow. For six months, maybe a year.'

She dropped her hands and stared at him, and her eyes filled with tears. 'No. No, please don't go. We've only just started. We've got something special here and we can't lose it now.' Christmas pulled herself up. That kind of emotional outburst wasn't like her, but she'd built this moment up so much in her mind and she'd prepared herself and her words over and over, and played out various scenarios of how he might react. Emily had convinced her this was a love that was meant to be, that it was destiny. She'd never imagined the news he'd just shared. The words were out before she could think twice.

'I agree that this has been unexpected and wonderful, and more real than anything I've ever felt before,' he said.

'Then don't go.'

'But this is what I do,' he said. 'This is who I am.'

Christmas knew then that there was no point in trying to change his mind. She'd known this about Lincoln. He'd told her from the start that he loved living his life on a whim and moving around as jobs came up, taking new experiences as they eventuated with no guarantees. And she'd built a life and career here, one that was just gathering momentum and moving into exciting new fields. Her family was here. Her life was here.

She stood up and folded her arms across her chest. 'I understand,' she said.

Lincoln looked pained. But it obviously wasn't enough pain to make him change his mind.

'You should go,' she said. 'I'm sure you've got a lot to do and you'll want to spend some time with Elsa before you go.'

'Yes.' He looked genuinely stricken about leaving Elsa. 'I haven't told her yet.'

'What about Caesar?' she said.

'I'm going to ask the nurse, Sarah, if she'll take him.' He grimaced. 'I'm actually really going to miss him.' He pushed the manuscript across the table. 'Can we can talk about the book via email?'

'Of course.'

He swung his legs over the bench seat and stood up, facing her, rubbing his hands together as though he didn't know what to do with them. She stared at the ground.

'I'm sorry,' he said.

She lifted her chin and looked him straight in the eye. 'I'll be fine.'

It would be a bigger heartbreak than she'd ever had before. And she would cry, probably for a long time. And she would feel sad, maybe for a lot longer than that. But she knew without doubt that she would be just fine because she was a different person now and she'd learned how to be happy. She'd learned how to be resilient.

And she had Val and the boys, and Joseph, Emily, Cheyenne, Rosemary, Tu and Lien, all of them a piece of the happiness puzzle.

'Thank you,' he said. 'For everything. I'll miss you.'

'I'll miss you too.'

And he was gone.

•

Emily was in the bath, shaving her legs and giving herself a pedicure for the wedding tomorrow, when her mobile phone rang, lying on the edge of the basin. She leaned out, dropping frothy bubbles on the floor. It was Christmas. And for some reason she had a feeling it wasn't good news.

'What's happened?' she said, sinking back into the water.

On the other end, Christmas was sobbing. 'It's over,' she managed to get out.

'What's over, what do you mean?'

'Lincoln . . . he's leaving!' And then she wailed and sobbed for so long that Emily told her to wait right there, she was coming straight over—because that was the job of the best friend.

28

The Leaning Church Vineyard was a twenty-minute drive out of Launceston, and resided in an elevated position about the town of Lalla, in the Tamar Valley wine route. The wedding cars were provided by one of Archie's motoring enthusiast friends. Archie drove himself and the three boys in a black 1930s Ford soft-top. When they reached the church at the back of the vineyard, their job was to light the tea lights inside twenty rice-paper lanterns that lined the aisle of the church. This would serve as the signal for all the guests to take their seats, and the boys would have their moment walking down the aisle. Christmas had kissed Archie's hairy cheek at home before the men left and thought he looked like a finely groomed shaggy dog, the fur of his paws just visible below the cuffs of his white suit. Willis, Nate and Braxton were all miniature copies of their dad, minus the excess hair—although that would likely only be a matter of time.

The bridal party—Val, Christmas, Darla and Joseph—followed in a teal Austin with white ribbons at the front and red leather seats. Joseph was at the wheel, Darla beside him, evidently working hard to keep her criticisms of his driving to a minimum, and the sisters sat in the back seat, holding hands, giggling, and inhaling the delicately scented white freesias in their laps. Cheyenne had dropped off the stunning bouquets that morning.

'Look at those clouds,' Val said, her eyes lit up as she checked the sky.

The weather was probably not what many brides would want for their wedding day but Christmas agreed that it was charming. The fat, low-hanging dark clouds surrounded the entourage and seemed to magnify the expectation in the air. Weak sunlight filtered through floating mist and intensified the green of the hills, giving everything an enchanted feel. It was perfectly quiet—a natural cathedral. The long dirt road to the church wound up and down and round, tall gum trees lining the edges, and the car bumped gently along past goats, grape vines and wizened houses with smoke pumping from chimneys.

Joseph pulled the car to a stop in front of the weatherboard church, and a few stragglers—a mother chasing a toddler in a pink tutu, one of Archie's pimply-faced apprentices smoking a cigarette, and an elderly woman on a mobile phone—all hurried inside. Christmas stepped out of the car in her sleeveless mint-green satin and ivory tulle and lace dress, shivering slightly in the cold and carrying her bridesmaid's bouquet. It was impossible not to feel happy in this moment, despite everything that had happened with Lincoln.

Darla opened her door and Christmas went to help her out.

'I'm not an old woman, Christmas,' she grumbled, but she allowed her arm to be taken and didn't pull away once she was on her feet.

'I know you're not,' Christmas said. 'But it's my prerogative as your daughter to be kind to you.' Darla looked a little startled, but Christmas just wrapped her in a hug before she could respond.

Her mother was flawed. Christmas had always known that, and now she realised that it was unfair, perhaps even cruel, to expect her to be anything other than what she was. She had to stop blaming her for not knowing more about Gregoire. It was what it was. No one could turn back the clock, change the past. It was simply time to move on.

Joseph opened Val's door and took her hand as she inched out. From across the roof of the Austin, Christmas could see the strong emotion he struggled to suppress. Her own nose began to tingle, heralding tears, but she forced them away.

Val's peacock-blue duchess satin floor-length dress made her look like Audrey Hepburn, and the peacock feather pinned at her crown added a regal touch. She might have had rouge on her cheeks but she didn't need it; she was as radiant as any young bride could be. She adjusted the material around her waist, positioned the freesias in her arm and turned her eyes questioningly to Christmas and Darla.

'You look gorgeous,' Christmas said.

Darla nodded. 'Yes,' she agreed, 'you're a vision.'

'Thanks, Mum,' Val said. 'I'm really glad you're here.' She squeezed Darla's hand and her mother pulled her in for a last embrace before the walk down the aisle.

Then it started to rain, lightly at first as they made their way up the petal-covered footpath, and more heavily by the time they reached the rose-covered walkway leading up to the church entrance. The lanterns cast flickering lights against the church windows, and the sound of relaxed jazz piano music floated from inside. By the time they got to the arched doorway, the rain was pelting down, hammering the roof and ground, loud enough to muffle the music. Far from being upset by this, Val glowed with pleasure.

The four of them walked between rows of pews filled with smiling people. They passed Emily, sitting on the end of the fourth row from the front, wearing a festive hat of Australian leaves and gumnuts, and Christmas gave her a grateful smile for all her support, especially yesterday when it had felt as though her heart was tearing in two. Emily beamed back and gave them a little wave. In the front row were Val's other half-siblings, Paula and Sacha, and their mother, Gloria, holding up cameras and wearing a buttonhole and corsages that matched Val's flowers.

By the time they reached the groom's party standing with the celebrant, the noise of the rain was deafening. Val kissed her three sons and handed her flowers to Darla, who stood close by with Christmas at her side. Joseph stood next to his ex-wife and put his arm around her shoulders as her bottom lip began to quiver. Val faced Archie and took his hands. The celebrant tried to welcome everyone but she couldn't be heard over the noise. Everyone laughed and for a few moments there was nothing but the sound of water drops hitting the roof. The reverie was only broken by a hiccupping, hee-hawing, blubbering noise that turned out to be issuing from the hairy man holding onto Val's hands at the front of the church, hands he would promise never to let go, just as soon as his words could be heard over the rain.

The reception was supposed to be a garden tea party affair in Val and Archie's backyard but the relentless rain made it impossible, so the whole thing was moved inside with an air of jovial chaos. Old jam jars holding candles were scattered throughout the house. Petals were sprinkled over tables. Bath towels were laid down in doorways and hallways to mop up excess water and mud. Body heat steamed up the windows. Braxton brought out his dinosaurs to decorate cheese platters, Nate put on an apron and set himself up in the kitchen to help make the food, and Willis fulfilled the role of runner, ducking and weaving through the crowd with ice, drinks, music and trays of canapés.

'Are you disappointed we can't do this outside?' Christmas asked Val as they were pressed into the corner of the kitchen by a mass of people moving through to the dining room.

'Not really. This is life. You can't plan it.' Val moved off happily to speak to an old school friend.

Emily approached her then, a drink in hand.

'Where's your hat gone?' Christmas said.

'I had to take it off because I kept knocking it on doorways and things. I think Braxton is using it as a bush setting for a dinosaur role play.'

They both watched the scene playing out around them, ties being loosened, shoes flung into corners, plastic cups overflowing with bubbles, groups posing cheek to cheek for informal photographs, smartphones being tapped and shared, laughter, chatting, the inevitable awkward guy in the corner with his arms crossed, and the bored and likely deaf grandmother ensconced in an armchair waiting for someone to bring her a plate.

'I can't believe you're leaving,' Christmas said, suddenly overwhelmed and tired and a little teary.

'I know. It's the end of an era. But we've survived distance before, when you lived in Sydney.'

'And then I ran back to you,' Christmas said.

'Well then, if it all goes badly for me I'll run back to you and sleep on your couch and eat your chocolate for a few months while I get myself together again.'

'Promise?'

'I promise.'

Just then, Frank Sinatra's voice boomed out of the stereo, tables and chairs were pulled to the edges of the lounge room, and Paula, the bossier of Val's other siblings, ordered everyone onto the dance floor.

Joseph manoeuvred into their corner, kissed Emily on the cheek and asked if he could steal Christmas away for a dance.

'I'll let you borrow her,' Emily said, and squeezed Christmas's hand as they moved off.

'Where are Val and Archie?' Christmas said, taking a space on the dance floor with Joseph.

'I'm not sure. I haven't seen them for a while.'

'Probably cornered somewhere by someone talking their ear off.'

Joseph sway-danced with Christmas to 'Come Fly with Me'. 'Have you been taking lessons?' he asked. 'I don't remember you being this coordinated before.'

'I would object to that if it wasn't so true,' she said, twirling under his arm. 'And yes, I had to dance in France as part of my chocolate course.'

'That's an unusual teaching method,' Joseph said, stepping in towards her and then out again.

'It certainly was.'

'Did it work?'

'Yes, I think it might have.'

'Huh.'

She put her hand up onto his shoulder. 'You know what?'

'What?'

'I'm really glad you're my stepfather/ex-stepfather/father-figure person.'

'Well, that's nice of you to say so. I'm glad you're my step-daughter/ex-stepdaughter/daughter-ish person.'

'And if I ever get married, I'd be so happy if you would walk with me down the aisle.'

Joseph stumbled and stepped on her toe.

'Ow!' She laughed.

'God, sorry. Are you alright?'

'I think I'll live, but my pedicure might be ruined. Sorry if I threw you off.'

Joseph's voice was thick with emotion. 'I'd be honoured to walk you down the aisle.'

'Because do you know what I've just realised?' she went on. 'You can't choose your parents. You can't even choose your step-parents. But I *can* choose my ex-stepfather as my own. You're the only father I've ever had and I'm so lucky and grateful for that. And I want it to stay that way forever, no matter how many other faux, transient, step- or biological fathers come my way. All my life I thought I was missing a father when really you've been here all along. Or mostly all along.'

Joseph pulled her to his chest and hugged her hard. 'I choose you, too,' he said. And his hand fluttered at hers briefly before he excused himself and left the floor, heading towards the under-cover patio at the back.

The wedding cake was a Victorian sponge tower made by Archie's mother and decorated with freshly whipped cream, strawberries and rose petals and a generous dusting of icing sugar. It was simple, elegant, beautiful and absolutely delicious. Christmas's miniature wedding cake chocolates were handed around on silver platters and were a huge hit with the crowd. She fielded endless compliments and enquiries about her shop and her work, with promises of several solid bookings to come.

But it was at around this time, when the rain had finally ceased and the guests started to drift off, a frosty wind shooting through the constantly opening front door, that she began to feel the weight of all she'd lost with Lincoln and what she would lose with Emily's departure. She put down the plastic cup of champagne she was drinking, suspecting that it was now having the opposite of the intended effect, making her maudlin rather than festive, and raided Val's wardrobe for a coat. Bracing herself, she stepped out into the cold, pulling the thick coat tightly around her, shivering as the wind skittered up her exposed legs and under the hem of her dress.

Cars lined the street on both sides but the footpath it was empty except for one man heavily rugged up and walking a small dog. She began to walk too, with no plan in mind other than to force herself into a better mental state by blasting away any self-indulgence. It was her sister's wedding day. She should be happy. But suddenly she'd run out of cheer. And battling the cold wind wasn't enlivening her; it was merely making her more miserable. Tears filled her eyes, only to be whipped away by gusts as soon as they dared to fall.

She kept walking, heedless of her direction, wiping under her eyes carefully to try to halt any makeup runs.

A car wended its way up the street towards her, moving carefully past all the parked vehicles, and then slowed as it neared.

She stared through the windscreen. It couldn't be . . . but it was.

Lincoln.

Christmas stopped, and he pulled on the handbrake right where the car was idling in the middle of the street and got out. He was wearing only a long-sleeved cotton shirt above his jeans and the wind flapped the open material at his chest.

'What are you doing here?' she called. 'It's freezing. And why aren't you on a plane?'

He stopped in front of her. 'I'm not going,' he said.

'What do you mean?'

'I couldn't get on the plane. I was sitting in the terminal and I just felt . . .' he waved his hands around as he looked for the right word '. . . miserable,' he finished. 'You make me happy and I'm miserable without you. I love you and I want to be with you. I decided to grow up and chart the course of my own ship instead of sailing wherever the winds take me. I'm staying here, with you.'

'But what about Ecuador?'

'Ecuador? Never heard of it.'

She burst out laughing and then tears mingled with her laughter.

'That country's been there for a long, long time and it will be there for a long while yet. It can wait. Right now, I want you. Is that okay?' he asked, grinning.

'It's perfect.'

He pointed to the Honda. 'Now, if you would be so kind as to step into my chariot, I'd like to take you home and make love to you all night.'

She nodded. 'Yes, please.'

'Just promise me one thing.'

'Anything.'

'Promise me you'll never again kiss me and push me out the door.'

'I promise.'

He grabbed hold of her and kissed her hard, and then shep-
herded her to the car. He opened the creaky door and bowed low.
'Madam, your chariot awaits.'

'Let's go,' she said, took his hand and stepped into the car and
the new chapter, only just beginning.

29

Lincoln entered the door of Elsa's bungalow carrying a bouquet of yellow flowers.

'Why are you still here?' Elsa said, flicking the remote control to turn off the television. 'I thought you had to leave.'

'The plan changed so I thought I'd surprise you,' he said, handing her the flowers.

She sniffed them; they had no smell, which was always a disappointment, but it was no matter because she had Lincoln back with her for another day or so, and she'd take any time she could get before losing him again. 'Thank you, they're lovely.'

Lincoln perched on the edge of the couch. 'I have some news,' he said, his eyes alight with the secret. 'I'm staying in Tasmania and I plan on coming over with Caesar every day to visit you.'

'Don't be absurd. You can't stay in Tasmania for me. I shouldn't ever have asked you to do that. It was wrong.'

'I'm not staying for you; I'm staying for Caesar,' he teased. 'I'm settling down a bit, as you suggested.'

'I shouldn't have said that, either,' she said, hot with shame. 'It's your life. You need to do what makes you happy.'

'I am.'

Elsa bit her lower lip, not daring to believe that what he was saying was true, and yet inside her was a flicker of hope that was growing in strength by the second. She let it sink in: Lincoln was staying here in Tasmania and she would be seeing him every day, along with that mad Caesar dog.

'You better get me some water,' she croaked. 'This is quite a shock.'

He jumped up. 'Of course.'

But she caught his hand as he passed and looked up into his eyes. 'This makes me very happy.'

He leaned down and put his arm around her shoulder and squeezed her to him. 'Me too.'

Two months later

ECUADOR

It has been raining for weeks. Heavy, drumming, soaking rain that no one and nothing can escape. Rivers burst their banks, rush towards villages and engulf crops. The surface of the land is fluid. Nothing is dry. Nothing.

Everything and everyone has had to retreat and wait, patiently, for as long as it takes, for the waters to subside.

And when they do, they will find that the earth has changed shape and long-buried secrets will emerge into the light.

Christmas had her textbooks open on the workbench, bunches of dried herbs and little blue bottles of pure essential oils nearby and a tank of chocolate beside her. She was working on a new range of chocolates, infused with medicinal levels of oils and herbs that had reputed pain-relieving properties. She'd recently found a course in France that taught aromatic medicine—ingesting essential oils for medicinal benefit—and the brochure was plastered to the stainless-steel fridge door, right next to Jackson Kent's thank-you card for his DVD of *The Sound of Music*, which had arrived safely in Johannesburg.

Studying in France for a year was a mouth-watering prospect, not least because she'd reconnected with Mim and would love to spend more time with her, Hank and Margot. And Mim had sent her an email from America, saying that Margot had recently confided in her and told her about her first true love and true heartbreak—and that was what had been keeping Margot distracted and tight-lipped. Away from Paris, the boy in question and her circle of peers, Margot had let down her defences and Mim said she hadn't felt this close to her daughter in a long time. Christmas wanted to hug them both, and she could do that, if she was back in France. She wasn't yet sure how she could make a one-year course in France happen, but she was letting the idea sit for a while, to see if it might take root and grow into a real possibility.

Now that Cheyenne and Wilbur were settling in well together, Cheyenne might just be able to manage The Apothecary in Christmas's absence. Christmas would have to work a bit harder at her French lessons, though, if she was going to be able to get by in France. She'd have to catch up with Lien, at least. Lien loved the fact that she was the star of their language cohort. And it made Christmas happy to see her succeeding and gaining confidence.

She leaned back on the stool and stretched her arms up high above her head, then let her left hand fall to the vintage brooch pinned to her shirt. It had been a gift from Elsa, from her very own collection.

'It's the bluebird of happiness,' Elsa had said, placing it in Christmas's palm and closing her fingers around it. 'It's brought me much luck over my life and now I want you to have it.'

'It's a great honour that you would give it to me,' Christmas had said, looking to Lincoln quickly for approval. 'Are you sure?'

Elsa sat back in her wheelchair, defiant. 'No arguments.' And then she reflected some more. 'Besides, it's as much for me as it is for you. Seeing you two happy together makes me happy too.'

'Well, it's beautiful, thank you. I'll take great care of it.' Christmas reached out her free hand to hold Lincoln's, while his other hand rubbed methodically at Caesar's ears on the bungalow floor beside him. Caesar was dressed in his Super-dog cape.

'I always knew you two were supposed to be together,' Elsa went on, while Christmas poured her some more tea.

'Did you?' she asked, genuinely surprised.

'Oh yes. Rita tried to tell me it wouldn't happen because we couldn't see the light.'

Lincoln tilted his head to the side. 'Light?' And then he shot Christmas a furtive, panicked glance because Elsa was talking about seeing the light.

'But I know now what happened,' Elsa said. She looked at Christmas. 'You were *hiding* your light, weren't you? You didn't want it to be seen.' She smiled gleefully at this as though she'd cracked an agonising mystery.

Christmas replaced the teapot on the table and considered Elsa, impressed. 'Yes,' she replied. 'I was afraid.'

Elsa clapped her hands and whooped. 'Gosh, I wish Lulu could hear you say that. But Rita—we must tell Rita. Next time you come, can you tell her what you just told me?'

'Sure,' Christmas said uncertainly.

'Excellent!' Elsa reached for another of Christmas's chocolate pralines. 'I can't wait to see her face.'

Now, sitting in the kitchen, Christmas smiled at the memory. Elsa was such a crafty old dear. And so sharp. She should take Rosemary and Gordon with her to visit Green Hills. Maybe they could put on a penny farthing display for the residents. And she was sure they'd get on with Elsa like a house on fire. Rosemary and Elsa were both so charismatic, and Gordon, she was discovering, had a cheeky sense of humour she knew Elsa would appreciate.

The grandfather clock—a recent addition to the store— chimed two o'clock, reminding Christmas to turn on the television. Emily, having originally gone to Melbourne as a researcher for the children's show, had quickly been identified as genuine, raw, unaffected talent and dragged in front of the camera. Now she was presenting three days a week and loving it. She was a total natural too, Christmas thought. All those hours playing dress-up and making crafts with her nieces had paid off. It was lovely to see her star rising. And from what she'd hinted during their last phone call, the producer hadn't just taken notice of her for her presenting talent. He liked her for a whole lot more than that.

Lincoln burst through the back door, startling her. A tower of biology assignments weighed him down. They were from his students; he was a lecturer now for an online university program, which meant he got to stay in Evandale and work from home. He hoisted the papers onto a bench, then pulled a beef bone out of a shopping bag and handed it to Caesar, telling him to stay outside in the garden. Then he turned back to face Christmas, a whirl of excitement, grabbed her by the arms and kissed her hard on the lips.

'Wow!' she said, coming up for air. 'What was that for?'

'I just got an email from the research station in Ecuador.'

'And?'

He picked her up and spun her around before hoisting her up onto the bench and standing between her legs and kissing her again. 'It's the best news!'

'What do you mean?'

'They found a new species!' He thumped the bench in triumph. 'It's incredible. And I think it's going to help you too. This might just be the magic cacao tree you've been looking for!'

She held his face in her hands, laughing. 'Slow down. What are you talking about?'

Pulling away in his excitement, he began to pace the room. 'There's been widespread flooding in the Amazon, and now that the waters are receding they've found all sorts of things—buried treasure, ancient sites, crypts. And a very old tomb that, evidently, a small fraction of sunlight had already penetrated, because there was a clay pot in there, with seeds in it, which were often placed in tombs, but one of those seeds germinated and has grown into a sapling, and now that the tomb has been exposed they've found it! They've found it! A whole new variety of *Theobroma cacao*! Do you know what this means?'

Hope exploded in her chest, though she was hesitant to embrace it. 'It's a new lead?' she said.

'Exactly!' He snapped his fingers, then ran them through his hair and laughed out loud. 'It could be the Holy Grail of chocolate.' He took a breath and calmed himself. 'Or, it could be nothing. But that's the thrill. That's the chase. It's what scientists love, and they want me to fly over as soon as possible and see what I think.'

Christmas slid off the bench. 'But for how long?'

'Just two weeks.'

'Oh! I thought for a minute you were going . . . like, leaving me.'

He wrapped his arms around her. 'No! I didn't mean to scare you. Quite the opposite. I want you to come too.'

'To the jungle? With snakes and leeches and poison darts?'

He let go of her and grinned again, his blue eyes sparkling. 'Yep.'

'Can I think about it?'

'Nope. We've got to go tomorrow.'

'*Tomorrow*?! Why can these people never give you more notice?'

'Because they can't plan a revelation like this. This is nature at her best—wild, unpredictable, dramatic and exhilarating! Come on,' he said, twirling her around the room once more. 'Think what this will do for your chocolate creations. You'll be going to the home of chocolate, the very source of everything.'

It *was* an incredible opportunity. And as Master Le Coutre had said, how could you make chocolate if you didn't even know where it came from?

'Will you keep me safe from the beasties?' she said, wincing.

'I promise.'

'What about Elsa?' she said.

'She's busy organising the inaugural Green Hills book fair,' he said, with an expression that suggested he knew Christmas was just looking for an excuse to back out. 'And Caesar will be welcome at Green Hills, so you don't have to worry about him either. And think about it—we're hunting for the Cacao Queen that Master Le Coutre told you about. We'll be right there, on the ground to find it!'

Her head spun. Her first instinct was to call Val to get her opinion, but she already knew exactly what her sister would say. She'd tell her to go and not think twice about it.

'But I have a cooking lesson with Nate in a couple of days,' she said.

'He'll understand. He'll be excited. What little boy wouldn't love to think his aunt was off to the jungle?'

'My fairy godmother projects?'

'Postpone them. Or delegate. Maybe Val would like to help.'

'No, she's too busy; she volunteered to organise the end-of-year concert at the boys' school and she's running around with a clipboard and a pen behind her ear at all hours.'

'Or maybe Lien's aunt . . . what's her name again?'

'Tu.'

'Yes! Didn't you say you wanted an assistant? Tu would be great, wouldn't she, having had firsthand experience of what you do?'

'Yes, she would actually . . .' But Christmas thought of another objection. 'What about the shop?' she squeaked. 'Abigail's busy at uni this term and Cheyenne's flat out organising the wedding.'

'Close it! Think how much more famous you'll be once we get some media attention for your jungle trek. Think about the next book we can write together. People will come flocking here from all over.'

'Close the shop,' she echoed, resolution settling in her mind. She looked at her research notes on the bench. All of that could wait two weeks. Nobody would die if the shop was closed for a fortnight. She'd feel guilty about letting the rest of the Evandale business owners down, but that would only last a day until she got on the plane. Then she'd be free.

And she only had one rule now: there were no rules. She touched the bluebird brooch once more. Had Elsa's gift already brought her and Lincoln luck? Really, there was no good reason not to go, snakes aside. It was too good a chance to miss.

'Well, I guess if life hands you cacao beans you should make chocolate,' she said, as calmly as she could. 'So let's do it. Let's go find the Cacao Queen.'

Acknowledgements

My love and gratitude to my husband, Alwyn Blayse, and my son, Flynn, for your immense talent, love, good spirits and general hilarity. You make everything worth it.

To my furry children who sat by my side with every word. The dogs: my gorgeous golden angel, Goldie, so fiercely loved and still so shockingly missed; Daisy dog, whose smile lights up the world; and the smallest of the canines, Molly (Cyrus), who came in like a wrecking ball and we're all the better for it. The fantabulous felines: Princess Jasmine, whose drool has been the glue for my bum to my seat, and whose parting was somewhat expected yet still so very painful; Sapphina Ballerina, for dancing crazily across our keyboards and hearts; and Bucket Man, for being the hugest Bucket of Love in the universe. The horses for grounding me to the earth every day (and especially the dark and dashing Lincoln, after whom our hero is named). And the goats for drinking tea and sharing cupcakes and never once compromising standards by eating a single weed like you were supposed to.

Clay Gordon, creator of The Chocolate Life, and all-round expert on everything to do with cacao and chocolate, for the inspiring podcasts, the wealth of written information, and infectious enthusiasm about the business of cacao from tree to mouth. Your knowledge and passion is so contagious I now wish to write ten books on cacao.

Kate Smibert for being such an integral support and guiding force in my writing life—I am so blessed to have you as my friend. Kathleen Lamarque for your great friendship, sense of humour, photographs and style, for answering endless questions about Paris and Provence and packing relevant scenes into your bag for a quick trip to France (though I want to stress that any errors or letdowns are entirely my fault), and to Philippe, Hugo and Margot for the same.

To my publisher, Annette Barlow, for your always-brilliant editing advice, Clara Finlay for adding so much value to the text (what a star!), Kate O'Donnell for guiding my words so carefully to the page, and the whole Allen & Unwin (Australia, NZ and UK) team for the hundreds of things I know you do (but generally don't get to see) to get my books out into the world. And my agent, Fiona Inglis, and the whole Curtis Brown Australia team for your support.

I was inspired by Chantal Coady's book *Rococo: Mastering the Art of Chocolate*, and Shannon Bennett's *28 Days in Provence*. Impressions of your recipes are found in this book. Likewise, *The Chocolate Tree: A Natural History of Cacao*, by Allen M. Young, is a now well-thumbed botany resource and helped me bring Lincoln van Luc to life. And *A Chocolate a Day Keeps the Doctor Away*, by John Ashton and Suzy Ashton, was just *too* wonderful to read—I always *knew* chocolate was good for you!

Thank you to Terese and Gerard Puglisi at Sweet Farm Tours in Cairns for so graciously allowing me to interrupt your cane harvest and ramble through your acres of cacao trees, cut open pods and taste the flesh and the seeds; and thank you Luis Felipe Valencia, Consul General of Ecuador in Sydney, for answering questions about Ecuador—I wrote so many scenes set in Ecuador that didn't make it into the final draft but they're there in the background; Phil Boyle for listening to my wild botany fantasy of an undiscovered miracle bean and finding a way to make it plausible; my dad, Brian, and my stepmother, Pamela, for sharing your gorgeous cottage and so much of Tasmania with me, and for willingly daydreaming about the Apple Isle with me at any other time; and Jane Shaw from Ingleside Bakery for sharing such vivid and funny anecdotes of what it's like to run a business in the town of Evandale.

To my mum, Geraldine, and my sister, Amanda, for accepting my shortfalls when my mind was elsewhere engaged; and Amanda, again, for suffering through the gruelling chocolate-making boot camp with me.

Lastly, thank you to all my readers for joining my characters on these fun journeys. You're the reason mine is the best job in the world.

Dear Reader

Thank you so much for joining me and my characters on this journey.
I do hope you have enjoyed their story as much as I enjoyed writing it.
Thanks to you, I get the best job in the world and for that I am
incredibly grateful. I write because I want to put joy out into the world,
a world I feel needs as much courage, creativity, kindness and
enthusiasm for life as we can muster.

If you would like to connect with me, you can find me on Facebook
at www.facebook.com/JosephineMoonAuthor,
on Twitter @josephine_moon, and on Instagram at josephine_moon.

You can always find me on my website at www.josephinemoon.com,
and you're welcome to email me at josephinemoon@live.com.au.

I hope we have the pleasure of each other's company again
for many more books to come.

Much love,

Jo xx

If you enjoyed *The Chocolate Apothecary* and would like to read more
from Josephine Moon why not try her previous novel, *The Tea Chest*

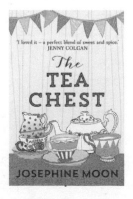